# The Maytrees

'In short, simple sentences, Dillard calls on her erudition as a naturalist and her grace as poet to create an enthralling story of marriage – particular and universal, larky and monumental' PUBLISHERS WEEKLY

'An anthropologist's eye and a poet's precision distinguish this superbly written novel, exploring the ritual complexities of life, love and death… The compact, elliptical narrative will continue to pervade the reader's consciousness long after the novel ends' KIRKUS REVIEWS

'The novel as a whole is beautiful, and the beauty is never digressive or ornamental. But when we see through Lou's eyes, it is as if the objects of her attention lift off the page. Her awareness invests the world with dimensionality and presence, summoning a sharp sense of the ontological strangeness of creation and the mystery of our place in it' WASHINGTON POST

'Every so often, a novel comes along that describes a relationship with such thoroughness that you almost feel better about love. Maybe, just maybe, it's a worthy use of our time alive. Annie Dillard's *The Maytrees* is such a novel. It is also a reservoir of oceanic language, thrilling and sophisticated assumptions of reader intelligence and elegantly lean descriptive detail' LOS ANGELES TIMES

'Dillard is expert at conveying the possible surprises of emotion – the degree to which the self is always terra incognita – and of how people change over time, or don't. Her evocation of her characters growing older is exquisite… *The Maytrees* is a love story of an unusually adult and contemporary kind' BOSTON GLOBE

'Dillard helps us see the universal in the specific. Her gift for giving weight to every detail of her material makes this "simple story" one you will return to, again and again' NY DAILY NEWS

'This novel is a treasure… Dillard writes beautifully about physical frailty, emotional complexities and the solace to be found in nature' USA TODAY

# The Maytrees

Annie Dillard

ET REMOTISSIMA PROPE

Published by Hesperus Press Limited
4 Rickett Street, London SW6 1RU
www.hesperuspress.com

*The Maytrees* first published by Hesperus Press Limited, 2007
This edition first published 2008
Copyright © Annie Dillard, 2007
The right to be identified as author of this work has been asserted by Annie
Dillard in accordance with the Copyright, Designs and Patents Act, 1988.

Designed and typeset by Fraser Muggeridge studio
Printed in Jordan by the Jordan National Press

ISBN: 978-1-84391-447-1

All rights reserved. This book is sold subject to the condition that it shall not
be resold, lent, hired out or otherwise circulated without the express prior
consent of the publisher.

for C.R. Clevidence

# The Maytrees

# Prologue

The Maytrees were young long ago. They lived on what still seems antiquity's very surface. It was the tip of Cape Cod, that exposed and mineral sandspit. The peninsula here was narrow between waters. Its average elevation was fifteen feet. It spiraled counterclockwise from the scarps of Truro and came rumpling over dunes to the harbor, Provincetown, inside the spiral. The town name of Provincetown was for a time 'Cape Cod.' Generations before Jamestown – let alone Plymouth – British fishermen loaded their holds with splitcod.

No Wampanoag Nauset tribes, not even Pamets, settled on Provincetown's poor sand or scrub woods; they were farmers. At river mouths as far north as Truro, however, Nausets stayed, and built permanent villages more thickly than in most of New England, for clams and oysters abounded, and south of the Namskaket creeks they found soil for squash and corn.

The Maytrees' lives, like the Nausets', played out before the backdrop of fixed stars. The way of the world could be slight, then and now, but rarely, among individuals, vicious. The slow heavens marked hours. They lived often outside. They drew every breath from a wad of air just then crossing from saltwater to saltwater. Their sandspit was a naked strand between two immensities, both given to special effects.

Toby Maytree grew up in Provincetown and spent most of his life there. His father was one of several guards stationed on the backside, on the cliffs by the Atlantic. Like some other coast guards, Maytree's father built for his family a rough shack on the bare sands near the coast guard station. Young Maytree and his mother camped out for summer weeks there in the one-room wood shack above the great ocean beach. They exchanged visits with the guards. Later, after the war, Maytree became a poet of the forties and fifties and sixties. He wrote four book-long poems and three books of lyrics.

His wife, Lou Maytree, rarely spoke. She painted a bit on canvas and linen now lost. They acted in only two small events – three, if love counts. Falling in love, like having a baby, rubs against the current of our lives: separation, loss, and death. That is the joy of them.

Twice a day behind their house the tide boarded the sand. Four times a year the seasons flopped over. Clams live like this, but without so much reading as the Maytrees.

They remembered the central post office – the post office where everyone met mornings and encouraged everyone else for the day and night ahead. They were young when passenger trains to Provincetown replaced freights. When he was eighteen, he joined crews all over the Cape to clear and rebuild after the big hurricane.

Toby Maytree wanted to engage the enemy – either one – in gunfight. Instead he spent the war at the San Francisco Office of War Information. He wrote broadcasts for Pacific troops. By then, Lou was in college. Later, married, both Maytree and Lou liked the idea of seeing the world. Neither, however, was willing to sacrifice free time for a job.

Maytree picked up cash by moving houses for friends and whacking up additions, at whim. They voted. They were not social thinkers, but their friends were. Their summer friends, in particular, harvested facts row on row from newspapers like mice on corncobs. The Maytrees were not always up-to-the-minute. Their city friends envied their peace.

She owned their house. Her mother bought it when Lou was a girl. Her mother and Lou had moved to Provincetown from Marblehead, Massachusetts, after the man of the family, a lawyer, left one morning for work and never came back. No one knew that ordinary breakfast would be their last. Why not memorize everything, just in case?

For a long time they owned no car, no television when that came in, no insurance, no savings. Once a week they heard world news on the radio. They supported striking coal miners' families with cash. They loved their son, Pete, their only child. Between them they read about three hundred books a year. He read for facts, she for transport. Nothing about them was rich except their days swollen with time.

Lou Maytree's height and stillness made her look like a statue. Her fair hair and her white skin's purity contrasted with the red she wore year-round to cheer the scene. Her courtesy, her compliance, and especially her silence dated from a time otherwise gone. Her size, her wide eyes and high brow, and her upright carriage gave her an air of consequence. Intimacy came easily to her, but strangers could not see it.

When she was old, she lived alone in the Maytrees' one-room shack in the parabolic sand dunes. She crossed the backshore dunes into the bayside town Fridays and stocked up. A straw hat kept her face clear. Year after year her eyes set farther back and their lavender lids thinned.

Throughout her life she was ironic and strict with her thoughts. She went dancing most Friday nights in town. People said that Maytree, or felicity, or solitude had driven her crazy. People said she had been an ugly girl, or a child movie star;

that she inherited fabulous sums and lived in a shack without pipes or wires; that she read too much; that she was wanting in ambition and could have married anyone. She lacked a woman's sense of doom. She did what she wanted – like who else on earth? All her life she found dignity overrated. She rolled down dunes.

Most of the few and unremarkable things Lou and Toby Maytree did occurred in their old beachside house on the town's front street, and in fact in its bed.

Their bed's frame was old pipe metal, ironstone. Lou Maytree painted its arched headboard and footboard white. Every few years she sanded its rust rosettes and painted it white again. This was about as useful as she got, though she stretched a dollar for food. One could divide their double bed into her side and his side by counting four pipes over, but the two ignored parity. He slept with a long leg flung over her, as a dog claims a stick.

Once while he slept on his side, his legs thrashed and he panted. She pressed his shoulder.

Chasing a rabbit?

He exhaled and said, tap-dancing.

It began when Lou Bigelow and Toby Maytree first met. He was back home in Provincetown after the war. Maytree first saw her on a bicycle. A red scarf, white shirt, skin clean as eggshell, wide eyes and mouth, shorts. She stopped and leaned on a leg to talk to someone on the street. She laughed, and her loveliness caught his breath. He thought he recognized her flexible figure. Because everyone shows up in Provincetown sooner or later, he had taken her at first for Ingrid Bergman until his friend Cornelius straightened him out.

He introduced himself. —You're Lou Bigelow, aren't you? She nodded. They shook hands and hers felt hot under sand like a sugar doughnut. Under her high brows she eyed him straight on and straight across. She had gone to girls' schools, he recalled later. Those girls looked straight at you. Her wide eyes, apertures opening, seemed preposterously to tell him, I and these my arms are for you. I know, he thought back at the stranger, this long-limbed girl. I know and I am right with you.

He felt himself blush and knew his freckles looked green. She was young and broad of mouth and eye and jaw, fresh, solid and airy, as if light rays worked her instead of muscles. Oh, how a poet is a sap; he knew it. He managed to hold his eyes on her. Her rich hair parted on the side; she was not necessarily beautiful, or yes she was, her skin's luster. Her pupils were rifle bores shooting what? When he got home he could not find his place in Helen Keller.

He courted Lou carefully in town, to wait, surprised, until his newly serious intent and hope firmed or fled, and until then, lest he injure her trust. No beach walks, dune picnics, rowing, sailing. Her silence made her complicit, innocent as beasts, oracular. Agitated, he saw no agitation in her even gaze. Her size and whole-faced smile maddened him, her round arms at her sides, stiff straw hat. Her bare shoulders radiated a smell of sun-hot skin. Her gait was free and light. Over her open eyes showed two widths of blue lids whose size and hue she would never see. Her face's skin was transparent, lighted and clear like sky. She barely said a word. She tongue-tied him.

She already knew his dune-shack friend Cornelius Blue, knew the professors Hiram and Elaine Cairo from New York, knew everyone's friend Deary the hoyden who lived on the pier or loose in the dunes, and old Reevadare Weaver who gave parties. Bumping through a painter's opening, picking up paint at the hardware store, ransacking the library, she glanced at him, her mouth curving broadly, as if they shared a joke. He knew the glance of old. It was a summons he never refused. The joke was – he hoped – that the woman had already yielded but would set him jumping through hoops anyway. Lou Bigelow's candid glance, however, contained neither answer nor question, only a spreading pleasure, like Blake's infant joy, kicking the gong around.

\* \* \*

Maytree concealed his courtship. On the Cairos' crowded porch, she steadied her highball on the rail. He asked her, Would she like to row around the harbor with him? She turned and gave him a look, Hold on, Buster. He was likely competing with fleets and battalions of men. Maytree wanted her heart. She had his heart and did not know it. She shook her head, clear of eye, and smiled. If he were only a painter: her avid expression, mouth in repose or laughing, her gleaming concentration. The wide-open skin between her brows made their arcs long. Not even Ingrid Bergman had these brows. The first few times he heard her speak, her Britishy curled vowels surprised him. He rarely dared look her way.

One day he might accompany Lou Bigelow from town out here to his family's old dune shack. He was afraid his saying 'shack' would scare them both. Without her he already felt like one of two pieces of electrical tape pulled apart. He could not risk a mistake.

Robert Louis Stevenson, he read in his *Letters*, called marriage 'a sort of friendship recognized by the police.' Charmed, Maytree bought a red-speckled notebook to dedicate to this vexed sphere – not to marriage, but to love. More red-speckled notebooks expanded, without clarifying, this theme. Sextus Propertius, of love: 'Shun this hell.' From some book he copied: 'How does it happen that a never-absent picture has in it the power to make a fresh, overwhelming appearance every hour, wide-eyed, white-toothed, terrible as an army with banners?' She was outside his reach.

Of course she glared at Maytree that fall when he came by barefoot at daybreak and asked if she would like to see his dune shack. Behind his head, color spread up sky. In the act of diving, Orion, rigid, shoulder-first like a man falling, began to dissolve. Then even the zenith and western stars paled and gulls squawked.

Her house was on the bay in town. He proposed to walk her to the ocean – not far, but otherworldly in the dunes. She had been enjoying *Bleak House*. Men always chased her and she always glared.

She most certainly did not ask him in. His was a startling figure: his Mars-colored hair, his height and tension, his creased face. He looked like a traveling minstrel, a red-eyed night heron. His feet were long and thin like the rest of him. He wore a billed fishing cap. An army canteen hung from his belt. She had been a schoolgirl in Marblehead, Massachusetts, when he went West.

—Just a walk, he said, sunrise. We won't need to go inside.

In his unsure smile she saw his good faith. Well, that was considerate, brickish of him, to say that they would not go in. She agreed. She had not seen the dunes in weeks. Maytree suggested she bring, as he did, a pair of socks, to provide webbed feet, and wear a brimmed hat that tied. In predawn light she saw the sunspokes around his eyes under his cap.

She followed him through the woods and up to the dunes. Morning dew under trees wet her socks. Sand stuck between her toes. She stuck her socks in her waistband. Heat would dry them.

Bursting uphill through scrubs into the open excited her. She saw a wild array of sand dunes inscribing a sphere of sea and sky. She saw three-hundred-foot dunes swirl around the horizon like a school of fish: bright side, dark side, moving downwind. The world of town vanished as if wind tore it off.

A low bump between dunes caught Lou's eye. It angled on a flat behind them near the trees they came through. She and Maytree neared it in a crescent of shade. It was a sail, a rolled canvas sail, a mainsail. From the roll's side, dark curls spilled like filling. They settled, these curls, on a green lobster buoy. It was their friend Deary Hightoe asleep and swaddled. Lou knew Deary slept in the dunes somewhere. She claimed to like the way starlight smelled on sand. Once Cornelius asked her how the smell of starlight on sand differed from the smell of moonlight. —More peppery. Beside Deary at the forest edge Lou saw, implausibly, a garden of shriveling chilis and kale. Deary woke, blinked, stretched, and opened the sail by rolling in it. Lou and Maytree moved fifteen feet to the slope where she fetched up.

—What brings you two out so early? While Deary talked and laughed – all her waking hours, it seemed – her mouth bubbled at gums and corners. At thirty-five she was six years older than Lou, small of body and round of face. Lou knew that this month she was playing drums with the band at a seaside bar and restaurant. She must have found her way over and among the dunes in the dark when the place closed at two o'clock. Lou resolved to give Deary bushels of seaweed to mulch these dry plantings. How could she carry water out here? Any rain vanished in sand. For soil Deary seemed to be substituting garbage, leaf litter scooped from under pines, fish racks, scrub oak leaves hard as harpoon points, and two stranded rays, one of which tilted, like a plane turning, over a head of kale it shaded and fed.

There were unsolved crimes out in this wilderness including murder. Not many years after Lou and Maytree met, someone murdered the Woman in the Dunes. The killer beheaded her and cut off her hands. Searchers found the rest of her, raped. They found only one sandy hand. No one ever found who she was, or her killer, or her other hand, or her head. Deary's Boston mother assumed she lived in a locked house in town.

Now Deary built a piney fire for making cowboy coffee. Her head was a globe. From a side part, her curls rose like a laurel wreath and set close behind her ears. A piece of green cloth, safety-pinned, bound one of her hands.

—What happened to your hand?

—I'm one step closer to death. She was enthusiastic.

—Who isn't? Maytree's height was drawing the smoke.

Deary crossed her legs. —You see, she said to Lou, as soon as you arrive, you start hurting yourself. You burn this fingertip. Later you cut yourself – right there, on the side. Paper cut in the webbing, and years later, another beside where it healed.

Lou knew all along that Deary originated theories. —Another time you bang a knuckle, and maybe twenty years later you pinch its other side. With each injury you learn how that patch of you feels. It wakens. Until it heals, you're aware of those nerves.

—This is a privilege?

—Of course. Every place you injure adds that patch to your consciousness. You grow more alive. And the point of all this is – she beamed up from the sand at Lou – that when you have hurt every single place on your body, you die! Once you have felt every last nerve ending, at least on your skin, then you have lived in full awareness. Then you die. Deary had a pleased toothy smile. Mysteriously, some years ago she earned the first degree MIT awarded a female in architecture. Her parents and grandparents were themselves educated.

The two left her before the sun got worse. Out of earshot Maytree told Lou that roaming in the morning from his shack, he often saw Deary sleeping loose. Sometimes she rolled in her sail near the ocean among beach peas. In storms she bivouacked by the swale's hollow in heather.

Lou followed him up the highest dune. Lightly he was teasing her about her many boyfriends and suitors. Lou found climbing loose sand, she said to herself, hellacious. When she gained a step up she slid halfway back. The dune top was nearer than it looked. It was a socket of light. Far away the rimming sea met sky and spread. Drying to death, like a fellow-crawling-in-a-desert cartoon, would not take long. There was no shade. She was hungry. From the high dune Maytree was trying to show her his shack on the horizon. Where could he mean? Would he touch her shoulder with his hand, or even arm, as he pointed? She had not let a man this close in years. Against blue sea she saw sand crests trace catenary curves against sky. Knee-high pines marked some hollows.

Beside the big dune's base she saw a house that sand had pushed halfway over. A broken line of brush paralleled the sea in a long hollow. Pointing, Maytree said those few right-angled planes on the horizon, each apparently the size of a playing card in relation to the collapsing house and the scrub, were actually shack roofs. If so, the forest was bonsai. Must one crawl in the shacks?

She could oversee the whole map: Provincetown harbor and piers and Cape Cod Bay one way, limitless sea the other way, and this dunefield. Pioneer bay dwellers cut this backshore for firewood, grazed it, and its topsoil blew away, leaving a

Sahara of dunes on the primordial sandspit. There was no rock anywhere, just that stretch of sand the coastwise current picked up from crumbling cliffs to the south and dropped here in a spiral.

Above the Atlantic's rim she saw a rain's fallstreaks curve. A stillness as of empty space marked all she saw. It was this loping shore of mineral silence people meant when they said 'the dunes.' The surface of the moon might look like this: rudimentary.

Losing sight of the sea, they crossed more dunes and dropped to a boggy swale. Trees grew below her knees and scratched her. Pollen scum lay on the swale's water like spray paint.

Beyond the damp swale they used a soft jeep track in sand that snakes crossed. They regained sight of the reeling sea where far waves broke in rows. Then, whoops, by her bare feet she saw a coiled pointy-headed snake, thick – a rattlesnake? Maytree dove for it. It escaped into poison ivy. It was a hognose snake, he said. Its first defense in life was to mimic a rattlesnake even where no rattlesnakes lived. He brushed his hands on his pants. —Pity… He watched the poison ivy as he spoke. You can do tricks with a hognose snake. In her mind she replied, as if bored, Oh can you.

The foam rows lined up in the offing marked shoals – Peaked Hill Bars, graveyard of the Atlantic, people said here, as on other coasts. Lou heard Maytree pronounce four syllables, Peak–ed Hill Bars. That those green shoals wrecked boats and killed people everyone knew. They bewildered her. Each offshore surf line contained commotion but got nowhere, like someone's reading the same line over and over. Sluggish waves rolled into wind. When they smashed, spindrift blew back in clumps.

On the foredune's crest, she saw the ocean's color change. Maytree's legs parted grasses and turned inland. She saw his shack. It rose off-plumb from driftwood stump corners. Her friend Josephine said of a shack like Maytree's that it looked like a big waiting bonfire. Maytree was telling her his father first built it while he was on lifesaving duty at Peaked Hill Bars station. Maytree said he had rebuilt the shack many times. Lou knew it would have an outhouse. But where.

He made no move toward the shack. Its deck was pine planks with popped knots. Its one room was twelve feet by sixteen feet. Lou could use a seat, so it was she who left him to sit on the first shack step, elbows two steps up. The sun was out and every second the sky's hues perished with no fuss. Behind him sand gave way to a band of dark sea and light sky.

She saw him walk away. Thirty yards down a slope he primed a pitcher pump from a water bucket. He came back and sat at a proper distance on her same step. He refilled his canteen. He spent the war at a California desk and bought the canteen at Wall Drug. Wind blew his shirt. Now again he was teasing her about her many suitors, possibly because she had not reacted the first time. He was only a bit taller than she was. She watched blue shadows on his white shirt stretch and shrink as he moved. The shirt flattened on his shoulder and ribs and blinded her. She looked away. It must be an old shirt of his father's. One of her arms felt one of his sleeves.

Only then did it strike her in fear that she could love this kind stranger. He knew everything, including, and perhaps specializing in, love. After VJ Day he came back near home for college. He returned to the West to cowboy for a few years. Then he came home at thirty. She knew nothing at all. How could he mistake her for sophisticated?

She opened her mouth to drink tinny water, but she did not open her mouth to correct his impression. What could she say? Nothing had been said between them. Their intimacy's height so far was drinking from the same canteen.

When Lou was a girl, her breasts grew both calamitously early and big. Boys came at her, shouting to one another. Alone or together, running, they competed to touch a breast, capture the flag. Had those boys put her off males forever? Throughout boarding school she thought all males younger than her teachers possessed neither fears nor noble hopes, let alone fine feelings – or even any inner lives at all. They were more like bumper cars than people.

Boarding-school boys rarely sought her. Considering her looks, and what one called her Betty Grables, they figured her dance card was full for years to come. In college she fell for a reckless cellist, Primo Dial, who played in the orchestra standing up. Whenever his music specified six or eight bars of rests, he lifted his music stand and cello at once, kept his eyes on the music, and wandered to set his stand in another part of the room. A new conductor fresh from Europe kicked him out. He took up the violin, the concertina, and blues harmonica. She had never heard blues. He dashed through town and its outlying cornfields making music. Lou was almost six feet tall. She laughed, held Primo's thin shoulder, and belted. It was a discovery of her reserve that she could sing if she belted, and never minded people about. Primo played 'Yes, Sir, That's My Baby,' 'Blues in the Night,' 'Heart of My Heart,' 'I Wish I Could Shimmy Like My Sister Kate,' 'Makin' Whoopee!,' 'Alabamy Bound,' 'Side by Side,' 'Hey Daddy.' Sometimes instead of singing she percussed: play a rat, play a rat, play a rat-a-ma-que, or ligga digga digga digga boom, boom she-boom.

She queried herself absorbedly in those ragged and trying years – for all their quick pleasures, the earnest years. Always she felt she was born to some heroism – but what? Only to abstractions, especially loyal love, and especially the specific love in the interest of which she and Primo Dial kept kissing each other. They kissed all over Ohio. Walking hand in hand or making music, she often discovered behind them a line of flushed girls like young quail barely keeping up.

She asked herself: Would she rather have his love, or hers for him? Would she rather have Primo himself, guaranteed to love her and only her forever, or would she rather have her love for Primo Dial forever, intact and untainted come who may? Astounded, she realized she would choose her love over his. Was she so selfish? Of course, if she lost him, and she did, the love might well dim – an apostasy to think, but lots of lovers lose. She took the chance, as any lover does, witting or not.

When Primo Dial and his concertina left her that May for winsome twins who played glockenspiels, she cried the whole of a Provincetown summer. She fed her love willfully on force-meats and tidbits from their strolling player days and dancing nights she knew by heart. She wrung her love. If the twins ever interrupted her memory, she reminded herself she liked them both. She drew her mind back to Primo. She liked loving, re-nounced being loved, and only rarely thought of slitting his throat.

Lou, singing to herself in the house on the beach, kept her misery and love alive in her single heart. Who but a passionate theoretician, of the sort those years produce, would burn down the house to finish cooking – just to see how it came out – a half-baked principle? It had been an appalling summer she cringed to recall, another failed go at interior life. Yet something about her hypothetical choice was right.

In the shack's outhouse Lou looked up now and saw a big blacksnake angled from the wall to float in the air over her head. Lou and Maytree started back. Every day she failed to tell him about herself and her solitude she led him further astray. She followed him up and down high dunes at the world's ledge. She looked at his neck. What kept him from taking her hand? In this charged air any touch would probably arrest her heart and disarticulate her joints, and so forth, but he should act soon because it could only get worse.

She was twenty-three. She could not imagine that a brave man could shrink from risking one woman's refusal. She wanted only a lifelong look at his face and his long-legged, shambly self, broken by intervals of kissing. After a while she might even, between kisses, look into his eyes. No time soon.

What could she do? She had gauged Maytree well: He never touched her. That is beauty's one advantage, she always thought, and might be its downfall. In town he left her at her walkway and waved off breakfast. She had been liking the way his hips set loosely, his shoulders tightly, his long wide-smiling face, pale eyes back under thick brows, alert. She stood in danger outside her door. What was she afraid of? Of her heartbeat, of his over-real eyes, of her breathing, everything.

Maytree had worked all year on a long poem, *Wood End Light and Race Point*. He worked mornings. Wood End Light and Race Point Light were Provincetown lighthouses. Race Point would embody sharp Aristotelean thought. Wood End would stand for Platonic thought. He rekindled his enthusiasm for the project every morning. He hauled lines of poetry like buried barbed wire with his bare hands.

On a frigid June fifth, he raced to Cornelius's dune shack to blurt his joyous scheme. While he was telling Cornelius that in his poem Race Point Light stood for Aristotelean thought and Wood End Light stood for Platonic thought – a distinction so obvious it scarcely warranted mention – abruptly the opposite correlations struck him as even more obviously right. It all sounded inane.

Still, he got back to it. In August, exhilarated, he loaned two sections to Lou Bigelow. He had by then kissed her, and she had kissed him back. Now he told her which lighthouse represented which thinker. She had a decent education and an ear – the woman he loved, beyond love as he knew or imagined it, in his hometown, had an ear! A week later he rummaged her spare comments. —Now all you have to do is reconcile them, she said. She smiled. What she said was sublimely true, and proved her stunning understanding, as if they were two halves of one brain. They were perched on the granite-block breakwater to Long Point, watching sunset in a spirit purely scientific.

—Right you are. Her level eyes were on him. The red light on her young face skin and mouth. —All I have to do is propose a metaphysic to cap Western thought. That year, Maytree was ready.

(After the book appeared, a poem in three parts, no one noticed its crucial – to him – structure. At thirty he feared being obvious, and any clarity, any saying what he meant, was ipso facto obvious. He never even mentioned the moieties Plato or Aristotle, let alone their reconciliation, lest he insult the reader, whom, in those days, one could posit. It was only his third book. Still, the poetry world and other Provincetown writers noticed the book, that there was one. Many storms. After that he told people he wrote about the sea, and steered talk ashore.)

Reevadare Weaver threw a crushing lawn party for the May-trees' engagement. Reevadare Weaver was a henna-haired old Provincetown woman, *un peu superbe*, who wore wax-fruit-elongated hats. As her party began she discovered that all her liquor was gone. Cornelius Blue wandered in from his dune shack. He had combed his walrus mustache and Walt Whitman beard. —Be a dear, Lou heard her tell him, and run get two bottles of everything. I'll pay you back, you're marvelous. Cornelius and all her guests, however, had long ago learned that to Reevadare's lawn parties, as to Deary Hightoe's beach picnics, they should bring everything but the place. Cornelius revealed a bottle of bourbon.

Reevadare wore a long purple cloth, low at the neck, and amber drop earrings that suggested her ears were draining. Deary brought, like a bindle, an oyster sack of beach-plum brandy in jars. She handed out conical Dixie cups no one could set down. She passed among them, refilling. Affixed to Deary was six-year-old Marie Koday, fist like a clothespin on Deary's skirts. Wild-eyed she followed on bare feet brown as buns. Everyone had bottles and bowls: linguica sausages, baked beans. Cairos toted out two hams, and Maytree brought smoked clams.

Lou hoped to be near Maytree, and knew he shared her hope, but the party's movements kept them apart. Reevadare hugged

Lou around the waist. —Marriage is wonderful, she said. She should know. Lou had learned Reevadare's past in bits. Reevadare had run through six husbands like a brochette. When she married Joe Jernigan, her first husband, family and friends gave her monogrammed towels and sheets. Subsequently when she married in succession the Messrs. Jarvis, Johnson, and James...

—I never needed to change monograms! She laughed, long-toothed, delighted all these years later. One husband, Chee, was the handsome grandson of immigrants. At the time she told Lou, on her college break, that she was then a Reevadare Chee. Reevadare made Mr. Chee nervous. He moved back to Boston. By the time she married Five, Trudeau, she was poor. Her friends and family had wearied of buying her presents, and monograms were out of the question. A year later Trudeau, suppressing laughter, sailed as one-way crew on a schooner for Papeete, Tahiti, and Reevadare resumed her maiden name, Weaver.

After a few hours the party moved to the Flagship restaurant. Reevadare had hired the place for the night and brought in a Boston band. The band played all night. Jane Cairo, a wild-haired schoolgirl, danced with most of the men and resumed reading. Lou was fond of brainy, tactless Jane Cairo. Her oval eyes were cynical. Deary sat in two sets on drums. When the band took breaks, Deary carried sleeping Marie Koday and kissed her hairy skull. Lou wished Maytree would dance. She knew the thick youth who was nodding at Deary and knife-knocking time on their table as Moses Lonn, a Long Island painter who lingered. Deary was a girl who could jitterbug, and so, Lou soon saw, could Moses Lonn; he flipped her like a baton. They returned breathless. He turned to Lou. —Anyone ever tell you you look like... Ingrid Bergman? Ever since the war, she thought. She smiled. To retaliate she whispered in his ear, Why do so many painters come to Provincetown? She wanted to see if his answer varied the usual, It's the light.

—It's the light, he explained. What about the light? He could not say.

During a band break, Cornelius proposed his usual toast from Santayana: 'If pain could have saved us, we should long ago have been saved.' It cracked him up every time and he hit his knee. Cornelius had one eye deep-set and one swimming, low eye, like Blake. Lou thought Cornelius was a man of sorrow, only because his mustache made him look sad unless he was laughing. He laughed constantly in company, splitting mustache from beard unexpectedly, and flashing pale teeth. He looked around. —The downwardly mobile we have always with us, he said, and sat. Lou and Maytree sought each other's eyes. They would talk later. When the band quit and the Flagship closed, half the revelers returned by the street to Reevadare's. Lou heard Elaine Cairo say she was up to her eyeballs in highballs.

Reevadare pulled Lou to a pinching metal bench. How constantly, Lou thought, old people claim to have been once young. It is as if they don't believe it. That old people were old never jarred her, but it shook the daylights out of them. They could count. They did not feel old, they said. Lou wondered if they felt as estranged from themselves at her age as she felt estranged from herself at ten.

Reevadare's grandmother on Hilton Head inherited a rolled-steel fortune in Birmingham, Alabama. Reevadare's mother was organizing peach pickers' time in Georgia, and her father was seldom in. Leaving the South, Reevadare served as a WAVE in the war, then moved to Provincetown because she was too odd, as a red-diaper baby, for anyplace else. The summer Reevadare was fifteen, she was a striking beauty, she told Lou, but the Duke University senior she loved ignored her. She tried to drown herself off Hilton Head, but turned back because the water was black muck and sucked her into oyster shells that cut her so blood striped down her black legs. Here in Provincetown she bought a house and collected friends' art. Of course she married people.

There in her garden under a locust, Reevadare told Lou her favorite part of marriage. —It's a marvelous way to get to know someone! Reevadare wore a Gibson girl pouf that perhaps also filled her glass-cherry-piled hat.

Lou asked point-blank, Can love last? (Rural people get to philosophizing, and will say anything.)

—Oh, darling! No, not that heart-thumping passion. Give that eighteen months. But it's replaced by something even better.

Lou waited.

—Lovers!

How they prized Reevadare, upright people did. She fought their battles for them like a mercenary. —Why do people fret about such a simply marvelous thing as love? After a bout with Reevadare, her friends' gargoyle scruples dropped from their shoulders and did not climb back for hours. Maybe she would even go to hell for them! She was already a southerner, from Virginia or Oklahoma or Mississippi or one of those.

That night on her pinching bench Reevadare offered Lou advice. With many killing rings she pressed Lou's hand and said, Keep your women friends, darling. Men come and go.

It was only lunatic here in part, Lou thought, looking around. Among their friends were people who wrote, people who painted, people who taught, people who carved or welded sculptures, and poets barefoot, lefty, and educated to a feather edge. They wore Greek fishermen's caps, frayed shirts, and huaraches. J. Edgar Hoover warned Congress about their ilk in 1947, noting Communist plans 'to infiltrate the so-called intellectual and creative fields.' They talked: Did the United States have a culture – apart from making money? Could a moving picture be a work of art? Among the older generation of their friends, almost no one remained a party member; Stalin's purges purged them. Did existence precede essence? Did somebody say martini?

Lou stayed late. South above town the Milky Way tangled Mars in its slack nets. Laughing, locust leaflets in her face, Deary related to Lou every least event from this very party they had not left. With Maytree and Cornelius, Lou emptied ashtrays and tossed Dixie cups. Reevadare, Sooner Roy, and Deary switched to whisky sours. Lou walked home by the water, at stars' level. She held her shoes and avoided trash. In the open, starlight was plenty of light. Of course Reevadare's exotic life led her to think men came and went. No one knew what she and Maytree knew.

The following noon, walking Commercial Street as everyone did many times a day, Lou saw Deary posing for a painting class on the beach by MacMillan Pier. Maytree recently told her that old Cornelius said of Deary, quoting someone about a Hollywood star, that she had curves in places where other women didn't even have places. Lou watched the painting students. Lou knew that vagabond Deary tended to marry painters, inter alia. Her marital history rivaled Reevadare's. Deary was the marrying kind. Between marriages she had boyfriends.

Lou and Maytree both liked a recent suitor of Deary's. That was articulate Slow Sykes, who wore green shoes and held down third base. A serious painter in oils, he also read good books. He always showed up for sunset drinks on Maytrees' beach, and acted out a new joke or two a day. Lou heard at once when, within two hours of Deary's marrying him, the new groom motored from Fishermen's Pier for their honeymoon cruise without her. Later Lou visited Deary's cold-storage shed and saw by lamplight the letter this gentleman wrote Deary on linen bond.

He apologized and sought divorce as kindly as possible. He noted in apparent misery that he had realized on the pier, for the second time on their one wedding day, how long it took a woman to change clothes. Deary found that sensible, and told the story on herself, laughing helplessly and anew each time. She was, Cornelius said, easily amused.

Before Lou knew her, Deary wed a New York painter who came to Provincetown every summer. Lou's mother used to find him surly. He divorced her for a Boston orthopedic surgeon, and both seemed to cheer up. Then she married a sweet-talking Azorean fisherman, a dragger. Everyone knew the dragger's family froze him out because Deary was not Catholic. He obviously missed his gregarious kin, just across town, so Deary sadly released him. One summer Lou returned from college to find Deary married to an old Rocky Mountain abstractionist who wore a gaucho's rawhide hat. She saw his few clothes and many primed canvases in the cold-storage shed. There he told Lou he found Provincetown provincial. Later Deary, weeping, told Lou that he moved to a Greenwich Village studio and returned only once, bareheaded, to load his canvases on the bus. And once she married a Red Sock, a reliever who never came back from spring training.

Standing on the road by the beach Lou studied the painting class. Alarmed, Lou saw the students *en plein air* ripple green and blue and cadmium yellow and red around Deary's form in glare. She herself hoped to paint, soberly, when she got old. The more she saw of the Provincetown school, the more she favored *grisailles*.

After they married she learned to feel their skin as double-sided. They felt a pause. Theirs was too much feeling to push through the crack that led down to the dim world of time and stuff. That world was gone. They held themselves alert only in those few million cells where they touched. She learned from those cells his awareness and his courtesy. Love so sprang at her, she honestly thought no one had ever looked into it. Where was it in literature? Someone would have written something. She must not have recognized it. Time to read everything again.

She shipwrecked on the sheets. She surfaced like a dynamited bass. She opened her eyes and discovered where on their bed she had fetched up. She lay spread as a film and as fragile. Linked lights wavered on the wall. The linked lights looked like chain mail. They moved blindly over the wall's thumbtacked Klee print of Sinbad. The tide rising on sand outside bore these linked lights as if on a platter. She loved Maytree, his restlessness, his asceticism, his, especially, abdomen. Where is privacy, if not in the mind? It is your temples I kiss, where they dip. They should bulge, from all your mind holds. Their hollows are entries; they allow me near your brain. Forever and aye, my jubilee.

Maytree, flexed beside her, was already asleep. He usually fell asleep as if dropped from a scarp. From above he would look as if his parachute failed. Intimacy could not be unique to her and Maytree, this brief blending, this blind sea they entered together diving. His neck smelled as suntan does, his own oil heated, and his hair smelled the same but darker. He was still fresh from an outdoor shower. Awareness was a braided river. It slid down time in drops or torrents. Now she knew he woke. The room seemed to get smarter. His legs moved and their tonus was tight. Her legs were sawdust; they were a line old rope shreds on sand. All her life the thought of his body made her blush.

—We should get up, Maytree said, and moor the dory. Tide's coming in.

Now he stood and brushed sand from his side of the sheet. They always had sand in the bed. It was a wonder she was not slimmer.

– Mayo's duck sandwiches, cheddar, beer
– hard-boiled eggs in waxed-paper twists (3)
– two red-speckled notebooks, fountain pen, 2 lbs 10d. nails
– *The Circus Animals' Desertion; Fathers and Sons; Sons and Lovers;* Eddington, *The Nature of the Physical World*

Maytree left town on impulse and headed toward his shack. The planet rolled into its shadow. On the high dune, sky ran down to his ankles. Everything he saw was lower than his socks. Across a long horizon, parabolic dunes cut sky as rogue waves do. The silence of permanence lay on the scene. He found a Cambrian calm as if the world had not yet come; he found a posthumous hush as if humans had gone. He crossed the low swale and climbed a trail his feet felt. He ate a sandwich. Now he knew, but did not believe, she loved him. Her depth he knew when he kissed her. His brain lobes seemed to part like clouds over sun.

He massed three glass lamps on the shack's table beside the speckled notebooks. The question was not death; living things die. It was love. Not that we died, but that we cared wildly, then deeply, for one person out of billions. We bound ourselves to the fickle, changing, and dying as if they were rock. *The young / In one another's arms, birds in the trees / – Those dying generations – at their song.*

Every book he read was a turn he took. He ran aground. He started new notebooks without having made the least sense of any old notebook. He pitched into the world for plunder, probed it with torches, filled his arms and brain with its pieces botched – to what end? Every fact was a rune. Whole unfilled systems littered the kitchen and beach of the house he shared with Lou. He wanted to spend himself broke in the brain, to master something and start again. Since everything fit with everything else, how could anyone begin to think or understand?

He took off his shirt. Love itself raised other honest questions, more than several. Was romantic love a modern invention? How long could it last as requited, as unrequited? Does familiarity blur lovers' clear sight of essences and make surfaces look significant? Since love intensifies in parted lovers, presumably because the lovers forget and reimagine each other, is love then wholly false? How false? Thirty percent false? Sixty percent? Five?

Later he stood on the foredune's lip and looked at the stars over the ocean. A wider life breathed in him, and things' rims stirred and reared back. Only the lover sees what is real, he thought. Only the lover sees the beloved truly, inwardly. Far from being blind, love alone can see. Watching the sky now, and forever after, doubled his world. He felt he saw through Lou's eyes as an Aztec priest, having flayed an enemy, donned the skin. Or somewhat less so.

A week after their wedding, Reevadare stopped by their house – Maytree had moved into Lou's. Raising a coffee cup as if to toast, she said,

*You went in as twoski*
*And came out as oneski.*
*Now aren't you sorry,*
*You son-of-a-gunski?*

He knew Lou was not at all sorry. The quatrain was new to Maytree. It posed a question he was circling then: Do women in love feel as men do? Do men love as women love? His virgin bride shared her pipe-frame bed all smiles and laughter. When they were intimate to the last degree on that bed, did Lou's experience join his, did his experience match hers, during this moment and that moment?

In the course of his reading he could survey, informally, what ground other students of the matter had won. He seized their green kitchen table as a desk.

Later while Lou bathed, Maytree copied from a volume of Keats's ever-young letters a possibly unrelated but similarly unanswerable question: Who enjoyed lovemaking more – the man or the woman? He popped it into that spotted notebook in dimeter and trimeter:

> *Who shall say*
>   *between Man and Woman*
>   *which is the most [more] delighted?*

The woman, everyone knew Tiresias said, but Tiresias was made up. On what grounds had the Greek man let full-fictional and full-switched Tiresias answer, The woman? Did lovemaking then and now run to male, or to female, noisemaking? Speaking of wild surmise?

For lovemaking nearly killed Lou. Was she all right? Abashed, he held her steady until she opened her eyes. Was he a brute? What ailed her? —Whoo, she answered once, and another time, Yike. He stopped worrying. Hours afterward he used to see her, firm and young as she was, gripping the rail to check her descent downstairs.

He proposed Keats's question to Lou one morning as they shared the last of the tooth powder. —Say, Lou – here's a question. Keats put it, 'Who shall say between Man and Woman which is the more delighted?' What do you think?

—The woman. Rather prompt of silent Lou. Much later that night in their shack bed she added just as he was rolling asleep, If the man is John Keats.

Two months after their wedding, Lou helped Deary shift to her shed. Year-round Deary kept rough headquarters in an abandoned cold-storage shed on Cold Storage Wharf. Provincetown's painters depicted this long shed so often they called it 'motif number one.' Deary looked now to be wearing several dozen layers of bright-print cloth. Her hoop earrings were the size of parrot perches.

Usually Deary lived there all winter, often sheltering a loose person or two who needed a roof. To Lou, the shed smelled of gasoline, engine oil, and shellfish. For utilities, Deary used a woodstove, and a pier hose till it froze. Everyone helped her by buying the oyster-shell sculptures she glued for tourists, purple eyes out. One winter Deary lived in Cairos' summer cottage. If almost anyone had a baby winter or summer, Deary moved there to watch the older kids, to shop, cook, and shift laundry. One October she moved into Cornelius Blue's dune shack to tend him when he broke his pelvis at low tide flying from a horse that bucked. Bauhausy in fits, Deary carted to wherever she was staying a pedestal chair sculpted as a hand. Lou liked it. She sat on the plastic palm and leaned on the black fingers. In summer when Deary slept on the dunes or on Cairos' porch, the chair stayed in the shed. So, often, did Crazy Joe, a harmless bum.

Last year on this pier by a creosoted piling Lou met Deary's mother, pearls and pearled hat, suit, and heels, on a rare visit: Ruby Hightoe. Glaring and calm in her tailored suit, she steered her red alligator-skin high heels around a pile of cord net that seaweed and beer bottles fouled. Deary's mother reminded Lou of Mrs. Buff Orpington, whose *husband invented the chicken* and portions of whose car stretched across four panels of *Blondie.*

Deary had floored her long shed and painted it yellow. Where Lou's eye wanted a window, Deary tacked the Modigliani print – the long-drawn-out red-cheeked woman's head and neck – that they all had. The opposite wall showed Picasso's usual blue clowns on a beach. A brass porthole was a window. Three bushel baskets hung from nails and served as dresser, closet, and pantry. Her bed was a cot mattress on a door on iron milk crates; Crazy Joe's was a mattress across the room. Some of her wool skirts stretched between wall nails like tapestries to block wind. Her bookshelf was a stepladder. Lou liked to peer down the gap between planks and wall where she saw fish swim. Now Deary handed Lou an old corn dodger to drop in. The fish were on the corn dodger before it hit.

Lou walked back from the pier, hoping Maytree was home. Vietnamese legend calls the earth the realm of desire. When Maytree laughed he loosed his legs. His collarbones and Achilles tendons were thin. He whistled, wore loose pants, and rattled on.

Moving houses was Maytree's paid work. Since he returned from out West and the war, Maytree hauled whole houses for hire, on afternoons only. He got paid for hijinks. He worked some afternoons with his old college friend Sooner Roy. They started as carpenters, turning porches into rooms, adding apartments, and raising roofs. Then for friends they moved the Protos' house on a Monument Hill traverse. They detached the pump, braced corners and doorways with two-by-sixes, jacked the mildewed house, and with advisers pushed it onto a hay-wagon hitched to a mule team. The mules were having none of it. Maytree forbade whacking the mules with planks.

Old Flo Proto, inside, chopped onions and carrots. People could hear her knife hit, or was it a hatchet. Maytree guarded the mules while Sooner rounded up two tractors and Flo Proto cranked up her woodstove. The tractors, themselves whacked, worked. Splay-legged in her wobbling kitchen, Flo Proto cooked on the woodstove a slumgullion to feed the crew. The chimney smoked, and its smoke marked their route. School-children broke out to trail the house.

The more houses they moved, the more house-moving jobs offered. People dragged anchor to a patch of trees, or a hollow cheap to heat, or a patch of waterfront exposed but eminently rent-outable. The process stimulated Maytree, and Lou, too –

and children, and retired sailors, and off-duty coast guards, and neighbors – by its many routes to disaster.

That summer Lou watched Maytree and Sooner move a house or two a month. Most larky, they floated houses alongshore – if half the hawsers in town and Sooner's truck, two veteran jeeps, two tractors, and the milkman's piebald cob could ease a house down to the bay without a wreck. Lou followed the trek. When they gained the beach they propped railroad ties as ramp to logs on the beach. They pushed the house to slide on the logs. Bystanders propped low walls. Lou stood at water's edge as one of their house tows rolled into the drink. It would have turned turtle but the bottom snagged the stovepipe. It got epic quickly. Where was Winslow Homer when you needed him? After that day, they breasted to the top-heavy raft four gasoliners to power the contraption and act as Mae Wests.

Maytree was no more finicky than house owners or the town about who might own lots' titles. During the war, property bills, if any, lapsed. Yankees paid back taxes and taxes on empty lots. After the war they owned them all.

Sooner Roy wore a slouch hat, its brim a sawdust gutter. He followed the Red Sox in frenzies terrible to behold. He was trying to borrow land on which to build, under a canvas canopy, a forty-foot sloop or yawl to sail to Maine. He grew up in Missouri. Maytree was tall, and Sooner was strong as Babe Ruth.

Two years later they were dancing in the kitchen to 'Lady Be Good.' Maytree turned down the radio and ran his notion by Lou. It is an unnameable boon love hauls down, that people rightly prize as the best of life, and for which it fusses over weddings. Not only will a cave-dwelling pair cull food and kill so kids thrive, but their feeling for each other, not to mention for the kids, brings something beyond food people need. Each felt it between them when they danced. It was real as anything the mind could know. Her eyes' crystal, her split-faced smile, agreed. He rolled the volume knob. Oh sweet and lovely.

After their first year or so, Lou's beauty no longer surprised him. He never stopped looking, because her face was his eyes' home. No, what so endeared her now and forever was her easy and helpless laughter. He felt like the world's great wit. She worked, walked, stood, or sat like a mannequin, shoulders down and neck erect, and his least *mot* slayed her. Her body pleated. Her rusty-axle laugh sustained itself voicelessly and without air. At table, if she was still chewing when the laugh came rolling on her backward like a loose cart, she put a napkin on her head. Otherwise she dropped on the table. If it slayed her yet more, she knocked the table with her head in even beats. Or her long torso folded and her orbits fell on vertical fists on her knees. Unstrung with hilarity, she lost her footing and rolled down a dune. More than once – anywhere – she dropped backward and straight-legged like a kid in diapers.

He fell in love with Lou again and again. Walking, he held her hand. She seemed, then and now, to roll or float over the world evenly, acting and giving and taking, never accelerating, never slowing, wearing a slip of red or blue scarf. Her mental energy and endurance matched his. She neither competed nor rebelled. Her freedom strengthened him, as did her immeasurable reserve. Often she seemed the elder. She opened their house to everyone. Actively, she accepted what came to her, like a well-sailed sloop with sea room. Her face was an organ of silence. That he did not possess her childhood drove him wild. Who was this impostor she sang with in college – how dare he?

Their intimacy flooded. Love like a tide either advances or retreats, Maytree opined into a recent notebook. Their awarenesses rode waves paired like outriggers. Maytree thought Plato wrong: physical senses and wordless realms neither diverge or oppose; they meet as nearest neighbors in the darkness of personality and embrace.

They named the baby Peter and called him Petie. From his first interview with this implausible son, then purple, Maytree curbed his vision of teaching it to read and love literature, to row, fish, hit and pitch, miter corners, frame walls, sail, and rebuild motors. His sole intended fatherly prohibition – that his son never draw his living from the sea – was superfluous. He seemed incapable even of drawing breath. He was not so much delicate as hopeless, predating vulcanization.

A pity because his plainly not-viable person, unfit for the grating air, enchanted Lou, of whose taste for primate fetuses or naked hatchlings he had no previous clue. Lou saw something in the organism that bypassed him, but apparently hit other females, including tourists, as if the quality inhered in females as a class rather than in babies as a class. Even managing his wormy limbs was an ordeal beyond Petie. If Lou handed the creature to him, Maytree had to remember to hold its head up, or his own Lou would scold him.

Once on a renovation job he deliberately described Petie as 'time-consuming' to Sol Raposo, a mason. Daily Maytree watched Sol's three kids make a reunion party at the site by bringing him the lunch he ate playing with all three. Sol looked up incredulously through his bison curls and shrugged. He said, Have more.

One day they settled with Petie under a bamboo-and-canvas beach umbrella. A red scarf held Lou's hair. The tide was out; the flats were mud. The sun was low; soon their friends would show up with drinks and bottles. Friends would help drag Petie back by the heels and try to get sand from his mouth's ungraspable drool.

When he first moved in after their wedding, Maytree got to work enlarging the beachside crawl space. Now they had a wedge-shaped basement furnished with a galley and head. He finished it off by installing many-paned French doors right on the beach. When storms came, he removed both doors so the seas could pour in without breaking glass. In ordinary weather, friends entered the front door, went downstairs, and opened the French doors to the beach.

Until the daily party dropped in they were reading on beach towels and leaning against the basement. The chairs were for visitors. Lou realized years ago that the sight of her reading impelled Maytree to try to drag her into his reading. She always went back to her book without a word.

—If you were a prehistoric Aleut –

—What?

—If you were a prehistoric Aleut and your wife or husband died, your people braced your joints for grief. That is, they lashed hide bindings around your knees, ankles, elbows, shoulders, and hips. You could still move, barely, as if swaddled. Otherwise, the Aleuts said, in your grief you would *go to pieces* just as the skeleton would go to pieces. You would fall apart.

He watched her close her book on a finger and train on him a look. He knew she hated his interrupting her reading.

—But the troubadours, she said. They made up romantic love.

—Where did you learn that?

—In college. And she added, Maybe only the husbands fall apart. The men.

What made her say that? What of life had she seen? Had not her mother fallen apart when her father left?

—Anyway, she said, prehistoric means only: before those people wrote. They could have learned to understand sealers' or whalers' love songs, long after the troubadours.

Maytree well knew peoples had managed swoons of their own devising having never heard of Europe. Archaeologists find love poetry in unopened pyramids. She was unreasonable. That he could fix.


—Until you have a baby, her mother had said, you don't know what love is! Her mother volunteered this on the day of Lou's one and only wedding. —Oh, Lou wanted to say, go soak your head. After Lou brought forth Petie, she at once recalled her mother's words, forgave, and endorsed them. That her mother was so often right no longer irked her. As she would never irk Petie, now joyful in her arms. He sucked her nose. Later his pointy fingers made faces with her face. She never put him down. She must feel his skin on her, feel his cranium in her arm's crook, his belly on her belly, and smell his breath, his scalp, etc., etc. He obviously felt the same way. They were pieces of each other foully parted.

When they had to separate, she took ever-deeper breaths as if air had no use. Her sternum and her ventral torso and arms ached. Maytree had some horseshoe magnets in the kitchen. She gave each a wrench to hold.

She and Petie laughed to flout fate by smashing together, thigmotropic. Or they met staring forehead to forehead, then twisted and laughed.

Lou saw that she had hitherto wasted her life. When he was six months old, she asked Maytree, Can we have more?

—Sure, he said. More what?

When he was fifteen months old, Petie could say 'anemometer' and 'horseshoe crab.' Sometimes he sang to the sand, Hyannis, Hyannis.

—Hold him while you can, Reevadare Weaver told Lou in her smoky voice. In the history of the world, Lou suspected no one had ever asked Reevadare for advice. She perceived others' needs so keenly she anticipated them every time. What an odd thing to say: anemometer.

At four Petie took to yelling at the heavenly bodies: —Hey, orbs! Wait for me! or, Orbs… listen to this! A genius, Lou thought; he commanded constellations. Clearly a poet. —A tyrant, Maytree said. —They are all tyrants, Deary said. His milk teeth separated neatly, like unripe corn on the ear. More children were evidently not in store for them. A sore spot, but she knew she could never love another so much.

Maytree and Lou were learning night skies together and trying to teach Petie. Star-watchings-with-child were now a moral imperative. They had read in *Wolf-Children and Feral Man* about Caspar Hauser, locked from birth in a low German attic he later called a hole or cage. His captor taught him to talk, fed him, and removed his waste. He played with a wooden horse. When he was a big seventeen his captor took him outdoors for the first time and abandoned him at a Nuremberg intersection. The groping boy carried CASPAR HAUSER written on paper. Bright and curious, he could scarcely use or understand fast speech. After a newspaper fuss (the criminal was never found), a benefactor adopted him and helped him adapt. He never complained of his captor's treatment but once, early. Then he wept to see for the first time – in the city! – those scattered thousand stars he realized everyone else on earth had been able to see all along. 'His astonishment and transport surpassed all description.' Caspar said that the man ought to 'be locked up for a few days,' for withholding the sight of the stars. It was the only indignation at his captivity he ever showed.

The first thing Lou and Maytree learned about skywatching was to lie down. Since town's light blanked skies, they watched from the dunes. Friends joined them. Once they settled down on the beach at sunset Lou saw terns nock their spines to bowstrings between their crossbow wings. At the last second the terns looked, cocked one wing, and smacked. A bluefish boil blackened the water. If she looked away, the bluefish sounded like popping corn. Geography laid their position bare. Overhead clouds cracked the last light like crude.

From deep water Lou saw a seal head appear. Deary stuck two fingers in her mouth and whistled. The seal perked and, without diving or moving its eyes from Deary, came inshore to her feet in lappets of foam. The creature came to Deary without stirring the water. It rolled in surf, dark and half on sand. Its nose touched Deary's painted toes. She had conjured a seal. She talked to it. As they quit the beach the seal searched all around, even up in the sky. It was Deary's pure heart – why should not a seal love it as they all did?

'A silkie,' Cornelius said of Deary.

In darkness they watched Venus, fastidious, track the downed sun. Alterf, the glance. Diphda, second frog. —Do you feel a fool for trying to learn what the Stone Age people already knew? Maytree did not. Lou saw the Milky Way's two bands merge over the sea. There, scoopings of stars made an oval where suns mixed it up in a spree. And that – that oval – was the galaxy's core. But – how do we know?

—We're complex jellies, Cornelius said. One animal among many. Well, the others didn't know jack, and scientists knew a lot. Lou watched stars bang their burning knuckles on the dome.

Now between his parents outside the shack on a blanket, Petie raised his head. He unfurled an arm and placed a boneless hand on his father's forearm. He had shed that clouds-of-glory, that leaving-of-fairies glaze by which newborn people keep parents in thrall till other charms appear. Like his mother, he did not say much. His eyes gleamed dark beneath low brows, and everything struck him as funny.

His parents murmured, a sound unnamed like foghorn or wind. Above him the shack's pitcher pump's handle, a shape like a hungry monster's neck, loomed. He looked at the stars around it. He felt cold sand at the back of his head. His mother covered him with her sweater.

He knew their name: stars. They rustled in place in the black sky. Unrelated to him, they made as much sense as most things, and more than some, for their harmlessness and calm. Of which he instantly tired, for nothing changed or required him. For a second on the blanket between his parents and watching stars, Petie knew he was alive.

* * *

Lou took a part-time job at Jen and Barrie's art gallery. She could read there, and stare at action paintings. She saw no reason to subject Petie to the austerities she and Maytree enjoyed exchanging for free time. Maytree must not give up his mornings writing poetry, and from her wages, baby got a new pair of shoes.

At six Petie with his friends made lemonade from ants and sold it on wharves. A scallop-edged new front tooth just cleared gum. His other, deciduous, teeth were the size of graph-paper squares. He could not yet build a fire; he could build a smoke. Cornelius called Petie 'Spotey-Otey.'

At eight Petie wrote for school, 'Mice are a small creature who come in.' In rain Maytree helped Petie carve whistles and daggers. One May three blizzards dropped eight feet of snow. When school let out Deary played with a two-year-old and a child, and carried around a baby or two, while she kept an eye on Petie. With Deary, with the Cairos from New York and Cornelius from the dunes, Lou and Maytree sat outside the basement doors on the beach during a southerly. They watched Petie and the neighbor Bonobos boys race up the beach and dare incoming waves like pipers. Overhead skies loosened.

Lou and Maytree saw their marriage as unique. Of course they rarely fought; she rarely spoke. They both knew love itself as an epistemological tool. As if mechanical, a halyard, love drew up something new that raised an everlasting flap and sped. How? Why?

\* \* \*

On holidays, ancient Greeks reddened the marble face of Jupiter with cinnabar. Maytree celebrated Thanksgivings by beginning work on a book. He wrote book-length poems. Three of his books, at four stressed syllables a line, took three years apiece to write. Others split like mica books.

Maytree hoped to inspire his Boston publishers to tout those books widely by showing up unannounced. As if they were idle. He was riding the bus back from such a surprise visit when he thought of a new book-length poem to start this Thanksgiving. Boston or New York embodies our condition in one aspect: We are strangers among millions living in cubes like Anasazi in a world we fashioned. And Provincetown shows, by contrast, that we live on a strand between sea and sky. Here are protoplasmic, peeled people in wind against crystal skies. Our soft tissues are outside, like unearthed and drying worms'. The people in cities are like Mexican jumping beans, like larvae in tequila bottles, soft bits in hard boxes. And so forth. The length to which we as people go to hide our nakedness by blocking sky!

There was a fatal problem. There always is. Provincetown people too, and all people worldwide who could swing it, were also bare tissues living under roofs. An honest way through, all but changing the whole idea, would be a set of interleaved narratives, Boston people and desert villagers. He would stress only certain aspects. Dwellers. And! – or, but! If he moved adobe dwellings from Arizona to Mexico, he could use *holi, holi, huqui, huqui*, to Mayans the sound of grinding corn on a metate. The words would console him for losing *Anasazi*, a word he had just learned from the *Globe*. Some year, somehow, he would work into some poem *rini, rini, manju, manju*, the sound of bullock-cart axle in Hindi.

So he added his playful bits to the world perceived. How much better to heal and prevent disease; feed and inoculate and teach kids; provide sturdy breeds of animals and seeds! But poetry seemed to be his task, and the long poem his form as it had been Edwin Arlington Robinson's. Quarterlies and reviews, like some anthologies, printed his short lyrics. He endorsed Edwin Arlington Robinson's view that anthologies preserve poems by pickling their corpses. Always omitting Robinson's real, long work that future readers would never know, anthologists forever reprinted 'Richard Cory' who went out and put a bullet through his head, and no wonder.

Petie at eleven surfcast the backshore for bluefish crashing bait, and in the fall for stripers. He freed a wing-hooked cormorant that slashed his throat. His mother fed his many friends ship's biscuit and honey. They overturned outhouses on Halloween. He met the fleet every night. He jigged squid by lantern light and leaned on pilings on piers. He had an old dory and often kept it running, afloat, or both.

His fondness for humans did not extend to girls, who were less interesting than frogs, and noisier. Girls had no skills but clustering and jacks – a ball game they played sitting down. Girls had no higher wish than to get old enough to wear makeup. He owned rocks he respected more. From afar, very far, he studied one high-school girl.

\* \* \*

Winter in calm air Pilgrim Lake froze. When it froze without snowing, everyone skated. One night Lou and Maytree skated arm-in-arm on black ice in half a gale. The lake lay in the expanse between dunes and highway. Others from town brought wood for a bonfire from which sparks joined stars. The two warmed each other on an iced marsh-grass hummock by the fire. They watched Petie dash among his friends. Now she saw bigger boys at one end of the lake jumping barrels. She watched Petie join them. Not tall, he was sturdy. When he jumped a laid-down barrel and skated away, the boys added another barrel. He cleared those two side-by-side, so they added another. Petie had been a marvel all along. By the time the boys quit, each had smashed up gloriously at least twice. When they landed, they slid on ice until stopped by the foot of a dune. These were the boys she used to watch Maytree coach at football.

Lou turned to Maytree and saw his firelit pupils deepen to hers. He was letting her in, as always, and holding her there. His skin glowed; she slipped from a mitten to warm his cold cheek with her palm. For three days it had blown 30 knots from the west. He put his arm around her, and she leaned her face near his face so she could hear him in wind. She tilted and felt his jaw move before he kissed her forehead.

> ... *If I don't talk about your hair, your lips, your eyes,*
> *still your face that I keep inside my soul,*
> *the sound of your voice that I keep inside my brain,*
> *the days of September rising in my dreams,*
> *give shape and color to my words, my sentences,*
> *whatever theme I touch, whatever thought I utter.*

He pressed her close to say part of the poem in her ear. She touched her forehead to his. How absurd that brains could not embrace, although she favored the present arrangement.

They walked all the way home. She longed for the life she already possessed, a life large as clouds'. Mightily, as she had these three days, she opposed the wind's push. Her coat pressed her back; cold blew through her wool slacks. All at once, as they walked still in the open, the wind died. Someone shut a valve? Her stance nearly toppled her; he caught her. Her ears pricked. The silence unnerved her. The air's emptiness felt like Maytree beside her had died. They looked at each other. —I feel like I've lost consciousness, he said, hoarse. He was in his early forties. His face was open. He seemed not to have noticed that consciousness in him was a wind.

The next morning, as Maytree's skull pinched off arterial flow to her arm, she told him – she grew talkative at such times – that when her mother left for New York, she had asked her how she

47

could leave Provincetown. —What do you like better in New York? —You'll laugh, her mother said. —No I won't. —All right: It's the light. Lou had laughed. She loved the silver light in New York canyons too.

And where was Lou's father? No one knew. In Marblehead, when she was a tall and bookish twelve her mother asked her one night to set the table for two. Her father often missed dinner. She and her mother sat to chilled consommé madrilène, roast potatoes, and lamb. Beyond the dining room windows, Marblehead harbor grayed. The sea floated a red oval: a cloud reflecting the sun now down. Her lovely mother's composure broke. She covered her face and left. Lou ate in silence and eyed the cold water. The next day her father missed breakfast.

At middle school a day later her friend Phoebe told her, You didn't know? – that her father had left town with her eponymous aunt Lou, her mother's sister. Of her tall father she retained several small memories and one big one. He loved her; they loved each other. She stood behind his chair and smelled his hair. She never saw him again, or heard from him. Someone said he married her aunt Lou and was spending the summer in Rough and Ready, California. Her mother's face hardened and stuck. She never spoke of the man. Lou knew then that her mother was tallying her father's faults and perfidies. She did not know then that polishing this grudge would be her mother's lone project for the balance of her life. Lou was in college when her mother moved to the West Village and gave her the house on Cape Cod Bay.

Sometimes now Lou searched old albums to test her proposition that nothing so compels a woman as the boyhood of the man she loves. She saw a snapshot of boy Maytree in cap and knickers dwarfed by his cross-eyed father on a wharf. In the prints, Maytree's cap's shadow blacked most of his face. Here again he crouched on the beach, as at a starting block, between his hairy mother and his visibly half-dead grandmother, in a wind harsh with that present's brine. In those prints she saw unease in the boy, as if he had been scanning the offing for the man.

No, it was she who sought for the man in the child. She could not find him, so the boy seemed to her lost in a deafening wind. The boy seemed – wonderfully – to need her without knowing it. But he did not, not yet. Perhaps, she asked later, he never did?

# Part One

That winter the crowd on the frozen corner parted for Lou, saying, He's okay, it's all right. She saw Petie across Maytree's arms; his legs dangled. She saw Maytree's bent head and his bombardier jacket's fleece. He was passing his chin back and forth across Petie's forehead. —Just a hurt foot, someone said. No one fools a mother. Fractures to both legs, probably pelvis, possibly back: quadriplegic. With one hand Petie held his right leg. His eyes lodged back just beneath his shed-roof browbone as Maytree's did. Maytree's pale eyes were lights glimpsed in a cave; Petie's eyes were themselves caves. When he saw her, he smiled and turned his head away. —It's all right, Lou said. Maytree rubbed his cheek against Petie's forehead.

Lou reached for Petie and saw Maytree secure his knees as he started to hand him over. Petie jerked and said, Yipes. No use moving him. She felt his cold pea jacket. She saw he was not going to cry.

Lou stroked Petie and sought Maytree's eyes. He looked up the street and said that a Zevar brother had examined Petie, guessed a simple fracture, and drove to fetch local Dr. New.

How could any mother let her child ride a bicycle? Petie lodged in the lobing sheepskin elbow of Maytree's bombardier jacket. Possibly in shock, he lifted his head and waved at friends.

—Where is the driver? Maytree bit his lips. She knew he would not curse in public. —They chased him on bikes. Someone had moved Petie's mashed bike to the road's edge. Petie often, as even now, seemed to be running for governor. At this intersection, face square and white, he hollered and joked and grabbed hands.

The narrow town favored bicycles over cars. Presently some men appeared far up the silver road, cap flaps down. A mainland man walked between two adult cyclists. She did not know him, which usually meant nobody did. Taller than the others, he wore a brimmed felt hat and a double-breasted coat down to his flat shoes, suggesting the silent-movies landlord who says to war widows with children, 'You must pay the rent!'

Dr. New drove up in his Ford and nodded at Maytree, who lowered Petie – Whoop – to recline on the backseat, and Lou climbed in front and cranked the window down. The driver of the car who hit Petie neared. He stood against a telephone pole and crossed his arms. By then many witnesses had told her, told them all, that the car pushed the bike off the road by hitting it. The man's coat's shoulders lifted and he looked up as if sighing. As the Ford pulled out for the hospital, Lou saw him look expressionless at Maytree, who had started in a low voice,

—Why in the living hell… The crowd closed in to hear. Not much happened in winter on land.

\* \* \*

—It was probably not the stranger's fault, she said. She was waiting at the hospital. How would she feel if they owned a car and she hurt a child with it? She saw Petie and other children flying over handlebars all around town, everywhere she drove her putative car. Low-flying children. They would be a danger in themselves. The poor man. Poor everyone. Petie had wide bones. Tomorrow, she and Maytree could maneuver their own ironstone bed down two sets of stairs to the half-basement by the beach. Petie could recuperate handy to bathroom and kitchen, they could see and hear him to help him, and he could watch through panes the day change, the tides, and the stars.

That night Lou watched Maytree pour brandy in a glass. He still wore a navy blue sweater under his overalls. Petie had a broken leg. Did she want brandy? She shook her head. She sat at the green kitchen table.

Brandy he drinks? The tenth-anniversary-present brandy from four years ago we've sipped on Christmas mornings only?

It was okay if he did not move. The cast was heavy; its edges scraped. In his own bed that night under low eaves, whenever he drowsed he rolled over his handlebars again and hit the street. Odd – his friends usually broke their collarbones. He heard raised voices from the kitchen. Once he heard his name. His mother came in, stooping under the eave; she soothed him and sang him 'Take Me Out to the Ballgame' – how touching of her, really, though funny. He used to like the song when he was little. His parents had always been swell. After another sleepy interval of handlebar-flying, his father entered with his hair sticking up, sat lightly on the bed, and handed him a flowery teacup of brandy.

—Brandy all around? his mother said.

—That ought to help, he said, and pretty soon it did.

—It might not all be the man's fault, she had said when they came down.

Gently Maytree knocked over his chair and cursed back and forth and in toto implied in rare words that he, by contrast and on balance, found the man grievously at fault. The series ended 'son of a sea-cook.'

Maytree sat and covered his face with his hands. Lou found herself by habit checking whether his sweater's elbows rested on spills. He rubbed his eyes. These last two or three weeks, something bad had worsened. Lou did not know what, but it was her, something about her. He had been close-shaven or unshaven, gone to the dunes, sleepy, jumpy. In her company he wrapped himself in misery like a robe. Between them self-consciousness bulked as a river silts its channel. They sat to smoked mackerel and turnips and plied Petie with questions. Only these few weeks. They chewed and chewed. She dumped her plateful and washed. She sought to avoid him and secure privacy.

Sometimes these past weeks at dawn he started between them a deliberate chat. —And what's your plan for the day? His bad acting was worse than silence. When friends came by, both of them roused: they ate, and Maytree told knock-knock jokes.

During all their other years' short silences – but not this one – while they slept, while stars held fast their spots beyond the window and seas concussed the beach, they woke together as if at a temblor. They turned and rolled. They met and sought and hit. Then they talked under the blankets, holding each other's arms or ribs or hands. She searched out his eyes in the dark, and regarded him in the long way of longing and knowledge, and in the longer way of love. There had not been much of that this past year.

At the green kitchen table Maytree was biting his lips from the inside. This meant a speech. He bit his lips from inside before he chewed Pete out. It meant a speech he would rather skip and she would rather miss. She held her head erect. A gust shook the glass and jerked the lamps' reflections. She rose to wash dishes.

Now he was crying. He rose and held her as if he just remembered something. Tears traced his face creases and dripped. She held him. Crying – Maytree? He had sniffled a bit when his mother died. They disliked drama.

—I will always love you. Believe me.

Now what. She removed her arms and stepped back. Fast as shock she knew now what, what alone could come next, and her blood in every vessel tripped. Not her Maytree. Never her Maytree, who loved her, as he just unsaid.

Maytree and who? She waited for it. She squared her shoulders. If this was not shaping up to be Maytree's finest hour, it might as well be hers.

He composed his mouth and backed till the old stove stopped him. Why could he not have launched this speech when they were both looking out at something, or tending to Petie with his broken leg? Did she know him or not, this wet-faced epistomeliac? He put his hands in his overalls' pockets, slid them out at once, crossed his arms, and finally uncrossed his arms to stand before her as if before a firing squad.

—I'm moving to Maine.

He's moving to Maine.

—When?

—Tomorrow. Petie will be fine with just you. I'm sorry.

—Where in Maine?

—An island in Casco Bay. Why?

—I'm just used to… it's a habit. She thought she might take a seat.

—When will you come back? She saw Maytree draw a breath and in his decency let it out in silence.

She would not ask why. An island in Maine was just the place for a carpenter poet. When had he seen this island, if he had? Last summer, when he crewed on Sooner Roy's schooner *Joyce Shatley* for three weeks. Who else was gone then?

—I never did love… anyone…

Go, you idiot, she merely thought, and he stopped cold. At the kitchen table she held her head still and cocked, as a robin listens for worms.

He waited standing, as if his being less comfortable at this moment would be his just deserts, all of them.

Everything familiar to her altered, as if she only now remarked his red lids, his lips he was still nibbling from within, the deep pair of lines by his mouth, the hollow cheeks his smiles cracked, his – very fine! – small oval head – enough. My. Time expanded. What was keeping him?

Reappraising Maytree and his every act and word for the past few years could wait. She would have the rest of her life to pace lost ground. How were she and Petie to live? On alimony, like everyone else. In fact, she bought almost nothing, food and fuel. Maytree was evidently ceding their house. She would not run to her mother in New York, unless for funds. She had no say. She had a son with a broken leg.

Maytree had not moved. Truly? He stood forlorn as a clown. Give him not the hook but the gaff. He rubbed his face and felt for his Luckies and went out. Her kitchen: its limed walls where they hung their friends' frenzied paintings, the dry money plants whose ovals clicked in the vase, the kindling box, mismatched chairs, the cast-iron gas stove whose warming oven took wood, the Bakelite radio, red pie chest, blue teapot, iron kettle; apple-jack on a shelf with poetry books, a shell sculpture, a cotton bag of chessmen, the stenciled breadbox, and her apron on a china hook. Petie was asleep upstairs, or drunk if he drank that whole cup.

Tomorrow? Just like that? He must have been packing in secret. When did he decide, make lists, figure, and pack – so that at this last minute, on the day Petie broke his leg, he was set to go?

How were he and Deary going to live? Both elbows on the green table, she rolled her head's weight from one fist to the other. No reason to be surprised. This sort of thing happens all the time.

Maytree walked far on the black beach. His hot eyes cooled. Invisible clouds blocked the sky and its atmospheres where noises of people dissolve. The sea beside him, a monster with a lace hem, drained east.

What happens to a person! Of all life's pitches, you notice only the curve. Or, late, the beanball. He had not meant to say that about his loving her! A brutal, terrible thing to say when you leave someone, even someone who made allowances. Low tide smelled like green pennies.

Before Lou, Maytree had traveled here and there around the heart, the raucous heart. Byways, dim-lit bars always changing hands. Once a great handful of girl out west told him – I never did love you, I just thought I did. They were watering their horses at an irrigation ditch. How mean of her to salve her spitcurled conscience by trying to take away their past! In the kitchen he had started to use those very words on Lou – they sprang readily to mind, as wounding words do – but he stopped himself.

He heard but could not see water. The beam from Wood End Light flicked. Count on me, it said to helmsmen. To him it said nothing.

Probably not the man's fault! The car flat-out rear-ended the bike. Thank God he was leaving. Past time. He might have stuck around not knowing that Lou's universal solvent had unmanned him. How he had admired it in her, that deep patch of calm! She seemed to live from it and expand it year by year. Now he despised it. An inner self that expands to include more and more runs to compassion, for which he had no belly. A woman's forgiveness weakened a man's arms and back. So did its sob sister, pity. It would not stand up to fight. Who could prevail against it? Conrad called pity a form of contempt.

Probably not the man's fault. Let's see her forgive this one, his leaving her for Deary. He passed the garbage fire. Reef Thayer nodded, —Dark night.

Holding Petie in his arms that afternoon, seeing his unmarked skin, Maytree wanted to take him to Maine, to let Deary mother him as she longed to. His leaving condemned Petie to being spoiled. And stuck with Lou's pauciloquoys.

One long-ago summer day, Petie was little, playing in low waves. Maytree watched Lou swim out to the bars and stand up wet. There were two kinds of stinging jellyfish out there, as well as Portuguese men-o'-war and sharks. She looked to be standing on the sea's skin offshore in dazzle. When she came in, he asked, How was the water? and salty Lou kissed him. Petie, old charmer, reached out his chilled jelly arms to be picked up. Not a baby lover, Maytree loved Petie more the older he got. Of course he had to cede her everything, including Petie. What cost. He must really be in love.

\* \* \*

Seaweed around beer bottles made another tide line. He saw the high tide line – shell bits and turnip parings, paper, fish racks, shark cartilage, culch. A line of stranded baitfish. Driftwood full of salts that would make blue and green flares in flames.

For all he knew, those new black clouds bottomed just above his head.

Even the mudflat was matte. Last spring in the mud at Drummer Cove, two men oystering the bay at low tide got stuck. Their struggles drove their boots and legs deeper. It was April in an area of summer cottages; no one heard their shouts. Drummer Cove off Blackfish Creek had a ten-foot tidal range. When the tide came in, it drowned them. Later at a sunny half tide their torsos stuck out again, bent. The harbormaster in his boat dragged their bodies out chained under the armpits.

On the black beach he stepped on a jellyfish mesoglea, the hard gel that spread the medusa from which the bloodless colony dripped. He felt the thing give under him like raw meat and his foot slid.

Of course he thought he would love Lou and stick by her forever. He believed a lifetime was not long enough. (Why did he bother to train his memory if it was only going to torment him?) Of course, through almost all human history, life expectancy was eighteen. His honoring his fourteen years' marriage to Lou would probably have set a world endurance record once. He already spent with one person several monogamous lifetimes. He was forty-four. He never really loved Lou. He saw that now. He loved only himself in her eyes. Her silence was paper on which he wrote. She always thought and felt precisely what he hoped. She loved making him happy. Was he his own or not?

When he was alone with Deary, he saw that her own desire scared and sapped her. He must relieve her. Absurdly, in the past week his duty was not to stir her. And today that blue-spangled jerk broke Petie's leg.

If he had known when he was fifteen how completely women would color his life, that he would sacrifice project, position, and ambition for this woman or that, and drop all he gained; if he knew that a woman's happiness could float or sink his own, decade after decade – why, he would have jumped ship. Jumped ship before he met the girl with a spitcurl in Wyoming. Tonight was no time to relay his sorry wisdom to Petie, Petie whom he was forfeiting for a woman's stubbornness over a technicality. Some uncharacteristic natural mercy prevents boys' foreseeing what they would do for one woman or sacrifice for another. It was just as well.

Would he walk all night? The beach's debris spread wider. He remembered reading that on a beach Ian Patterson encountered the sole of a human foot. The writer thought at first he was seeing a shoe sole. But it was someone's plantar skin, callused, striated with ridges like isobars. Its toes were gone. And the dogs had eaten Jezebel by the wall of Jezreel, ate her all but her palms.

His tongue felt tidal ridges on his palate. A night without stars restored a person to his place. He offered himself as proof to favor his plan: Would a good man like him leave his family for no extraordinary reason? He was moving not from but toward.

Forty-two is the most dangerous age, the Japanese say. He soldiered on two years past that. Why use strength of mind to fight love? Love was stronger. The bout was rigged. Willpower was an idea that appealed to everyone, especially kids. Was it not by using teeth-clenching force of mind that his grandfather stopped drinking, that Roger Bannister broke the four-minute mile, that boys stanched weeping and men marched sleeping? As a force, willpower proved almost null. Attraction beat strength of mind every time. Reading and writing poetry drew him. He loved it because he knew it. As a way out of himself it was a chance, however small, of his hand's catching from nowhere the gift of writing something good, however small. He could not force himself. Neither would Roger Bannister have trained unless his hope of breaking the four-minute mile inspired him. He, Maytree, had no more strength of mind than any other decent man.

Lou would be asleep now. She would get over it. The solitude of immensity lay round about him. A piece of mono-filament snagged one shoe. He found and pocketed the hook. From nowhere, snow touched his mouth. It must be snowing into the water and mud.

Lou's being an angel was the damned trouble. Or was it Deary's fixity. No: there was no trouble – he frowned – only joy. He never thought to be in love again. Since Lou he sought only Lou. He hated sneaking. It marred his love and respect for Lou. This afternoon while they tended Petie in the hospital and at home, Deary had driven a borrowed clunker of a car ahead to Maine with their things. They would meet over the bridge off-Cape. Best go right away. Goonight Lou.

Earlier he could not believe it of Deary. Except now he must. It was true: free spirit Deary forbade him her bed. She denied him, Deary the biddable, the generous warm heart. No hanky-panky. Made betrayal sound cute. He had never suspected her of this quirk. The much-married and much semi-married Deary who slept loose in sand? Who enjoyed one boyfriend after another? And he, her true old friend, could not be one?

Deary balked on a fall day. They had rowed and floated down the Herring River. They spilled into light. Among marshmallows they saw a brown cow. Later he and Deary were back at the shack. She sat two steps down and rested her head on a box. One dimpled arm looped under his knee. Up his trouser leg, she fingered his hamstring.

—You don't want Lou to find out? Neither do I. The only person apart from Petie she loves more than you is me.

—No, that's not it at all. Of course I don't want Lou to find out.

He waited. A habit he picked up from Lou. A pepper scent of winter already, sea dense. How could falling in love, surely a good, drop one like a mantrap into lies? Was love a fruit that soiled your hands? My, she was relaxed. They had just been kissing on the bed. He felt like a child again, humiliated and in thrall, and at his age. Or as if he were courting Lou, who had similarly held him off – but he had expected Lou to hold him off.

—I've never had a love affair. She pulled his knee toward her. He welcomed the strain of misery that thinned her voice.

—What, never?

She unhanded his knee. —And my loving you all of a sudden has nothing to do with it. I'll never have a love affair.

—What, never?

—It's a decision every woman makes again and again.

In the distance blue crescents of cast shade draped from dune cornices and blowouts. Deary who loved him and desired him, who played snare drums in a bar careless of her ever-looser dresses, was too good for him? When it was breaking his heart even to imagine stooping so low and risking, and losing, Lou? His wife to whom he was forever joined in love?

—What about the flyboy from Otis? Rudy Dupeau?

Dupeau spent his leaves with her. —You lived with him. She stood to face him from the bottom step. —A nice change of scene for him. He slept twenty-four hours. Hands on hips. —I made him cornbread, boiled kale with fatback, hotted up some clams. He griped about the higher-ups, polished his shoes, and slept some more.

He must have looked skeptical.

—Certainly, we kissed. It settled him down.

It did not settle Maytree down. Why else had he brought her to the shack? Why did she go along? Why so stubborn over a technicality?

In all the years he had known Deary she did not lie. She met his eyes stricken. What did they both fear? Or was it excitement? He drank a gallon of water; nothing wet his mouth. Deary licked her cracked lips. They were a mess. From the shack steps he saw three clouds long as pickets charge from over the sea. A fishing boat set out. Its transom's tin patch flashed.

Far more onus attached to divorce than to a discreet affair. No wonder she kept marrying. What if everyone married every lover? Any number of women he knew held open house. His past month's turmoil whenever he caught himself imagining he might one day betray his Lou and their marriage he loved – was in vain? Not even hardly ever? He thought Deary promoted divorce and remarriage as Reevadare did, for its bracing effect. Those were high ideals, in his own, his brave girl. Her warm limbs hooked his heart to the world.

He lifted her curls. Her head quivered. He cupped his palms over her hot ears. Her ears were soft as Petie's, flat to her head. He held them for dear life.

To enjoy simple and god-given loving she thought at first that she required the folderol of marriage, and even, save the sailors, of wedding? Was she so terribly old after all? At forty-seven, she had no gray hair. She was born during World War I. Could three years' age difference mean separate worlds? A few years after the war, when, historians said, European class bounds broke, and others said aristocracy had dropped both its faith and its duties, Deary would have been six years old – scarcely an age by which a girl's sexual mores entrench. She got it somewhere, or it got her, this business of waiting for marriage. 'The littler the maid, the bigger the riddle, to my mind.' Damned if Maytree would marry again. His parents were dead. She would have to settle for cohabitation. Which was not at all the done thing. —Until Lou knew they were serious lovers, and gone, she now specified, whether or not they married. Maytree thanked bohemians everywhere.

That day with Deary at the shack gulls again rose from the beach to blow over the dunes like ashes. He had to go. He wanted to think, but at home he had to act – here on this thrust stage without walls at what someone called the limit of the world. Where his tongue died in his mouth. Do I want to be this young again? Your sweet life I do. With Deary under his shoulder he entered the moving edge of air.

That was in the fall. It struck him often, even then, that a real affair with Deary might last only a month and do less harm.

Now he trod black cordgrass where the beach narrowed. Burning trash limned a stick figure ahead. At his feet Maytree made out a bird's neck bones. His jacket's collar, turned up, shielded his neck only a bit. How had it come to this? His telling Lou sickened him. Best go right away.

The Nauset tribes on Cape Cod had nothing with which to build monuments. They marked big events' sites by digging ceremonial holes. They kept these sand holes well dug out, here and there and year by year. Everyone who passed, seeing the hole, recalled its occasion.

The Maytrees and their crowd marked occasions by getting lit, as did, it must be admitted, most peoples on earth.

The Maytrees' story was not worth a hole in the ground. The Nausets – the Pamets, the Wampanoag – told a story like the Maytrees', or perhaps they did not, wherein their founder, now a star, was originally a whale from the deepest waters of antiquity. Some winters this divine whale beached himself to feed famishing villages. Villagers offered his bones back to the sea, where he put on weight. He came again in famines when the people needed him. Then She, Corn, appeared from sunset lands rattling a pouch. She taught the people to sow, parch, and grind corn. The whale surfaced. The two fell in love.

The whale, knowing his people would never again starve after they learned to parch corn, was free to go. He carried Her off on his mighty back and never came again. Often he sent to his people stranding whales – blackfish – as remembrances. The Maytrees performed no heroic deeds, neither Toby or Lou, and both acted within any decent heart's scope. They became not constellations but corpses.

The last anyone saw Lou alive, thirty-nine years later, she was doubled over, walking with two black canes up the steep dune to the shack. Her canes' tips she had fitted into rubber plungers to spread them on sand. Her legs like gutterpipes extended from corners of her red dress. Her arms worked the plunger-canes. From each wrist hung a full straw bag. That year she permitted her Pete and Jane Cairo, of the tormented hair already gray, to help her hoist two months' supplies straight up loose sand from the jeep track to the door. She let them prime and pump the well to fill gallon jugs and lug them up the path to get her started. Most years she shook her wide, white head and refused aid. — She's impossible, they said, fond and scared.

The grown son was a solid stump. In profile he resembled his father squashed – eyes set deep directly under browbone. He and his wife Marie and Jane Cairo tried to imagine Lou's carrying a full water jug up sand, her knees lacking cartilage. How did she manage – with two canes, with one cane, or no canes, and the jug? At least weekly one of them crossed the dunes to learn if Lou was alive, and if so, to refill, if only on the sly, buckets and jugs at her well, and carry them up to the shack. Old Cornelius still lived in the dunes, and checked on her, too.

One morning Jane Cairo learned that Lou Maytree was not alive at all, but, prone on the bed, was blue on her low side – ventrally – like a boat with fresh bottom paint. She was white above the waterline. Otherwise she looked quite like Ingrid Bergman, as people used to say when Lou and Ingrid Bergman were young.

That day Jane saw Lou had brushed and braided her hair and wound it in coils on her head. A neat trick, holding a hand mirror. She had dressed in a lace-bodiced nightgown and thoughtfully crossed her arms. Jane tried to close Lou's eyes. In the end she covered them with scallop shells from the windowsill. Already blowflies walked into Lou's nostrils. Greenbottle flies slipped under the scallop shells to find her eyes; one bluebottle fly worked a lip's corner. Where had the flies come from? How did they know? Jane smelled no odor. Lou had been eighty – not enough.

Jane lowered the bedspread. Her glasses fell on Lou's neck. She drank two quarts water. At the pump she filled every jug from the house. Where should she do this? For she must wash Lou's body now. Later the gown and bedding. Pete could haul the messed mattress to the dump.

The Cape's nonconformists, including the Maytrees, had consigned their burnt bone knobs, which they imagined as fluffy stove ashes, to a biplane pilot, Loopy Devega, who lived near the airfield. For a fee he would scatter ashes like a sower, over the sea.

Even Jane Cairo was old, decades hence, when the paper reported that Loopy Devega possessed on his bookshelves some 170 crematorium seven-pound cans. The first time he tried to scatter ashes (he said), and also the second time, 'they all blew back at me.' The newspaper never told what became of the ashes. The Maytrees liked bookshelves. It would all fall into the sea eventually.

When her husband returned from the beach walk he took after he told her he was leaving her, he got into their marriage bed as usual. Lou felt his chill. He started to speak. She felt his elbow dip their mattress. She heard his rangy voice turn toward her back in the dark. Was there nowhere else on the planet's face for him to sleep? On the whole, she did not want to hear it.

What in the name of God could she have done? They had had a good run. And if love itself, as well as Petie, was the fruit, she could keep loving if she chose, which she at forty-one did not. Petie once told them – he acted it out – that when fishermen gaffed a hooked shark aboard, to save their legs they slit its belly and gave it its own entrails to chew. She would not.

The next morning when Maytree actually left, Lou and Sooner Roy carried the white ironstone bed downstairs for Petie. They set it inside the French doors, so Petie could watch beach, sea, and sky. She pulled a chair beside him. Petie knew his father had left them. She dreaded putting what she saw as Petie's large-heartedness to test. She placed a hand lightly on his good leg near the ankle, and saw his dark eyes jump.

One of her speech difficulties was starting. The other was proceeding. Really, she could talk only to Maytree, Cornelius, and the Cairos, dry as they were. They could trace implications to their ends and respond as if she had said those very things aloud. She should say, Your father loves you very much and his leaving is not your fault. And she did repeat those things in the weeks and years ahead. She never brought up Deary at all.

Their first morning alone she and Petie, red and blue sweaters, watched through the doors the fall of the sea. The horizon crossed each pane at a fractionally different angle. The green sea made the glare in the sky accessible.

Soon despite cruel medical protocols – Children forget pain, the doctor explained – Petie could swing on crutches like a parakeet.

That first June after Petie's leg healed, his friends called him from the rain or frost and he left, and left her arm bones hollow. The Maytrees' crowd closed the gap Maytree and Deary left as if the two never were. Only Jane Cairo, suddenly twenty-three, registered her entire outrage at moral wrong, scandal, evil (etc., etc., etc.), by staying away and seething in New York all summer. She told her mother she never wanted to see another body on a beach. Jane Cairo was eighteen years Lou's junior. Lou missed having her around. Everyone else was so old. Last summer this Jane – with her professor parents and Deary and Reevadare – had cooled with the Maytrees waist-deep in the bay behind their house. Jane complained about *The Golden Bowl*; Maytree had put her on it. —You'll get used to James, he told her. —Not sure I want to. She wore her glasses into the water; a clothespin held back her hair. Off-season she was in Columbia's graduate program in comp lit.

One July morning, cold stirred Lou. The tide had withdrawn to the Azores. Wind through the windows smelled of mullions' dust. She knew Maytree had loved her. The perception was correct; only her inference was false. What should Maytree have done? Stayed in harness? She just had not known she was harness. Nor presumably does baitfish consider itself baitfish. Nor did she know how long she had been harness.

Why surprise? She remembered what the scorpion said to the camel: You knew what I was when you agreed to carry me. To marry me. What was Maytree? A man in love. Who else would a woman marry? Among Maytree's many early loves, both the rancher and the teacher lasted over two years. Is all fair? Is love blind? There must be some precept she could have heeded. On the beach below, the pram's red mooring buoy chained to a cement plug lay on mud. All over New England, it rained three days out of nine. She hoped Deary was worth it.

Downstairs she cracked kindling on her knee and boiled the kettle. Why sadder but wiser? Why not happier and wiser? What else could wisdom be? She drank coffee black. She would not fall apart.

She enjoyed benefits. Maytree no longer interrupted her to read aloud from his book. He never stopped doing it, though he knew it drove her crazy. And he never stopped talking. At last she had time to think. Plus she had his dune shack now, that Maytree's father built near the coast guard station. And she could eat crackers in bed.

She sorted and soaked beans; she would bake cornbread at five. What was it she wanted to think about? Here it was, all she ever wanted: a free mind. She wanted to figure out. With which unknown should she begin? Why are we here, we four billion equals who seem significant to ourselves alone? She rejected religion. She knew Christianity stressed the Ten Commandments, Jesus Christ as the only son of God who walked on water and rose up after dying on the cross, the Good Samaritan, and cleanliness is next to godliness. Buddhism and Taoism could handle all those galaxies, but Taoism was self-evident – although it kept slipping her mind – and Buddhism made you just sit there. Judaism wanted her like a hole in the head.

And religions all said – early or late – that holiness was within. Either they were crazy or she was. She had looked long ago and learned: not within her. It was fearsome down there, a crusty cast-iron pot. Within she was empty. She would never poke around in those terrors and wastes again, so help her God. Provincetown was better. She witnessed the autarchy of the skies.

—I have to blame Deary, Reevadare Weaver confided as though it cost her. Reevadare, wearing the first djellaba anyone had seen, held forth in her garden. Hazy air brightened as the sun fell. —But what can you expect? Fourteen years is too long to stay married. (Decades later Lou determined that one of Reevadare's ambitions had been to define a marital maximum, in years. It switched between seven or eight.)

—I hate to blame her, she was such a love…

So don't. Both Deary and Maytree could be material and final cause without being at fault. On principle Lou avoided blaming. Reevadare's lipstick smeared her wet corncobs.

—But she stole Toby Maytree pure and simple. Reevadare laid it out with a nod.

Lou lifted her chin. —He left freely on his own two legs.

Lou found no comfort in friends' disparaging either Deary or Maytree. What about her own loyalty to both? They had a right to live as best they could. Did Reevadare think Lou would hate them – once she got her bearings – as if either had changed?

—He wasn't a paperweight. No one can steal a man.

—I could, Reevadare said, in my day.


—Everybody's sweetheart not so sweet after all, is it? Jane's professor father had named her after his own father, Jeremy. Now he was bugging Lou about Deary. Everyone gets carried away sometimes, she thought. Hers a private matter, weightless in any possible world scheme. She dreaded her own friends. She could persuade no one she was not heartbroken. She had seen her own mother heartbroken, and knew she could do better.

When Marblehead school let out the year her father left, Lou's mother moved them to Provincetown's West End on the water. Child Lou had no inkling at Marblehead breakfast, say, if it was indeed at breakfast, that this was her final glimpse of her wonderful father. She could not remember what he ate, said, or read. She began to suspect that many moments were possibly last ones. She strove to impress what she could on her memory, which she imagined as a clay cylinder. Her mother's fingers around a Pink Lady, the Cape's fish flakes and laundry drying in yards, foghorn, seasmoke, school roll-down maps. In bed at night she inventoried that day's catch: her yellow-toothed teacher's deploring her penmanship, gulls in full cry above their dodgeball game, her friends' high voices, and mostly her mother's smell of talc, her smooth dress, her retreating as if kicked.

Why not drop all this saying hello and good-bye to every-thing, this effort both grateful and scared? That was an eventful year. Girl Lou liked her easy Provincetown friends – hard-working, laughing girls, half of them Portuguese, who directly stuck her like spat to their clump. Aware how keenly she would miss any who vanished, she never considered loving less. Presently she forgot about memorizing. New Provincetown and then boarding-school friends caught her up. Still, she attended the smallest college she could find. There she learned to skate and sing.

Now Petie went back to school, and streets and air replaced crowds. Cairos and Lou's other summer friends would bear her abandonment tale to Boston and New York. She eased her guard and got sucker-punched. I am not going to fall apart, she had told herself, but this was an edge from which she could only slip.

Do not drive in breakdown lane, said the Route 6 signs. Do not break down in driving lane. The sea poured over the stone lip at Gibraltar and emptied.

In late September, when Lou could stir at all she moved like a glacier, the queer sort at which dogs bark. Reading Hardy always distracted her in rough patches, as when her father vamoosed. Now she might enjoy the company of solid Farmer Gabriel Oak. She read, 'It may have been observed that there is no regular path for getting out of love as there is for getting in.'

Lou (and Maytree, too) shunned drama, inside and out, as, at least, bad taste.

*Deep as first love, and wild with all regret;*
*O Death in Life, the days that are no more!*

Why ever had she neglected to become a Buddhist? Low blood pressure. Anyone could see how fat the Buddha was.

She had no force to fight what held her as wind pins paper to a fence. She was a wood horse, a rock cairn, a jerry can of pitch. She found herself holding one end of a love. She reeled out love's long line alone; it did not catch.

She fell apart. She should have lashed her elbows and knees, like Aleuts.

Ablaze, she scraped the pot. She boxed her paints. She scoured the sink till the sponge reverted to spicules. Petie gave her wide berth.

One cold June morning Cornelius appeared. —Say, Lou, I wish you'd stop poisoning yourself. She did not whine or voice any grief or anger. Did it show?

After Cornelius left she climbed the steep street to Pilgrim Monument. She mounted the monument stairs in her camel's hair coat and red earmuffs. From the top she looked at flat sky, flat sea, and flat land. She was ready to want to stop this. Thereby she admitted – barely – that she could choose to stop. For one minute by her watch, she imagined liking Maytree impartially. For only one minute by her watch she saw him for himself. That day, having let go one degree of arc only, for one minute, she sighted relief. Here was something she could do. She could climb the monument every day and work on herself as a task. She had nothing else to do. Their years together were good. He was already gone. All she had to do for peace was let him go.

Within a month she figured that if she ceded that the world did not center on her, there was no injustice or betrayal. If she believed she was free and out of the tar pit, would she not thereby free herself from the tar pit? What was this to, say, losing Petie? Why take personal offense if two fall in love? She knew they reproached themselves. Maytree was party to fits of enthusiasm. Loving was Deary's nature. What would any of this matter two hundred years hence? She had many decades more to live. Whether she lived them or not was her call.

To drive her mental cylinders Lou climbed to and up Pilgrim Monument daily in every weather. Sometimes she entered fog. From the monument's top she loosed Maytree like sand. She saw the sand drop onto roofs and yards. After only seven or eight weeks' relinquishing Maytree, she saw the task would take practice, like anything else. She planned to work at it for a year, shedding every grain of claim. After seven months she had what she called 'a grip on letting go.' When anything unwise arose in her henceforth, she attended to it by climbing the monument, at whose top she opened her palm.

So she pulled her own stakes in the matter, stakes she herself pitched. That she could withdraw them was news. She could guy out Orion and spread him like a spinnaker, a chute to fly beyond her own self-love. If earth's sky got confining, there were plenty more. Why did monks fast? They had to be half dead to do this? For if you knew a continent was there, you could find it again and again. Could she detach from Petie? Of course not, not now when he needed her. But in our culture parents released a child's person like a balloon. Of course, they kept the love.

It was then Lou began to wonder: If overcoming self-centeredness was the goal, then why were we born into a selfish stew? And who even studied this question? Would the Cairos know any books to bring her? For she meant to keep this cast of mind and renew it.

Two decades later, as it happened, while she was washing around Deary's deepest and most noisome bedsore, she asked herself: If she, Lou, had known how long her first half-inch beginning to let go would take – and how long her noticing and renouncing owning and her turning her habits, and beginning the slimmest self-mastery whose end was nowhere in sight – would she have begun? Would she have turned herself over like a row of salt hay? Tossed herself to loose her own chaff? It took her months to learn that she could get clean for more than a minute at a time. Consciously she looked out for resentment, self-cherishing, and envy. Over years she formed the habit of deflecting them before they dug in. But she lived through those years in any case, and now she lived from that steady ground she won. More distances opened as she opened. Not that town, national, and world life as it was going did not give her fits.

Moreover, as bonus side effect, she got to do this – to dip terrycloth in a warm-water basin in sight of the sea, and wash Deary's old skin, and irrigate her bedsores' holes, and change the water and change the cloth and do it again. Plus, she now had a houseful. If having a houseful was a desideratum. She might have debated it – at this far-future point on Deary's bed's edge – if she had any time.

After his bone knit, Petie became Pete, who pondered facts. What did sweet-eyed Deary, his former beach playmate, who drew him even when he was eleven and triggered his fancy and remorse, see in his shriveling, peeling father – who must be well over forty, with his knuckly hands too big for their wrists, his white hairs in his nose and ears, the wrinkles in front of his ears, and his notebooks fusty, and his jokes embarrassing, and the books he wrote so thin you could use them as shims? Surely Deary loved and was loved generally; she could take her pick. Why pick a man who kept saying *a priori*? Surely his father had aged beyond any passion save his old chore of amassing lore to take to his grave. Maybe Deary needed a live-in carpenter. That badly? He did good work.

On his mother's dresser and on the kitchen wall he saw his father in photographs she likely left up for his benefit: his father raising a striper by a gill; his father and himself in silhouette, rowing. He saw in the photographs his father's tight shoulders, loose smile, long limbs, and eyes a stripe of shadow hid like the blindfold of a man about to be shot.

A few winters ago he broke his leg at that frozen intersection. His father, holding him across his arms, had openly kissed his head and muttered something. His father, it turned out, knew he was running off with Deary the next morning.

What gave adults the cheer to tolerate their hypocrisy? Even his mother praised generosity and hoarded; she preached industry and barely worked. Perhaps every generation passes to the next, to hand down to yet more children, an untouched trunk of virtues. The adults describe the trunk's contents to the young and never open it.

Pete no longer told his mother much. When he was ten he had ensured, kindly enough, that she stop instructing him. If she would only quit telling him it was cold when it was cold. At fifteen he gave her little time. She was probably struggling. When his father left, she had cut her hair. Outside he used to see her by the monument then, or on another of the seven hills, hatless and red-nosed from sun or frost. Once she abruptly and without antecedent said —He is the most noble and considerate man I ever met. Pete nodded, ducked, and kept moving, fast.

Now in summers and falls Pete passed clear nights on a sleeping porch. If he woke, he saw Orion's torso rise beyond Truro and climb. At dawn the hunter was all abroad and fading, like his memory of his father, like a dead man's arising weak. He rolled on his belly; he bit a fingernail and turned west to Bonobos' house. In classrooms he imagined real Orion – the Orion of the dunes' black night, whose visible arms held visible weapons – as the hunter was crossing behind the hot sky invisible as an Apache.

\* \* \*

To what goal might a young man's ambition run? He hoped to crew on a fishing boat and finally own a boat and catch and sell each fish in season. And privately –

Walking to school one morning through sleet, he began tracking his alewife thoughts as a game. He learned he did not think. He witnessed ghost parts and motes on parade disappear.

A girl named Marie several grades older; her smile; his spinster teacher who for all he knew was once the object of his father's lascivious eyes; his damnable father who didn't know even how to take care of his mother. These bits deployed before his gaze as football fans after the last kick swarm. Now he and others roamed the world feeding or vaccinating people, palpating mastitis in zebus. Crowds came, girls in saris, there they went. He had no idea this gabble reeled and garbled his head ever, let always.

Quailing, he imagined aiming his mind as a knight aims his sword. Could anyone, has anyone ever tried to, master his own mind using only that mind as tool? Did his brain contain a pack of selves like Musketeers, each smaller and farther back and waving a sword? And what might such a stunt win, apart from peace of mind? What man his age wanted peace of mind? His agitation fueled his power. Right? But what kind of power did a man have when screaming meemies ruled his thoughts?

For the next few years especially, and long after, Pete played at maneuvering his own ephemera like toy boats. Surely, he thought, it must be easier to drill a troop of baboons. Either the task was impossible or impossible for him.

He failed to still his bilge. He could replace its slosh with only more slosh. Why was this basic control so almighty tough? Other people appeared to think. He easily persuaded his fingers to write. He could not get his brain to do anything. Was he crazy? In real life he never stole cars or slugged guys or raped girls – so how could these stale schools of resentment, these monotonous flappings of weed, how could these minnow film-strips unman him? They were not wishes or instincts. They were floating junk the tide rocked. He was taking pains to watch his brain take out trash. Indifferently, those windrows buried and blinded him. Why attend this nonsense? Because his hope of mastering himself attracted him.

How hard could it be? Someday he would appear before his awed father as a perfected human. A fisherman who fed hungry Africans. So perfect he never felt superior, even to his weak and contrite father. A youth's thought no less idle than any wind-blown straw, it still stuck him like a dart.

The following summers he grew; he set and pulled fishnets all night from a wagging boat; he worked on himself. Winters in his solitudes he worked on himself. He had begun by remembering his father's coveralls. One leg's pocket held a wood carpenter's rule that folded, foot by white foot, to make a ten-ply stack.

# Part Two

Within two hours of their crossing the Sagamore bridge, on a motel bed, Deary welcomed Maytree into her arms with gales of laughter that beaded on her gums. Then she slept palms together under her cheek like a charade for *sleep*.

Maytree prized fidelity like everyone else. He looked at the motel's knotty pine ceiling. Was he evil, and Deary evil? Who has not loved twice? More than twice? Who has never broken a heart? Should his first high-school sweetheart have stayed true to him as she grew on ahead? He saw her often. Jolly, she wrangled grandchildren.

Surely he must have been, at thirty when he courted Lou, shallow. Nothing had ever vaulted him to such an elated pitch as his slow awareness these past weeks of good old Deary Hightoe, during a general glance he saw only peripherally – of her high-arched eyes across Cairos' porch scorching the skin on the side of his face as a flatiron burns.

He recognized that when, after two years, his infatuation with Lou dwindled, neither love nor happiness withdrew. Often he fell in love with her clarity or her eyelids afresh, and he whistled 'Clancy Lowered the Boom.' After eight years or so, had he forgot to marvel at her depth of spirit their intimacy revealed? His lasting marriage mightily outweighed and banned the puny flirting and responding-to-flirting that topple others. He and Lou trusted;

they confided. They made love with less urgency and more sustenance. Theirs was not a fire they rushed to douse, but one they fed slowly. They loved and reared Petie. They maintained the shack as a demented project. She listened to him; she always knew what he was talking about; she laughed. They loved and read good novels, good poetry. Had he stopped loving Lou? Not at all. His abiding heart-to-heart with her merely got outshouted.

By equating fidelity with neither flirting nor responding to flirting, Maytree left a flank open. He never flirted with Deary. She never flirted with him. They fell in love, love unlooked for. The same thing took place at least once before. Relieved, oblivious then, he read it in a book and copied it. 'Try and realize' – Levin told Oblonsky – 'that this is not love. I have been in love but this is not the same thing. It is not my feeling but some external power that has seized me... such happiness does not exist on earth.'

Try and realize. Maytree admired Tolstoy's giving Levin the truth to say and his making fun of it fondly.

They rented on the Maine island they saw with Sooner Roy. Maytree repaired five of the twelve wood-framed houses on the island. Deary baked gingerbread in square pans and steamed for it a translucent lemon sauce. He saw her carry the gingerbread on heaped, waxed-paper-wrapped plates. She billowed through woods and fields all summer barefoot to give it to neighbors. She took turns with Maytree rowing ashore for food, gas, lumber, asphalt tile. They bathed in a clawfoot tub. Once while he knelt to dry her she asked, How many roofs could you do a year? He laughed. Her flesh dipped wherever he pressed – pure woman.

—I'm not a roofer. Now your other side.

—I'll give your harness bells a shake, she said when it was his turn. He smelled her vapor. He noticed, not for the first time, that rowing had callused her palms.

Increasingly he found her working over ruled books and newsprint tablets at their table, wielding a knife-sharpened pencil. She told him, surprised daily, that she liked keeping his business books. Business? he thought; I charge only materials and time. She told him that, short of burning cash, there was no more expensive way to light a room than burning candles. She bought three Aladdin lamps, and prophesied the week two years hence when the lamps would finish 'paying for themselves' – a usage that always amused him. She replaced her torn filmy clothes first with shirts and dungarees, then with blouses and slacks.

On the bed she curled under his arm. Of course, she told him, she missed Provincetown and its sky. Of course she would take Maytree home to die, or he would take her – promise? Maytree humored her. He tried not to think of Provincetown at all, not to remember Lou and Petie. Who would both hate him now. He had chosen his own disgrace. He would probably do it again.

Maytree worked at building both on the island and off. Old Mainers had settled rivers and coves. These new people built on bare coasts and hilltops, as if they meant to heat with wind. He turned down most jobs, to save his mornings for poetry. On a September day Deary looked up from a ledger.

—You could take up lobstering. Her baby face! She was older than him, let alone Lou; she sprang to her impulses like a child.

—Lobstering? For a living? Sun heated his shirt and clavicle through the window.

—For half a living. The other half is working on houses.

—The other half is poetry, my love. We don't need more money.

Best not tell her how dramatically, if he got rich enough to learn lobstering and to start up, local lobstermen would discourage him.

—How many roofs can this small island need? How many summer people's screened porches? He bent his nose to her hair; its smell stirred him.

—I thought you liked the island. Shall we move to the mainland?

—Could we? To Camden? We can get our licenses.

What? He kept forgetting she had a degree in architecture. By suppertime they were moving to Camden.

Maine's beauty was not of sky but of earth. Sunlight hit black spruces and died, or sprawled in fields. This cold forest stopped his eyes. Brown needles underfoot became his sand. He smelled black humus and rock like wet pipe.

Their new house smelled of mildew and smoke from a long-ago house fire. Deary insisted they buy a respectable, meaning too-big, house. He heard everyone split and stack wood. Year-round he heard chain saws. They got their licenses.

Maine, he found, had social classes. Educated people sat at dinner parties discussing the news and drinking – all of a sudden – wine. Only the children knew how to enjoy themselves. Enjoyment required, in his view, at the very least, easy people, a record player, or a drummer, or a piano player, or a deck of cards and chips, jokes or funny stories, or some sort of ball. And not before or after dinner, but alongside a big buffet. He granted his was a general failure to mature.

Once Deary whispered from his lap, I miss being poor! And could they adopt a baby? He felt her lips and breath. He knew she was only keeping him abreast of her flitting thoughts. Yet he never knew – *connaître, wissen* – what she was in essence. On the Cape he had fancied her not quite of this world, Ariel asleep on sand. Or was she of this earth, earthy?

Six years after Maytree and Deary flew the coop, Lou and Cornelius were making a mess eating sea-clam chowder at her green kitchen table. Lou saw the sun spread like a gull for its landing on the sea. Cornelius had wandered in from the dunes for food and mail. Lou knew that five or six times a year, for these six years, his mail included a letter from Maytree. A new one came today. He read it and passed it across the table. Lou saw that Maytree had typed the letter and Deary appended a note, apparently written against a ruler, wishing everyone – *everyone* twice underlined – all best. Did they give architecture degrees to people who bubble-dotted their i's? Like the others, this letter of Maytree's was easygoing and reticent. To Lou, Maytree and Deary both had changed into old friends whose life together she followed with an affectionate interest almost like Cornelius's. For years she had read his letters without turning a hair.

It shamed him, Maytree wrote, to be a builder filling the coast. How many rooms could the new people actually need? — As many as they can pay for! Deary wrote in the margin. What wives would clean the houses? New people asked for many bedrooms because they truly believed their children and spouses and grandchildren and their own friends and their friends' children would pass all their summers, if not all their free time, there with them, simultaneously. The empty bedrooms amounted to cargo cult, clearing airstrips to attract planes that never came.

Lou liked reading Maytree's letter in his familiar voice. That they were once, to put it mildly, intimate, belonged to the realm of far-fetched facts, like Io and Ganymede's circling Jupiter. Lou pictured his freckled stick figure slap-dancing on a shake. Deary managed his business. How? Lou and Cornelius had to laugh.

The next day she ordered Maytree's new book from Wesleyan. When it came, she saw it was a long poem: boy-girl twin halves – Plato's old thought. He set the twins in modern Greece. From his usual poetic line he had subtracted a foot. Perhaps the cold took his breath away.

That November Lou began painting again. It was never too late to record the faces you love. She thought watercolor suited beginners. Pete's frontal portrait looked like a beady-eyed fanatic or a police sketch. Next Lou painted Jane Cairo in profile, too-small hands holding *Victory*. Perhaps if she could draw. She burned her tries. People praised her humility because she so seldom spoke. They did not know her ambition: a show in town.

One year she found a scheme and stuck with it the long balance of her life: foreground of disturbing beach, middle distance disturbing sea, and sky above, disturbing. Iced trash, tarnished waves, clouds like glyphs. Graywacke stones, dirty sea ice, stubby far plane. Waves of varying length, like words, and in parallel lines, like type, moved left to right on prevailing wester-lies. So watching storm waves in the bay made her eyes move just as reading did, and seas looked like lines of italic type she tried to read. She painted Nekkar in Boötes ('ox driver'), and the elusive 'loincloth.' She liked nocturnes. Vega was a blue dot that taught nothing. Scorpio reared over chalkline breakers. Hercules held his club fast over the roof gutter. Soon in Provincetown's expanding glare Hercules would not have a club, or even arms.

In thin oils she depicted clumsy beaches and clouds. Their foregrounds and middle grounds showed jetsam and wrack, stained waves, brown bottles, steamer shells, broken china, waxed paper, church keys, foil, nails sticking through in lumber, clamshells, tires, purses, shoes – only two or three objects on each canvas. With a sable brush she graphed each torn string of a crab trap against dirt pink sky. Color was local. It allowed an ocean like red marcelled hair. Everything was littoral. Sandpipers pecked child footprints in mud. Storm sea like a ripsaw blade, and clouds in a mumble nearing. She would no more scumble a cloud than kill a child.

One evening of those twenty middle years she was watching Pete sop gravy from his plate with a biscuit. She had already handed him that day's mail: a letter to him from Camden in Deary's hand. He threw it away and smiled without guile. Lou could imagine his fearing that his father was making it clear he wanted nothing to do with him. Pete had moved to two rooms a few streets over. His friends and their ways called his tune. It took years for her and Maytree to grasp that he was not going to college but to sea. When she used to wash his face, he screwed his skin so hard it got dark as a tire.

Just as few men love their wives so much as their daughters, few, if any, women love anyone so much as their children. Parents love adopted babies with the same passion. Often she missed infant Petie now gone – his random gapes, his bizarre buttocks. How besotted they gazed at each other nose-on-nose. He fit her arms as if they two had invented how to carry a baby. While she walked, he patted her shoulder in time with her steps. If he stopped patting, she stopped walking. If his pats speeded up, she stepped lively. He was driving her; they both died laughing.

Later she washed his filthy hair and admired his vertebrae, jiggled his head in toweling that smelled like his steam. She needled splinters and sandspur spines from his insteps as long as he let her. Every one of those Peties and Petes was gone. That is who she missed, those boys now overwritten. Their replacement now sat at the green table wiping crumbs onto his plate. Pete's friends came by to get him for a party no one wanted to attend without him. He was good-natured; could he also be the life of the party? Did she ever know a noisy fisherman?

His friends hauled Pete away. She confronted the sink. How she wished she could see all those displaced Petes and Peties once more! She imagined joining picnic tables outside by the beach and setting them for 22 Peties and Petes, or 122, or however greedy she was that day and however divisible Pete. Together the sons at every age and size – scented with diaper, formula on rubber nipples, salt-soaked sand, bike grease, wax crayon, beer, manila, engine oil, fish – waited for dinner. Who else knew what each liked? It was a hell of a long table. She gave herself a minute to watch them – Petie after Petie barefoot near his future self and past. They pinched or teased or shoved one another. All but the babies ignored the babies. What mother would not want to see her kids again? When this sort of thing got out of hand, Lou called herself 'Poor Mom.' She dreaded 'Poor Mom,' her periodic walk-on role as grieving and piteous victim. Lou spied her from a distance floating long-skirted over the sand, hands on face. Lou gave the hag a short hearing to shut her up, and tea in a cup. 'Poor Mom,' she commiserated: her child grew up.

A bank wrote her. Her vamoosed father, who left their Marblehead house and never came back, had died in Edgartown – so near, all these years, and here he was, gone – and left her money she split with Pete. She bought telephone service because Pete might need to reach her from any port.

She wrote Maytree and Deary to stop alimony. She described Pete's new boat and detailed his fish hauls. She reported that Jane Cairo had washed ashore for good. Chiefly Lou wrote to persuade him and Deary she was content, good-willed, and long past regrets. She urged them to take a vacation to the Cape. — Everyone misses you both. Please come and stay here. Or move back! Was this a bit thick? Well, they both knew her.

In the next few years she painted two canvases she could bear. One showed kapok spilt in clots from ripped red cushions, a blue kite in a dead man's float, and gassy sky. Another was cirrus cloud high over a rusted-out boiler in a dune. She read the Russians again, just about every novel, and Cather, *Middlemarch*, Hardy, Hemingway, Conrad, etc. One night Jen and Barrie twisted her arm until she agreed to let them hang some of her own paintings in a locals' show. The night before it opened, she used her key to break into the gallery and steal her stuff back.

Three years after he threw away Deary's letter, Pete was over-nighting on his boat offshore. He wore red sea boots. Eating hot dogs from a can made him hungry for old-fashioned work. He was manning a square-rigger rounding the Horn. When he saw that a given South Sea wave would overcome the ship, he jumped to the yardarm and hooked one leg over it and water poured from his boot. He saw green water scrape the deck and drown the ship. Then it moved off, heavy as land. His ship hit and entered one sea after another and rose streaming. Like his parents, Pete was a reader. He knew more about Cape Horn than about Boston.

On watch Pete ignored cold hands. Why not ignore every other feeling that dropped his way, instead of biting and getting hooked? Long ago when he was a boy he tried to talk himself out of hating his father. It worked for a while, until the years' silences piled up.

Now he was frying in crumbs. Helplessly he imagined those two there in Maine doing what. He did not hate them. Observing, he saw that hatred is rare. Envy and begrudging wreck a man first. Other people lived in peace without knotting their brains. Pete's boat partner was Sooner Roy's son. In a bigger boat they could fish Georges Bank in winter and the Gulf of Maine. The hauls were heavy offshore, halibut and swordfish, as well as those winter waters' unending cod. Till that big boat materialized, they handlined near shore for turbot and witch flounder, for haddock, redfish, whiting, pollock, and striped bass. They used trash bluefish, sliced squid, and dogfish to bait bass.

Pete & Co. also owned a mackerel seine and averaged decent hauls. If only decency sufficed. Every few decades, on one ocean or another, someone lucked into a bank-buying, hundreds-of-thousands-of-dollars' haul of mackerel or herring or something. It could be that Greenlanders made the mighty haul off Baffin Island, or purse seiners made it in salmon three thousand miles away in Haro Strait. It could be that the sum in dollars had swelled to a lie. That haul nevertheless set the benchmark for everyone forever. Their neighbor's son Heaton Vorse saw a boat unload 138,000 pounds of halibut. Any great haul anywhere, however, in any fishing port's imagination happened recently and nearby. Pete heard of catches that sank boats to the gunwales. One guy, somewhere, once, would not trim the load that was sinking him, refused to toss out fish at fifty cents apiece. He saw he would sink before he could dock. He limped to the buyer boat and got himself and his boat winched aboard in a net. The buyer boatmen dumped fish from his hold to theirs, and lowered him and his empty boat away. When they heard about it, others in the fleet considered that saving the fisherman's haul was unfair.

Pete multiplied possible pounds by possible price per species next year. Mackerel could yield $6,000 in one haul. He might then dare speak to Marie Koday. He saw fish scales thick on deck like doubloons, gold bullion dragging down the hoppers below denting two thousand fathoms of ocean that lesser boats could never ply. No one would envy and begrudge him, because he did not envy or begrudge anyone else.

Onshore a headlight pair appeared on High Head, illumined the rain in a cone, and came about. Through his teeth he whistled 'Nel Blu, Dipinto di Blu.' Could he surmount his trash-ditch thoughts and work above them? Could he let them come and go without bias, minnows schooling about his feet? Simply slosh through them and let the waves wash over? He could build on the mainmast a crow's nest. With his life, with his mind, he would build him a crow's nest, rope by rope and plank by plank for as long as it took. Ahead dwelt some heart-pure Pete who rode whatever came. So might a seeing white statue, aware and at ease, over whose feet and plinth wash wild seas, guard a greasy harbor.

Late one blackfly morning Maytree was supervising a crane operator smashing with a wrecking ball a house across the marsh. He
saw Deary driving her new Buick to the site. Maytree pulled an
eight-penny nail. He felt its hot point cool in his fingertips.

Deary brought forks, linen napkins, and a rhubarb pie. She
wore a suede jacket and cashmere scarf. She asked, On Cape
Cod, did I ever tell you why I liked poverty? Because she could
no longer remember. By then Lord & Taylor knew her measure-
ments. She ordered three tailored skirts a year, eight or so small-
print McMullen blouses, Papageno (as she said) low heels, navy
cable-knit cardigans grosgrain outside… she never dreamed she
would remember those things, she told Maytree, who thought,
What things? When at a college reunion he saw she resembled
and outshone other well-to-do wives, it gave him pause. What
impelled her to revert to a lady now? She was sixty-two years
old. Years ago she scuttled her palm-of-hand pedestal chair and
retrieved her overjoyed mother's ancestral carved-cherry furniture, and her flatware, linens, and jewelry.

Her old mother subsequently yelled into a telephone, I knew
it was just a phase! By then Maytree understood that Deary's
mother adored her in any form or function. She was merely rejoi-
cing over the cherry furniture's staying in the family – possibly,
Maytree thought, as she herself would like to stay in life.

Deary's mother dwelt at the peak where old Stockbridge families met atop old legacies. She sent Deary to Concord Academy and Smith before MIT. A stoneworker could chisel on the tomb of everyone she knew: good taste. Only once did Maytree himself see Deary's mother. Erect, wearing a slant-brimmed hat, she drove an open car down Commercial Street. She commanded the steering wheel from its bottom. Shortly after the furniture arrived in Maine, Deary's mother's final illness came. Deary lived with her in New York for six months to tend her. After she died Deary spent another month emptying the apartment. Deary's absence felt as if it would kill Maytree.

After she got back, he exchanged Blackwell's shipments with his Maine friend, an abstract expressionist painter who played Brubeck while he worked. One winter day the men skated on a beaver pond and sliced each other's shadows.

—We must buy land around those ponds, Deary said that night, and you can build on spec. Where did she get these terms? She continued, We must buy every waterfront lot available. Deary spoke into one of her full-length mirrors. He saw her gauge his reaction.

Keep her happy, Maytree thought.

—Who can afford a waterfront lot?

—We can, if you work full time.

How happy? Maytree thought.


Her curls took well to permanent waves. To Maytree they looked like Peaked Hill Bars at low tide. One evening, over rows of her colored hair's parallel waves, she was fastening a dot-veiled hat, to go out. She was starting to look like the Queen Mother. A fine figure of a woman, and one to whom he was vowed.

Maytree knew Lou read his letters. Why not? He loved her and had long ago forbidden his deep thoughts to turn back to her. He dreaded learning she hated him. Surely by now would she not have let it all go? Her letter said she had. She even invited them to stay with her. And would she not think of him fondly but not regretfully, as he thought of her fondly and stopped himself? Though surely not so often. Year after year Cornelius urged him back home.

Maytree could no longer find red-speckled notebooks. He got his first one over twenty years ago. In Camden, he bought a batch of black-speckled notebooks. In the black ones he kept random notes. He glued red ribbon to the binding of one of these. He wrote on the binding the letter L. Damned if he would write *love*. He was studying not love but consciousness. Insofar as he still saved time to read.

On a hot day he and his friend drank on the back steps. The friend was a hangdog giant with a crew cut. He had introduced Maytree to Henry Green and Borges. Now he asked if he liked Stevenson. Maytree brought out some old notebooks. 'Marriage,' he read, 'marriage is a step so grave and decisive that it attracts light-headed, variable men by its very awfulness.'

Now in the same notebook Maytree found a passage from *Under the Greenwood Tree*. Someone wonders of a couple, How could they be in love? They are distant in manner. —'Ay,' says a rustic, popping up. 'That's part of the zickness. Distance belongs to it, slyness belongs to it, the queerest things on earth belongs to it!' He read aloud. His friend liked Baudelaire's calling lovemaking 'the lyric of the masses.'

After his friend left that day he found Deary inside manning the telephone like a howitzer. For clients she drew up similar plans and elevations. She fooled with rooflines. Deary and he convinced each new client that his or her personal needs – for bedrooms, kitchen, bath, living room, porch – showed unique taste.

Tonight they expected ten for dinner. On the extended cherry table he placed crystal and sterling in phalanxes on linen and lace. Maytree foresaw tonight's distinguished crowd repeating information from the newspaper. Some of their guests wrote excellent articles and books. Consequently Maytree knew them to be – somewhere in there – vastly more learned than social life permitted.

Seeing friends used to be easier. Was it their age? Did anyone actually like adult social life? Ping-Pong brought laughter as respectable entertainment did not. He and Deary wasted their many-paned dining room on dinner parties instead of ongoing games and music. Portuguese and Azorean old-timers in Provincetown – calling themselves respectively Lisbons and picos – enjoyed whist, singing fados, and taking grandchildren out in boats. Maytree envied them their noisy parties. He could not change Maine alone.

After they cleaned up the party, Maytree helped breathless Deary upstairs and into bed. Then down on the back steps he paged through another old red-speckled notebook by the back-door light. It intrigued him still, what an art historian wrote of Michelangelo's poetry: 'The tensions deepen in the twenty or so poems of the middle period as the poet who is working deeply to complete the Sistine frescoes of the Last Judgment suffers the torture of loving two women and one man.' Maytree thought, Torture?

Decades' reading had justified his guess that men and women perceive love identically save for, say, five percent. Reading books by men and women showed only – but it was something – that love struck, in exactly the same way, most, but not all, of those few men and women, since the invention of writing, who wrote something down. An unfair sample.

—Keep your woman friends, Reevadare told Lou long ago. But Lou ignored friends when she met Maytree. After Maytree ran off, people imposed on her the unwelcome dignity they accorded new widows or Nobel Prize winners. They blamed her for their own distance, fancying she caused their feeling by a vaunted opinion of herself. It drove Lou bats. At parties she danced silly dances, made far-fetched puns, sang camp songs, and all but wore lampshades. She could not imagine a friend more lively, and loyal, than Jane Cairo turned out to be. Jane seemed not to resent or begrudge anything Lou was by birth or hap, such as tall, or made-into-myth.

Jane often visited Lou or Cornelius or both in the dunes. Once she invited Lou to Cornelius's shack when he was gone. Sitting on the shack bed, Lou watched Jane ladle water. She hooked the ladle, took three steps to the bed, raised an arm, and, whoops, detained a big black snake that was speeding up the wall by Lou. Thumbing the back of its head like a tick's, Jane seemed to persuade the snake to be caught. She peeled it from the wall. When its front half coiled on her arm, she offered it her other arm, as if for a quadrille. It curled its weight on Jane's two arms and kept moving balanced between them. It was over six feet long, and unduly thick.

—They relax, she said, when they know you've got them.

She was short and nearsighted like her parents. She freed the snake outside, saying, Let them eat mice. Were not people who tolerated snakes going against human nature? Did that mean they were cultured?

Jane came back blinking. —Why is it always a big black snake? Have you ever seen a small one? Imagine their eggs. She looked at Lou, who had not budged. —Oh, you and your marble calm! Lou laughed and knocked down her water.

All Lou's life after she got her height, only Maytree mocked and teased her as an equal, and now Jane. How generous of Jane to chaff her. Jane worked at the Art Association. She and Lou met often. Her general knowledge surprised even Lou. Jane looked roguish through her glasses, tapped her temple, and said, Like a steel trap!

Lou walked through the dunes back to her house. The tide was out so far the metal mudflat smelled, Lou thought, like the moon.

Reevadare knew a thing or two when she told Lou to keep her women friends. Jane was a teenager then. Come to think of it, Reevadare herself could not have been much over fifty at that party. Lou was now fifty-eight. Was Lou now old, or had Reevadare been young? Lou knew herself to be young. She touched her mouth. So Reevadare had been young? Hands veiny, her mottled face and arms, lipstick ascending, much-married, thin-voiced Reevadare? – had been younger then than Lou was now? Old people were not incredulous at having once been young, but at being young for so many decades running. Then what is old? Old must be... out of the ball game.

One windy Thanksgiving Lou joined the Cairos visiting Jane behind the Art Association counter whence she sold paintings, prints, posters, and magazines. These academic parents of Jane's, in whose summer house she lived above the harbor, were waiting for her to finish – that is, to write – her dissertation.

Their shining prodigy was throwing herself away in a backwater so rural that four digits dialed the phone. Was her dissertation not finished – except the actual writing? Jane faced her father. Her glasses lenses miniaturized her eyes. —That's why there's no need to write it. She could easily defend it. She quoted Einstein on abandoned doctorates: 'The whole comedy has become boring.' Walking back, Elaine Cairo, nonplussed as she put it, appealed to Lou. —Help her find some ambitious man who will sweep her into the mainstream.

Summer people loved the Cape and never for a minute mistook it for real. By which Lou guessed they meant skyscrapers? opera? She realized the older Cairos meant, at bottom, universities. Her parents said that while Jane dallied in Provincetown not writing her dissertation, she might as well insulate, paint, and reroof their house. So she did. When Lou and Jane were alone, Jane told mean stories about her mother. She disdained her mother's academic outlook; she said her mother treated her father like dirt. Lou thought Jane was getting too old to regard her bitterness as the natural effect of a cause outside herself.

Often from her shack Lou saw Jane slog through sand to visit either her or Cornelius. She thought nothing of it until one summer, those two, Jane and Cornelius, more than twenty years apart in age, married. Only Lou and Edna Raposo, county clerk, witnessed the civil to-do. At Lou's kitchen table afterward, Cornelius popped corks. Lou saw his profile; his beard hid a bow tie. He kept a bow tie in his shack? He spent that night in town at Cairos'. The next day on the Upper West Side, Jane Cairo's mother Elaine, on the telephone, threw a rod.

Hollyhocks spattered Reevadare's West End house. Perhaps so many spattering painters for that reason chose it as motif. Jane Cairo arrived at the gate as Lou did. Jane's hair overwhelmed two barrettes and a rubber band. Since her mouth was wider than her teeth, whenever she smiled or laughed, dark triangles pointed up her lips' corners. Knowing, Lou looked hard and saw Jane was already showing.

—You look wonderful, Jane told Reevadare. Reevadare's humpback, which she named Surtsey, was now almost higher than her head.

—Honey, I got enough troubles without looking good. Reevadare never used to call people honey. She was playing old age like a bass.

—'The tragedy of old age,' Jane said, 'is not that one is old but that one is young.' Reevadare led them to a red table in the garden. Unseen, a catbird sang baroque. The wind was clocking east. It cracked the cold sea line.

Jane and Cornelius would keep living apart. What if they have a baby? Especially if they have a baby, Lou thought. Cornelius claimed to abhor both the form baby and the concept baby. Town had a Laundromat. Wait and see.

Reevadare's hair's part sunburned red. She was going hatless these days like everyone else. To Lou as a girl, old people's following fashion was just as sickening to watch as old people's not following fashion. Reevadare's ears looked like Buddha's. Her tea smelled like grass clippings. Over egg-salad sandwiches, she asked Jane if they planned to have children. Jane said Cornelius always wanted to name a baby girl Tandy, after a character in *Winesburg, Ohio*. A what? A girl. In a book?

—A drunk man names a seven-year-old girl Tandy, which he says means something like, the quality of… Jane looked off high to her left, revealing her jawline. —Tandy means… 'The quality of being strong to be loved. It is something men need from women and that they do not get.'

Why would anyone saddle a baby with a made-up name that means 'the quality of being strong to be loved'? Jane said she liked the name fine. Tandy Blue?

Lou asked herself, yet again, What happens to people out here on the lower Cape, a mid-ocean sandspit, what happens even to intelligent and educated people, that they take to plying skies like cows in Chagall? From solid citizens they sublimed to limbless metaphysicians. Their minds grew lucent as gels. Or they slipped from supersaturation to superstition without passing through crystal. Lou decided that the lower Cape's ratio of gases and fluids to solids must be out of whack. Otherwise, she agreed with many out here who like her (and Maytree, Deary, and Jane) found it prudent not to waste life's few years cultivating and displaying good taste. To whom? She could be reading.

—I wonder what women need from men that they do not get. In Reevadare's garden, Jane looked dreamy.

—Courage would be nice, Reevadare said. All my husbands were afraid, every last man jack. She laughed and waved her spotted hands. She looked to Lou like she had gotten over them, every last man jack.

During one snowy Saturday morning cartoon commercial Deary asked Maytree, Did you know that back in Provincetown I could see children's auras? Petie's was blue! He did know that. She repeated herself at ever-closer intervals. When did he notice he tuned her out like wind, like halyards' knocking masts? He had vowed himself to their life together, not to every word she spoke.

Maytree stepped into his study and rubbed his face. He heard the television playing the Poet and Peasant Overture in full orchestra. Things must be working out for Bugs Bunny.

How had he now loved Deary for – almost – twenty years? Or did he. He used to listen on edge, for years and in vain, to uncover where, in any anecdote's avalanche, dropped the flake she thought might interest him.

Early with Lou, then with Deary, and again now, he returned to this: Why can love, love apparently absolute, recur? And recur? Why does love feel it is – know for certain it is – eternal and absolute, every time? He opened a notebook and found a passage he had copied from Kafka's letters to Felice. 'I have no crazier and greater wish than that we should be bound together inseparably by the wrists.'

Of course Kafka wrote letters to Felice only when they were apart. Love letters do not so much document daily love's long hours as precede them. Now after these many years in Maine, Maytree wondered if Kafka ever felt that being bound to Felice by the wrists was a wish crazier than he knew.

He began on a blank page. Three explanations for love's recurrence presented. Perhaps everyone gathers or grows an enormous sack of love he hands whole from one beloved to another. In this instance, the beloved is love's hat rack. Or, second, perhaps love is delusional. The heart never learns and keeps leaping the length of its life, rising to lures made of rubber hiding hooks. Or, third, perhaps he never really loved Lou, let alone his other girlfriends, and, having learned love by loving, had found in Deary his true mate at last.

All three – even the usually irresistibly tempting true-mate-at-last hypothesis, for which both Maytree and Deary were by now many years too experienced – apostasized. They apostasized by saying love between man and woman, or anyone and anyone, beyond those eighteen months that science allows for infatuation, was imaginary or theater, or inertia, or convenience. A view looking to Maytree ever more plausible, but he knew he had truly loved Lou for years and still did. Since all apostasized, he was missing options, unless the premise – that there is such a thing as love, and it recurs – was false, so that apostasy was really a lapse into truth, like Galileo's. But then which belief was largest, which afforded hope, by which could we live? Was romance hierophany, or some fowler's snare that yanked a culture by the toe? Lucretius declared that love was only a shudder mammals used to procreate. Lucretius drank a love philter, fell in love, and died of suicide from a broken heart – doubtless, Maytree thought, to the delight of everyone.

Deary's legs felt weak, she told him later; she could hardly get up the stairs. She was out of breath. She had back trouble. She was old. Her neck hurt. Would he rub her back? Was her back still beautiful? Could he build them an addition – a bigger dining room in which to hang three chandeliers?

The lasting love he studied, not mere emotion, might be willful focus of attention. It might be a custody of reactions. He circled this view for years. Love as directed will did not sound like love's first feeling of cliff-jumping. Call that period eighteen months or seven years – call it anything but infatuation! It must be acknowledged and accounted for. Recently science had nailed down its chemistry: adrenaline. After eighteen months, the body balks at more adrenaline. Then what? He had loved Lou for years and years. On and off, mostly very much on. Those loving years, and their persistence, must also be credited. People used to die so young! Maybe lasting love is a rare evolutionary lagniappe. Anthropologists say almost every human culture on earth gives lip service, and lip service only, to monogamy. He was scrupulously loving in mind and body toward Deary in order to make reparations to the moral universe. He was grateful for the chance.

Lasting love makes no scientific sense after the kids can hunt and gather. Yet statistics note that if one of a long-married couple dies, the other often dies soon after. Maybe love in that case is a term so wide it includes both infatuation and mutual, habitual dependency. Screw that. Why? Because he knew better. That it was outside science's lens did not mean it did not exist. As Maytree aged, lasting love was starting to seem more central to a man's life even than work. Even than building a career and even writing poetry! Anthropology had proved against its expectations that the ideal of lasting love and also its undeniable (if minority) presence was well-nigh universal, in culture after culture from the Stone Age on.

Say that evolution came up with the eighteen months' infatuation. That might be long enough to get Baby on his feet and arranged for, if only by Grandpa or siblings. Then the man can go off and impregnate someone else. Why then do old people fall in love? Why stay loving? The feeling of love is so crucial to our species it is excessive, like labor pain. Lasting love is an act of will. It is a gentleman's game.

To Lou's raised light Maytree had once set his face. 'Time was,' said a Wessex rustic, 'long and merry ago now!' He loved her, whatever that was, merry ago or not. He skipped over his undeniable knowledge that he had also loved Deary deeply for a while at first, a *while* he had been prolonging. He was obliged to love Deary. Now with and for Deary, he had wrapped his hands around oars, iced them fast, and kept rowing.

Lou hoped scandalously to live her own life. A subnormal calling, since civilization means cities and cities mean social norms. She wanted only to hear herself think. She admired Diogenes who shaved half his head so he would stay home to think. How else might she hear any original note, any stray subject-and-verb in the head, however faint, should one come?

She pushed the tiller hard over, came about, and set a slashing course upwind. The one-room ever-sparer dune shack was her chief dwelling from which only hurricane or frost exiled her. Over decades, she had reclaimed what she had forfeited of her own mind, if any. She took pains to keep outside the world's acceleration. An Athens marketplace amazed Diogenes with 'How many things there are in the world of which Diogenes hath no need!' Lou had long since cut out fashion and all radio but the Red Sox. In the past few years she had let go her ties to people she did not like, to ironing, to dining out in town, and to buying things not necessary and that themselves needed care. She ignored whatever did not interest her. With those blows she opened her days like a piñata. A hundred freedoms fell on her. She hitched free years to her lifespan like a kite tail. Everyone envied her the time she had, not noticing that they had equal time.

The bay and ocean and daytime sky did not change. Lou lived in color fields. By habit, she ignored the Cape's man-made changes. In town it was tough to break the habit of checking skies every hour or so. These new people kept imaginary beasties away using streetlights and spotlights. Not one of them asked about burglary rates. They thought they knew. They unknowingly brought their big-city obsession with crime and appearance and status as rats bring etc.

When winter forced her back to town she braced to enter the same low-ceilinged cave most Americans lived in unknowingly. Always in May the Milky Way returned to belly overhead, as if equinoctial storms made of the galaxy a spinnaker that opened to north winds. Any fuss reached her anyway, even though she ducked just as, swimming, she took a breaking wave by diving under it.

Three days a week she helped at the Manor Nursing Home, where people proved their keenness by reciting received analyses of current events. All the Manor residents watched television day and night, informed to the eyeballs like everyone else and rushed for time, toward what end no one asked. Their cupidity and self-love were no worse than anyone else's, but their many experiences having taught them so little irked Lou. One hated tourists, another southerners; another despised immigrants. Even dying, they still held themselves in highest regard. Lou would have to watch herself. For this way of thinking began to look like human nature – as if each person of two or three billion would spend his last vital drop to sustain his self-importance.

In September and October, Lou stayed in the dunes to surf-cast. After sunset, the sky drew out its dying. The sea climbing her legs was suddenly warm, a wonder. Until a wave knocked her down, she was herself sea and skies in equipoise. A hitting bass jump-started her. She caught the shrieking reel as the fish ran the line; she set the hook.

The next day Jane Cairo visited Lou's shack on the way to Cornelius's. And she brought swaddled Tandy! who was the size and shape of a one-quart thermos. Tandy's yellow face (previously purple) was peaceful. When Lou held the light baby, she said, You forget. Jane said everybody without exception studied the baby's face at length and eventually said, You forget. Cornelius called her You Forget. Later that night Lou felt a friendly greeting from Maytree in Maine. She felt his surprise jig several times a year. Did it rebound from that old backboard the moon? Hallo, she said back like Toad, amused.

Maybe someday a thought or two would come. In the meantime she cleared the landing strip.

Newly ashore in Camden, Maine, Pete wore his sweater belted into his pants. A Greek cap, canvas land shoes. He liked this time of evening, yellow pier lights, indoor rooms glowing blue as the sky's last edge, and Cassiopeia asprawl. When his vessel *Marie*'s motor cracked in the Gulf of Maine, he hauled out the two-stroke, the old eggbeater, and they limped to the nearest boatyard. In Camden, if this tiny outboard could make Camden within their lifetimes, they would seek a cheap boatyard, wait for a new engine, and fix or replace the pump. How would he and his estranged father act? Pete at thirty-two was ready to meet him man-to-man and father-to-father.

Once on the wharf as Pete dropped his duffel from dock to deck, his father's face appeared behind the water – narrow skull, laugh creases, alert eyes under brows like shakes – and Pete felt the barometer needle swing over like a helm. SET FAIR. He had hopped aboard. The needle stayed over ever since.

He remembered playing catch, rowing. His father let him open and shut his folding ruler. They dug clams. Sometimes his parents danced to Louis Armstrong on the radio and sent him aghast out the door. When his father looked up from the flats, or looked beyond the downstairs French doors to the bay, he tended to say,

*Where is there an end of them, the fishermen sailing*
*Into the wind's tail, where the fog cowers?*


These memories were thin tokens. Long ago Pete had forgiven Deary's betrayal. She was the one adult in town who had a good time.

And what would his own firstborn, little Manny, remember of him? Everything! His son was extra conscious.

Pete climbed the steep Main Street sidewalk. He found the couple's side street named at its top. He knew the house number. He could always join the rest of the crew at the boatyard.

He saw her dark slacks on a porch, a green couch, knees up, white ladylike bun showing over a pillow; she was reading the *New York Times*. He saw lamps, a sideboard, a heater, and a Persian rug. He opened the screen door and walked in. What if his face rang no bell? She gave a cry, and he helped her rise. She held him fast. She was short. She tilted her face up and said, Petie! Your room's ready.

My room?

—What is it? That voice came from inside. His father entered the porch, thin as a pipefish, tall, orange-and-white eyebrows, loose limbs, full head of white hair, nice-guy face. He wore his belt high. Their eyes met over Deary's head.

Here was the look he used to dread. The sticking point for Pete had been his father's twenty-year silence. Often Pete's partner Sooner reported that his own father had seen Maytree at their college reunion. So he even came to Massachusetts every five years, and still never even called.

Pete saw his old father's smile kindle and tremble. So many easy lines crossed his skin that his eyes looked like pokeholes in screens. Pete held out his hand. Maytree surrounded him as if for keeps, and, in the process, Deary. At his collar Pete smelled the man's neck like warm copper. His hair smelled like him alone. I must hold back, Pete thought; he knew his enthusiasm could scare people. Then he saw his wet-faced father, not holding back. Oh – he used to read him books, that's what he did. Pete felt his father's tensile arms, felt his knobbed shoulders' heat and tone. He remembered the round faraway voice in which his father read him stories aloud day and night long after Pete himself could read. Blue carpenter's chalk smudged the pages.

Why had he waited? Why had he not – as his mother urged him to – invited him, both of them, to his and Marie's wedding?

—Hell's bells, his mother had said back at home. You poisoned yourself after all. —It's not that, he said. He did not say that meeting his father would embarrass them both. He knew his mother would ridicule his using embarrassment as an excuse not to do what was right. Yet surely she understood embarrassment?

Now in Camden father stepped back, possibly lest Deary suffocate. —Whiskey? he said. Vodka? Gin? Here was the same long face blushing, the same shambling friendliness. His wild brows arced down and his wide mouth arced up, giving him a hopeful look. Pete had seen this expression squinting in deckel-edge snapshots. Now the rays pleating his father's temples were deep. He was sixty-four, Pete knew – much younger than Deary, younger than Cornelius, three years older than Lou Maytree. He had the zip of a tern.

—Gin, thanks. His father carried his head a bit forward. What should he call him? His short orange-and-white beard angled like a train's cowcatcher. Deary, hanging like a toddler, still had Pete hooked with both arms.

What sort of love was twenty years' silence? It made no sense. A father's shame, fearing his son's censure? Pete had no idea. He knew how a parent falls wild for a child. Nothing could breach his intimacy with their own amazing baby, gleeful, passionate

Manny. No one who adored you like that could ever hate you. Pete's once wanting to stone his father with beach cobbles had dropped from his mind, and so had the memory of all his internal work just to bear the thought of him.

Later that night he climbed Camden's Main Street again with his kit. The sidewalk under trees was like a cave. In twenty years he had never once imagined – in the little time imagining takes – that his father loved him all along. His father had waited for him to figure out it was his, Pete's, move. But Pete's movement was all internal. He never let his father know.

When had scruples not hobbled or wrecked love or affection? He could have won Marie Koday several years earlier, years in which he so cautiously refrained even from saying hello that she finally had to kiss him. She met the boat and kissed him. His blood bolted and his town cap dropped. Their life began. Scrupulously not rattling his father's presumed privacy or indifference, he had wasted more stupid years.

Deary tried to show him down their polished hall. She looked like summer people – gold bracelet, earrings, tailored skirt, lipstick. He remembered her tatterdemalion. Still striking, she was newly a limping matron. A bit far between, the curls at her crown. Her eyebrows barely traced their ruts. Deary's eye area, he guessed, opened a vertical third of her face. Good looks at any age required only big eyes under high brows.

She was sixty-seven. Maytree helped her show Pete down the hall. —Remember, Deary said. She winked across his father's potbelly no bigger than a chowder bowl. Promise me. When I die I want to go out like a gypsy queen. Big smile, great false teeth. Burn my carriage with me inside it, she said. In Provincetown.

—You bet, Pete said. Consider it remembered. Burn in carriage, Provincetown.

—Where are you keeping your carriage these days?

—He's humoring me!

—Actually, Maytree said, I am. At the kitchen sink later he told Pete that two years ago he had tricked Deary into letting the town's tall white-haired physician, whom Maytree now referred to as Dr. Eminent, check her. Speaking to Maytree, Dr. Eminent implied that everything was all in Deary's dimply head, likely because she never had a baby. —Find another doctor, Pete had said.

—They're all quacks! Deary squeaked from the porch. The cure is lost in a jungle! Her hearing was excellent.

Pete stayed four days in Camden, shoulders on walls (his friends called him Eileen), while the boatyard waited for parts. During breakfast daily, a broad-hipped, plaid-clad young woman named Sarah Smither let herself in. Maytree had already told Pete that Sarah's Irish-immigrant parents had so many children that he and Deary privately called the offspring, collectively, Smithereens. Sarah joined them in the dining room. His father said Sarah looked after things. Later Sarah filled a thermos jug with coffee, helped Deary to her office, and put away dishes within earshot of Deary's bronze handbell.

The first full day, he saw his father and Deary were partners. —I've come up in the world, Deary said. —Isn't that the point? Recently she sited a house on a once-wooded lakeshore. She drew plans and elevations to the last spec. Her architectural weeks on this project were ending if clients approved. Maytree and men would stick-build the house, roof it, and dry it in. Deary got permits. Before her vitality waned, she had risen early to chase forestry crews, haulers, suppliers, the furnace installer, plumbers, electricians, the insulation people, the plasterer, and the stonemason. She had accounted, billed, and paid.

Near Deary at the oak kitchen table, Pete peeled the potatoes she washed. She told him old Provincetown stories in her familiar, if aerated, high voice. He picked up potatoes she dropped. He wished she knew his childhood less and his manhood more. But how? He could have let them know him, any time.

—Marie Koday? She spent all one summer upside down with her head in the water, walking on her hands. Adorable child. Was she not considerably older than you?

—Not now.

Deary wanted to play spit, double Canfield, and slapjack. She insisted he grab hard and slap fast. She lost her breath. Her hands whirred and her rings clobbered. She laughed. Evenings after coffee, Maytree rubbed her shoulders. She kept her chin raised, as Pete had noticed in Boston that only beautiful women do. His father cleaned up.

—Are you writing poetry?

—Maybe over next winter. They say Georges Bank is over-fished – that right?

—They have never been there.

—So you fish the Gulf of Maine?

—Sometimes. We keep an eye on both cod stocks.

Deary double-shuffled. Ventrally, her hands were yellow except between the bones, where they were blue. He never imagined coming here to slap her around.

Here in his father's Camden house, Pete had his own head. Its window looked into what his father told him was a maple. Thinly in the maple he saw his own mirrored face that boughs scratched. He missed Marie.

'What we have together,' Pete and Marie called it to them-selves, for want of a single noun. While both sets of parents, when very young, had coupled for certain once, or in Marie's parents' unthinkable case thrice, those parents' matter-of-fact ways, like everyone else's, showed they never suspected, and must be shielded from, the secret and unearthly properties of what we have together. A good man like his father – he always heard his father was once a good man – could go bad and run off?

Obviously his father and mother never had anything together. But what about his father and Deary, twenty years ago? His father would have been forty-four then: twelve years older than Pete now, but of course much older inside, as befits a parent. At that age, couples patted the remains of each other's hands on porches. Deary was even older now than Marie's coal-tar-dyed mother who still plunked herself on the old man's knees after ice cream. Grotesque, all of it.

The maple outside and his own face showed equally in the window. As a boy, Pete noticed that old people like Reevadare Weaver and Cornelius Blue could horrifyingly persist in oldness for decade after decade, no end in sight, without shame. Old people were those who lacked will to leave, or tact to know, when their party was over. At thirty-two he had begun the rocketry recalibration of what constitutes old people – whose merry ranks he did not plan, in any case, to join. Drowning at sea was a likely option. Better, when the time came, was shooting himself. This was America.

Once a day either Pete or his father wondered why they waited so long. —Men! Deary said, but she had not contacted him, either. Still, no use wasting time regretting time they'd already lost. That now he made his father happy with a few words – come see your grandson – shamed Pete for once begrudging them.

On their final morning when *Marie* would launch again, Pete watched fog pool up the street. A sprucey scarf of fog entered with Sarah Smither. Her eyeglasses' frames were plaid.

—I like the fog, Deary said, except when it catches in trees.

—You like the fog, Sarah replied, except when it catches in trees.

Sarah was studying clinical psychology. Maytree told Pete he wondered whether to strangle her or give her a cracker. He gave her a raise. What would they do when her school started? On the stone steps the men pounded each other's shoulders. Deary tried to squeeze Pete, wept brightly, and said, Don't be a stranger. Again his gaze met his father's over her head.

Dr. Cobo, cardiologist, kept offices in his house's basement. As a young man board-certified in both cardiology and internal medicine, Dr. Cobo had immigrated from Cuba and had to undergo recertification as though Cuba's were the lesser health-care system.

Granite steps delved from a Main Street sidewalk to Dr. Cobo's door. Maytree carried Deary down the steps' pitch.

—A heart murmur, Dr. Cobo said. Tests. Her leaking mitral valve lost to backwash more than it pumped. —Congestive heart failure, Dr. Cobo said, addressing Deary.

—We can try to get you into Texas transplant trials, he said. In the meantime, we'll monitor you in the hospital. A ventilator will help you breathe easily. Deary half closed her eyes and bestowed her lipsticky smile. —I'd rather die.

Maytree settled her in the car. She would refuse any treatment, let alone any physician or hospital. —I could get roller skates, Deary said as he carried her in their front door. —I love old ladies who roller-skate.

An hour later: —They even admit they don't know everything! Look on their licenses, O ye mighty, and drop dead! Almost everyone they knew who went to a hospital, or consulted physicians, or submitted to surgery, died in pain. *Post hoc non ergo propter hoc,* Maytree thought.

In the kitchen he cupped a pinna against her sternum. Murmur! The backwash of her heart's pump sloshed. The mitral valve was no seal but a rubber pet door that flapped both ways.

Maytree set up a bed in their living room by the wheelchair. He moved tables. Deary called for her hairdresser to come once a week. She gave Maytree instructions for gardener, cleaner, and florist. Happily in bed she named another dozen people who had surgery and died in pain. They filled the cemetery.

Dr. Cobo had asked Maytree to stop by later. Then he told him that cardiology could only palliate. Deary's heart muscle had swelled and thinned past saving. In any case she would not suffer. He made sure Maytree understood he was no prophet. — Soon, he said. Pressed, he said, Maybe many months, maybe fewer. Maytree hoped Deary would not get pious on him, and she did not.

—You took her to Dr. Eminent before? his painter friend asked from the porch. He tells women it's all in their heads.

Maytree quit work and handed others both his projects to finish. He bought robes. He learned 'Black Watch plaid' and 'chenille.' Their friends the painter and his wife visited self-consciously. Maytree loved this guy but knew their friendship was not intimate. When they came, he turned off the television. As its screen darkened, it contracted to a dot of light that snapped out.

Deary let only Sarah Smither visit what she called her crypt. Sarah Smither read orange-bound children's biographies aloud. Wrapped in blossom-print silk, Deary smiled when Abe Lincoln played a trick: he lifted and flipped a local boy who tracked muddy footprints on a friend's ceiling.

When the wheelchair or bed tired her, Maytree carried her like a doll. She raised her palm before his eyes while he bore her to the bathroom.

—Look at my lifeline. What does it tell you?

—That I can't see where we're going.

For dying, she was ready as for any other party. —Messages for anyone dead? she asked Sarah Smither and the scared mailman. Her eyes half closed. She could no longer belt her exhilarating favorite, 'Antonio Spangonio (the Bum Toreador).' Maytree joined her. —*When I catch that blighter I'll kill him, I will… I'll cut out his heart with a dagger, I will.* One morning Maytree heard the song's finale, —*He shall die! he shall die! when I plant an onion on his Spanish bunion, when I catch Antonio – tonight!* Pause.

—You forgot the *boom boom!* Maytree said. —No, you. Meaning, you sing the *boom boom!* because I can't. – Boom boom!

One morning after a December snowstorm he slipped on ice and dropped her. Rather, he threw her – just a lob.

He was carrying her down to Dr. Cobo, the sight of whose Castilian face soothed them. It was voodoo after all.

The day he dropped her, he was bearing forward like a tray. She weighed ninety pounds. He felt his foot slip on iced stone. In that instant he tossed her in the fresh snowbank by the steps. At the toss he recoiled, and his slip became a wreck.

—Honey? she whispered. She usually called him Maytree.

—Are you all right?

—Are you?

She told him later she, too, heard his bones snap like carrots. Nothing hurt for almost an hour.

In the strictly-for-profit hospital, professionals did their best shorthanded. They let him wait behind curtains on a bed. Deary, unhurt, waited, too. Someone glanced at Deary and ran out. Someone else listened to Deary's heart.

—I'm just taking her vitals, the emergency-room nurse told Maytree.

—No, he said. You emphatically are not.

Deary refused admission, stonewalling ever-higher-ups, and signed a hundred release forms. She held the pen among blue fingernails. She sat on a wheeled steel stool until she slipped and the stool bowled into the nurses' station. Then Sarah Smither's mother appeared carrying Deary's oxygen-tube stand – she refused it – and her pillow. This worthy, who made squash doughnuts, held Deary on her lap to balance and warm her. Maytree watched her slip a fingerful of petroleum inside Deary's nostrils. He wished she would shoot them both.

Much later he learned that he had broken his left humerus just above the elbow. He broke his left clavicle. He broke his right radius twice. He broke his right wrist and thumb; he snapped his right ulna in two at the elbow. One lumbar vertebra cracked – the crucial one, he felt, that every twitch cracked anew. Without puncturing his lungs, his fourth and fifth ribs sustained greenstick fractures dorsally. Far from 'sustaining' anything, he thought, his bones broke. The orthopedist reduced Maytree's four arm fractures in memorable jerks, and unrolled wet plaster casts over both his arms, one high, one low.

He pictured his fall down those six stone steps as so spectacular he chose not to picture it again. His X-rays looked like the Tunguska event, the Siberian forest after a meteorite hit. An old woman entered and taped his broken ribs as if they might flee. She tucked his right cast under her arm, eyeballed his thumb to align it with his invisible wrist, and splinted it. On doctor's orders she gave him only acetaminophen – as he learned later from the itemized bill. We Americans possibly enjoyed a right to suffer needlessly that lesser peoples miss.

Mrs. Smither, driving them home, wore a green felt hat. He addressed her hat from the backseat as loudly as he could. — Mrs. Smither. I know you both work hard. I wonder. His ribs broke again every time he breathed. His vertebra halves ground like floes. His two broken arms. His head lay on his coat folded on Deary's lap. All day since he fell, or since he pitched her on the snow, she seemed dumbstruck. No choices for them or even chances presented, if he could not carry her and wait on her. She knew it, too.

He had no one to turn to. Under tires dry snow yelped. His bones jolted as if the car had triangular wheels. Moving to Provincetown for now would content Deary and keep his word. Since he botched life with Lou twenty years ago, he honored his every word sometimes to absurdity, like skating with friends after his viral pneumonia had turned to lobar pneumonia.

—If you, or if Sarah… If we offer you twice whatever you earn… Could you help us out for a few months while I mend? In Provincetown on Cape Cod, some nice house? Or (this in a rush) do you think Sarah would help us now and postpone graduation? Has she ever seen Cape Cod? She would have her own room and no other duties. Whether he could use his arms or not, Deary was still dying. Why had they not moved to Provincetown yesterday?

Sarah, Mrs. Smither said, was starting in June as a counselor for the county. Nor could Mrs. Smither herself leave her squash doughnut supervisor post.

Could Pete take care of them? Good Pete would never spring this family of strangers for weeks on his wife. They had their baby boy and only two rooms.

That night Maytree drank vodka from its bottle as Deary gasped beside him in their bed. Their walkway lamps below the window yellowed the iced maple's glaze. Deary's breathing stopped sometimes, as always, and resumed with a snort.

What had they injected him with, hummingbird feed? Had none of them ever broken a bone? How about half a lethal injection? At least in capital cases they treated the whole person.

He could buy Pete and Marie a house of any size – but Pete would not accept. He still had his young pride. How could they move when she had just had a baby? He and Sooner could hoist Pete's house to a wide flatbed… No, Sooner had gone back to Missouri for the winter, and he could hoist nothing. That was the point.

He reminded himself that perhaps a billion people like him worldwide were lying awake in pain now and at their wits' end. In Provincetown he could rent a place off-season, for Deary and him and a live-in helper or two, if Deary could stand strangers whose accents and clothes betrayed sloppy families. For what purpose had he amassed so much money if it was useless? Well, for three private nurses in eight-hour shifts, if there were any nurses. And again, if Deary would permit as witnesses strangers who would misplace everything in a twinkling, and pat her head. Reportedly Cornelius Blue and Jane lived in separate dune shacks and separate places in town; they visited. With Jane lived a bundled baby, Tandy. Cornelius's town room! It was one room. If the old bachelor would not tend one sack of helplessness in the form of Tandy, he would not tend three.

Reevadare took in strays, of which Deary had been many. Reevadare also loved throwing parties, loved being waited on herself, and talked too much. He rejected the Manor – the nursing home. Now what to hope? For he had known all day he would appeal to Lou. He knew it as he fell.

If he could flex his elbows, he would hide his face. Practiced – he was at least practiced – he faced his embarrassment down. The iced maple trunk near the windows had a translucent double. He would slither back so his real wife could carry Deary from bed to bath till she died. Lou had kept his name. And she would take them. He would welcome them in her place, and he knew her spirit to be generous. Not because troubles whipped him and he had no one else to appeal to, though troubles certainly whipped him and he had no one else to appeal to, but because Lou might actually help them, pronto.

And forgiveness had nothing to do with it. They were both whole people, he and Lou. Whole old people. At their age forgiveness could be child's play if you knew the ropes, and so could be the nod that accepted forgiveness of course and moved on. Young, he would have thought any end, even dying, beat being forgiven, let alone by a woman, and beat asking for help, too, let alone asking the wife he left for help. Now he and Lou – if Lou was like Pete, whom he more wronged – could meet as equals. His asking would honor her goodness. His willingness to ask was part of what he now knew best: to think well of those you have wronged, let alone those who have wronged you. He hoped Lou's thinking had brought her there, too. He really hoped. Just till Deary died.

Mrs. Smither would drive Deary and him to Provincetown tomorrow in her car. If Lou refused them, she would at least help him think what else to try. Would he and Lou even recognize each other? She kept inviting them to visit – but she was kidding herself. No, no possible course could be worse. They would leave early. He sprang to life. He fell asleep.

It was after two o'clock the next day that they hazarded the Orleans rotary. He sat by Mrs. Smither while Deary dozed and jerked in back. The Cape land was flimsy; it lacked stones. If Nausets discovered a glacial erratic, they wore paths to it to grind corn; later surveyors reckoned by it. Maytree saw gaudy roadside shops clear to Eastham. A gas-station map showed that the green-tinted National Seashore takings, which they had all fought, had saved the lower Cape. They passed dead Pilgrim Lake. Ahead a moving dune was crossing the road footfirst like a snail. He saw half a dozen highway employees (convicts?) trying to sweep the dune back with brooms. Left toward the bay. Pulling up to his own old house, Mrs. Smither found no parking space. Town had shrunk and multiplied walls as crystals form facets in vials. They parked back on Bradford. He asked Mrs. Smither to leave the ignition on so the heater worked. His hip hit the car door shut. He would walk. His jacket hung open over his casts and slings.

How would he start? He had outgrown eloquence. He started the first time by introducing himself. Lou might well not be amused. He needed more air. He would be able to tell from her face.

On the top step he knew she was gone. He rang the bell, waited, walked into the house that smelled like sea and her skin, and called. The empty house where they had lived still seemed hospitable. Back in the car he told Mrs. Smither how to find Pete's.

Pete's Marie opened the door where the outside stairs ended. Maytree identified himself. She held the door for him. Marie stood taller than Pete, slim-faced and exuberant. Her laughing chatter was either her habit, or, more likely, extra happiness. She displayed for him, in her thrust arms, black-eyed baby Manuel who stared at air. The baby had more eyebrows than Cary Grant. Braced to confront Lou, Maytree found himself undone by this in-the-translucent-flesh grandson who set him blinking. Pete's boat was due in after sunset, Marie said as if she had known Maytree all her life. He sat and knocked back a beer. His bones' pain was a siren in his ears. It wore him out all over every instant, and he could barely strain to take in the world behind the blare. Marie said Pete's mother was out closing the shack. In December? Bowing, Maytree left. He had to walk to her there before dark.

There was a new motel off-street on Bradford. —Where are we? Deary whispered when the car stopped. Oh, look, it's Provincetown. The lives we live! She reached in her bag for a mirror. Last week she almost stopped eating. She was shutting down one tube at a time. In the motel lobby Maytree checked them in. From the bed Deary could watch sky stir over the bay. Maytree's broken bones registered each wave's break as a bomb. Mrs. Smither handed him water to drink. She buttoned his jacket over his casts and pulled his watch cap over his ears. He set out north for the dunes.

When Maytree was young, men, women, and children found their way in starlight alone. When clouds covered the night sky, as now, the whole Cape knew it: Dark night! they said, in a greeting then as common, and almost as frequent, as —Fine day! The answer was, Sure is, or Real dark night. Night was their familiar parlor, a scented time all its own. Now that electric lights wrecked the night sky, he mourned as if the great universe had died within his own lifetime. People forgot to look up. Maytree knew his remembering starry nights dated him as the war did. Except that the war, unlike humans' sight of stars, had lasted fewer than ten years.

Dark would catch him somewhere in the dunes. At this thought he turned back and kicked his motel door politely. Mrs. Smither obliged him by removing his shoes so he could feel his way. Deary smiled. He wondered if she remembered the dunes.

That morning at the shack, Lou unhooked the long-handled tinsnips. She cut a coiled copper scouring pad into strips, and knelt with a palette knife to force the strips to caulk holes and cracks in the walls and floor. The task required her moving everything in the room, including the bed. Scouring pad and steel wool worked as razor-wire for mice. If she failed to jam it, it blew out. A few mice and snakes always got inside anyway, perhaps through the gaps between nuclei and electrons. The mice, from scrapings of pillow, made nests the size of basketballs.

A flying wedge of cirrus was coming in high. She watched the sky fill, crowd, and close. By noon low cloud shut it. The foghorn started. That evening from her shack Lou saw blurred lights white and red in dark. The lights meant that most of the fleet, alerted by forecasts, had drawn inshore to dunes' lee. Always ominous, the sight scared her for years, until she learned that in hurricanes she would see no boats at all. Was Pete there? If the storm were going to be worse, those boats would have made for the breakwater and the harbor behind Provincetown's seven hills, or at very worst gone offshore for searoom.

\* \* \*

Maytree crossed the cold highway. His feet had softened in shoes for twenty years. He entered the woods and felt pine needles give way to sand as he climbed. All he had to do on this part was climb straight up sliding sand. It was like walking up a down escalator.

The first high clearing with its 360-degree prospect comprised all the dim dunes left and right. Here forest backed horizon's arc. Behind him a strand of lights, now blurring, dotted both Provincetown and its reflection. The lights burned no holes to relieve the black but instead seemed glued to its cloth. No matter how dark the night, sand's albedo was barely lighter than bushes' and trees'. Foundering behind a blowout, he rehearsed his bearings. The dunes and the people's path through them might have moved. The southwest wind at his neck could not serve as direction finder because it might shift.

Maytree was – as their old friend Mary Heaton Vorse said – 'night-footed.' Up and down and veer up and veer down and veer left and with luck find the swale's hard sand. Farther along in the night's burrow, he must strike the wavy jeep trail south behind the big rise to the foredune. He must stay in the jeep trail's ruts through each curve without bumping a scrub tree or the old coast guard station's broken wall. Then if he could balance atilt on the tracks' left edge in order to feel with his feet any sand dip wider than a toad track in the foredune's lee, and if he could by chance count these footpaths, then he might even find the thready shortcut left to the foredune's ridge and the last hard right to the shack. If, as likely, that failed, he could climb the foredune anywhere – unless he unknowingly passed the shack – and keep just at its grassy edge till he hit a shack or trail he knew. If he walked into the sea he had gone too far.

He started balancing across these steeps with his sore arms tied across him. He knew only the old route, and where he was now, where the shack was, and which way the sea. Not enough. Surely if the foredune and shack had fallen in the sea, Cornelius or Pete would have told him.

In the dark he could not walk fast enough to keep warm. Why during that eight-hour drive had he never once stopped to buy, say, soy sauce for Lou? He could have brought her anything. Asking, yes or no, for a month or two's room and board and twenty-four-hour nursing for two – especially for these two – called for one superb hostess gift. After two decades the A&P he saw on Conwell must carry soy sauce. He remembered Lou's translucent beauty of twenty years ago, her still carriage, and her friendly note above all. He was shaking from cold. The worst she could do was say no and mock him and kick him out. This worst was looking worse by the minute.

His head hit a dead branch and it broke. Last night awake in Camden he had fabricated some convoluted formula proving one minus one plus two equals just fine, downright dandy, in the presence of vodka and yelling pain and the absence of alternatives. How did it, impossibly, go? Something like... He, Maytree, would return home in courage – he had of course grown in courage – and part of courage is thinking well of people, even people you have wronged. He climbed the sand. Of course: never mind Lou, never mind Pete, never mind Deary, he was the bloody glorious hero. Fortunately a favorite aphorism from *Howards End* came to mind; he and Cornelius repeated it for years: 'Unworthiness stimulates woman.'

A tall pale dog joined him from nowhere. It was going to be the dog of this particular walk. An unknown dog *ex nihilo* often found him and joined him for one walk, a dog he never saw before or since. A strange dog might appear in Camden to escort him around his own block. This dog waited. Its muzzle seemed white. Such dogs never wore collars. They came up beside his leg and took him as charge. Maytree never patted or spoke to any of this otherworldly breed.

Presently his clothes were wet, from ground fog or sweat. He should have worn another watch cap or two. He fancied some tea. His cracked vertebra, people said, like his ribs, would knit in time. That was just yesterday. Near the great second dune's foot he felt with every plantar nerve for the slim berm of clay, or the hard sand beside it, that would lead him 'round the swale. He found it and hazarded the swale's bog. Cranberry patches felt good underfoot but meant he was off course. Dried grass stalks bloodied his insteps. The danger was a fall or a tree limb in the eye. The wind had clocked clear around to northwest, at him now, and soon at his back. The new wind was wildly cold, but it might beat back a line squall or two. He shook through atmospheres of blackness and blank.

Actually, he would rather turn back and find the lee of a beach plum in the swale, discover some brandy, and sleep abutting the strange dog. And not ask Lou what he had to. Still, he held the rigging. To be safe he nixed the shortcut and climbed the foredune on a known steep path. Of every step he gained, he lost half as his foot slid down sand. At the top he turned east. Thornbushes were colonizing this final ridge. From pre-eternity the ocean ahead lashed and threw salts. There far on the right was her light.

To Lou he appeared in the doorway as a watch cap and orange-white eyebrows. It was in-the-flesh Maytree. Lord love a duck. Empty sleeves hung from his bulged jacket, as if behind his buttons he held a new baby he happened across. The kerosene lamp blinded him and paled his irises.

—Well, come on in. He nodded without moving. You'll let the heat out.

Tall thin fellow, neck a bit forward. His skin had shrunk over his temples, nose, and cheekbones, revealing a round skull. —Take off your hat, she said, and plucked it up for him, handless as he was. His hair was thin, but there. He stood at a loss in the one room. She started tea.

Then she saw Maytree could not shed his jacket. She unbuttoned it and bared two plaster casts from which his blue fingers dangled like squid arms. She found herself amused for no reason. She drew for him his usual chair. She stuck a quarter-round and another in the stove. You would think plucking a man's hat from his personal head and so naturally unbuttoning his jacket would relax him, and it seemed to. He sat and shrugged the jacket halfway off, and sat in his damp socks. He had a short red beard. Pete had mentioned a beard, she recalled. She herself was easy as ever. She could see his creased face had a smiling habit it cost him to sober. He rose, opened the door, and looked around.

—What?

—There was a dog. He stepped outside. Without bumping him, she too looked into the living night for a moment.

From where they sat, the windowpane made of one lantern two. The weaker one trembled like a moth outside. He turned. What big ears you have! Aging had thinned his mouth as it thinned hers; they were drying up. Only stubby rows of white lashes propped his eyelids. The lines at his eyes' edges splayed like the comet's tail in the Bayeux tapestry.

—Pray, what brings you out here? She stopped herself. There was no reason to kid him. She was pretty sure she knew: If he had hurt his arms he could not take care of Deary whose heart was failing.

—Maytree, she started again, and smiled. Good to see you. He was the one who used to overdo things.

He bent to his tea mug and looked worried into it.

—You used to do the talking, she said. How are you both?

Had they no close friends after twenty years in Maine? Had Deary no mother? She used to possess quite a well-tailored, competent-looking mother who fled Provincetown eons ago when she saw a topless sunbather on the beach, then two men holding hands. Had Deary a brother or sister? No. No hospitals in Maine? Nursing homes? Visiting nurses? She knew Deary thought medical science killed its victims. Lou's only sincere question was this: Should she break into Maytree's travails now, and put him out of his misery, or let him dangle a bit for the sake of the long-lost jilted Lou? Of course she would take them in. Anyone would.

—Deary's dying real soon. He looked up at her like the gentleman he was. Maybe you've heard. She nodded. —Actually, she doesn't know she is dying. I always promised to bring her to Provincetown to die and here we are. I can't take care of her anymore. I broke my arms. I can't take care of myself for now.

—I will take care of her, of course, she said, as he went on without seeming to hear – Pete and Marie live in two rooms.

He would think of imposing on betrayed Pete and Marie and their baby Manny? He and Pete were all patched up – but did he fear her, Lou, that badly? And with her no patching was needed, never mind what he or anyone else might think. Maytree and Deary were her old friends.

What would ease Deary? Lou would have to learn. She bade her solitude good-bye. Good-bye no schedule but whim; good-bye her life among no things but her own and each always in place; good-bye no real meals, good-bye free thought. The whole fat flock of them flapped away. But what was solitude for if not to foster decency? Her solitude always held open house. When was the last time anyone needed her? She was eager to do it, whatever it was.

—Come, of course. Not really hearing herself, she went on, We'll move Pete's old bed downstairs by the beach, so Deary can look out, and you can use the couch. Or instead of the couch I could bring in this shack's cot mattress, and find it a frame. Surely it would be more comfortable than that old couch.

—Or we could take apart our big bed and carry the frame down in pieces, then the mattress. That would be best. It has a good mattress – and I'll take Pete's old bed.

Across the table he was regarding her wide-eyed as if she were deranged. She recalled this only later. Possibly she had never spoken so long. Possibly he found crucial household mechanics peripheral. He looked as though he had never given mattresses even a thought. Lamplight made the night shack look like one cell in a beehive.

He stood; their heights matched. Why not name the shack Shrunken Heights? He looked away, not uncomfortably. He asked her to button his jacket. He expected to walk back that night.

—Don't be silly. He resisted and relented, though cloud cover was breaking up. When he stepped out for a minute Lou remembered that in the last decade or so invading Japanese wild roses crowded the shack. She wondered if a rosebush would trap him. How could he unstick himself? Well, he would just have to call out. She would be helping both of them, her arms serving as everyone's. How soon do broken bones mend?

He slept as shack guests always slept, in a sleeping bag on the cot mattress on the floor. When he settled, she blew out the last lamp. After some time she heard him speak from the floor in the dark, now sounding tight-throated, making light.

—Not going to slug me?

—I considered it, when Petie was a baby and you wore earplugs.

—Earplugs? I don't remember any earplugs. Actually, I ran off with Deary.

—I did notice that. You brute. Get some sleep.

—You're wonderfully…

She growled and he stopped. He was treating her like a stranger who was helping him change a tire.

She could not sleep. Should she pretend to find it all difficult, and not so much a matter of course, to ease his chagrin, or at least to make it seem apt? She declined this ploy as tiresome. Or did he think so poorly of her, and so well of himself, that he fancied his chucking her and Pete for Deary had left her ruined and angry for twenty years? Surely he knew her better than that. Surely! – or else he really would insult her.

She opened her eyes in the dark to make lists. In town Deary and Maytree would draw their old friends to visit. She needed tumblers, cups, plates, bowls, forks, and spoons. She would drive to Snow's in Orleans, in Mrs. Smither's car. She needed sheets, many, and towels, also many. Chairs. The laundromat was across town; she could borrow Jane's car. Thinking up meals above all, and shopping for them, cooking, serving, and cleaning up, cleaning up and organizing everybody's everything: That was the hell of it.

Would a wheelchair fit through the bathroom door? How did Deary move from wheelchair to bed? Maybe that was another place she came in.

* * *

At breakfast on the hoof by the woodstove he told her that in the motel lobby yesterday he heard a tourist tell his son that the Milky Way was a star formation over Arizona. Later he stepped from the shack and then called, Where did the outhouse run off to? She laughed and told him; it must have been in its new location at least fifteen years.

—Where's the mirror?

—I took it down. There's a hand mirror in the drawer.

—Took it down? Why?

—It wanted products.

—Products? He was smiling as she supposed she was, to see how readily they slipped back. He was starting to yield to her stubborn view that they had indeed previously met. When he smiled and also when he did not, she saw parallel lines in his cheeks like presliced bacon.

He was leaving for town. Outside where they paused, white mist obliterated the lowlands. —I'd forgotten how unearthly this place can be. From a white lake of fog opaque as paint, the tips of dunes, and only the tips of dunes, arose everywhere like sand peaks that began halfway up the sky. Dune tops protruded from a flat fog line evenly as atolls. She could see every stick and pock on their tan tops against dark blue sky. These sand peaks lacked nothing but connection to earth and a cause for being loose. They looked like a rendezvous of floating tents. She looked down and could see only a white fog wall under which her own feet showed.

Mrs. Smither would drive back to Camden soon, he told her, and fetch Maytree back to Maine after Deary died. When was she going back to town? He still avoided her gaze.

—It'll take a day or two to close the shack. You two go right into the house. Pete and Marie can help you set up.

Lou watched him take off jagged, arms inside his jacket, across the dunes. He walked as if his legs and feet were prosthetics. He entered the fog as into a wall of fresh plaster. It enfolded his foot. She watched him contract and vanish as he moved on, leg hip shoulders head, as if he were walking into solvent. She had never imagined seeing him again. They could all be in town as soon as tomorrow night. She should get busy.

How would she stock the house? She changed her mind and decided to leave the shack now; it had no part to play. Pete could close it. Now she wanted to clean the glass on those beachside doors and beg, borrow, or buy bedding, food, bowls, and plates. She regularly visited friends and helped the staff at the Manor. Her friends there would lend her a wheeled overbed table. What sort of bright painting might Deary like by her bed? What did heart patients eat? She hoped it was potatoes, cabbage, turnips, winter squash and greens, clams, short ribs, and fish.

She drank water, hooked the outhouse door, and stuffed laundry and the brown garbage bag in her knapsack. She had to hurry – so much to do in two days. Why not keep daylight savings time forever? Weren't farmers about one percent of the population?

The fog was burning off. She angled down the foredune crest to the jeep ruts. A pale dog joined her out of nowhere and zigzagged over the dunes with her. She never heard Maytree mention a dog. The sight of Maytree lamplit and filling the door, night over his shoulder, had taken her breath.

Dew wetted the sand and made it brown. Maytree's footprints, and now hers, broke through the brown film to the dry sand below. Dry sand in footprints looked blue. The swale drained the dunes like a vein. She stopped to drink from the almost-permanent pond. There grew archaic plants from the world's first wags: club mosses, lichens in mounds, puffballs, sea stars, and bug-eating sundews. She stepped over this saurine landscape, and over heather, and started climbing. The pale dog raced ahead and looked back over its shoulder as if chiding her for not running.

Deary must be very helpless, more desperate than he, for him to come to her, not quite crawling, but crawling must have crossed his mind. She could better imagine a cloud in pain than Deary, the sapling eternal. Can disease kill painlessly? Any hope of getting a doctor in the picture? Maytree, had he but arms and hands, would make an ideal houseguest. He would lure Pete and Marie to visit often while Maytree and Deary stayed in town till he healed or she died, whichever came last. And Pete and Marie would bring little Manny.

Did Maytree, before he fell, still climb ladders? His knees were obviously shot. There was a roof leak she wanted him to look at. She needed a new hot-water heater. Windows stuck, and their frames parted. A live-in carpenter: Here comes Santa Claus. With dying and beloved old Deary in his sack.

She was throwing a deathwatch house party. Had she ever been so astounded?

Suddenly she descended the last leg to the oak-pine woods by the road. Where was the dog? From the trees overhead she heard a red-eyed vireo's call: —Do you see it? Do you hear it? Do you believe it?

# Part Three

Lou watched Pete carry Deary into the house. Deary rolled her head over his arm and smiled loopily. —Hello, Lou. Lou saw Deary's twenty years' change. Her skin grayed, her eyelids tripled. But why would she wear a Harris tweed suit and earrings? Deary must see this incursion, Lou guessed, as a particularly tricky social call.

—I can barely move my arms and legs, she confided as Lou turned down the bed. I should have been a belly dancer! Lou privately agreed.

Pete and Sooner Roy's son had angled the big bed's sections downstairs by the French doors so Deary could watch the sea, and moving sky, or any beach walkers. When Pete carried her around the house and spread her bones on the bed, she remained exactly so till Lou raised her shoulders to put a pillow under her head and straightened her skirt.

—These things happen, Deary said.

Whatever things Deary meant, Lou thought – dying, or running off with your friend's husband – she said, They sure do. Her amusement appeared to put it to rest. —Did you bring a bathrobe?

—A freight car full.

Helping Deary into a gown, Lou saw she was mostly dead already. But a miss at that line is, for a while, as good as a mile.

Deary removed her emerald ring, then rested. She took off her other rings, rested, and her bracelets, rested, tried to unclasp her heavy necklace, and at last, wincing, her gold earrings. Lou guessed how good it would feel to throw in the towel. The gown was silk. The backs of Deary's hands were darker blue than they were a few months ago, Pete said later. Yellow bones straight as meteorites crossed pools of dark blue.

Lou gazed through the glass doors and remembered seeing Deary cut bait. Bait was horseshoe crabs from Cape Cod Bay. Deary baited her own eel traps. She was living on an alley that May. Lou came across her cleaving horseshoe crabs with an axe. Beside her, horseshoe crabs scratched in a garbage can. One such she placed on its back on a beaverboard square in the alley. Raising the axe, she split it. Then, as its halves crawled apart and away, she gathered them back as one would join the halves of an onion, gave them a half turn, and split them again. Lou remembered that the animal's four quarters also tried to crawl away. Deary threw their kicking pieces in a basin, drew out another crab by its telson (Nausets used these for awls), and lifted the axe again. Lou looked on. Deary gave her many eels for bait.

At first she talked. The third full day, rasping, Deary told both Lou and Pete about rocks. She was passing on a last-minute legacy. It took about two hours on and off, and it was this: Frames of film comprise every rock in the world. (—Have you got that?) If you slice a rock thin enough, and splice the slices serially as frames, you have a documentary film. The film displays the long history of the world from that rock's views. Together the world's rocks hold a visual record of all time. You splice the frames and store them in reels by continents and by some rough stabs at their more or less infinite subdivisions of regions and times. It all badly needed film editors.

—It's not my idea, she said. I just heard it. Lou begged her to name whatever she would like to eat or drink. She licked her lips.

—At any stage after the splicing, one need only run the films through projectors to see it, any of it, eventually all of it, the world from everywhere and all angles in all its times. At least up to a random cutoff point when someone – wild with curiosity – called a halt and began slicing again. During and after the big work, ever-new rock would record films of the ongoing life of their sites: people showing up on the planet, and moving over it.

Was she off her head? Lou let her face ask Maytree. He stood beside the bed stiff in slings. —She has always had theories. Lou was glad Deary had not worn through his chivalry. How did he stand it for twenty years? She wondered again what Deary learned in school. Oh, but – how does anyone stand anything?

—How do the cormorants stand it? Deary piped up. —Stand what? They looked. —Stand the cold water. It was that chrome winter day's last light; the smoke of sea-frost blurred the horizon. Did Deary eat? Barely; applesauce.

Pete Maytree and Charlie Bonobos widened door frames for Deary's wheelchair. In the event, Deary never left her bed. Maytree slept on the couch, and Lou moved Pete's old bed to her room.

Deary shrank, and her face thinned. There did not seem to be much to her head but lobes and draped skin, ears long and yellow, lipless mouth, and eyes emerging from ziggurat levels like their turtle Yankee's. What would she like? Pete and Marie let their Manny climb on her. She never winced. Manny at that time was fat as a Macy's float. Manny climbed the bed, and crawled knee by knee across the covers over her body. He leaned against the wall, knelt back over Deary, who fingered his calf, and descended sock by sock to the floor, whence he launched repeats. Then he tried to engage Yankee the turtle in play.

Pete's Marie demanded that they all try to make Deary drink hourly around the clock. Or at night she could suck a wet towel. Marie said her grandfather had survived lobar pneumonia in his twenties solely because his whole family heard old Dr. Gaspar shout, Your life depends on how much water you can drink!

Everyone saw Deary's eyes follow the people and dogs who used the winter beach as road. Some were friends stopping by. Everyone strained at wind. Children played on. Every few minutes a gannet fired itself aslant and raised a white foam wedge. Black ducks, buffleheads, and loons glided around the bay for their southern winter. They looked like decoys.

Lou and Maytree and Pete took turns going out. Each got out once a day. Dumping garbage was an outing; they breathed the wind. Maytree mailed bill payments; Lou drove Deary to Dr. Gaspar, Jr., who, while Deary forced their exit, was trying to get the emergency room in Hyannis to take her if she would go. Jane and Reevadare, the Roy boy, Irene Bonobos, the Kodays, Cornelius, Pete's friends, and many fishermen and painters called daily with chowders, macaroni, Skully Joes, clam pies, kale soup. Most days, one of the Macaras brought haddock or scallops straight from the water. Twice a week someone left eggs in a bowl inside the door. Jane offered to trade places with Lou for a week to relieve her. Lou declined; it would take the week to teach her when to do what and how.

Pete replaced his watches on the boat and kept ashore for the duration. He took charge of dump runs and provisions for both houses. When his friends asked how they could help, he said, Walk by our beach. He and his mother dug a deep hole in sand near the glass doors. They mixed cement in a paper paint bucket, poured it, and mounted a bird feeder Lou loaded with leftovers and lard. Pete thought a woodpecker that hammered lard would get stuck. Cornelius came in from the frozen dunes;

he stayed with Jane in town. Jane clothed Tandy to a fare-thee-well, and Cornelius walked her mitten-to-mitten back and forth in boots on the beach beyond the French doors – her first long walks. Inside, it was Lou who peeled Tandy down a few layers and sat her red-cheeked in bed by Deary. Deary's eyebrows were circumflex furrows. The mighty sight of a baby's face by a crone's lasted only a second before Tandy escaped.

Reevadare had absconded to Brewster, where she married an old Brewster man who hailed her with, Thar she blows! or Thar she breaches! – a habit that Lou found literary. It swept Reevadare off her feet. Pete had met him once and asked, You got your sou'wester for the nor'easter? Pete of course said no'theaster. Lou would not admit Reevadare as a caller until she sounded her out about Deary's perceived moral status. Maytree told Lou he knew from her green-inked letters over the years that Reevadare bore Deary no malice. —A long time ago, they said.

When Reevadare arrived in the sickroom, in sable coat and lined boots, she ordered Pete to go home, and tried to shoo Maytree and Lou: —Go take naps. Baths. A powder. Every day from Brewster Reevadare brought something needless.

One day from a chair by the bedside Lou asked Reevadare why, since she had all her horsepower, she sold her house and moved away. Deary liked to listen to talk. —Because of the garden, of course. She was heating cocoa at the basement stove. —My knees staged a strike and refused to work on the garden, even to maintain it. I hated to leave home.

—Why not just let the garden go?

Lou could not remember anything's so scandalizing Reevadare. —Oh, no! she said, You can't let a garden go! – as if Lou proposed infanticide. Now Reevadare spent her days driving Route 6 and 6A, her hat barely clearing the steering wheel.

She had expensive new teeth and looked like Burt Lancaster. People said she was so sociable she would appear for the opening of an envelope. To Provincetown's galleries Reevadare drove her rich Brewster friends. Lou heard her telling one trapped painter that intellectuals lacked common sense. She could prove it in two words – natural childbirth. Or how about open marriage?

Nights after Lou changed Deary's nightgown and turned in, she heard Cornelius and Maytree downstairs, often with Pete, drinking and telling stories at her green kitchen table late – good. She and Deary would sleep. But would Deary breathe better if they sat her up?

Propped behind the headboard, slings akimbo, Maytree lifted Deary's stuck curls. He let them slip. He blew across her scalp. Her head felt swampy. Pete had gone out and Lou was asleep. Lou never had the grip to hold a grudge. Here Maytree was at home – with Deary, Pete, and Lou. Lou and he worked the days as smoothly as fishing partners drew nets. Their old ease together calmed and slowed him. He had not noticed his speeding up. He put his wristwatch aside. He reset himself to the tides.

He stayed at his post those twenty years in Maine. Deary seemed to regard their stockpiling stuff and money as a natural part of aging. Had Deary been happy with him? She was born happy. He remembered Reevadare's leaving parties saying, I'm going on to the Whites'. The whites were her sheets. She wanted her hosts to think she was going to another party (possibly a party to which no one invited them). Now Deary was staying with the obliging Whites indefinitely. She bit at the air and lunged at it. She twisted from the oxygen mask he tried. It dried her out.

One of the last things Deary said was about the war, dancing stateside with sailors in Dixie cup hats or GIs, dancing to – what were all those numbers? (Maytree's mother's version of the war, to which she gave much war-bond money and years of volunteer work, was that grinning sailors and grinning GIs somehow defeated cartoon Hitler and cartoon Hirohito with nylon stockings, chocolate bars, Luckies, and lard.) Deary whispered a song: *Go in and out the window, Go in and out the window, Go in and out the window, As we have done before.* Lou recognized it and sang along. Once Deary tried to sing 'Happy Birthday,' always a tough one. On the sill outside Maytree saw a chickadee whose breath was condensing just beyond its beak into a white pellet. It looked like a cartoon balloon that should inscribe chickadee wit inside. One pellet vanished and another appeared, and behind that another. The chickadee was shooting a cannonade of pearls. A few days before she died, Deary whispered for the record that she had felt worse with Hong Kong flu. Maytree recalled that winter; they skipped Christmas. Now he laid sleeping Manny beside her bent arm. Both bodies perspired.

The next day she stopped using the chamber pot. Her feet and ankles bulged to the size of four-by-fours, then locust logs, then melons. Her slit attention opened seldom. In those waking moments her cross-eyed courtesy suggested to all that their small talk was boring her to death. —Head, she said once. She stopped following motion with her eyes.

Deary was charring and buckling like a leaf. Maytree watched Lou change wet cloths on Deary's forehead. No one wanted to leave the bedside where Deary slept noisily so long as they talked. She still turned from every wet fruit they thought might tempt her, and from water, ice cream, and chipped ice. He thought people died in three days without water, but no.

It took eight days for unconscious Deary to die her death. It was eight weeks since they had come. She lowered without fuss like a pilot light. A process within her, far behind her eyelids, evidently piqued her full attention. What could it be but the big blank's advance? She weighed maybe sixty-five pounds. She turned blue and rattled away. Once she spooked them by lifting an arm in the air, as long ago she had hailed seals or first sun. In her last few days, dying made her face young. Her skin smoothed on her forehead, eyes, cheeks, and the corners of her mouth, and reflected light. Pete lifted her wrist, turned it to rest on his thumb, and felt it with three fingertips. The radiator banged. *Stars sang in their sockets through the night.*

Yankee the turtle crawled out from under the couch and stretched his snake neck. He stood square as a pack mule waiting its load, like the lowest totem-pole animal resigned to shouldering all the rest, or resigned to lifting the seas that floated the lands, if this was that kind of world. He regarded dead Deary with the obsidian calm of a god.

When Deary died, Maytree got Pete to help him shave his beard off. He got Mrs. Smither to help wrap Deary's washed body in sailcloth as she used to sleep in the dunes. Then Mrs. Smither drove back to Camden. That night was dark and drizzly. Time to sneak Deary out to the Provincetown dune wilds. Maytree walked holding a burlap bag of bayside stones. Lou and Pete and Jane took turns carrying Deary like duffel. Cornelius carried Tandy, and Pete carried Manny on his shoulders. Jane made faces at Tandy. She and Marie trailed carrying spade and box. They buried Deary in a stretch of forest where dunes encroached. Despite her fixed hope to set every boat in the harbor on fire posthumously, they curled her body in the mainsail and tucked it, pastrylike, in a box, and buried the box too, piled with stones.

Mettle fatigue, Maytree called it. Lou and he slept most of a week. Maytree slept in Pete's old room, now again a spare room with its single bed. Pete was back at sea. From the area by the many-paned doors in the basement all Deary's tables and pillows and chairs were gone. With Cornelius and Jane, Maytree and Lou shifted Lou's pipe-frame bed in sections back up two stories.

Maytree's casts – most – were off. At the kitchen window he hefted mason jars – first jars empty, then full of water, then full of sand – to regain his strength. He thought rehabilitation might take a few days, as it had when he was young. He and Lou returned everything they borrowed.

The baldness of Deary's death – and where did she go? was individuation a waste? – was an insulting reminder, a blow from reason to reason. The belief that we were all pieces of a cosmic whole he found less wishful than pointless. His mother, for instance. And the frozen fishing crew they watched drown one day at Peaked Hill Bars thirty yards off the beach where the townspeople stood helpless, for instance.

When he was a boy, his mother took him along the night she went to see a fishing boat aground on Peaked Hill Bars in a storm. Frisch Fragonelle was the first to go. In the blackness Toby Maytree knew him by his narrow shape, as everyone on the beach knew every man clinging in the rigging by shape. He squinted into spray and happened to see Frisch Fragonelle let go. Seas ruptured on bars in rows behind the vessel and before it, so streaming foam silhouetted Frisch Fragonelle's drop an instant before it covered it. He fell upright and straight as a plumb bob.

—Hell, young Toby's mother said close by, the very hell. The whole frozen town on the beach groaned.

His father and the other coast guards at the Peaked Hills Bars station had already tried everything: firing the breeches buoy; launching their boat into the breakers; and even launching an old whaleboat that Captain Mayo's tractor hauled down the beach from town. At first the men hooked in cordage and spars were waving to the people on the beach, as if hallooing them in midnight high spirits, or as if pointing out their situation, or as if warming their blood by saying *até a volta, adeus,* good-bye. Seas, spray, and sleet froze on them. Toby and the others onshore waved and jumped and all useless else, as if their encouragement would lighten the men's hearts, and maybe it did.

The stranded crewmen dropped all night like acorns. More groans low under the high wind. Toby saw something like laundry roll in a breaker. The next wave presented it as Frisch Fragonelle's body. Maytree's father and another coast guard brought it in and laid it at his wife's boots without a word. Mothers were turning their children and heading back toward town.

—Do I have to go home now? Toby was eight. He hoped she would say, Yes, darn tootin' go home. You must shun the sight of the men of our own fleet, your friends' fathers, dying almost an arm's length from shore, and us helpless to save them.

His mother bent to his face and looked at him. Her face was chapped. Two wool shawls covered her head; she had wrapped her fingers in their fringes.

—No, she said. You don't have to go home. This is part of life.

Damn, he thought – not that he would watch his neighbors drown, but that it was part of life.

If Maytree's mother and that drowned crew, and Deary, were now sticks or star-gas, *cui bono*? It was all brittle. That dying was at least nothing personal had comforted Marcus Aurelius. But what could be more personal than a person?

Of course everyone had tended Deary. Was that tending love genetically or socially determined convention? The idea of love as irresistible passion died hard in Maytree long after he knew better. Was he 'in love' with Deary all those years? No, but he never dreamed of shipping his iced-over oars. What, carry off the Maine poet's fetching wife or – for that matter – their stunner of a daughter?

Still less was Lou in love with Deary. Nor was noble Pete. Then what guides will – reason? The darling of dead Greeks, that guarantor of the science he loved? Surely reason never trafficked in a man's love life. Science rinsed love's every scent from its hands. Maytree had been sensible of no particular sentiment except the natural wish to help Deary find comfort. That steady wish for her comfort on which he had acted for years and Lou and Pete had acted for eight weeks – was *love*?

Wishing and doing, within the realm of the possible, was willing; love was an act of will. Not forced obeisance, but – what? The obvious course of decency? Innate knowledge of goodness? Was it reasonable to love the good and good to love the reasonable? What a crashing bore. The painter's wife was such a peach.

At the garage he bought three new tires and rotated the old. He replaced windshield wipers in front of the gallery across from the house. Inside he washed and hung Deary's nightgowns and later rolled them and her tweed suit around her jewelry. He wrapped newspaper over the bundle, tied it with string, and set it in the trunk beside her newly anachronistic purse. How they used to search when she lost her purse.

✳ ✳ ✳

Now behind Lou's house he leaned cross-armed on a neighbor's handrail by three stairs to the beach. The reeling sea rose before a silence as if the neighbors' houses were prehistoric children asleep and drying from the primordial mudflat that formed them. Cold seemed to be chipping his ears to flakes of chert.

He missed Camden's big trees. Ahead of him in Maine was time to read and write. He would commandeer the dining room table and sideboard as study, click up a card table or two, and leave their three television sets at the curb. In his former study he would build stacks for books. Moor a Hobie cat and get a mutt and let it run. The Camden building market would pick up in May. Or he could retire. He already had much more money than he could use even if he died in a hospital. The process of retiring itself would swallow two or three years. He would have to find and train new people so his and Deary's business could thrive without them. Then he wondered: Exactly why did his business matter? It took them years and years to build it up. Why would he devote more years to keep it going – to keep his memory alive when he was dead? Like a pyramid? What nonsense. He could plain walk away. That was a revolution.

He watched a gull pace the iced-over tide line before him. Actually, he had an idea, a structure, for a long poem all these last many years. But not so much as a phrase for it.

At rare intervals he granted that he would die like everyone else, only, of course, worse. He read that four in five of us die slowly, attended by family or strangers or generic Smithereens. Waves bounded up the beach. He pinched his nose's bridge. Behind him dead grasses changed directions together like a horse's hair whirling from its loin.

Had he redeemed himself with Lou? By any chance? Just by doing the chores he caused? He would welcome her general knowledge and intelligence. She was in his view too old to live alone. Arthritis in her spine, knees, elbows. At the Bronx Zoo years ago a lion and a tiger were milk brothers. Lions and tigers hail from Africa and Asia respectively, and would fight if they met. In the zoo these two were close. Neither had ever seen himself, only the other. Each had looked at the other for as long as he could remember. So the lion thought he was a tiger, as it were, and he feared adult lions. The tiger feared adult tigers. Only in the face of the other did each find home. Maytree watched sky's turmoil and a scallop dredge heading out.

He stayed on the first of three steps to the beach. Had not Lou herself once been a peach? Monument of unaging intellect and all that? He and Lou used to have a way about them he recalled vividly. *One man loved the pilgrim soul in you.* Would she be thinking such a thing? Anyway, how ever could he start when now was far too soon, and later was impossible? A movie, a chocolate soda, and two straws if they could stay awake? On the other hand, nothing was more common than courting your wife. How meek you had to be varied with the depth of the particular creek you were up. He and Lou knew the same past. Their fourteen years' marriage vastly outweighed their twenty years apart. Of course she might disagree. It never struck him that she had anything to do. What did she ever do?

This was how Lou found him at the neighbors' beach rail, pants over potbelly. He was rotating one wool ankle after the other in a circle whose hub was his heel. She recognized that gesture. She had forgotten it. She smiled and pulled in her jacket. Would he stay in Maine or – save the sailors! – ask to move back?

She stilled there by the back door so he would not hear her. Sky ran its candid lengths round the hoop of horizon. Weak swells spent themselves in muddy sea ice. A tide line of frozen froth like lees stranded in dead rye.

This winter before Maytree came with Deary, Lou had been orbiting one galaxy of ideas as close as she dared. Could a person hold all people past and present in awareness? She further wondered if doing so was, by some errant chance, the point – toward what end she had no clue. Not that life required a point. But she found herself starting to sway toward eventually considering that there might be one. A point. Any point.

Books must know something. She dug from every direction. The bravest foray would be to try it, to hold all human consciousnesses, past or present, etc., in awareness…. Or just stay aware that… or just stay aware. She was wary. Conceding that there could be a point – merely granting it as a long shot – might lead to a mess. Both time's back wall and front wall fell open. As a mire in which to wallow, it had housework beat all hollow.

She kept her eye on Maytree by the beach. His ears looked cold. She felt she had gained, oh, half a millimeter on these questions over her lifetime. That is, her sense of the vastness of each aspect multiplied, and the more it expanded, the denser with questions it grew.

The draining tide was leaving a ring of debris. Terns made hullabaloo over a crinkled patch of sea – must be a herring ball. Had she by hap made of her solitude a moral stance? Talking lately on and off, she and Maytree touched on their recent lives, mostly his. Was there any poet left in him? She did not say how she liked the recklessness of her own venture into simplicity. How many decades had she spent listing, like Diogenes, all she did not need? Her thoughts' motion accelerated in giant paces down the steep unending dune that revealed more dunes, each comprising all time and every place – a real rabbit hole. Taking those flying steps and not crashing! It reminded her of an old parody of Ripley's Believe It or Not: *DUCKS CANNOT FLY! They are merely GREAT LEAPERS!*

Maytree would resume his life in Maine, and she could pick up her subjects' edges anywhere – in other cultures, in any mind's track, in paleontology, old peckings and runes on stones, in Asian philosophy – … and poke up at the bottom of things with a stick, or however she used to work. She kept an eye on the rifling, fletching, skeg, or keel that trued her aim. What was it, that hum? Did generations make it or hear it? She forgot herself like a cloud. This was the out-of-earshot life she cobbled from her freedom. Maytree fit in like a couple of aircraft carriers.

The sea's line was sharp. Beyond Maytree's form, waves were crashing in spaced convulsions – a big storm out at sea, and the clouds blowing two or three ways. What was in her awareness after Maytree brought Deary? Why, nothing; she was busy. When she bumped into something that needed to be done, she did it. Then she wet a cloth and went to Deary.

What in her bare awareness might Maytree expand? And his car, and Deary's car and their boat. Their business and tax records. And the new stuff he mentioned – stereos and speakers, tape player, radio, televisions, 35mm film camera, VCR, skis. Let alone the old things, the tools, notebooks, and lordy the books! Anyone rich could move to Provincetown and buy a big house. She needed him and his junk like a hole in the head – except for the shack. He would take back his shack and fix it up. That she loved him and his depth had nothing practical to do with anything.

He still stood tall on the beach rotating his ankles. Maybe it helped ease arthritis as well as yearning. Wind covered her approaching him from behind. He was leaning on the two-by-four as if he needed it. What kept Maytree far from her these twenty years? She doubted it was Deary, who trilled over bumps as they came. She hoped it was not shame. On the other hand, she knew it was shame.

She crept up and put her arms around his waist from behind. Instantly, one of his hands – the one with the good thumb – covered hers. How did he do that? His touch was light. He was exactly with her but not holding, not pressing. Neither he nor she crossed the line beyond fond.

How she had enjoyed having him around, his easy compe-tence and camaraderie. How grand of him to help her take care of Deary! (Oh, they don't make them like that anymore; it's just as well.)

The creases behind his neck made him look like the survivor of several beheadings. She knew that any note at all, of even so much as inquiry, was up to her. Her inquiry was: What did she hope?

A few days now before he returned to Maine, he crossed the dunes with Lou to check the shack. For twenty years he had sacrificed his shack as well as everything else. Where a footpath forked, Lou made straight for the ocean to swim. It amazed him, that the custom of some people here was to swim the ocean – the Labrador Current! – every summer day through October or until they dropped dead. They seemed never to drop dead. Jellyfish stung them, and Portuguese men-o'-war. They saw sharks. He remembered young Lou in a red suit waving at him from far out in the ocean at a spring ebb. Half her torso was out of water; she was standing on a bar as a stunt. When she came in, he asked, How is the water? Still in her twenties, she spoke three languages and held her tongue in all of them. Now up the shack steps. Through his socks he felt two of four planks dip. He was carrying Pete's Manny.

Storm sands had blasted shutters silver. An hour later between mattress and wall Lou found a shed snakeskin. She held the translucent husk by Maytree's crown; the tail skin trailed on the floor. They found mouse poops like jimmies and nests of shredded newspaper. (Why had she left pillows and paper out? Was she losing her wits?) They found a crack in the floor between planks.

You could leave the woman, but not, it turned out, the shack. He seemed to have toiled on it all his life. When he was a boy his father, whacking it up, used him as clamp. Now he walked outside and under the shack to study the floor timbers' crack. His father had buried chainsawed driftwood logs – trunk bottoms – to prop the floor. The heavy crawl of the dune pushed these logs half over. For fourteen years Maytree had buttressed and shimmed them. Now he found the cornerposts askew and deeper in the same crisis. On the floor timbers he saw his old flat-pencil marks.

—Who did this work? he yelled pleasantly up at Lou, like a new dentist. —A mess under here! You should sue! She was up there feeding Manny. Easy as it was to make Lou laugh, he never wearied of it.

He reckoned he had not seen the shack in twenty-one years. No, by crikey, no – only six months ago he slept on this very shack's floor. Six months ago. He had not noticed the propane tank and hose. He had not noticed much that night. He remembered himself bone-cold and old and furious with pain laid out on the floor as if gut-shot.

When Lou opened the shack door that night he almost fell forward through the frame on his broken arms. Heat and light seemed to blast him up. Behind her head in the doorway yellow light shone and wreathed her hair. He saw the dark red-bowled lamp smoking on its wall shelf behind her head. She was using cheap kerosene. He felt his blood pulse in his eyeballs. And that night she had said, Sure, of course she would house and help Deary and him, in town for the winter and for the duration. She wore a red shirt open at the neck. Familiar she was, and unsurprised.

Exactly what might surprise the old witch? Come in, his ex-own Lou said, and he saw her oval face and her wide eyes still affectionate, or affectionate again, or affectionate by habit. Or she didn't recognize him.

As soon as he saw her easy-eyed look that night he started falling asleep. Yet he had to crank himself up and speak more carefully than ever. Then he would drink water and cross the dunes to the motel. She had unbuttoned his jacket for him. He drank from a hot and too-heavy cup. That night, he thought now, they would have sat at this table. His feet's thawing under the table had turned out to be his chief woe. That and deciding if he was crazy or she was.

Now kerosene lamps made the room hot. She said, Certainly, of course, as if they two had already hashed this out for months on end, Deary's dying and his broken bones – and she had already told him yes long ago. Or as if, after his bad fall on Dr. Cobo's steps, she had naturally bade him and Deary to come live with her in Provincetown so she could tend Deary, and he had agreed, and it had all slipped his mind. So he had crawled the wild dunes in the dark and stood late in her doorway half-dead just to secure what they already decided? It gave him the royal creeps. He broke his bones the very day before Mrs. Smither drove them to the Cape. Was Lou expecting him in the doorway any minute? After breaking his bones he had no intention of bothering her, not for hours.

Oh, yes, his knees and thighs had unstrung that recent sneaky day when Lou wrapped her arms about him from behind. He could only barely remember why he had dreaded seeking refuge for Deary with Lou. Of course she was too wise to blame them for long. That cold night in this shack she was matter-of-fact and he was drained. Keeping this ever-lasting smash of a shack upright and dry might again, if he failed to watch his step, become his job. Maybe she foresaw that.

Later Manny fell asleep on the four-plank deck against a knap-sack. Dozens of mosquitoes were feeding through his skin when Lou fetched him in. When he woke, Maytree picked him up and thumped him like a cask. —He couldn't be hungry again, Lou told Maytree. He just ate!

# Epilogue

*Nothing restores the sense of being alive less
ambiguously than the birth of the unexpected,
the finding of a person who one did not know one
loved so much.*

– Ralph Harper, On Presence

Sometimes in the middle of their sleep, in the black of the night
with the metal wind and stars forcing the room through the
window, they woke together as if at a quake. If passion
returned they burst out laughing.

Sometimes by day or night he heard them breathe old as
oceans – experienced. They enfolded each other and looked
over each other's shoulders at the world's wreck where all shattered, at bareness they held at bay. Or they cradled the world
between them like a mortally sick child, loving it and not telling
it all they knew.

Now in compassion they bore, between them, their solitudes
each the size of the raveled globe. Everything looked better since
they were old.

By day a smell of her lingered in sweet sheets. Intimacy
with Lou had no bounds. Half his life he had sounded her
and never struck bottom. Perimeters edged Deary, and the girls
of his youth, and for that matter himself and everyone he

knew. Lou held nothing back, but he knew he never reached it all.

—Let's pretend we're old, Lou remembered saying back when they were young. They had been watching hurricane waves rip the outer beach. To walk back they aligned adjacent legs like a pair in a three-legged race.

—Those days will come soon enough, Maytree said. His gravity had startled her. Now those days were here. Lou remembered when his forehead's skin stuck tight as an apple's. She pressed a finger to her own forehead and drew a circle. She was loose in her skin as a rabbit. She felt French knots on her shins. Now she wanted a book not to knock her out but only to move her. And when will the days of wisdom come?

The first week after he showed up again, he built bookshelves. He asked, Should I grow back a beard? She liked his beard, but gave no answer. The last opinion she voiced had concerned Deary's cherry furniture. —Why not sell it or give it away? She was sorry she had spoken. Afterward, she accorded his Maine life with Deary a sanctity never to broach.

Tonight Maytree wanted to help her chop one onion. Now after supper he planned to walk the beach with her in moonlight. A fine activity, but she wanted to draw inside with vine charcoal. He seemed to like her within earshot. She guessed she saw for the very first time his lifelong exposure to enemy fire, probably because he had watched Deary die. For her the shelling never ceased, and beauty ditto – nothing hostile, nothing won. He possibly needed her as bulwark, foxhole, at best a trenchmate who could cook. Maybe a big dog would suit him, a very big dog.

From the green kitchen table she could see him moving up the beach, head bobbing like a marionette's. She was getting charcoal on her shirt. She had once tinted or dyed her one life the hue of his, this one man's out of billions mostly unknown. She no longer leaned her life on anyone.

Well, one time she fell in love; the next minute – in an apparently unrelated event – an unprecedented short person played with a roller skate on the floor. Without this new one (and presumably his ilk) she had absurdly considered her life full. When Petie was young, she assumed Petie would make his life around her – were they not miraculously, deliriously as one? Then the next minute this same one propped his own boggling-new, hitherto-nowhere child in his arms to display to her as if she had never seen such a thing. Who had? It was as if the tide came in under the door.

In her last years Lou puzzled over beauty, over the tide slacked holding its breath at the flood. She never knew what to make of it. Certainly nothing in Darwin, in chemical evolution, in optics or psychology or even cognitive anthropology gave it a shot. Having limited philosophy's objects to certainties, Wittgenstein later realized he broke, in however true a cause, his favorite toy, metaphysics, by forbidding it to enter anywhere interesting. For the balance of Wittgenstein's life he studied, of all things, religions. Philosophy, Lou thought and so did Cornelius, had trivialized itself right out of the ballpark. Nothing rose to plug the gap, to address what some called 'ultimate concerns,' unless you count the arts, the arts that lacked both epistemological methods and accountability, and that drew nutty people, or drove them nuts.

June 24 was the first – and as it turned out, the last – warm day in June. They cut each other's hair on the front steps. She asked him to cut for her short bangs. Her braid was so thick it popped hairpins, as if surprised.

In early July before they moved to the shack they drove out to what they called the New Beach. Others called it Herring

Cove. They brought their respective books. Lou ran into the waves. Maytree took a walk. There was a lot to see. Locals had divided the beach informally. Half a mile left of the parking lot, that is, counterclockwise, he saw many talking women on towels. These women, as he had heard, wore nothing anywhere except bright plastic eye shields. Most were over forty, some probably in their seventies. 'God and the neighbors,' his mother used to call that *plein air* jury that, so long as you were outside, was everywhere in session. He had never seen so many naked women, let alone naked women who could not see him. God and the neighbors had seen a lot worse – given earth's thirty million years of hominid behavior – but not much weirder. The close-set eye shields – two hollowed ovals a nosepiece joined, like glasses – made all the women look cross-eyed.

Beyond the women was a stretch of naked men sunbathing their every detail. What the Sam Hill? He hurried scandalized back to Lou, to their folding chairs and their two books.

Lou asked him, Didn't he remember Ross and Milo? Of course Maytree knew their parents' openhanded friends, who had nothing to do with the situation at hand. These people on the beach ignored God and the neighbors, even little children! Ross Wye and Milo Matheson lived together on Pearl Street almost fifty years. Ross was an educated impressionist painter. Milo bred dachsunds.

—At least they kept quiet about it.

That night Lou dragged him to a drag show. Afterward, they walked home upstream in the crowd.

—What are we supposed to think?

—That it's all a big joke, all pretence, and certainly 'what people think,' and you can drop dead laughing. You're going to drop dead anyway. He thought, She talks more in her old age. He thought, You wouldn't catch any man in Camden going around as Carol Channing! He almost said it. He stopped himself just in time.

Maytree would write one last book-length poem: *There Will Be a Sea Battle Tomorrow*, Aristotle's conundrum. Can we establish the statement's truth or falsehood? He had by no means finished with the sea, embattled or bare. Truth and falsehood were a barrel of laughs. He would for starters read Willard Quine, and *The Odyssey* again, and Aristotle and the history of the 1812 blockade. Why the 1812 blockade? Readers would see.

\* \* \*

They stayed in the dunes till mid-October that first of many new years. Cranberries came on. Dune people met at cranberry patches. Among them were the Maytrees' favorite young friends, smart and funny, whose work over years had convinced the National Seashore not to demolish the shacks. One night an early frost capped ice on the pump jug. Clouds began to withdraw to their winter heights and thinned.

They boarded up the shack. This fall as every fall, they guyed the outhouse ever more strongly against storm winds. Maybe this winter the outhouse would stay upright. They knew it would not.

When they returned to their equally windy house by the bay, leaves had gone. In the neighbors' wisteria they saw a nest. Maytree extricated it and showed Lou. Flown birds had lined it with her blond-white hair in threads and his red-and-white hair in threads. Their hair made a smooth cup inside twigs. Perfecting the circle, he knew, were the nestlings' wars. Ants ate the ones that got pushed out.

As they aged they grew more avid of beauty, the royal sea in their eyes in town, the dunes' scimitar shadows, the ever-perishing skies. The two were storing all this – for what? Blind death's long years. Bay tides amazed them again. Bay tides re-created the world, stink and all. Twice a month spring tides multiplied seas without diminishing sky. For three nights and days after full and new moons, the bay drowned the beach and climbed steps. It bore flat clouds upon it. From her kitchen window Lou looked down to the beach and saw clouds. People vanished. The sea swelled over ground without a sound and invisibly, as stars cross sky. Lou felt her eyes brimming with tears, but it was illusion. Dying fish stranded, as did party balloons that strangled sea turtles who mistook them for their chief food, jellyfish.

Six hours later the same seas had withdrawn to Europe. Acres and acres of mud showed brown. People walked this absorbent surface, or sucking muck, cooling their eyes. They strayed among listing boats tied to dry moorings. Beyond, and back of beyond, Lou saw human forms wavering in distance wandering stretches at whim. Out there on the mudflats Lou wanted to wave her arms exhilarated, as did many dizzy children, children she had never seen. There were no paths or bounds, only the planet's bare skin. Children could run anywhere and did. Only adults got stuck.

Lou memorized the faces of her friends, of children, Maytree's face and knees, clouds, the paintings she loved. She played Pete Fountain. They drove hours to see fireworks. She asked Maytree, Are these new people afraid of the dark? Why light everything? (Etc.) And, Would they look up more often if they had to pay?

He once hoped to acquire what Pico della Mirandola had: Keats called it 'knowledge enormous.' Maytree had settled for knowledge slim. Manny was pretending to be a truck. What was it, exactly – or even roughly – that we people are meant to do here? Or, how best use one's short time? For a decade or so in Maine he read ethnographies and prehistory to ask people of every culture past and present, How did you divide your time? The Toltecs, Olmecs, et al. usually gave him the willies, till he read an old Mayan book, the book of the dawn of life:

*The first beings gave thanks to the gods:*
*– Truly now, double thanks, triple thanks*
*that we've been formed. We've been given*
*our mouths, our faces.*
*We speak, we listen, we wonder,*
*we move… under the sky.*

Thanks a million? They sounded like good sports. Plus the Mayans saw in the Pleiades four hundred boys. Could skies ever have been so clear? For the Greeks, counting seven sisters was ordinary, and counting nine was perfect. Maybe Mediterranean mists dispersed another 391 sisters or boys? On a good north-wester now he saw five or six Pleiades, not even the seven of his youth.

All these peoples voted on what we are supposed to do here by portioning their time. Our forebears' chief acts were raising children and gambling. Not even getting food. Getting food never took long before storing grain showed up. The few people tended to starve instead. Also popular: getting high, eating the salty, oily, and sweet, whittling, weaving, invading, and placating gods. Were people missing something? If we are missing something, why the big secret?

Soon, but not soon enough, a Modern Library anthology of modern American poetry would appear containing slivers – as he poked a few pine needles between pages – from two of his book-length poems, likely alongside Aiken's 'Morning Song of Senlin.' With the book-length poem, the long-range cannon full-bore, Maytree had had a blast. Whether his work lasted was less crucial now than whether Manny would straddle his shins a little while longer.

Tomorrow is another day only up to a point. One summer five years later Maytree began to die all over the place. Pete used to tease him about reading as if there were no tomorrow. There never were a hell of a lot of tomorrows, as Pete would see. Why should he live upstairs, he asked Lou, or even inside? The terms of the peace he had forged in these past five years with social convention had made convention surrender its tangle of keys. Lou reminded son Pete that Maytree always liked a change of scene. Those two broke down the ironstone bed once more and tilted its mattress and frame down one flight of stairs to the kitchen, then down another flight to the basement floor by the doors to their yard's strand of cordgrass and sand and sea. On fair nights, they carried Maytree himself, long and light, through the doors and spread him in bed open-eyed.

They were Arabic: Enif, Markab, Achernar, Hamal, Alfirk, Scheat, Rasalhague. They moved evenly over the black desert. They spread and kept their places as searchers sweep a field. Algenib and Denebola had gone before. Fomalhaut kept alone. Alpheratz and Saiph trailed out of sight.

Long-necked Cygnus from afar pointed to the water like a spear and spent all night falling southwest unflinching. The breast of Cygnus was Sadir. Deneb, Altair, and Vega cornered a triangle overhead. The Milky Way smeared through it. The galaxy shed lights from far shores. It seemed to split in two streams that plied side by side over the top, north to south. Meteorites fell, six an ordinary hour. Ursa Major swung on its mooring as if tide loosed it. 'But my eighties are passionate,' someone said in a book.

Pete strung a tarp like a Baker tent to catch dew without closing sky. Lou slept like a mummy outside at the edge of their mattress. All Maytree's adult visitors read to him in the dew. He wanted the stories of his childhood, 'The Apple Tree, the Singing, and the Gold,' and 'The Country of the Blind.' He wanted the lasting feelings only books could provide. If anyone asked, he would probably admit that he was unlikely to be up and around, really, again.

Nights he rose to take companionable leaks with Jupiter. Comically, when he took his last outdoor shower a week ago, he did not know it would be his last. Nothing marked or would mark his last piece of pie, swim, tune – as presently he would see his last everything, kid, dawn, spoon, and familiar face – if he had not already. When he knew he would die, he found it first impossible, then sad, to near the falls' lip, to yield to the ripping loss of the colored world and himself in it. Where would – say – literature be, if everyone mattered less than a speck? In all his work he avoided sentimental topics, say love and grief. But they came along, didn't they.

One morning Lou told him that their sleeping outdoors on fair nights was scandalizing neighbors – always invigorating. Sunny days she shielded him with a Red Sox cap – not that such shielded the Red Sox. She had a book of Trask Provençal lyrical poems and an anthology of old lyrical poems from East and West. She read to him in a murmur. Everything amazed these ancient poets as if they had just awakened to a world already moving and full of astounding stuff like hills, or a round of white cheese. Tandy often sat by the bed listening and gnawing her knees. Maytree refused the tapioca she kept sticking at him.

When Lou woke beside him one rainy morning on their bed moved inside the doors, she watched his blue hand feel for a nautical chart. His hands' backs looked glued over with blueberry skins. That his face was gray as a kneaded eraser she ignored. Now a month had passed since he could hold a book, a week since he asked her to read. After he took to bed he hoped, he told her, to learn more constellations. Cartoons of suns that look adjacent only from here, Lou thought, attracted her too. But learning why, now? Would he dead reckon among stars? And now learning a nautical chart? Lou watched his hand find it curled on the floor. He tried to fold it into submission. How little time – less than the *verblasteder* turtle's. Today he would surely not try to memorize what muck anchors brought up whence. She creased the blue chart to display local waters north to Stellwagen Bank. For the next few days when he was alert she gave his hand the chart, right side up. His thumb pressed it to his fingers and he lapsed away. Any section she gave him was fine.

Here came sneaking the tide. Its raised rims caught starlight that streaked along the beach like lighted eels. The son picked up a fish rack spangled in blood and threw it on the mudflats, where its stink would meld in the brine they rarely noticed but loved. Then the son sprawled on sand by the old ones and looked up. He and his mother watched the night with Maytree while they could.

*I scarcely knew how pleasantly the moments were falling, until now, when looking them over through the telescope of years.* Last month he had read this to the woman from a book. He interrupted her reading. Had his moments fallen pleasantly? As a boy he sold cod cheeks door-to-door from pails.

*Diomede exulans exulans,* the wandering albatross. He heard girls laughing down the beach. Orange and black specks rose from distant bonfires. Breeze lifted a blanket corner. The woman rose and tucked something over his feet. Which feet – he had seen and forgot – were turning black. The sea's curve neared. The lighthouse turned; everything extended. His arms cooled. His eyes roved. Carina, the keel. Overhead Hercules ran like a turpentined horse. Cepheus, that crazy little house.

\* \* \*

*Your face I keep inside my soul,... the days of September rising in my dreams... , whatever theme I touch, whatever thought I utter.* These Cavafy lines recurred as he went in and out of sleep on the beach. Maytree's adoring grandmother, always good in a crisis, showed up fitfully to encourage him. A radio said, Here's the pitch! Mornings a bird repeated, *You hit me and I'll tell Mom! You hit me and I'll tell Mom!* He realized he had been hearing this bird's whine all his life, and it would be his death song.

He knew a crew had buried his grandfather at sea. The men sewed shut the canvas they shrouded him in. The mate used a leather palm to ram a curved sewing needle again and again through all the layers of canvas on either side of the corpse's nostrils, and, in the middle, through the nostrils' gristle.

By day, dimming people circled. Cornelius brought Tandy. One day he faced Maytree. Wide whiskers wagging, Cornelius began,

—Doc says, You have three minutes to live.

—Anything you can do for me, doc?

—Well, I could boil you an egg.

When he woke at night, he saw Altair in Aquila, Corona Borealis, and the wild swan sluicing down the Milky Way. The Little Dipper looked like a shopping cart. They should rename it.

Lou lay beside him, silent as bandages, her immense solitude so gloriously – he might say, for who will fault a dying man's diction? – broached. *I wither slowly in thine arms, here at the quiet limit of the world.* She got up to stretch in her long dress, and his body drooped to the low and midgey spot she left warm. What was he trying to remember? Was Alterf 'the glance?' He thought he witnessed, and was now witnessing, the cutting edge of things. Had he helped cut? *I scarcely knew how pleasantly the moments were falling.* He had enjoyed what Brits call good innings. He had seen downy feathers on eggs. He saw auroras from the dunes. Once he saw a fireball.

Now the rising sea drowned the flats with no struggle. The heavens slid down. Was dragging the bed outside Lou's idea? He would trail off into skies like a cloud or sonic boom. *Addio terra, addio cielo.* Maybe like Lou he was more ironist than he knew. Around him her body, sawgrass, trash, seas, and skies altered, reeled, and gave way to dark. The gods in the night jumbled with beasts there, and moved through tools, thrones, machines. Their legs tangled in one another's chariots. Their wings disrupted lovers. Horns' tips ran through eyes. A mess up there.

Only now did he reckon beauty itself was the great thing. As a deathbed revelation this required – like most, he suspected – more thought.

Lou changed their sheets without getting him up, as she did in the rest home. Shifting him, she guessed he weighed about what his skeleton and teeth did. His rib cage through his shirt reminded her of a newsreel of the Hindenburg. Two days later he rarely opened his eyes. Still they moved him in and out; now he was out. Even in fog he wanted the bed on the beach. A gliding gull dropped its head, swiveled its neck, and peered under its tail to keep him in sight like a car crash.

Frowning, he looked as if he were trying to scry the back of his skull like a cave wall. She and Pete hated to interrupt, to chivvy him forth and try to make him drink. He was tied up elsewhere. He was lowering away. Davits started to swing.

Lou wondered where his information would go when he died. Would filaments of learning plant patterns on earth? Would his brain train the sinking plankton to know their way around the seafloor from here to Stellwagen Bank? Her brain would deliquesce too, and with it all she had learned topside. Which was not much, she considered, nor anywhere near worked out. Bacteria would unhook her painstakingly linked neurons and fling them over their shoulders and carry them home to chew up for their horrific babies.

She watched a wave strand a white skate inverted. It scraped back and forth in the waves for an hour, openmouthed.

Clams squirted in the bucket by the door. Pete dug them at low tide. Now the ocean ponderously tilted in its basin to flood North America a grain at a time. She and Pete sat by the bed where Maytree had lain indoors and unconscious, or bored stiff, for two days. He neither ate, drank, eliminated, opened his eyes, or turned. She watched his clavicle. A piece of brilliance found his face through the French doors; it wrapped his features in shape-shifting trapezoids as clouds passed. The room and all its glass faced south. Yankee the box turtle stretched like a blindworm to warm its neck.

She told Pete that Maytree would live till the next ebb. — Since when are you superstitious? Pete said. The clams had soaked his blue jersey. It's even odds. She did not answer.

Maytree made a fist. The woman wore a long red shift. She stroked him – Algreba, the brow. The little she retained; all she had yet to think through in her time left. Replaceable gulls. For all she knew she had seen the same gulls over and over.

She lifted thin slips of his hair between spread fingers and let them slide. He used to fall asleep when she cut his hair. She dripped water between his lips from a clean cloth's corner. With her finger, she painted his mouth in bacon grease.

Would he remember, at least at first, to watch for its own blue seas' palming the earth?

# CONTENTS

# INTRODUCTION

In the strange days towards the end of 2001, I was in Thailand preparing to go location-scouting for a film I'd co-written and was intending to direct, based on a novel by Eric Ambler. I'd brought with me Ian McEwan's novel *Atonement*: I always look forward to his books, and this longish novel, I thought, might be the ideal distraction from the gathering conviction that a piece like Ambler's *The Night-Comers*—which deals with the quiet, deadly power struggle in Indonesia between moderate and fundamentalist Moslems—would, in the current climate, never even reach the starting gate. So, sitting by the hotel pool, far from the prewar English country landscapes so vividly evoked in the novel, I felt myself sinking into the world of Briony Tallis, so entranced that I could scarcely bring myself to move when the fierce sun shifted and fell across my feet or shoulders.

By the time I came back to England, I was convinced that, complex and interiorized as it was, the novel could still be the basis of a powerful film. I contacted my agent, who told me that several writers were already interested in the project and that Ian, who had retained a position as Executive Producer, had reserved the right to interview, vet, or otherwise audition the candidates. A dinner was arranged with Richard Eyre, an old friend and colleague of both Ian and myself; Robert Fox, the producer; and Ian. I gave a somewhat halting (and, in retrospect, totally inaccurate) account of the approach I was thinking of adopting and, in due course, to my great excitement, was offered the job.

Over the next couple of years, I produced three or four drafts, each of which was analysed and dissected in meetings at Richard's house, before being discussed in considerable detail with Ian. In the version that emerged, the story was framed by the return of Briony Tallis, celebrating her seventy-seventh birthday, to the country hotel into which her childhood home had been converted; the voice of the old writer, whose actions one blazing summer's day in 1935 had profoundly affected, not to say blighted, her own life and the lives of those most precious to her, was heard from time to time, reflecting on the implications of this or that event, while she herself was glimpsed occasionally like a ghost from the future; and the second and third sections of the novel (the flight to Dunkirk and Briony's wartime service in St. Thomas's Hospital), which happen more or less simultaneously in time, were rearranged and interwoven. The intention was always to remain as faithful to the spirit of the novel as possible—I'm always baffled by the widespread notion that when a high price has been paid for a much-loved play or novel, the first thing to do is to set about it with a hacksaw—and to translate it into a calm and measured overview of a series of irredeemable catastrophes, somewhat in the manner of Harold Pinter's spare and heart breaking account of L. P. Hartley's *The Go-Between*.

Time drifted on, and a familiar anguish began to make itself felt: the fear that for one or another unfathomable reason, the film might in the end not be made. A pretty expensive art film about a writer and her very particular sufferings and temptations might well seem a hard sell, and eventually Richard Eyre moved away in the direction of a sure thing: his exquisitely acted and entertainingly malevolent version of *Notes on a Scandal*. It seemed to me as if a whale I'd been riding for a number of years was about to disappear into the deep: and then I was called into the Working Title offices to meet Joe Wright.

Joe wasted no time in uttering one of those formulae that strike dread into a screenwriter's heart (others might include, "This is a really good first draft" or "Who exactly are we supposed to be rooting for?"). He said: "I'd like to start from scratch." Furthermore, he meant it. But the good news was he knew what he wanted: to bring the screenplay back even closer to the form of the novel, and he had good, specific ideas of how this might be done. For him the first move was to kick away the crutches: the explanatory voice-overs, the framing device, the linearity of narrative. This would mean that the story would have to be told primarily in images and that the actors' thoughts would have to be readable on their faces rather than audible on the sound track; and that, echoing the bold strategy of the book, we would be dealing in big, self-contained chunks of narrative, where the focus would shift unapologetically from one character to another.

This had one major unforeseen advantage: the twenty-minute gap between seeing Briony at thirteen and Briony at eighteen made it far easier to think of casting two separate actors, an idea that had not really occurred to us before, when our structure had appeared to insist on a teenage actor capable of aging up and down. The reclaiming of the first half of the story, so that it could be seen through the eyes of a genuine child, made an immeasurable difference to the understanding of Briony's crime, if that is what it is. And the holding in reserve of old Briony, who now appears only in a relatively brief epilogue, means that the viewer of the film, no longer alerted by premonitory hints, can suffer the same dislocating shocks at the end as the reader of the novel.

The entire process was long and arduous: a couple more full drafts, followed by constant revision of one section or another, until finally, at the end of 2005, Joe and I went to spend two weeks on a property not far from Florence, belonging to Susa Gelpke, an extremely sympathetic and hospitable friend of Joe's, out of which came a final draft which proved to me the truth of something I had often heard asserted: nothing can be more time-consuming or effortful than the work required to make a piece of writing seem simple, lucid, and effortless.

A word, finally, about the passage we always referred to as "the Dunkirk section." Formally troublesome in itself, it was also the most serious victim of the budget restrictions that had, quite sensibly, been applied to this adventurous project. There were to be no columns of refugees strafed by German Stukas, no Panzers rolling northwards, no carpet-bombing of the retreating armies. Instead, illustrating another old adage about the creativity unleashed by imposed limits, there would be three soldiers tramping north through a phantasmagorical landscape of literal death and dreams and memories of many other kinds of death. The teeming chaos of Dunkirk had to be portrayed in a kind of composite scene, brilliantly organized by Joe into a single, spectacularly executed Steadicam shot. Not exactly a case of less meaning more, although it meant that the thousand extras were required only for one day, it gave a genuine sense of sweep and size and a true feeling of the sorrow and pity of war. Here and elsewhere I can say, almost as an objective bystander, though with great pleasure and pride, that the film found its own compelling way of conveying the novel's particularly eloquent balance of the epic and the intimate.

A word about the text itself: what you have in your hands is a transcription, made after the event, of the finished film. The dozens of scenes that fell by the wayside like exhausted soldiers on their way to Dunkirk had their place in the overall scheme of things, but to include any or all of them might seem like a criticism of the completed object: the film *Atonement*, of which this is the written record.

—Christopher Hampton
December 2007

# ATONEMENT

Screenplay by
Christopher Hampton

Based on the novel by
Ian McEwan

CREDIT SEQUENCE

The SOUND of a typewriter, irregularly struck, now fluent, now creating an urgent rhythm that forms the percussive element of the opening score.

A doll's house, in the form of the Tallis house, an enormous Victorian Gothic pile. The CAMERA moves from room to room, from the nursery and spare bedrooms on the second floor, to the main bedrooms on the first floor, where puppet versions of mother, daughter, son and baby sister are neatly ordered, to the ground floor with its library, drawing room, dining room and kitchen. Finally the CAMERA moves to the hall through which a young gardener puppet wheels a wheelbarrow.

The CAMERA PULLS BACK through a downstairs window to reveal the whole impressive facade.

A CAPTION: **ENGLAND, 1935**


INT. BRIONY'S BEDROOM. TALLIS HOUSE. DAY.

The doll's house is kept in BRIONY's bedroom. At 13, she's the youngest of the family, an intense-looking child with a wilful temperament. Her room is meticulously tidy, with model animals arranged with military precision, all facing in the same direction, two by two, as if queuing for the Ark.

BRIONY is typing out a version of her just-completed first play, a battered copy of the Oxford English Dictionary open on the desk. As the CAMERA arrives at her manuscript, she is typing, with a confident flourish, the words THE END. Having done this, she leans forward to pull the page from the typewriter and add it to a small pile (the play is no more than 8 pages) of manuscript, the cover page of which reads THE TRIALS OF ARABELLA by Briony Tallis. It's still early in the morning, but the beads of sweat BRIONY brushes from her forehead tell us that the day is already exceptionally hot.


INT. LANDING, STAIRCASE AND HALLWAY. DAY.

Holding her manuscript, BRIONY hurries along the landing, past a door opening on to a spare bedroom. Inside, a HOUSEMAID is singing as she makes up twin beds. BRIONY descends the servants' staircase, which leads to a black-and-white tiled hallway. She doesn't even glance into the library, a vast, gloomy room glimpsed through its open door, but turns to move towards the back of the house.

INT. KITCHEN. DAY

BRIONY glances into the empty dining room and passes through the scullery into the huge old kitchen, where GRACE TURNER, the housekeeper, sits at one end of the kitchen table polishing the silver, while BETTY, the cook, is supervising two or three KITCHEN-MAIDS, who are peeling mounds of potatoes, scouring oven-trays, etc.

>                    BRIONY
>          I've finished my play!

>                    GRACE
>          Well done, dear.

>                    BRIONY
>          Have you seen Mummy?

>                    GRACE
>          I expect she'll be in the drawing
>          room.

>                    BETTY
>          I hope you're not going to be getting
>          under our feet today, Miss Briony,
>          we've got a dinner for ten to prepare.

BRIONY's already on her way out of the room, not listening.


INT. HALLWAY. DAY.
BRIONY hurries back down the hall, reaches the drawing room door and is about to enter when she sees ROBBIE TURNER, an impressive-looking young man of 24 in working clothes, outside an open door leading to the formal gardens. He's putting on a pair of muddy gardening boots.

>                    ROBBIE
>          Hello pal. I hear you're putting on a
>          play.

>                    BRIONY
>          Who told you?

>                    ROBBIE
>          Jungle drums.

>                    BRIONY
>          Will you come and see it?

>                    ROBBIE
>          I'm not sure that would be quite...

He breaks off, quickly finds another tack and stands.

> ROBBIE
> Why don't you let me read it? You used
> to make me beautiful bound copies of
> all your stories.

> BRIONY
> I still want you to come.

> ROBBIE
> Let's see.

BRIONY enters the drawing room. Inside the morning news plays on the wireless.

> BRIONY
> Mummy, I need you!

She closes the door behind her.


INT. DRAWING ROOM. DAY.

The drawing room is an enormous corner room looking out onto a terrace. EMILY TALLIS, BRIONY's mother, a slightly faded woman with pale skin and raw nerves, finishes reading BRIONY's manuscript. The radio has been turned off. BRIONY hovers above her, anxious and excited. EMILY looks up and smiles warmly at BRIONY.

> EMILY
> Stupendous! It's stupendous, darling!
> Your first play!

> BRIONY
> Do you think Leon will like it?

> EMILY
> Well of course he will. 'The Trials of
> Arabella' by Briony Tallis.


EXT. TALLIS HOUSE. GARDENS. DAY.

It's no later than 10am, but the sun is already high and blazing down on the monumental facade of the Tallis house, recognisable from its miniature version seen earlier. Lying on one of the rolling lawns is CECILIA TALLIS, BRIONY's sister, a beautiful, restless-looking girl of 23, who is making a desultory attempt to read a fat edition of Richardson's <u>Clarissa.</u> She turns back a page to re-read something, then sighs, rolls on to her back and shuts her eyes against the sun. BRIONY is lying a few feet away.

                    BRIONY
          Cee?


                    CECILIA
          Yes.


                    BRIONY
          What do you think it would feel like
          to be someone else?


                    CECILIA
          Cooler, I should hope.

Pause.


                    BRIONY
          I'm worried about the play.


                    CECILIA
          I'm sure it's a masterpiece.


                    BRIONY
          But we only have the afternoon to
          rehearse. What if the twins can't act?


                    CECILIA
          You have to be nice to them. Think how
          you'd feel if your mother had run off
          with Mr. What's-His-Name who reads the
          news on the wireless.


                    BRIONY
          Perhaps I should have written Leon a
          story. If you write a story, you only
          have to say the word 'castle' and you
          can see the towers and the woods and
          the village below... But in a play
          it's... it all depends on other
          people.


                    CECILIA
          Mm.


BRIONY rolls over. Some way off, ROBBIE TURNER pushes a
wheelbarrow up to a flower bed and parks it.

                    BRIONY
          Cee?


                    CECILIA
          Yes.

                    BRIONY
          Why don't you talk to Robbie any more?

                    CECILIA
          I do. We just move in different
          circles, that's all.


Down by the flower bed, ROBBIE glances across at CECILIA and
BRIONY. But he's very focused on his immediate task which is the
planting of a row of cuttings from the greenhouse. He wipes the
sweat off his forehead and begins to dig with a trowel.


INT.  NURSERY.  DAY.

Rehearsals are taking place in a now disused room on the top
floor, the former nursery, occupying the front corner of the
house. BRIONY has wedged herself into an old high chair and
looks down at her red-headed cousins: LOLA QUINCEY, 15, and her
twin 9 year-old brothers, PIERROT and JACKSON. They're all
clutching handwritten copies of BRIONY's play.

                    JACKSON
          Do we have to do a play?

                    PIERROT
          Why do we have to?

                    BRIONY
          It's to celebrate my brother Leon's
          visit.

                    PIERROT
          I hate plays.

                    JACKSON
          So do I.

                    BRIONY
          How can you hate plays?

                    PIERROT
          It's just showing off.

LOLA crosses her legs, revealing an ankle bracelet above her
sandals, and a set of brightly painted toenails; she speaks
quite calmly.

                    LOLA
          You'll be in this play or you'll get a
          clout and I'll tell the Parents.

                    JACKSON
          You're not allowed to clout us.

                    LOLA
          We're guests in this house and what
          did the Parents say we were to make
          ourselves?  Well?  Pierrot?

                    PIERROT
          Amenable.

                    LOLA
          Jackson?

                    JACKSON
          Amenable.

                    LOLA
          Amenable, that's right.

She turns graciously to BRIONY.

                    LOLA
          Now, Briony, what's your play about?

                    BRIONY
          It's about how... love is all very
          well, but you have to be sensible.

LOLA frowns, dubious.

                    LOLA
          I suppose you're going to be Arabella.

                    BRIONY
          Well... Not necessarily.

She's been surprised into this, but LOLA takes immediate
ruthless advantage.

                    LOLA
          In that case, do you mind if I play
          her?

                    JACKSON
          Lola was in the school play.

                    LOLA
          Do say yes, it'd be the first decent
          thing to happen to me in months.

BRIONY can't see any way to get out of it.

                    BRIONY
          Well... all right.

                    LOLA
          I suppose we should start by reading
          it...

                    BRIONY
          If you're going to be Arabella, then
          I'll be the director, thank you very
          much.

                    LOLA
          Sorr-ee!

                    BRIONY
          I'm going to do the prologue.

She looks down and begins reading.

                    BRIONY
          Prologue.
          This is the tale of spontaneous Arabella
          Who ran away with an extrinsic fellow.
          It grieved her parents to see their first born
          Evanesce from her home to go to Eastbourne...

The door opens; BRIONY breaks off and looks up to see DANNY
HARDMAN, the seventeen year-old spotty son of the head gardener,
standing in the doorway.

                    BRIONY
          Yes?

                    DANNY
          Nothing. Just thought I'd watch.

                    BRIONY
          Rehearsals are private, I'm afraid.
          You can see the play this evening.

                    DANNY
          I'll have to work then.

                    BRIONY
          Well, I'm sorry, Danny.

DANNY reluctantly prises himself away, closing the door behind
him. BRIONY turns back to the OTHERS.

                    JACKSON
          Can we have a swim now?

                         PIERROT
               Yes, yes, yes!

                         BRIONY
               There's no time!

                         PIERROT
               Cecilia will let us.

Before BRIONY can respond, the TWINS are charging towards the
door, pretending to fire guns at one another and shouting for
CECILIA.

                         LOLA
               I'm sure a half-hour break would do us
               all good.

LOLA saunters casually after the twins, leaving BRIONY alone.

She sits on the floor, her back up against the wall, fanning
herself with her script, her expression morose. A wasp is
buzzing irritatingly, trapped between two panes of the open sash
window. BRIONY gets up and goes over to liberate it. She's about
to lower the sash, when something outside catches her attention.

Below, to one side of the house, is a terrace, dominated by a
monumental fountain. Beside the fountain are ROBBIE and CECILIA
glaring at each other.

As BRIONY watches, ROBBIE stretches out a hand and says
something, as if issuing a command. In response, although her
expression is mutinous, CECILIA immediately kicks off her shoes,
unbuttons and removes her blouse and strips off her skirt, so
that she's standing before ROBBIE in her underwear.

BRIONY gasps and steps back from the window. The wasp buzzes
frantically.

When she returns, ROBBIE is standing motionless by the fountain
and CECILIA has disappeared. Then, suddenly, the surface of the
water breaks and CECILIA emerges from the fountain. She picks up
her clothes, turns her back on ROBBIE and pulls them on to her
still dripping body. Then she bends and rises again, this time
holding a previously invisible vase of flowers, and strides off
back towards the house. ROBBIE, left by the fountain, reaches
out a hand and lays it on the surface of the water.

BRIONY lowers the sash with a bang, liberating the wasp.


EXT.  WOODS.  DAY.

CUT BACK IN TIME.

CECILIA, with an armful of wild flowers, runs through the woods, enjoying the sheer exhilaration of movement. There isn't a cloud in the sky.

EXT./INT. NURSERY. DAY.

CLOSE on BRIONY, seen through the window, staring out.

EXT. WOODS. DAY.

CUT BACK IN TIME.

CECILIA runs on through the woods.

INT. HALLWAY. DAY.

CECILIA crosses the hall, as the TWINS come clattering and shouting down the stairs.

> JACKSON
> Can we go for a swim please, Cecilia?

> CECILIA
> I don't see why not, as long as you
> don't go near the deep end.

And the TWINS rush away as CECILIA steps into the drawing room.

INT./EXT. DRAWING-ROOM. DAY.

CECILIA crosses to the window. Outside, ROBBIE is standing rolling himself a cigarette.

CECILIA goes over to a cherry-wood table, where there's an early 18th-century Meissen vase. She drops the flowers untidily into it and pulls out a crushed packet of cigarettes, which turns out to be empty. She glances back out of the window, picks up the vase, checks her reflection in the mirror and strides out towards the terrace.

EXT. TERRACE. DAY.

CECILIA speaks a little sharply, startling ROBBIE.

> CECILIA
> Can you do me one of your Bolshevik
> roll-ups?

She doesn't stop; and he follows her, making the cigarette as
she heads across the lawn towards the fountain.

> CECILIA
> Beautiful day.

> ROBBIE
> I suppose so. Too hot for me.

They move on in silence.

> ROBBIE
> How are you enjoying your book?

> CECILIA
> Not at all.

> ROBBIE
> It gets better.

> CECILIA
> I'd rather read Fielding any day. Much
> more... passionate.

CECILIA suddenly feels awkward and hastens to change the
subject.

> CECILIA
> Leon's coming down today, did you
> know?

> ROBBIE
> I'd heard a rumour.

> CECILIA
> He's bringing a friend with him. This
> Paul Marshall. The chocolate
> millionaire.

> ROBBIE
> Are the flowers for him?

> CECILIA
> Why shouldn't they be? Leon says he's
> very charming.

They reach the fountain: CECILIA puts the vase down on the top
step leading up to it. ROBBIE hands her the cigarette and lights
it. They obviously know one another very well; yet there's some
definite, perceptible constraint between them.  There's more
than a hint of accusation in what CECILIA says next.

                    CECILIA
          The Old Man telephoned last night. He
          says you're planning to be a doctor.

                    ROBBIE
          I'm thinking about it, yes.

                    CECILIA
          Another six years of student life?

                    ROBBIE
          How else do you become a doctor?

                    CECILIA
          You could get a Fellowship now,
          couldn't you? With your First.

                    ROBBIE
          But I don't want to teach...

He breaks off, looks away for a moment; then turns back to her.

                    ROBBIE
          I said I'd pay your father back.

                    CECILIA
          That's not what I meant at all.

There's an edge of real hostility in her voice. She puts her
cigarette between her lips and bends to pick up the vase,
preparing to dunk it in the fountain, having first taken out the
flowers and laid them on the step.

                    ROBBIE
          Let me do that.

                    CECILIA
          I'm all right, thanks.

But ROBBIE persists, reaching for the vase.

                    ROBBIE
          You take the flowers.

                    CECILIA
          I'm all right!

He gets hold of the vase, just as CECILIA turns away; and with
the crisp sound of a dry twig snapping, two triangular sections
of the rim of the vase detach themselves in his hands. In his

shock, he lets them go; and they drop into the fountain and sink
slowly, spiralling to the bottom, almost three feet down.
CECILIA looks at him, horrified.

>           CECILIA
> You idiot! You realise this is
> probably the most valuable thing we
> own.

>           ROBBIE
> Not any more, it isn't.

The hint of truculence in his voice serves to agitate CECILIA
even more. She sets the vase down. Then straightens up, aware
that ROBBIE has begun to unbutton his shirt. She takes a step
towards him, then, confusedly, a step back. ROBBIE, afraid she's
going to step on the vase, throws out a restraining hand, a
gesture so abrupt as to seem peremptory.

>           ROBBIE
> Careful!

CECILIA's response is to kick off her shoes and, in front of
ROBBIE's transfixed gaze, to strip down to her underwear.  Then
she steps over the lip of the fountain and lowers herself into
it.

She gasps at the unexpectedly cold water, but doesn't hesitate
to plunge her face beneath the surface.

ROBBIE, watches, unable to look away, his expression a queasy
mixture of fear and longing. CECILIA'S hair fantails out across
the surface of the water.


UNDERWATER.  DAY.

CECILIA reaches down to the bottom of the basin and carefully
retrieves the two triangular shards of porcelain.


EXT.  TERRACE.  DAY.

CECILIA lays the two pieces of pottery down by the vase and,
with her back to ROBBIE, scrambles back into her clothes.  Then
she gathers up her sandals, tucks them under her arm, picks up
the pottery fragments and puts them in her skirt pocket, takes
up the vase of flowers and marches back towards the house.
ROBBIE stands there, watching her go. Then he reaches out a hand
and lays it on the surface of the water, as if to calm it.

EXT./INT. NURSERY.  DAY.

BRIONY, seen through the window, closes it and stays where she is for a moment, staring out. Then she turns back into the room and crosses it, grabbing up her notebook.


EXT. PERGOLA. DAY.

BRIONY strides through the rose-covered pergola, moving away from the house.


EXT. TALLIS HOUSE DRIVE. DAY.

A cream-coloured Rolls-Royce makes its stately way up the drive.


INT./EXT.  CECILIA'S BEDROOM.  DAY.

CECILIA's room is heroically untidy. The bed is unmade, the floor is littered with papers, clothes, and open books, the ashtrays are overflowing and the dressing-table is a disaster area. CECILIA herself sits, painting her toenails, when she hears the SOUND of the approaching motor. She crosses to the window gingerly, so as not to ruin her nail polish.

In the distance she sees ROBBIE striding across the lawns on his way down to the lodge, where he lives with his mother. The Rolls-Royce slows and stops alongside ROBBIE and the passenger leans out to speak to him.

CECILIA frowns in obvious annoyance.

>           CECILIA
> No need to encourage him.


INT.  HALLWAY.  DAY.

The two young men, LEON TALLIS, 25, and his friend PAUL MARSHALL, 28, surge into the house, followed by DANNY HARDMAN, struggling with their suitcases.

>           LEON
> Cee! Mother!


He turns to DANNY.

>           LEON
> Where is everyone, Danny?

                    DANNY
          Dunno, sir.

                    LEON
          I'm gasping for a drink.


He steps into the drawing room. DANNY, still with the luggage,
follows confusedly.


INT. DRAWING ROOM.  DAY.


LEON is moving over to the drinks table.

                    LEON
          Will you have one?

                    MARSHALL
          Rather.

                    LEON
          Whisky?

                    MARSHALL
          Please.

As LEON fixes the drinks, CECILIA bursts into the room.

                    CECILIA
          Leon!

LEON takes her in his arms.

                    LEON
          Here she is!

                    CECILIA
          Oh, I've missed you. I've been going
          completely doolally up here.

LEON turns to include MARSHALL.

                    LEON
          This is my sister, Cecilia; Paul
          Marshall.

                    MARSHALL
          I've heard an awful lot about you.

                    CECILIA
          Likewise.

                         LEON
               Where are we putting him?

CECILIA turns to DANNY.

                         CECILIA
               In the blue room.

DANNY starts off up the stairs, then stops, looking gormless.

                         CECILIA
               Mother's lying down, she's got one of
               her migraines.

                         LEON
               Not surprised, this heat.

CECILIA looks up at DANNY, somewhat irritated.

                         CECILIA
               The big room next to the nursery.

DANNY sets off, grunting with effort.

                         CECILIA
               Is the Old Man staying in town?

                         LEON
               Looks like it. There's some sort of
               rush on at the Ministry.


INT. EMILY TALLIS'S BEDROOM.  DAY.

EMILY is on her bed in her darkened room, propped up against two
pillows, her eyes protected by an eyeshade, cooled by an
electric fan that whirs on her bedside table.

From the nursery comes the regular thud of a bouncing rubber
ball.

EMILY sighs and pushes up her eyeshade.


INT.  NURSERY.  DAY.

The TWINS are sitting in their still wet bathing suits, bouncing
a rubber ball against the wall.

LOLA lies on the couch, flicking through a fashion magazine.

                         PIERROT
               So aren't we doing the play?

>           LOLA
> No.

>           JACKSON
> Why not?

>           LOLA
> Don't ask me.

>           PIERROT
> I don't like it here.

EXT. LAKE. DAY.

On the lake floats a white pontoon. CECILIA is wearing a white one-piece swimsuit and nursing a glass of punch. MARSHALL and LEON are also in bathing suits. We're looking at CECILIA, lying on the diving board in the blinding heat, as MARSHALL's droning voice nibbles at the edge of her attention.

>           MARSHALL
> And currently our main challenge is
> whether or not to launch the new Amo
> bar, the *Army* Amo. You see, Pass the
> Amo!

CECILIA turns her head to look at him for a moment.

>           MARSHALL
> My source at the Ministry of Defence -
> I used to clean his shoes at Harrow,
> so he's very reliable - assures me
> we've a good chance of getting the Amo
> bar included in the standard-issue
> ration pack. Which means I'd have to
> open at least three more factories,
> more if they bring in conscription,
> which I'd say is bound to happen if
> Herr Hitler doesn't pipe down - and
> he's about as likely to do that as buy
> shares in Marks and Spencers, wouldn't
> you agree?

CECILIA's been making a valiant effort to seem interested; now she takes a sip of her punch.

>           CECILIA
> This isn't very good.

                    MARSHALL
          I make a cocktail with rum, crushed
          ice, and melted dark chocolate.
          Absolutely scrumptious!

CECILIA manages to catch LEON's eye and make a discreet vomiting
face; LEON is obliged to rise to his feet to conceal an
irresistible burst of silent laughter. To recover, he turns away
to speak to CECILIA.

                    LEON
          Guess who we met on the way in?

                    CECILIA
          Robbie.

                    LEON
          I told him to join us tonight.

                    CECILIA
          Leon! You didn't!

                    LEON
                (to Marshall)
          So Robbie the Housekeeper's son, whose
          father did a bunk twenty years ago,
          gets a scholarship to the local
          grammar and the Old Man puts him
          through Cambridge; goes up at the same
          time as Cee and for three years she
          hardly speaks to him! She wouldn't let
          him within a mile of her Roedean
          chums.

                    CECILIA
          Anyone got a cigarette?

MARSHALL produces a gold case, brings it over to CECILIA and
lights the cigarette she's taken.

                    LEON
          Don't know what the hell he's doing
          these days, messing about in  flower
          beds...

CECILIA is standing on the diving board now.

                    CECILIA
          As a matter of fact he's planning on
          doing a medical degree.

                    LEON
          And the Old Man said yes to that?

                         CECILIA
               Look, I think you ought to go down to
               the lodge and ask him not to come.

                         LEON
               Why? Has something happened between
               you?

                         CECILIA
               Oh, for God's sake.

CECILIA dives into the lake.


UNDERWATER.  DAY.

CECILIA swims by, powerful underwater breast-stroke.


INT.  BATHROOM IN THE LODGE.  DAY.

ROBBIE surfaces in his bath: he settles back, brooding, looking
up at a skylight, a small pane of glass directly above him, a
square of bright blue sky, through which flies an RAF plane.


INT.  NURSERY.  DAY.

LOLA, PIERROT and JACKSON are hanging about aimlessly, already
at a loss as to what to do.

                         JACKSON
               When can we go home?

                         LOLA
               Soon.

                         PIERROT
               We can't go home: it's a divorce!

                         LOLA
               How dare you say that?

                         PIERROT
               Well, it's true.

LOLA grabs PIERROT by the shoulders and shakes him.

                         LOLA
               You will never ever use that word
               again. Do you understand?

PIERROT nods miserably. Eventually, JACKSON breaks the silence.

                    JACKSON
          Now what are we going to do?

                    MARSHALL (O.S.)
          I'm always asking myself that.

They're all startled by PAUL MARSHALL's sudden appearance in the
doorway. He advances into the room, hand extended.

                    MARSHALL
          My name's Paul Marshall.  And you must
          be the cousins from the north.  What
          are your names?

They tell him, as he shakes hands with them.

                    MARSHALL
          What marvellous names.

                    JACKSON
          Do you know our parents?

                    MARSHALL
          Well, I've read about them in the
          paper.

This causes consternation, from which LOLA is the first to
recover.

                    LOLA
          What exactly have you read about them?

MARSHALL realizes it may be time to back-pedal.

                    MARSHALL
          Oh, I don't know. Usual sort of
          nonsense.

                    LOLA
          I'll thank you not to talk about this
          in front of the children.

MARSHALL turns to the TWINS and speaks with glutinous solemnity.

                    MARSHALL
          Your parents are absolutely wonderful
          people, that's quite clear and they
          love you and think about you all the
          time.

LOLA's expression changes; he's successfully appeased her and
follows swiftly through with a compliment.

                         MARSHALL
                Jolly nice slacks.

LOLA smooths them down, visibly pleased.

                           LOLA
                We went up to see a show and got them
                at Liberty's.

                         MARSHALL
                What was the show?

                           LOLA
                Hamlet.

                         MARSHALL
                Ah, yes: to be or not to be.

                           LOLA
                I like your shoes.

MARSHALL tilts his brown and white co-respondent shoes, serenely
self-satisfied.

                         MARSHALL
                Ducker's in the Turl. They make a...
                wooden thing shaped like your foot and
                keep it for ever.

                         PIERROT
                I'm starving, when's dinner?

                         MARSHALL
                I might be able to help you out, if
                you can guess what I do for a living.

                         JACKSON
                You've got a chocolate factory.

                         PIERROT
                Everyone knows that.

                         MARSHALL
                Ah, so it wasn't a guess.

He takes a slab of something wrapped in greaseproof paper out of
his pocket and unwraps it to reveal a shell of khaki sugar which
he taps with his fingernail.

                    MARSHALL
          There'll be one of these provided in
          every kitbag of every soldier in the
          British Army. Sugar casing so it won't
          melt.

                    PIERROT
          Why should they get free sweets?

                    MARSHALL
          Because they'll be fighting for their
          country.

                    JACKSON
          Our Daddy says there isn't going to be
          a war.

                    MARSHALL
          Your Daddy is wrong.

He's snapped at the boy, and now smiles wolfishly in an attempt
to make amends.

                    MARSHALL
          We're calling it the Army Amo.

                    LOLA
          Amo amas amat.

                    MARSHALL
          Top marks.

                    PIERROT
          It's boring how everything ends in O.
          Polo and Aero.

                    JACKSON
          And Oxo and Brillo.

                    MARSHALL
          Sounds as if you don't want it then. I
          shall have to give it to your sister.

Which he does. She takes it, smiling triumphantly at the
disappointed TWINS. She glances flirtatiously at MARSHALL, who
watches with frank interest as she wraps her lips around the end
of the bar. His voice is soft and breathy.

                    MARSHALL
          Bite it. You have to bite it.

EXT. GROTTO. DAY.

Beyond the formal lawns at the bottom of the garden is an old crumbling grotto. This is BRIONY's place: she sits in the shade, scribbling furiously in her notebook.

>           BRIONY (V.O.)
> The Princess was aware of his
> remorseless wickedness, but that made
> it no easier to overcome the
> voluminous love she felt for Sir
> Romulus...The Princess knew
> instinctively that the one with red
> hair was not to be trusted...As his
> young ward dived into the depths of
> the lake in search of the enchanted
> chalice, Sir Romulus twirled his
> luxuriant moustache...Sir Romulus rode
> north with his two companions, drawing
> ever closer to an effulgent sea...So
> heroic in manner he appeared, so
> valiant in word, no one could guess at
> the darkness lurking in the black
> heart of Sir Romulus Turnbull: he was
> the most dangerous man in the world.

INT. ROBBIE'S STUDY/BEDROOM IN THE LODGE. DAY.

ROBBIE sits at his typewriter, pensive. His tiny room is stuffed full of books; open on his desk is a copy of Grays Anatomy. He reads back what he's just written.

>           ROBBIE
> Dear Cecilia, I thought I should write
> to apologize for my clumsy and
> inconsiderate behaviour...

He sighs, pulls the paper out of the typewriter, crumples it up and throws it in the waste-paper basket, where it joins other rejected drafts.

INT. CECILIA'S BEDROOM. DAY.

CECILIA is studying herself in the full-length mirror. She's wearing a black dress and a jet necklace.

With a profound sigh, she shakes her head and lets the dress fall to the floor.

On SOUND: the final duet of Act 1 of <u>La Boheme.</u>

INT.  ROBBIE'S STUDY/BEDROOM.  DAY.

The music is on ROBBIE'S gramophone. He leans back, wrenching
the paper out of the typewriter, again, crumpling it and
throwing it in the waste-paper basket.

A series of JUMP CUTS: ROBBIE moves over to the gramophone,
stands a moment listening to the climax of the duet, picks up
the arm and moves the needle back to replay the high note. He
paces his small room. He feeds another sheet of paper into the
typewriter, stubs out his cigarette, pulls the sheet out of the
typewriter and starts again. Decisively, he begins to type.

As he types, the words appear on the paper: "In my dreams I kiss
your cunt, your sweet wet cunt. In my thoughts I make love to
you all day long. Robbie."

ROBBIE sits back with a small gasp and laughs; he's surprised
himself.  Then he pulls the page out of the typewriter, sets it
down on <u>Gray's Anatomy</u>, pushes the typewriter aside and reaches
for some notepaper and a fountain pen. After a pause for
reflection, he unscrews the pen and starts writing.

He writes: "Dear Cecilia..."

                    ROBBIE (V.O.)
          ... you'd be forgiven for thinking me
          mad-the way I acted this afternoon.


INT.  CECILIA'S BEDROOM.  DAY.

CECILIA is now wearing a green halter-neck evening gown and the
jet necklace has been replaced with a rope of pearls. A couple
of other dresses lie on the floor beside the rejected black
dress.

                    ROBBIE (V.O.)
          The truth is, I feel rather light-
          headed and foolish in your presence,
          Cee, and I don't think I can blame the
          heat. Will you forgive me? Robbie.

CECILIA fixes on a diamond hair-clip, contemplates her
reflection for a moment, this time with satisfaction and leaves
the room.

INT.   STAIRS/FRONT ROOM.  LODGE.   DAY.

ROBBIE comes downstairs in a vest, carrying a shoe brush and a
pair of black brogues. His mother, GRACE TURNER, whom we've
already encountered in the Tallis kitchen, is sitting in the
front room with her eyes closed, her feet up and her slippers
dangling from her toes. ROBBIE spreads out a double page of the
Daily Sketch, before sitting to polish his shoes.

                    GRACE
          Off out, then?

                    ROBBIE
          Yes; Leon asked me to join them for
          dinner.

                    GRACE
          So that's why I've been polishing the
          silver all afternoon.

                    ROBBIE
          I'll think of you when I see my face
          in the spoon.

He stands up. GRACE watches him for a moment.

                    GRACE
          You're not a bit like your father. Not
          in any way.

                    ROBBIE
          That's because I'm all yours.

ROBBIE kisses his mother's forehead.

                    ROBBIE
          I'll be late.

                    GRACE
          Your shirts are hanging upstairs.

ROBBIE starts to leave.

                    GRACE
          Son?

                    ROBBIE
          Yes?

                    GRACE
          Nothing.

INT. ROBBIE'S STUDY/BEDROOM.  DUSK.

ROBBIE, rushing now, does up the front of his shirt and at the
same time finds an envelope, folds his letter, looks for his
cigarette case, puts the letter in the envelope and seals it. He
puts his jacket on, tests his lighter three times and leaves the
room.


EXT.  LODGE & PARK.  DUSK.

ROBBIE leaves the bungalow, impeccable in his evening dress, the
envelope in his hand and a spring in his step; he looks for all
the world like a young man with a glorious future.


EXT.  DRIVEWAY.  DUSK.

ROBBIE walks down the drive towards the Tallis house, his letter
still in his hand. He comes to a monumental bridge that crosses
a small stream. Below he sees a figure at the water's edge,
slashing at nettles with a hazel switch.

                    ROBBIE
          Briony? Is that you?

BRIONY turns, obviously startled and straightens her hair.

                    ROBBIE
          Are you all right?

BRIONY nods, her face flushing.

                    ROBBIE
          Do you think you could do me a favour?

BRIONY scrambles up the slope to join ROBBIE.

                    ROBBIE
          Could you run ahead and give this to
          Cee? I'd feel a bit of a fool handing
          it over myself.

                    BRIONY
          All right.

She takes the envelope from him, turns and runs off without
another word. He starts to roll himself a cigarette.

ROBBIE watches her go, leaving the drive to take a short cut
across the grass, running all the way.

Suddenly ROBBIE gasps, as if punched in the solar plexus, and lets drop the makings of the cigarette.

> ROBBIE
> Briony.

INT. GARDENS. DUSK.

But BRIONY  is out of earshot, running across the gardens, clutching the envelope.

INT.  ROBBIE'S STUDY/BEDROOM.  DAY.

CUT BACK IN TIME.

Again ROBBIE tests his lighter three times and leaves the room. But this time the CAMERA PANS back to ROBBIE's desk and moves in on the hand-written letter, still lying on his copy of Gray's Anatomy.

EXT. DRIVEWAY. DUSK.

ROBBIE, panicked now, cups his hands around his mouth and yells at the top of his voice:

> ROBBIE
> Briony!

INT. HALLWAY. DUSK.

BRIONY runs into the hall and stands for a moment, alone.  Then, impulsively, she rips open the letter, stuffs the envelope into her pocket and reads.

The SOUND of a typewriter, builds to:

INT. ROBBIE'S STUDY/BEDROOM. DAY.

The hammers of ROBBIE'S typewriter in extreme close-up, crashing down with the word: C - U - N - T

INT. HALLWAY. DUSK.

WIDE on BRIONY, a tiny figure isolated in the vast hall, transfixed by what she's just read.

INT.  DRAWING ROOM.  DUSK.

CECILIA and LEON, both holding gin-and-tonics, sit in a window
seat overlooking the gardens.

>           CECILIA
> I suppose he's what you might call
> eligible.

>           LEON
> Rather!

>           CECILIA
> He certainly seems to think he's the
> cat's pyjamas. Which is odd,
> considering he has pubic hair growing
> out of his ears.

LEON snorts with laughter.

>           CECILIA
> I imagine he'd give you a lot of very
> noisy boneheaded sons.

>           LEON
> He's quite a good egg, actually.

>           CECILIA
> You say that about everyone.

LEON'S face lights up as BRIONY bursts into the room; he goes
into his Arthur Askey impersonation.

>           LEON
> Rummy, if it ain't my little sis!

BRIONY thrusts the letter into CECILIA's hand without a word and
flings herself into LEON'S embrace.

>           BRIONY
> I wrote a play, Leon. I wanted to do a
> play for you, The Trials of Arabella.

CLOSE on CECILIA as she unfolds the letter and reads. She
blushes hotly, looks up to make sure her shock has not been
observed and bows her head to read it again.

>           LEON
> There's still time, doesn't have to be
> this evening.

                    BRIONY
          No, it's impossible!

                    CECILIA
          Briony?

BRIONY completely ignores CECILIA, pretending to hang on LEON's
every word.

                    LEON
          Tell you what, I'm good at voices and
          you're even better. We'll read it out
          after dinner.

                    CECILIA
          Briony, did you read this letter?

                    BRIONY
          Yes, let's, that's a wonderful idea!

                    CECILIA
          Briony...

CECILIA's about to speak, but she's interrupted by the sudden
appearance of PAUL MARSHALL, who's carrying a silver tray, on
which stand five cocktail glasses containing a sludgy brown
liquid. He has a faint scratch running down his right check.

                    MARSHALL
          Here we are, my chocktail; I insist
          you try it.

BRIONY tries to take advantage of this to slip out of the room;
but CECILIA grabs hold of her arm and hisses at her.

                    CECILIA
          Wasn't there an envelope?

BRIONY wriggles free and hurries out of the room.


INT.  BRIONY'S BEDROOM.  DUSK.

BRIONY, not yet changed, paces restlessly up and down, trying to
make sense of the events of the evening. There's a light tap on
the door and she looks up, very surprised to see LOLA.

                    LOLA
          Do you mind if I come in?

Before BRIONY can answer, LOLA comes in and perches on the edge
of the bed; her expression is tragic. She's dressed for dinner
and wearing make-up and lipstick.

                    LOLA
          I've had the most appalling evening.
          The twins have been torturing me.
          Look.

She pulls up a sleeve to reveal a blue bruise on her upper arm.

                    BRIONY
          How awful!

As she speaks she notices LOLA's wrist is blotched and sore-
looking; she reaches out to take it.

                    BRIONY
          Chinese burns?

                    LOLA
          That's right.

                    BRIONY
          But why?

LOLA is beginning to weep softly, in the presence of BRIONY's
obvious sympathy.

                    LOLA
          They want to go home. They think it's
          me keeping them here.

                    BRIONY
          Lola, can I tell you something?
          Something really terrible?

                    LOLA
          Yes, please.

                    BRIONY
          What's the worst word you can possibly
          imagine?


EXT.  LAWN/TERRACE.  DUSK.

ROBBIE approaches the towering bulk of the house, dragging his
feet. He looks up at the lighted windows and comes to a halt
outside the front door, not at all sure he can bring himself to
proceed. Finally, he takes a deep breath and tugs at the bell-
pull.

INT. BRIONY'S BEDROOM. DUSK.

LOLA seems to have made a complete recovery. She's staring at
BRIONY in undisguised fascination.

> LOLA
> He's a sex-maniac!

BRIONY nods seriously, struggling to find the correct mature
response.

> BRIONY
> That's right.

> LOLA
> What's Cecilia going to do?

From below, a ring on the doorbell.

> BRIONY
> I don't know.

> LOLA
> You ought to call the police.

> BRIONY
> Do you think so?

> LOLA
> He said he thought about it 'all day
> long.' All you need do is show them
> the letter.

> BRIONY
> You won't tell anyone, will you?
> Promise.

> LOLA
> I promise.

> BRIONY
> If he found out, there's no knowing
> what he might do.

> LOLA
> You're right.

> BRIONY
> You'd better tidy your face. I've
> still got to change.

LOLA goes to the door, turns back in the doorway.

                         LOLA
              Thanks, Briony, you're a brick.

She leaves the room.


INT.  STAIRCASE AND HALLWAY.  NIGHT.

BRIONY, now changed for dinner, crosses the landing and starts
down the last section of staircase leading to the hall. As she
reaches the bottom step, she notices a diamond hair-clip lying
in front of the door to the library. She crosses to the hair-
clip and picks it up. A moment later she hears a low moan,
recognizably CECILIA'S voice, coming from behind the door.


INT.  LIBRARY.  NIGHT.

BRIONY opens the door quietly and stands, framed in the doorway,
peering apprehensively in.

The library is cavernous and dark, lined with floor-to-ceiling
bookshelves. The only light comes from a desk lamp that points
directly into BRIONY's eyes. Silence. BRIONY takes a tentative
couple of steps into the room. As she does so, there's a sound
from the far corner.

                     CECILIA (O.S.)
                   (whispering)
              Someone's come in.

BRIONY edges closer and suddenly, revealed in the corner, frozen
against the bookshelves, are ROBBIE and CECILIA. ROBBIE, who has
one of CECILIA's wrists pinned against the wall, appears to be
attacking CECILIA, while CECILIA has a hand round his head,
gripping a handful of hair.

BRIONY, bewildered, stops by the desk.

                        BRIONY
              Cecilia?

SOUND of a doorbell.


EXT.  TALLIS HOUSE.  DUSK.

CUT BACK IN TIME.

CLOSE on ROBBIE'S hand, tugging at the bell-pull.

When the door opens, it's CECILIA, the folded letter in her
hand.

```
                    ROBBIE
          It was a mistake.

                    CECILIA
          Briony read it.

                    ROBBIE
          Oh God. I'm so sorry. It was the wrong
          version.

                    CECILIA
          Yes.

                    ROBBIE
          No one was ever meant to...

                    CECILIA
          No.
```

INT. HALLWAY. NIGHT.

CECILIA turns away and moves briskly towards the library.
ROBBIE, after a second's hesitation, follows her, almost
stepping on the hair-clip which has dropped from her hair.

INT. LIBRARY. NIGHT.

It's dark in the library.

ROBBIE waits in the doorway, until CECILIA has switched on the
desk-lamp; then he closes the door behind him and advances
tentatively into the room. CECILIA crosses almost the full width
of the room, before turning to face him.

```
                    CECILIA
          What was in the version I was meant to
          read?

                    ROBBIE
          I don't know, it was more formal, it
          was less...

                    CECILIA
          Anatomical?

                    ROBBIE
          Yes.
```

CECILIA doesn't know whether to laugh or cry. ROBBIE begins to
inch towards her as she begins to back gradually into a dark
corner, until she's up against the bookshelves.

> CECILIA
> It's been there for weeks and then
> this morning by the fountain... I've
> never done anything like that before
> and I was so angry with you, and with
> myself. I thought if you went away to
> medical school, I'd be happy. I don't
> know how I could have been so ignorant
> about myself. So stupid.

Tears well in her eyes. He's moving closer and closer.

> CECILIA
> You do know what I'm talking about,
> don't you? You knew before I did.

> ROBBIE
> Why are you crying?

> CECILIA
> Don't you know?

> ROBBIE
> Yes, I know exactly.

He reaches out and draws her to him, until their faces are
inches apart. He kisses her briefly and pulls back; then they
look at each other and kiss again, this time a long, passionate
and breathless kiss, that draws from CECILIA a falling, sighing
sound. He pushes her back into the corner and she starts tearing
at his shirt, pulling at his waistband. He buries his face in
her breasts and she drags his head up by the hair and bites his
lip. She links her hands around his neck. He reaches down under
her dress and into her underwear. She kicks off her shoes and he
raises one of her feet on to the lowest shelf. He undoes his
buttons, lifts her dress and enters her. She turns her head
sharply, biting her lip. They stop moving and slowly turn to
look into each other's eyes. Then, after a long, still pause
they whisper to one another, barely audible.

> CECILIA
> Robbie.

> ROBBIE
> Cecilia.

> CECILIA
> I love you.

> ROBBIE
> I love you.

She gasps as he starts moving again, crushing her against the creaking shelves. He takes her wrist and holds it back against the wall.

The door opens. CECILIA and ROBBIE freeze.

                    CECILIA
               (whispering)
          Someone's come in.

                    BRIONY
          Cecilia?

CECILIA doesn't answer. ROBBIE steps back from CECILIA and begins adjusting his clothes, keeping his back to BRIONY. CECILIA tidies herself up, steps out from behind ROBBIE and pushes past BRIONY without a word. BRIONY watches her leave the room, at a loss, then turns back, startled, as she senses ROBBIE turning towards her. She takes a step back, frightened; but he merely fumbles with his bow-tie and, staring coldly past her, leaves the room.


INT.  DINING ROOM.  NIGHT.

BRIONY enters the dining room to find ROBBIE holding CECILIA'S chair for her to sit. Also around the table are LEON, MARSHALL, LOLA and, at the top of the table, EMILY. DANNY HARDMAN is rather sloppily pouring wine for LEON, whilst leering across the table at LOLA.

                    LEON
          In Charlotte Street last week, people
          were sitting out having dinner on the
          pavement.

                    EMILY
          It was always the view of my parents
          that hot weather encouraged loose
          morals. In high summer my sister and I
          were never allowed out of the house.

                    LEON
          What do you say, Cee? Does the hot
          weather make you behave badly?

CECILIA flushes red, taken by surprise.

                    LEON
          Good heavens, you're blushing.

                    CECILIA
          It's just hot in here, that's all.

> EMILY
> Lola, wipe that lipstick off. You're
> far too young.

> LEON
> What about you, Briony? What sins have
> you committed today?

BRIONY, now seated, looks across at him indignantly.

> BRIONY
> I've done nothing wrong.

She turns to look meaningfully at ROBBIE and CECILIA. Meanwhile
EMILY speaks to LOLA,

> EMILY
> Have you seen the twins recently?

> LOLA
> Er...no.

Following some nervous impulse, ROBBIE suddenly finds himself
joining in the conversation.

> ROBBIE
> They didn't look very happy last time
> I saw them, poor little chaps.

> BRIONY
> You know nothing about it.

> EMILY
> I can't imagine what's got into you,
> Briony. I've never known you be so
> rude.

CECILIA dabs her lip with a napkin to find a tiny spot of blood.

> BRIONY
> Well, they're not poor little chaps:
> just look what they did to Lola!

> EMILY
> What are you talking about?

> BRIONY
> Jackson and Pierrot. Bruised her arm,
> gave her Chinese burns.

> MARSHALL
> She's quite right, I'm afraid, I had
> to pull them off her.

He indicates the scratch on his cheek.

                    MARSHALL
          That's how I got my war wound.

                    EMILY
          The twins did that? Lola?

LOLA doesn't reply.

                    MARSHALL
          It all turned into a bit of a wrestle.
          Still, no harm done, eh, Lola?

                    EMILY
          Would you go and find these boys
          please, Briony?  Tell them dinner's
          ready and where are their manners.

                    BRIONY
          Why do I have to go?

                    EMILY
          Briony, you'll do as you're told or
          you'll go straight to your room.

BRIONY rises from the table, her expression mutinous; EMILY
turns to inspect LOLA's arm. Under the table, CECILIA reaches
for ROBBIE's hand.


INT. TWINS' ROOM. NIGHT.

BRIONY switches the light on and is surprised to find the room
empty. There's a large ragged piece of paper on one of the beds.
As BRIONY moves towards it, she sees it's headed in big red
capitals: TO WHOM IT MAY CONCERN. She reaches for it.


INT. STAIRCASE AND HALLWAY.  NIGHT.

BRIONY comes flying down the stairs, the piece of paper in her
hand.


INT. DINING ROOM.  NIGHT.

All heads turn as BRIONY flings open the door. CECILIA lets go
of ROBBIE's hand.

                    BRIONY
          It's a letter!

CECILIA immediately panics.

>           CECILIA
>      Give it here.

Then she sees what's in BRIONY'S hand and relaxes; BRIONY, meanwhile, is advancing towards the head of the table.

>           BRIONY
>      They've run away.

>           EMILY
>      Who has?

>           BRIONY
>      The twins.

BRIONY reads from the piece of paper.

>           BRIONY
>      "We are going to run away because Lola
>      is so horrid to us and we want to go
>      home. Also there wasn't a play."

She hands the sheet of paper to EMILY. LOLA has gone pale.

>           MARSHALL
>      Not to worry, we'll send out some
>      search parties, they can't have gone
>      far.

>           LEON
>      Cee, you come with me.

CECILIA manages to catch ROBBIE's eye and half-shrugs, as if to say it can't be helped.


EXT/INT. TERRACE/DRAWING ROOM.  NIGHT.

BRIONY comes out on to the terrace; she hesitates a moment and then moves off into the darkness.


WIDE SHOT: the house with torch beams fanning out across the grounds. VOICES calling out the twins' names.


EXT. LAKE. NIGHT.

BRIONY crosses the small bridge that crosses from the bank of the lake to the small island, her torch switched on.

Seeing what might be the flash of another torch in the distance, she stops and listens.


EXT. BOAT HOUSE. NIGHT.

BRIONY comes down a narrow stone alley and peers into the watery darkness under the boat house. Suddenly, a duck splashes away from under a boat, startling her.


EXT. GROTTO. NIGHT.

BRIONY climbs down the steep steps into the bowl of the grotto. Then, once again, she hesitates and slows to a standstill.

Suddenly, out of the darkness, there's a painful gasp; and BRIONY whirls round, pointing her torch. For a fraction of a second there's an image of LOLA, on all fours, her dress hiked up and a tall male figure, kneeling behind her. BRIONY drops her torch in shock; it shines up in her eyes, blinding her, so that the man, rising to his full height, turning and scrambling away up the bank, disappears before she can pull herself together. LOLA'S voice breaks the silence.

             LOLA
      Briony?

BRIONY picks up the torch and shines it at LOLA, who by now is in a sitting position. She hurries over to join LOLA, dropping to her knees beside her.

             BRIONY
      Lola. Are you all right?

             LOLA
      I'm sorry, I didn't, I'm sorry...

BRIONY puts her arm round LOLA's bony shoulders; she seems strangely invigorated.

             BRIONY
      Who was it?

LOLA doesn't answer. She's sitting up now, her arms wrapped round her knees, rocking slightly. They talk in whispers.

             BRIONY
      I saw him. I saw him.

             LOLA
      Yes.

                    BRIONY
          It was him, wasn't it?

                    LOLA
          Yes. It was him.

                    BRIONY
          Lola... Who was it?

LOLA doesn't answer.

                    BRIONY
          It was Robbie, wasn't it?

Silence.

                    BRIONY
          Robbie.

                    LOLA
          You saw him.

                    BRIONY
          Like you said, he's a sex maniac. And
          you don't even know what happened
          before dinner. I caught him attacking
          my sister in the library. I don't know
          what he'd have done, if I hadn't come
          in...

                    LOLA
          You actually saw him.

                    BRIONY
          Of course I did. Plain as day.

                    LOLA
          He came up behind me.  He pushed me to
          the ground and then he put his hand
          over my eyes. I couldn't actually, I
          never actually...

                    BRIONY
          Listen, I've known him all my life.
          And I saw him.

                    LOLA
          Because I couldn't say for sure.

                    BRIONY
          Well, I can. And I will.

INT. HALL. NIGHT.

LEON crosses the hall with LOLA limp in his arms, followed closely by BRIONY and CECILIA. He speaks to EMILY in an urgent undertone.

>           LEON
>     Call the police. And she'll be needing
>     a doctor as well.

INT. DRAWING ROOM. NIGHT.

As the party surges into the room, following LEON, LOLA bursts into noisy tears, which continue as LEON lays her down on one of the sofas and EMILY tries to comfort her.

>           EMILY
>     It's all right, dear, you're all right
>     now.

>           CECILIA
>     Is Robbie back?

>           EMILY
>     I haven't seen him.

All this is very fast and chaotic: then BRIONY, who's standing just inside the French windows, makes a quiet announcement.

>           BRIONY
>     I know who it was.

INT. LIBRARY. NIGHT.

BRIONY, her face sharply lit against the dark library wall, is being interrogated by a stony-faced plain clothes INSPECTOR. EMILY is scarcely visible. He rattles out the questions intimidatingly; but BRIONY'S answers are firm and unhesitating.

>           INSPECTOR
>     You saw him, then?

>           BRIONY
>     Yes, I saw him.

>           INSPECTOR
>     Just as you see me.

>           BRIONY
>     I know it was him.

                          INSPECTOR
          You know it was him, or you saw him?

                          BRIONY
          Yes, I did. I saw him.

                          INSPECTOR
          With your own eyes?

                          BRIONY
          Yes. I saw him, I saw him with my own
          eyes.

EMILY rests a comforting hand on her daughter's shoulder.

                          EMILY
          Well done, darling.


EXT. TERRACE.  NIGHT.

CECILIA paces on the terrace, drawing hard on her cigarette, as
she peers out into the darkness, looking for ROBBIE.


INT.  LANDING.  NIGHT.

BRIONY hesitates outside CECILIA's room, then tries the door
gingerly. It's dark in the room.


INT. CECILIA'S BEDROOM.  NIGHT.

BRIONY steps into the room, closes the door, turns on the light,
crosses to CECILIA's dressing table, opens one of the drawers
and begins to rummage around in it.

We pass through the wall into -


INT. LOLA'S BEDROOM. NIGHT.

- LOLA's bedroom, where LOLA, is being examined by a DOCTOR,
watched by BETTY the cook.


INT. CECILIA'S BEDROOM.  NIGHT.

BRIONY continues to rummage, opening CECILIA's desk.

INT.  LIBRARY.  NIGHT.

CECILIA is being interrogated: as with BRIONY, she's brightly
lit, the INSPECTOR and EMILY are in shadow.

>                    CECILIA
>           My brother and I found the two of
>           them, down by the lake.

>                    INSPECTOR
>           You didn't see anyone else?

>                    CECILIA
>           I wouldn't necessarily believe
>           everything Briony tells you; she's
>           very fanciful.

CECILIA'S BEDROOM.  NIGHT.

BRIONY throws back the covers on CECILIA'S bed and finds, there
on the rumpled sheet, what she's looking for. CECILIA's handbag
and in it ROBBIE's letter.

INT.  LIBRARY.  NIGHT.

DANNY HARDMAN is being interrogated. He's flustered, almost
tearful.

>                    DANNY
>           When they went looking, I went up to
>           my Dad's. I did, honest..

>                    INSPECTOR
>           Why was that?

>                    DANNY
>           To tell him all about it.

INT. LIBRARY.  NIGHT.

CLOSE on the letter as EMILY reads it, the INSPECTOR waits in
the background.

>                    BRIONY
>           I know I shouldn't have opened it.

>                    EMILY
>           No. You should not. But at least
>           you've done the right thing now.

INT.  DRAWING ROOM.  NIGHT.

Tea is being served to the various POLICE OFFICERS.

MARSHALL is on one of the sofas, fast asleep, his mouth open.

LEON, sitting isolated in an armchair, sighs and consults his watch.

BRIONY sits at the piano. Suppressing a yawn, she reaches forward and plonks on one of the notes two or three times. At the window, CECILIA has seen something.

A WIDER SHOT reveals a CONSTABLE stepping into the room.

> CONSTABLE
> Sir, there's someone coming.


EXT.  TERRACE.  NIGHT.

CECILIA emerges from the house to join EMILY, BRIONY, LEON, MARSHALL and the three POLICEMEN all of whom are watching, motionless, the approach of a strange apparition through the mist: which eventually reveals itself as ROBBIE, with PIERROT on his shoulders and JACKSON, clinging on to his hand. EMILY speaks sharply to BRIONY.

> EMILY
> It's time you went to bed.

> BRIONY
> But...

> EMILY
> Now.

Obediently, BRIONY turns and vanishes into the house. ROBBIE, closer now, stops in his tracks as he becomes aware of the POLICEMEN.


INT.  BRIONY'S BEDROOM.  NIGHT.

BRIONY is awake, crying into her pillow silently. She stops, hearing the sound of a car starting, and jumps out of bed.


INT/EXT.  LANDING/STAIRCASE/DRIVE.  NIGHT.

Briony runs across the landing and jumps up on to a window ledge to look out. Below is a police Humber with all four doors open.

Then ROBBIE appears, his wrists handcuffed in front of him, moving between the two CONSTABLES. One of them rounds the car to get into the back seat. ROBBIE stops suddenly and turns back towards the house. At the same time, EMILY'S VOICE rings out.

>                    EMILY (O.S.)
>          Cecilia!

BRIONY cranes forward to try to see what's happening.

CECILIA, ignoring her mother, runs to ROBBIE. ROBBIE moves towards her, catching the CONSTABLE off guard for a second; she catches hold of ROBBIE's lapel and whispers into his ear. The CONSTABLE arrives and disengages her hand, gently but firmly, then leads ROBBIE to the car and pushes him down into the back seat. CECILIA bursts into tears, as the door closes. The car begins to pull away from the house. Visible through the back window, as he twists round to look over his shoulder, is the shocked, white face of ROBBIE.

The car is only about twenty yards away from the house, when it's obliged to slow down by the irate figure of GRACE TURNER, clutching an umbrella, marching down the very centre of the drive. As the car passes her and before it can accelerate away, she brings the umbrella down with a great crash on the shining paintwork, roaring out at the top of her voice:

>                    GRACE
>          Liars! Liars! Liars!

BRIONY'S P.O.V.: CECILIA stands motionless, isolated below on the driveway.

TRACKING SHOT: the CAMERA  slowly CLOSES IN on BRIONY's eye, unblinking at the window.

INT. BARN.  NIGHT.

ROBBIE TURNER, in a private's uniform, is a good deal thinner than when we last saw him, pale and unshaven. He's with two corporals in the loft of a French barn: TOMMY NETTLE, a young, skinny Cockney and FRANK MACE, a giant of a man, black, with a once-white bandage round his large head, holding a patch over one eye. He's stuffing sacks with straw to make rough mattresses, while NETTLE tries to light a stub of candle.

A CAPTION: **NORTHERN FRANCE, 1940.**

                         NETTLE
              ...so I says to him: "you can sit
              round here twiddling your thumbs,
              waiting to get your head blown off if
              you want to, I'm off out of it"...

                         ROBBIE
              Ssh.

He's heard footsteps approaching the barn. NETTLE and MACE reach
for their rifles and ROBBIE takes out a revolver. Two figures
appear in the doorway, carrying something, possibly weapons,
it's too dark to tell.

                         VOICE
              Bonsoir, Messieurs.

                         ROBBIE
              Bonsoir.

He whispers to the CORPORALS

                         ROBBIE
              Let me do this.

                         VOICE
              Anglais? Belges?

                         ROBBIE
              Anglais.

                         VOICE
              On a quelque chose pour vous.
              (We have something for you.)

                         ROBBIE
              Quoi?
              (What?)

                         MACE
              What's his game?

                         ROBBIE
              He says he's got something for us.

                         NETTLE
              Fucking hell.

The two FRENCHMEN take another step and ROBBIE and the CORPORALS
release their safety catches.

                    VOICE
          Laissez vos armes!
          (Put away your guns.)


                    ROBBIE
          Vous aussi!
          (Put away yours!)


                    VOICE
          Attendez!
          (Wait!)

One of the FRENCHMEN reaches in his pocket and brings out a
torch, which he uses to reveal that the two of them are carrying
loaves and bottles. The two FRENCHMEN are obviously brothers and
in their fifties.

                    1ST FRENCHMAN
          Ou a du manger pour vous. Du pain, du
          sucre...
          (We have some food for you. Some
          bread, some sugar.)


                    2ND FRENCHMAN
          Et du vin!
          (And some wine!)


                    1ST FRENCHMAN
          Vive l'Angleterre.


                    ROBBIE
          Er, Vive la France.

Later. The two FRENCHMEN sit in the loft with ROBBIE, MACE and
NETTLE, circulating the wine bottle.

                    2ND FRENCHMAN
          Qu'est-ce que vous faites ici?
          (What are you doing here?)


                    ROBBIE
          Tout au commencement de la retraite,
          il y avait un attaque de Panzers et
          j'ai été séparé de ma section.
          (When the retreat started, Panzers
          attacked and I was separated from my
          unit.)


                    1ST FRENCHMAN
          Ah, c'est vrai, l'armée anglaise se
          retire.
          (So it's true, the English are
          retreating.)

                    ROBBIE
          On va disparaitre, avant qu'il fait
          jour.
          (We'll be gone at first light.)

                    1ST FRENCHMAN
          On s'est battu toutes ces années, tant
          de gens sont morts. Maintenant les
          Allemands sont de nouveau en France.
          (We fought all those years, lost all
          those dead. Now the Germans are back
          in France.)

                    ROBBIE
          On va revenir. On va les chasser.
          C'est promis.
          (We'll come back. We'll throw them out.
          I promise you.)

Later. Below, the FRENCHMEN smile and wave.

                    1ST FRENCHMAN
          Bonne chance!
          (Good luck!)

They disappear into the night. NETTLE turns to ROBBIE.

                    NETTLE
          Come on, then. How come a toff like
          you, talks French and everything, ends
          up a private?

ROBBIE hesitates, then decides to be forthcoming.

                    ROBBIE
          Not eligible for officer training if
          you join direct from prison.

                    NETTLE
          You're pulling my tit.

                    ROBBIE
          No, I'm not: they gave me a choice,
          stay in prison or join the army.

They're looking at him with increased respect, as he adds,
quietly:

                    ROBBIE
          And, for the record, the last thing I
          am is a toff.

He leans back against the wall, lost in thought.

INT. JOE LYONS CORNER HOUSE IN THE STRAND.  DAY.

CUT BACK IN TIME.

ROBBIE, in uniform, looks through the glass separating the foyer
from the café and sees CECILIA, in her nurse's uniform, sitting
at a table near the back. Suddenly overcome with nerves, he
turns away, facing the cloak-room, where he tries to get the
better of his fears. When he turns back, CECILIA, lit by a shaft
of sunlight, is standing by her table, looking at him. ROBBIE
pushes into the cafe and moves over to her. For a moment, they
stand in awkward silence.

                    ROBBIE
          I'm sorry I'm late, I got lost.

                    CECILIA
          Hello.

                    ROBBIE
          Hello.

A short silence.

                    CECILIA
          Shall we sit down?

                    ROBBIE
          Yes, of course.

She's already ordered tea and now she pours him a cup. Her hand
hesitates over the sugar bowl.

                    CECILIA
          I'm sorry. I'm afraid I can't
          remember...

                    ROBBIE
          Two, thank you.

He begins stirring his tea; CECILIA puts a hand over his. A
moment passes, then he gently takes his hand away.

                    ROBBIE
          Where are you living?

                    CECILIA
          Tiny flat in Balham. It's ghastly. The
          landlady's rude and horribly nosey.

                    ROBBIE
          You look the same, apart from the
          uniform of course.

                    CECILIA
          I have to be back at the hospital in
          half an hour.

                    ROBBIE
          Oh, God, that's...

He breaks off, mastering his dismay. Two OLD LADIES are
gossiping at a nearby table.

                    CECILIA
          I'm sorry.

                    ROBBIE
          No...Have you been in touch with your
          family?

                    CECILIA
          I've told you, I'm not going to. Leon
          came and waited outside the hospital
          last week. But I just pushed past him.

                    ROBBIE
          Cee, you don't...owe me anything.

                    CECILIA
          Didn't you read my letters? Had they
          let me visit you, had I been
          allowed...every day...I'd have been
          there every day.

                    ROBBIE
          Yes. But if all we have rests on a few
          moments in the library three and a
          half years ago, then I'm not sure...I
          don't know if...

CECILIA puts her hand on his.

                    CECILIA
          Look at me.

He does so. He's close to tears.

                    CECILIA
          Come back. Come back to me.

She reaches out and puts a hand on his cheek; he inclines his
head, holding her hand between his cheek and his shoulder.

INT. BARN. NIGHT.

ROBBIE lies awake, hearing the snoring of the CORPORALS. A white
barn owl sits on an adjacent beam staring at ROBBIE, who's
composing a letter in his mind.

          ROBBIE (V.O.)
    Dearest Cecilia...
    Dearest Cecilia...
    Cecilia...


EXT. WHITEHALL. DAY.

CUT BACK IN TIME.

ROBBIE is walking CECILIA to the bus stop, through milling
crowds, many in uniform, past sandbags piled high in shop
entrances.

          CECILIA
    A friend of mine has a cottage by the
    coast; she says we can use it when
    you're next on leave. White clapboard
    with blue painted window frames.

They look at each other; then he kisses her, a long, deep kiss.
CECILIA starts to cry. A bus pulls up beside them. CECILIA
hurriedly produces a photograph of the cottage and hands it to
ROBBIE.

          CECILIA
    Something to think about while you're
    away.

She tears herself away and scrambles aboard the bus. She stands
on the platform, looking back at ROBBIE and the bus starts up
and moves away.

          ROBBIE
    I love you.

ROBBIE starts to run after the bus, but soon it accelerates
away, leaving him marooned in the middle of the road, the
traffic passing either side of him.

EXT. BARN. DAWN.

ROBBIE sits outside the barn in the pearly dawn light. He's
looking at the now somewhat battered photograph of the cottage
which is attached to a bundle of letters, which he now puts back
in an inside pocket. Then, checking to make sure he's not being
watched, he opens his shirt to reveal, at his solar plexus, a
wound about the size of an old penny. It doesn't look too bad,
just red and sore. But when he presses on it, he gasps in pain
and the wound releases a flow of colourless liquid.


EXT. FIELDS. DAWN.

The three soldiers move across a field, silhouetted against the
rising sun.

They move along the bank of a narrow canal, in which are
reflected the shapes of three German bombers, passing overhead.

> NETTLE
> Some poor sod's going to catch a
> packet.


EXT. STREET IN BALHAM. DAY.


CUT BACK IN TIME.

CECILIA moves briskly down the street with a letter in her hand.

> CECILIA (V.O.)
> My darling, Briony found my address
> somehow and sent a letter. The first
> surprise was she didn't go up to
> Cambridge. She's doing nurse's
> training at my old hospital. I think
> she may be doing this as some kind of
> penance. She says she's beginning to
> get the full grasp of what she did and
> what it meant. She wants to come and
> talk to me.

She kisses the letter and posts it.

> CECILIA (V.O.)
> I love you. I'll wait for you.

INT. POSTBOX. DAY.

The letter falls on to the pile of other letters.

          CECILIA (V.O.)
    Come back. Come back to me.

          ROBBIE (V.O.)
    Come back.


EXT. APPLE ORCHARD. DAY.

ROBBIE, MACE and NETTLE  move cautiously through a mist-shrouded
orchard.

          ROBBIE (V.O.)
    Come back. Come back.

NETTLE, who's limping a little, comes to a ragged halt.

          NETTLE
    Where are we going, guv?

He suddenly sits down on the ground and, with a cry of rage,
pulls off his boots and hurls them into the distance.

          NETTLE
    I fucking hate those boots. I hate
    them worse than all the fucking
    Germans put together!

          ROBBIE
    You'll have a job getting back to
    England in your socks.

ROBBIE trudges off through the trees to retrieve NETTLE's boots.
He approaches the area where he thinks NETTLE's boots might have
fallen, a little out of sight of the CORPORALS, finds the boots,
picks them up, wearily removes his tin hat, mops his brow and
closes his red-rimmed eyes. When he opens his eyes again, he
notices something, frowns and advances a few paces.

In a clearing in the orchard, lying in neatly organised rows,
are the corpses of thirty GIRLS, all around 13, dressed in the
neat black and white uniform of a convent school.

ROBBIE looks down at them, appalled and moved.

EXT. RIVER-BANK NEAR THE TALLIS HOUSE.  DAY.

CUT BACK IN TIME.

There's a natural pool not far from the weir in the river which
flows through the woods at the far end of the Tallis House
grounds.

ROBBIE finishes dressing, picks up a damp towel and emerges from
the trees to find BRIONY, still in her swimsuit, standing by the
jump-off point, wrapped in a towel.

>           ROBBIE
> Come on, pal. You should be getting
> dressed.

>           BRIONY
> If I fell in the river, would you save
> me?

>           ROBBIE
> Of course.

As ROBBIE bends down to do up his shoelace, there's a loud
splash. He looks up. BRIONY has disappeared, her towel lies
where she stood. Horrified, ROBBIE moves forward to look down at
the river.

BRIONY surfaces for a second, then goes under again.  She's
drifting towards the weir. ROBBIE doesn't hesitate. He dives
into the river.


EXT. UNDERWATER.

ROBBIE  flounders around in the greenish murk. Then he sees a
flash of white and the bubbles rising round BRIONY's flailing
limbs. He swims powerfully towards her.


EXT. RIVER-BANK.  DAY.

ROBBIE drops BRIONY in the shallow water near the bank and
strides ashore, furious. BRIONY, on the other hand, seems
delighted.

>           BRIONY
> Thank you, thank you, thank you...

>           ROBBIE
> That was an incredibly bloody stupid
> thing to do.

                  BRIONY
         I wanted you to save me.

                  ROBBIE
         Don't you know how easily you could
         have drowned?

                  BRIONY
         You saved me.

                  ROBBIE
         You stupid child! You could have
         killed us both! Is that your idea of a
         joke?

She looks at him for a moment, shocked by his tone, but defiant
nonetheless.

                  BRIONY
         I want to thank you for saving my
         life. I'll be eternally grateful to
         you.

He strides away angrily, into the woods, leaving BRIONY
disconsolate amidst the cow parsley.


EXT. RIVER-BANK IN FRANCE.  DAY.

ROBBIE leads MACE and NETTLE northwards beside a broad river.

                ROBBIE (V.O.)
         The story can resume. Our story can
         resume. I will simply resume.

NETTLE's insistent voice breaks into his reverie.

                  NETTLE
         Let's see Jerry come and have a go at
         us in fucking Southend. Or, better
         still, Trafalgar Square. No one speaks
         the fucking lingo out here. You can't
         say "Pass the biscuit" or "Where's me
         hand grenade?" They just shrug.
         Because they hate us too. I mean,
         that's the point. We fight in France
         and the French fucking hate us. Make
         me Home Secretary, I'll sort this out
         in a fucking minute. We got India and
         Africa, right? Jerry can have France
         and Belgium and whatever else they
         want. Who's fucking ever been to
         Poland? It's all about room, empire.
                (MORE)

NETTLE (cont'd)
They want more empire. Give'em this
shithole, we keep ours, and it's Bob's
your uncle and Fanny's your fucking
aunt. Think about it.


EXT. SLUICE. DUSK.

It's late afternoon and the sun is low in the sky as ROBBIE and
the CORPORALS trudge past some kind of sluice which squats
across a broad canal. They're approaching the outskirts of the
industrial quarter of Dunkirk, close enough now to see the huge
pall of black smoke rising above the town.


EXT. RAILWAY BRIDGE. NIGHT.

ROBBIE is trying to get some sleep under a stone railway bridge,
watched by an impassive bullfrog.

                    ROBBIE (V.O.)
          Dearest Cecilia, the story can resume.


EXT. BEACH BELOW WHITE CLIFFS. DAY.

On a deserted shingle beach, beneath towering chalk cliffs,
CECILIA sits, looking out to sea towards France.

                    ROBBIE (V.O.)
          The one I had been planning on that
          evening walk. I can become again the
          man who once walked across a Surrey
          park at dusk in my best suit,
          swaggering on the promise of life; the
          man who, with the clarity of passion,
          made love to you in the library. The
          story can resume.


EXT. INDUSTRIAL QUARTER. DAY.

The three soldiers tramp along between narrow-gauge railway
lines.

                    ROBBIE (V.O.)
          I will return. Find you, love you,
          marry you, and live without shame.

A WIDE ANGLE reveals that ROBBIE, MACE and NETTLE are moving past an enormous burning steelworks ringed with deep bomb craters, with destroyed vehicles at precarious angles.

EXT. APPROACH TO BRAY DUNES. DAY.

ROBBIE and his companions move along a straight road between patches of scrub grass, the industrial quarter now behind them. Suddenly, ROBBIE raises his head.

>           ROBBIE
>      I can smell the sea.

He sets off at a run, along a path cut through long grass, MACE and NETTLE labouring behind.

EXT. BRAY DUNES. DAY.

ROBBIE scrambles up the final steep dune and stops. NETTLE and MACE join him, their jaws dropping in amazement.

They are looking down at an astonishing scene. Beyond them, the beach at Bray is teeming with SOLDIERS, hundreds of thousands of men as far as the eye can see. The few ships there are, out on the iron-grey Channel, are almost all capsized or ablaze; and, most striking of all, what looks at first sight like a series of jetties turns out to be columns of SOLDIERS, six or eight deep, standing out to sea for almost five hundred yards in the shallow waters, the closest submerged up to their knees, the furthest obliged to hold their rifles up above their tin helmets to keep them dry. The three MEN watch for a moment in silence, before MACE gives out a heavy sigh.

>           MACE
>      Fuck me, it's like something out the
>      Bible.

For once, NETTLE  is at a loss for words.

>           NETTLE
>      Jesus Christ.

ROBBIE shakes his head as if to clear it.

EXT. BEACH AT BRAY DUNES. DAY.

ROBBIE wanders with the others through what seems like a hallucination.

Harnessed but riderless horses gallop across the sand. A whaler with ragged black sails lies fifty yards from the sea. A football game is in progress. A small group of men throw off their clothes and splash into the sea for a swim. Another larger group huddles in a bandstand, singing a hymn.

A chaplain and his clerk are throwing prayer books and bibles into a bonfire; the thin pages catch and float into the air like black snowflakes. A YOUNG SOLDIER of no more than 17 sits quietly looking out to sea with tears streaming down his face.


ROBBIE approaches a group of NAVAL OFFICERS, as they stride down the beach with a clipboard, trying to do a head-count. They keep moving briskly throughout the conversation.

> ROBBIE
> We've just arrived, Sir. Can you tell us what we're supposed to do?

> NAVAL OFFICER
> Nothing. Just wait.

> ROBBIE
> Where are the ships?

> NAVAL OFFICER
> A few made it in yesterday but the Luftwaffe blew them to buggery. We lost five hundred men when they sank the Endurance. And high command in its infinite wisdom is denying us air cover. It's a disgrace, it's a fucking disaster.

> ROBBIE
> The thing is, I'm expected back, you see.

> NAVAL OFFICER
> There's over three hundred thousand men on this beach, private. So you'll have to wait your turn. Just be grateful that you're not wounded, we've had orders to leave the wounded behind.

NETTLE pulls ROBBIE away, as the NAVAL OFFICER continues up the beach.

> NETTLE
> Come on, guv, never trust a sailor on dry land. Best off out of it.

ROBBIE moves on, dazed, through crowds streaming across the
beach in opposite directions, past gutted and blazing vehicles.

From up ahead, the SOUND of a gunshot.

>           MACE
>       That's not right.

To one side is a detachment of French cavalry, each man
dismounted and standing to attention beside his horse. A FRENCH
OFFICER with a pistol moves slowly, almost ceremoniously, down
the line, shooting each horse in the head.

ROBBIE moves on, as another horse goes down in the background.
He rounds the back of the beached whaler where a deranged
SOLDIER is perched up on the mast, furiously waving and shouting
at the top of his voice.

>           SOLDIER
>       Can you hear me, laddies? I'm coming
>       home.

The seafront, or what's left of it was once a cheerful resort
with cafes and little shops. ROBBIE, MACE and NETTLE pass a
bandstand and merry-go-round decorated in red, white and blue.
Soldiers have opened up the cafes and a good portion of them are
raucously drunk. Some lark about on bikes. A solitary sunbather
in his underpants lies on a towel. A brawling couple rolls down
the bank on to the beach.

MACE climbs up on to the gazebo-shaped bandstand where a tight
knot of SOLDIERS  is singing "Dear Lord and Father of Mankind".
Then he catches up with ROBBIE and NETTLE as they plunge on
ahead.

>           ROBBIE
>       Come on. I have to get something to
>       drink.

>           NETTLE
>       You need one. You're grey.

He turns to MACE.

>           NETTLE
>       He's gone all grey, look.

They move on past another group of SOLDIERS, disabling vehicles
with their rifle-butts. Then ROBBIE points ahead to where a
cinema sits, perched unexpectedly at the top of the beach.

                              ROBBIE
                    There. Come on.

He scrambles up a wooden stairway and disappears into the
cinema, having taken one last appraising look out across the
raucous inferno of the beach.


INT.  CINEMA BAR.  DAY.

ROBBIE pushes his way through a tight crowd of SOLDIERS, who are
singing "The Long and the Short and the Tall" with the words
changed from "Bless'em all" to "Fuck'em all". He can't find
anything to drink, and, as a brawl starts up and bottles begin
to fly, he ducks through a door at the back.


INT.  BACKSTAGE AREA.  DAY.

ROBBIE finds a tap on the wall in a kind of box-room, cluttered
with film cannisters; he tries it, but nothing comes out. In the
background, the SONG has changed to "The White Cliffs of Dover",
but ROBBIE has heard, under this, the murmur of French dialogue
and he moves forward to investigate.


INT. CINEMA.  DAY.

ROBBIE scrambles down a ladder and finds himself at the foot of
a giant screen where the huge face, full of doomed melancholy,
of Jean Gabin leans forward to kiss the shining lips of Michèle
Morgan in Quai des Brumes. As Gabin kisses her a second time,
ROBBIE, dwarfed by the enormous black-and-white image, buries
his face in his hands.


EXT. STREET IN BRAY.  NIGHT.

ROBBIE  wanders down a rubble-strewn street, between blazing
buildings and vehicles; NETTLE, accompanying him, cups his hands
around his mouth.

                              NETTLE
                    Mace! Mace!


They turn a corner and NETTLE, demoralised, stops to light a
cigarette.

                              NETTLE
                    Hold up, guv.

ROBBIE , looking listlessly around, sees an elderly FRENCHWOMAN step into a shop with shattered windows. His interest abruptly aroused, he speaks crisply to NETTLE.

                    ROBBIE
          Wait here.


He sets off into the shop, leaving a bemused NETTLE.


INT. SHOP. NIGHT.

ROBBIE moves into a kind of parlour off the main shop. He looks around; he's sweating now and very pale. Suddenly, a familiar VOICE breaks into his reverie.

                    GRACE (O.S.)
          Why don't you sit down?

ROBBIE turns to find the reassuring figure of GRACE, his mother, standing in a doorway. Gratefully, he sinks into a chair.

                    ROBBIE
          It's so hot in here.

                    GRACE
          Take your boots off.

Later. GRACE is washing ROBBIE's feet. They exchange a tender smile.

                    ROBBIE
          I have to get back. I promised her. To
          put things right. And she loves me.
          She's waiting for me.

GRACE looks up at him, infinitely understanding. There's a loud explosion outside.


EXT. STREET. NIGHT.

ROBBIE strides out of the shop, carrying bread and wine, no longer wearing his boots. NETTLE, who's sitting waiting, is obliged to jump to his feet and hurry after him.

                    NETTLE
          Oi! Wait!


NETTLE catches up with ROBBIE.

                    NETTLE
          What you done with your boots?

No answer. NETTLE circles ROBBIE, trying to get his attention.

                    NETTLE
          You sure you're feeling all right?

                    ROBBIE
          Never better.

He moves on, frowning in concentration.

                    ROBBIE
          Now, I'm wondering if the beach really
          is the best place for dinner.


EXT. SIDE STREET.  NIGHT.

ROBBIE  and NETTLE  turn into a side street, as bombs explode
not far away, and the night is lit up by flashes of artillery.

                    ROBBIE
          I'm not sure, I don't recognise it...

NETTLE follows, scrambling over rubble and bomb debris. He
indicates a dark opening.

                    NETTLE
          This'll do. Down here.

                    ROBBIE
          No, no, it's a little further on.

                    NETTLE
          What is?

                    ROBBIE
          This place I know, an old cottage,
          white clapboard with blue painted
          window frames.

NETTLE finally understands he's delirious and decides to play
along with him, whilst manoeuvering him towards the entrance of
an abandoned ice factory.

                    NETTLE
          Oh, yes, that's right, that's where
          we're going.

                    ROBBIE
          It's close to here.

                         NETTLE
                 We're there. This is it.

He succeeds in leading ROBBIE into the side entrance of the
factory.


INT. ICE FACTORY.  NIGHT.

NETTLE  guides ROBBIE between ranks of sleeping SOLDIERS,
arriving at a steel staircase leading down to a cellar.

                         NETTLE
                 Here we are. Down here.


INT. STAIRCASE AND CELLAR. NIGHT.

ROBBIE  descends the narrow staircase, NETTLE following. The
cellar is also crowded, but they reach an empty stretch of wall
and NETTLE starts to help ROBBIE off with his pack. As he does
so, ROBBIE more or less collapses.

                         NETTLE
                 It's all right, guv'nor.

He straightens ROBBIE out and drapes a thin blanket over him.

                         NETTLE
                 That's right. Get your head down.
                 There you go. Tuck yourself in. Keep
                 yourself warm.

NETTLE hands ROBBIE a chunk of bread.

                         NETTLE
                 Chew on a bit of this but quiet like
                 or they'll all be wanting some. And
                 try and get some sleep. Ssh.

Having calmed ROBBIE, NETTLE settles himself down facing him.
Darkness. Then a match flares. It's ROBBIE: he has the bundle of
letters in his hand, and the photograph of the cottage on the
coast. SOUND of the sea. Slowly the match burns out.


MONTAGE

Key moments from ROBBIE's past, some familiar, some not, REPLAY,
some running backwards.

The fragment of Meissen flies back up out of the fountain and re-
attaches itself to the lip of the vase.

ROBBIE takes back the letter he's handed to BRIONY.

The hammers of ROBBIE's typewriter lift the ink from the page: T-N-U-C, leaving clean white paper.

ROBBIE, alone, advances through a poppy-field in France, under a blazing sun.

> ROBBIE (V.O.)
> Find you, love you, marry you, and
> live without shame.

The Dunkirk cinema is filled with SOLDIERS singing "The White Cliffs of Dover."

As Jean Gabin kisses Michèle Morgan, ROBBIE raises his face from his hands.

A SLOW TRACKING SHOT finds CECILIA, in her green evening gown, standing outside the Tallis House.

ROBBIE's arrest, played backwards: he backs away from the car, breaks away momentarily from the CONSTABLE escorting him.

CLOSE on CECILIA: She leans forward and whispers into ROBBIE's ear.

> CECILIA
> I love you. Come back. Come back to
> me.

INT. CELLAR. NIGHT.

ROBBIE comes awake with a start; NETTLE is gently shaking him.

> NETTLE
> Bit too much noise, guv'nor.

> ROBBIE
> Noise? What noise?

> NETTLE
> You keep shouting. Some of the lads
> are getting a bit peeved.

ROBBIE tries to lift his head but can't. NETTLE strikes a match.

> NETTLE
> Christ. You look a bit rough.

>               ROBBIE
> Thing is, I've decided to stay on a
> bit. I'm meeting someone. I'm always
> keeping her waiting.

NETTLE wipes the sweat off ROBBIE'S forehead; he begins to
speak, his voice soothing.

>               NETTLE
> Now listen, listen to me, guv'nor.  I
> went out for a Jimmy Riddle just now.
> Guess what I saw? They're getting
> themselves sorted out down on the
> beach. The boats are back and a geezer
> from the Buffs is marching us down at
> seven. We're away, we're off home,
> mate! So get some more sleep and no
> more of your bleeding shouting, all
> right?

ROBBIE looks peaceful. He speaks in a cracked whisper:

>               ROBBIE
> I won't say a word. Wake me before
> seven, would you? Thanks so much. You
> won't hear another word out of me. I
> promise.

>                         FADE TO BLACK.

INT. CORRIDOR AND WARD IN ST.THOMAS'S HOSPITAL.  DAY.

A broad, empty hospital corridor, simonized to an improbable
gloss.

A CAPTION: **LONDON, THREE WEEKS EARLIER.**

The SOUND of rapid, regular steps at the far end of the
corridor. Then they appear, a group of PROBATIONARY NURSES
following a WARD SISTER, like ducklings after their mother.

At the back of the group is BRIONY TALLIS, now eighteen,
dressed, like the others, in the constricting purple and white
tunic of a probationer.

SISTER DRUMMOND, a woman in her thirties with a narrow mouth and
a quiet but lethal delivery, and her NURSES sweep into a long
ward with high ceilings and windows.

> DRUMMOND
> Bed castors should be lined up and
> pointing inwards. I found three
> yesterday that weren't. You know who
> you are.

They keep walking, moving fast.

> DRUMMOND
> Which of you was responsible for
> putting away the blankets today?

An amiable-looking nurse, FIONA AVERY, pipes up apprehensively.

> FIONA
> I was, Sister.

> DRUMMOND
> I don't suppose you can tell us what
> you did wrong.

> FIONA
> No, Sister.

> DRUMMOND
> Labels are folded to the inside, are
> they not?

> FIONA
> Oh, yes, Sister, sorry, Sister.

> DRUMMOND
> Do them again. Nurse Tallis, I'll see
> you in my office. The rest of you are
> excused.

BRIONY follows SISTER DRUMMOND towards her office.


INT. SISTER'S OFFICE. DAY.

BRIONY stands across from SISTER DRUMMOND, who sits at her desk.

> DRUMMOND
> Is this job at all important to you,
> Tallis?

> BRIONY
> Very important, Sister.

                    DRUMMOND
          Yesterday you were seconded to men's
          surgical. When your patient came round
          from his anaesthetic, it seems the
          first thing he did was to ask for
          Briony.  Who might Briony be?

                    BRIONY
          Well, me, Sister.

SISTER DRUMMOND suddenly draws herself up and shouts at BRIONY.

                    DRUMMOND
          There is no Briony! You are Tallis.
          Nurse Tallis. Is that understood?

                    BRIONY
          Yes, Sister.


INT.  CORRIDOR.  NIGHT

BRIONY stands at a window at the end of a long corridor looking
out at a view of the Thames and Parliament beyond. The sun is
setting. Her focus shifts to her own reflection which she
studies impassively for a moment.

                    BRIONY
          There is no Briony.

She turns  from the window and walks away down the corridor,
past  people putting up the blackout shutters. Over this, the
VOICE of a RADIO NEWSREADER.

                    NEWSREADER (V.O.)
          This is the B.B.C Home Service. Here
          is the news. The B.E.F., with their
          French allies, are fighting a
          desperate battle in the Northern Zone
          of the Western Front. The Allied
          Forces have not lost cohesion and
          their morale  is high. The R.A.F.
          continues to give all the support  in
          its power  to the  Allied armies in
          Northern France...


INT.  NURSES' DORMITORY.  NIGHT.

The CAMERA moves slowly through the 20-bed dormitory, taking in
jars of cosmetics, overflowing ashtrays and tennis racquets. In
the corridor a NURSE stands at the wall-mounted telephone
talking to each one of her family in turn.

Back in the dormitory, NURSES are putting in curlers, writing letters, crying gently on one another's shoulder, dancing to a Flanagan and Allen record. Finally, we arrive at BRIONY, who is trimming the nails on FIONA'S right hand.

> FIONA
> Thanks, I never could make the
> scissors work with my left hand. Mummy
> always did it for me.

> BRIONY
> There. You're done.

She turns to her bedside locker, in which is the small portable typewriter she used as a child.

Somebody shouts "Lights out!" And the lights go out.

> FIONA
> Oh, bother.

BRIONY lies back on her bed.

> FIONA
> Good night, Tallis.


INT. WATER TANK ROOM. ST. THOMAS' HOSPITAL. NIGHT

The water tank room is high in a tower above the hospital. The SOUND of someone typing. BRIONY is perched on a step, among the pipes and tanks, typing furiously. Beside her, a small pile of paper.

A noise at the bottom of the stairs.  BRIONY is startled.

> FIONA
> Don't panic. It's only me.

> BRIONY
> Fiona! I almost jumped out of my skin!

FIONA climbs up. She's  wearing her dressing gown. She sits and fishes for a cigarette.

> FIONA
> So this is what you get up to after
> lights out. I thought you might be in
> the middle of some tempestuous
> romance.

She shivers.

                    FIONA
          Don't you freeze to death up here?

She moves to look out of the window.

                    FIONA
          I love London.  Do you think all of
          this will be bombed and just
          disappear?

                    BRIONY
          No. I don't know.

                    FIONA
          Do you write about Sister Drummond? Do
          you write about me?

                    BRIONY
          Sometimes.

                    FIONA
          Can I look?

                    BRIONY
          I'd rather you didn't. It's private.

She puts out a hand to cover the title page, which reads: <u>Two
Figures By a Fountain</u> by Briony Tallis.

                    FIONA
          I don't see any point in writing a
          story if you're not going to let
          anyone read it.

                    BRIONY
          It's not ready yet.

                    FIONA
          What's it about ?

                    BRIONY
          It's just...it's about a young girl, a
          young and foolish girl, who sees
          something from her nursery window
          which she doesn't understand, but she
          thinks she does...I probably won't
          ever finish it.

FIONA considers BRIONY for a moment.

                    FIONA
          I look at you, Tallis, and you're so
          mysterious.
                    (MORE)

> FIONA (cont'd)
> I've never been mysterious. Do you
> know what I decided tonight?

> BRIONY
> What?

> FIONA
> I could never marry a man who wasn't
> in the Royal Navy.

BRIONY thinks about this, then bursts out laughing. FIONA
shushes her, giggling helplessly herself.


INT.  HOSPITAL ADMINISTRATION OFFICE.  DAY

A sympathetic-looking ASSISTANT with an index-card in her hand
turns to speak to BRIONY, who's in uniform, waiting on the other
side of the counter.

> ASSISTANT
> Here we are, Cecilia Tallis, I think
> this is her address.

> BRIONY
> Thank you.


INT. WARD.  NIGHT.

BRIONY, on night duty, sits at her table studying textbooks.

> BRIONY (V.O.)
> Dear Cecilia, Please don't throw this
> away without reading it. As you'll
> have seen from the notepaper, I'm here
> at St. Thomas's, doing my nurses'
> training.


INT.  SLUICE ROOM.  DAY.

BRIONY, in a heavy rubber apron, sluices a bedpan, looking away,
holding her breath.

> BRIONY (V.O.)
> I decided not to take up my place at
> Cambridge. I decided I wanted to make
> myself useful, do something practical.

INT. HOSPITAL CORRIDOR.  DAY.

BRIONY and FIONA are polishing the floors using a heavy bumper
that they can hardly move from side to side.

> FIONA
> It says in the paper the army are
> making strategic withdrawals.

> BRIONY
> I saw that. It's a euphemism for
> retreat.


EXT.  HOSPITAL YARD.  DAY.

BRIONY works alongside a number of other PROBATIONERS, on her
knees in the centre of the yard, scrubbing the frame of one of a
number of filthy old beds.

> BRIONY (V.O.)
> But no matter how hard I work, no
> matter how long the hours, I can't
> escape from what I did...


INT. WASH ROOM.  NIGHT.

BRIONY  stands at the only (cold) tap, fiercely scrubbing her
hands with a scrubbing-brush and baking soda. Her hands are red-
raw, cracked and marked with chilblains.

> BRIONY (V.O.)
> ...and what it meant, the full extent
> of which I'm only now beginning to
> grasp. Cee, please write and tell me
> we can meet. Your sister, Briony.


INT.  STORE ROOM.  DAY.

BRIONY works in a corner near the doorway, with FIONA.  From
time to time PORTERS arrive with trolleys and leave piles of
boxes outside in the corridor. Other NURSES unpack and stack
kidney bowls and packs of hypodermics.

> FIONA
> So do you?

> BRIONY
> Do I what?

                    FIONA
Have a secret fiance in France? That's
what everybody thinks.

                    BRIONY
No. Of course not.

                    FIONA
Imagine not knowing if he'd ever come
back.

                    BRIONY
I've never been in love.

                    FIONA
What never? Not even a crush?

                    BRIONY
I had a crush once, when I was ten or
eleven. I jumped in the river to see
if he'd save me from drowning.

                    FIONA
Now you're teasing me.

                    BRIONY
No. And he did save me. But as soon as
I told him I loved him the feeling
sort of disappeared.


Outside in the corridor, there's a commotion. People are running
past. Another PROBATIONARY NURSE sticks her head through the
doorway.

                    NURSE
Something's happened.

BRIONY and FIONA put down the boxes they're stacking and run out
into  the corridor, where everyone is running towards the exit.


EXT.  ENTRANCE TO ST. THOMAS'S HOSPITAL.  DAY.

As BRIONY and FIONA arrive, out of breath, bloody and wounded
SOLDIERS are being unloaded from the lorries and ambulances.
Many of them are black with oil, coated in grime and dazed with
exhaustion. BRIONY has scarcely arrived, when a young REGISTRAR
barks at her.

                    REGISTRAR
You! Get on the end of this stretcher!

He turns away from her and picks up the stretcher, handles behind him, so that he doesn't see the vast effort it costs BRIONY to lift her end. The PATIENT is a large SERGEANT, his bare feet and filthy bluish toes directly below BRIONY's face, his thigh disfigured by an ugly wound. BRIONY struggles forward, each step plainly an agony for her and, even more distressingly, for the SERGEANT.


INT.  SECOND FLOOR.  CORRIDOR.  DAY.

The lift doors slam open and the REGISTRAR emerges carrying the stretcher. BRIONY is struggling desperately along behind the REGISTRAR, her teeth gritted, her face puce with effort. The PATIENT utters a fearsome groan. Tears begin to roll down BRIONY's cheeks as she gasps with effort, the fingers of her left hand begin inexorably to unravel. She hangs on grimly until they turn into the ward.


INT.  WARD.  DAY.

A NURSE and a SISTER wait by an emergency bed in a ward now crammed with extra beds. The REGISTRAR and BRIONY arrive alongside and stop. BRIONY's left hand gives way and she's obliged to catch the stretcher on her knee. This causes an anguished gasp from the PATIENT. The REGISTRAR glares at her.

BRIONY turns and hurries away, glancing surreptitiously at her red and dented left hand.


EXT.  HOSPITAL ENTRANCE.  DAY.

BRIONY emerges into a scene of escalating chaos as more and more field ambulances arrive and dozens of wounded soldiers mill about hopelessly or sit waiting on the pavement.

                    1ST SOLDIER
          Fucking shambles.

                    2ND SOLDIER
          Turner! Private Turner?

BRIONY spins on her heels. There is a slight man, his face filthy and black with oil. It is ROBBIE.

                    BRIONY
          Robbie?  Robbie!

ROBBIE turns away. BRIONY rushes to him, puts a hand on his arm and turns him forcibly. The man is not ROBBIE.

                    BRIONY
          Excuse me.


INT. BRIONY'S WARD.  DAY INTO NIGHT

A MONTAGE of BRIONY's work against a background of ceaseless
activity in the rest of the ward. BRIONY helps lift a man whose
leg has been amputated back on to his bed.

BRIONY swabs the oil from a long, stitched wound down a man's
back.

BRIONY leans forward, puts one hand on an AIRMAN's leg, grips
the end of a protruding piece of shrapnel with the forceps and
pulls it out, firmly and smoothly.

BRIONY rips a dressing off a man's chest, causing him to cry out
and vomit.

BRIONY joins a group of NURSES around the bed of a young man
whose body is entirely covered in savage oil burns.

Outside in the hallway, FIONA, overcome, turns towards the wall
and weeps.


INT.  WARD.  NIGHT.

BRIONY moves between rows of sleeping patients, checking them.
She's intercepted by SISTER DRUMMOND.

                    DRUMMOND
          You speak a little French, if I
          remember rightly.

                    BRIONY
          Only school French, Sister.

                    DRUMMOND
          The soldier over there in bed 13. Go
          and sit with him for a minute. Hold
          his hand.

BRIONY hesitates, looking over towards the soldier.

                    DRUMMOND
          Off you go.

BRIONY slowly moves down the length of the ward, full of
apprehension. Bed 13 is surrounded by screens. Inside the
screens is the patient, LUC CORNET, his head heavily bandaged.

He's asleep. BRIONY sits by the bed and hesitantly takes his
hand. He turns to her.

> CORNET
> Te voilà, enfin.
> (Here you are, at last.)

> BRIONY
> La soeur m'a envoyée. Pour bavarder un
> peu.
> (The Sister sent me. For a little
> chat.)

> CORNET
> Ah, oui, je me souviens de ta soeur.
> Elle était toujours très gentille.
> Qu'est-ce qu'elle fait maintenant?
> (Oh, yes, I remember your sister.  She
> was always so nice. What's she doing
> now?)

> BRIONY
> Erm, elle est aussi infirmière.
> (She's a nurse as well.)

> CORNET
> Est-ce qu'elle s'est mariée enfin avec
> cet homme qu'elle aimait tant? J'ai
> oublié son nom.
> (Did she finally marry that man she
> was so in love with? I've forgotten
> his name.)

> BRIONY
> Er, Robbie. Bientôt, j'espère.
> (She will soon, I hope.)

> CORNET
> Robbie, oui, c'est ça.
> (Robbie, yes, that's right.)

> BRIONY
> Et vous, comment vous appellez-vous?
> (And what's your name?)

> CORNET
> Luc. Luc Cornet. Et toi?

BRIONY hesitates.

> BRIONY
> Tallis.

                    CORNET
          Tallis. C'est joli.
          (That's pretty.)

A spasm of pain or bewilderment crosses his face. He grips her
hand tightly and looks at her, frowning.

                    CORNET
          Je me rappelle de toi maintenant.
          C'est l'Anglaise. Tu te souviens, ta
          première visite à Millau? Je
          travaillais avec mon père près des
          fours. J'ai entendu ton accent.
          (I remember you now. You're the
          English girl. You remember your first
          visit to Millau? I was working by the
          ovens with my father. I heard your
          accent.)

BRIONY looks at him, moved by his confusion.

                    CORNET
          Tu peux me rendre un tout petit
          service, Tallis?
          (Can you do me a little favour?)

                    BRIONY
          Bien sûr.
          (Of course.)

                    CORNET
          Ce bandage me serre terriblement. Tu
          peux le desserrer un peu? S'il te
          plaît.
          (These bandages are so tight. Can you
          loosen them a bit? Please.)

BRIONY stands to look down at the bandage. It's secured by a
pair of simple gauze bows. She begins to undo them.

                    CORNET
          Tu te souviens de ma soeur cadette,
          Anne? Elle joue toujours ce petit
          morceau de Debussy. Tu te souviens?
          (You remember my younger sister, Anne?
          She still plays that little Debussy
          piece. Do you remember?)

He starts to hum the tune. BRIONY continues to unwind the
bandages.

                         CORNET
          Elle prend toujours une mine si grave
          quand elle joue, tu ne trouves pas?
          (She always looks so serious when she
          plays, you know?)

All of a sudden, the sterile towel underneath the bandage slides
away, taking most of the bloodstained dressing with it. A
section of CORNET's skull is missing and BRIONY finds herself
looking directly down at his brain.

                         CORNET
          Et nos croissants? Qu'est-ce que tu en
          pensais?
          (What about our croissants? What did
          you think of them?)

Methodically, not panicking, BRIONY starts to replace the
dressing.

                         BRIONY
          Délicieux. Les plus délicieux à
          Millau.
          (Delicious. The most delicious in
          Millau.)

                         CORNET
          Oui, c'est la qualité du beurre.
          (Yes, it's the quality of the butter.)

                         BRIONY
          Oui.
          (Yes.)

                         CORNET
          C'est pour ça que tu venais tous les
          jours?
          (Is that why you came every day?)

                         BRIONY
          Oui, bien sûr.
          (Yes, of course.)

CORNET thinks for a moment. Meanwhile, with infinite care,
BRIONY is replacing the sterile towel.

                         CORNET
          Parce que, tu sais... Ma mère t'aime
          beaucoup.
          (Because, you know...my mother is very
          fond of you.)

> BRIONY
> Ah, bon?
> (Oh, yes?)

> CORNET
> Oui. À son avis, on devrait se marier
> pendant l'été.
> (Yes. In her opinion we should get
> married in the summer.)

BRIONY <u>falters</u> in her work, but recovers. She's tying the bows
of the bandage.

> BRIONY
> C'est plus confortable comme ça,
> j'éspère.
> (I hope that's more comfortable.)

> CORNET
> Tu m'aimes?
> (Do you love me?)

> BRIONY
> Oui.
> (Yes.)

She's spoken without hesitation. He's broken into a light sweat,
and she leans forward to wipe his face tenderly. He looks up at
her.

> CORNET
> Tu peux rester un peu?
> (Can you stay a while?)

BRIONY nods reassuringly. All of a sudden, it's as if an
electric current has passed through him. He jerks upright and
begins to topple forward. BRIONY catches him and his head slumps
forward, banging against her cheek. It's all she can do to get
him back to his previous position in the bed. She's settling
him, her face close to his, when his eyes flutter open. A tear
rolls down his cheek.

> CORNET
> J'ai peur. J'ai peur. Tallis.
> (I'm frightened. I'm frightened,
> Tallis.)

> BRIONY
> Briony. Je m'appelle Briony.
> (My name is Briony.)

She's suddenly aware of SISTER DRUMMOND standing above her. She
speaks with her habitual sinister softness.

                         DRUMMOND
                Stand up, Nurse Tallis.

BRIONY does, bracing herself for an onslaught which doesn't
come. Instead, DRUMMOND reaches out to straighten BRIONY'S
collar. Behind her, a NURSE covers LUC CORNET'S face with the
sheet. Finally, DRUMMOND speaks, an unprecedented note of
tenderness in her voice.

                         DRUMMOND
                Now go and wash the blood off your
                face.

Numbly, BRIONY turns away and sets off down the centre of the
silent, darkened ward.


INT.  HOSPITAL DAY ROOM.  DAY.

Open on full-screen newsreel footage: the return of the BEF from
France. The newsreel is being shown on a makeshift screen in the
day room, where it is being watched with various degrees of
disbelief and disgust by those of the patients well enough to be
up and about. In total contrast to everything we've seen in the
hospital and at Dunkirk, what's shown tells of a heroic rescue
and a triumphant return. We see the troops offering smiling
faces and giving the thumbs-up as train carriages roll into
London. We see Union Jacks waving, and happy wives and children.

                         NEWS REPORTER (V.O.)
                *The navy has earned our undying*
                *gratitude. The army is undefeated.*
                *Courage has brought them through*
                *unconquered, their spirit unbowed.*
                *This is the epic of Dunkirk, a name*
                *that will live forever in the annals*
                *of warfare.*

BRIONY stands at the back, watching this propaganda. The next
item in the newsreel is introduced by a title: ON THE HOME
FRONT.

                         NEWS REPORTER (V.O.)
                *In the course of a comprehensive tour,*
                *Queen Elizabeth is seen here visiting*
                *a chocolate factory in the North of*
                *England...*

On the screen the Queen is being given a tour of the ARMY AMO
factory. BRIONY begins to collect her things to leave. Suddenly
her attention is caught, as there, on the screen, she sees LOLA
QUINCEY and PAUL MARSHALL shaking hands with the Queen.

                    NEWS REPORTER
          *The confectionery magnate, and friend*
          *of the British Army, Mr. Paul*
          *Marshall, gave the Queen a tour of the*
          *Army Amo factory with his lovely soon-*
          *to-be-wed fiancee Miss Lola Quincey.*
          *And what a mouthwatering couple they*
          *are. Keep the Amo coming, our boys*
          *have a sweet tooth!*

LOLA looks at the camera and smiles, as if straight at BRIONY.


EXT.  CHURCH OF THE HOLY TRINITY, CLAPHAM.  DAY.

The church stands at the end of a street of terraced houses, an
imposing facade behind pillars and a flight of steps. BRIONY
approaches, moving up the street, taking note of an empty black
Rolls Royce parked outside the church. She hesitantly climbs the
steps towards the church door.


INT.  CHURCH OF THE HOLY TRINITY.  DAY.

The wedding is already in progress, as BRIONY quietly lets
herself into the church.

There are a large number of GUESTS. PIERROT and JACKSON, now
fourteen, stand between their estranged parents, HERMIONE and
CECIL. On the other side are the many GUESTS of MARSHALL. LOLA,
in full bridal white and heavily veiled, and MARSHALL in a
morning suit, face the VICAR, who is in full flow.

BRIONY slips into a pew at the back and watches.

                    VICAR
          Secondly for a remedy against sin, and
          to avoid fornication, that such
          persons as have not the gift of
          continence might marry and keep
          themselves undefiled members of
          Christ's body. Thirdly, it was
          ordained for the mutual society, help
          and comfort, that the one ought to
          have for the other...

The VOICE of YOUNG BRIONY breaks in, talking to the POLICE
INSPECTOR.

                    YOUNG BRIONY  (V.O.)
          I saw him.

BRIONY sits in her seat, an appalling knowledge dawning.

> VICAR
> Therefore if any man can show any just
> cause, why they may not be lawfully
> joined together, let him now speak, or
> for ever hold his peace.

BRIONY's fingers grip her seat.

> YOUNG BRIONY (V.O.)
> I know it was him.


EXT. GRASSY BANK NEAR THE TALLIS HOUSE. NIGHT. 1935.

BRIONY stands still, blinded by the torch.


INT. CHURCH OF THE HOLY TRINITY. DAY. 1940.

BRIONY's eyes widen.


EXT. GRASSY BANK NEAR THE TALLIS HOUSE. NIGHT. 1935.

This time it's clear that the figure scrambling away up the bank
is PAUL MARSHALL. A CRASH of organ music.


INT. LIBRARY. NIGHT.

YOUNG BRIONY faces the INSPECTOR.

> BRIONY
> I saw him, I saw him with my own eyes.

The church organ thunders on.


INT. CHURCH OF THE HOLY TRINITY. DAY. 1940.

BRIONY stands in her pew as LOLA and MARSHALL walk towards her.
They don't notice her until the VICAR swings open one of the
great doors of the church. A shaft of sunlight sweeps across,
shining straight on BRIONY. She stares at LOLA and MARSHALL as
they draw level with her. LOLA'S eyes meet with BRIONY'S, her
forehead crinkles with displeasure, her lips purse. MARSHALL'S
face reddens and then they are gone.

BRIONY is left alone in the church.

EXT. STREET NEAR BALHAM.  DAY.

BRIONY passes down a narrow terrace of red-brick houses. Coming
towards her is a MOTHER with four unruly BOYS, all carrying
cardboard suitcases and knapsacks.

                    MOTHER
          Leave off, let the nursey through!

The BOYS take no notice of her whatsoever, and BRIONY is obliged
to stand aside to let them pass.  The MOTHER smiles at her
apologetically.

                    MOTHER
          They're going down to the country
          today. Never been out of London
          before.

                    BRIONY
          I hope they get a nice family.

                    MOTHER
          They dunno what they're in for with
          this lot!

EXT.  DUDLEY VILLAS IN BALHAM.  DAY.

BRIONY walks down the long, drab street and stops at no.43,
outside which is an old Ford 8 without wheels, supported on
piles of brick.  She walks down the front path, rings the
doorbell and then, realizing it doesn't work, uses the heavy
knocker to knock twice.  The door is opened by a sour-faced
woman in her thirties, MRS. JARVIS.

                    BRIONY
          I'm looking for Miss Tallis.  Cecilia
          Tallis. Is she in?

MRS.JARVIS turns and yells up the stairs.

                  MRS. JARVIS
          Tallis!  Door!

Eventually, CECILIA appears in the doorway. She's wearing a blue
striped dressing-gown and men's socks.

                    CECILIA
          My God.

                    BRIONY
          I tried writing, but you wouldn't
          answer. I have to talk to you.


INT.  CECILIA'S FLAT.  DAY.

CECILIA leads BRIONY to her tiny kitchen/living room. Everything
- furniture, lino, wallpaper - is cheap and shabby. There's a
small table covered by a gingham cloth, a few books
(Shakespeare, <u>Gray's Anatomy</u>), an overflowing ashtray and a jam
jar containing a bunch of harebells. The door to the bedroom is
closed.

CECILIA is lighting a cigarette as BRIONY advances tentatively
into the flat. She sees CECILIA's uniform hanging behind the
door.

                    BRIONY
          So you're a ward sister now?

                    CECILIA
          Yes.

CECILIA forces herself to offer BRIONY a cigarette.

                    BRIONY
          Thanks.

BRIONY launches abruptly into what she's come to say.

                    BRIONY
          I want to go in front of a judge and
          change my evidence, Cee.

                    CECILIA
          Don't call me that!

She turns away, trying to control herself.

                    CECILIA
          Please don't ever call me that.

                    BRIONY
          What I did was terrible, I don't
          expect you to forgive me.

                    CECILIA
          Don't worry, I won't.

She turns away again.

                    CECILIA
          You're an unreliable witness, they'd
          never re-open the case.

                    BRIONY
          Well at least I can tell everyone
          else, I'll go home, explain to Mummy
          and Daddy and...

                    CECILIA
          What's stopping you?

                    BRIONY
          I wanted to see you first.

                    CECILIA
          They don't want to know.  That
          unpleasantness is all tidied away in
          the past, thank you very much.

BRIONY starts: the bedroom door has opened and ROBBIE stands in
front of them, in his uniform shirt and trousers. His shirt is
open revealing a square bandage taped over the wound at his
solar plexus. BRIONY is partly obscured from ROBBIE's view by
CECILIA who has turned to him. He talks quietly to CECILIA
without focusing on BRIONY, then briefly nods in her direction.

                    ROBBIE
          Excuse me.

Then he's gone again. Silence.

                    CECILIA
          He sleeps so deeply.

BRIONY holds onto the table for support. In silence CECILIA
begins to move around the kitchen area of the room. She fills a
kettle. Mixes milk and water to egg powder and lays a pot of jam
and three plates and cups on the table. Finally they hear the
click of the bathroom door and ROBBIE whistling as he crosses
the landing. BRIONY moves as far away from the door as possible.
She's in his sight line as ROBBIE opens the door. He sees her.
He can't even address her.

                    ROBBIE
          What is she doing here?

                    CECILIA
          She came to speak to me.

                    ROBBIE
          Oh, yes?  What about?

                    BRIONY
          The terrible thing I did.

ROBBIE <u>moves around the room</u>, putting his hands in his pockets,
taking them out again. It's clear he's furious, hardly able to
contain himself.

                    ROBBIE
          I'll be quite honest with you. I'm
          torn between breaking your neck here
          and throwing you down the stairs.

BRIONY  stands her ground, shaken but not afraid.

                    ROBBIE
          Have you any idea what it's like in
          jail? Course you don't. Tell me, did
          it give you pleasure to think of me
          inside?

                    BRIONY
          No.

                    ROBBIE
          But you did nothing about it.

                    BRIONY
          No.

                    ROBBIE
          Do you think I assaulted your cousin?

                    BRIONY
          No.

                    ROBBIE
          Did you think it then?

                    BRIONY
          Yes, yes and no. I wasn't certain.

                    ROBBIE
          And what's made you so certain now?

                    BRIONY
          Growing up.

                    ROBBIE
          Growing up?

                    BRIONY
          I was thirteen.

              ROBBIE
How old do you have to be before you
know the difference between right and
wrong? Do you have to be eighteen
before you can own up to a lie? There
are soldiers of eighteen old enough to
be left to die on the side of the
road! Did you know that?

              BRIONY
Yes.


              ROBBIE
Five years ago you didn't care about
telling the truth. You and all your
family, you just assumed that for all
my education, I was still little
better than a servant, still not to be
trusted. Thanks to you, they were able
to close ranks and throw me to the
fucking wolves.

BRIONY shakes her head. ROBBIE clenches his fist, looks as if
might attack her.  BRIONY prepares herself, flinching. But
CECILIA intervenes, holding on to him, calming him.

              CECILIA
Robbie. Robbie, don't.  Please. Look
at me, Robbie. Look at me.


She kisses him gently and lingeringly on the lips. BRIONY looks
away, something like shame in her eyes. We stay on BRIONY's
face.

              CECILIA (O.S.)
Come back, come back, come back to me.

BRIONY looks out of the window. ROBBIE and CECILIA are now
talking in low voices as BRIONY watches an OLD WOMAN outside in
the street below, pushing a pram.

              CECILIA
Briony.

BRIONY turns.

                    CECILIA
          There isn't much time. Robbie has to
          report for duty at six and he's got a
          train to catch. So sit down. There are
          some things you're going to do for us.

BRIONY and CECILIA sit in the kitchen. ROBBIE leans on the
table, looming over them.

                    ROBBIE
          You'll go to your parents as soon as
          you can and tell them everything they
          need to know to be convinced that your
          evidence was false. You'll go and see
          a solicitor and make a statement and
          have it signed and witnessed and send
          copies to us. Is that clear?

                    BRIONY
          Yes.

                    ROBBIE
          Then you'll write a detailed letter to
          me, explaining everything that led up
          to you saying you saw me by the lake.

                    CECILIA
          Try and include whatever you can
          remember of what Danny Hardman was
          doing that night.

                    BRIONY
          It wasn't Danny Hardman. It was Leon's
          friend, Marshall.

They both look at her, <u>astonished</u>.

                    CECILIA
          I don't believe you.

                    BRIONY
          He's married Lola; I've just come from
          their wedding.

Silence. Finally, ROBBIE exhales the breath he's been holding,
CECILIA looks across at him.

                    CECILIA
          Lola won't be able to testify against
          him now. He's immune.

ROBBIE straightens up and turns away, grappling with a riot of
emotions. Silence. Finally, BRIONY stands up and speaks, very

STILLS

Cecilia Tallis (Keira Knightley) emerges from the fountain, watched intently by
Robbie Turner (James McAvoy).

Grace Turner (Brenda Blethyn) receives a kiss from her son, Robbie, before he goes off to dinner.

Briony Tallis (Saoirse Ronan), age 13, is asked to deliver a letter by Robbie.

In the hallway, Briony is transfixed by the message.

Later in the drawing room, Cecilia blushes as she reads the message from Robbie, while her brother, Leon (Patrick Kennedy), frolics with Briony.

Lola Quincey (Juno Temple) listens to the shocking news from Briony.

Briony makes a discovery.

Cecilia and Robbie say goodbye at Whitehall before Robbie is shipped off to France.

Robbie in Northern France, 1940.

The evacuation beach at Bray Dunes.

Robbie witnesses more chaos at Bray Dunes.

Briony Tallis (Romola Garai), age 18, as a nurse at St. Thomas's Hospital.

Briony Tallis (Vanessa Redgrave), age 76, at a break from the television interview in 1999.

formal.

>                    BRIONY
>          I'm very, very sorry to have caused
>          you all this terrible distress. I am
>          very, very sorry.

>                    ROBBIE
>          Just do what we've asked of you. Write
>          it all down.

>                    BRIONY
>          I will. I promise.

She leaves abruptly, her eyes brimming with tears.


EXT.  DUDLEY VILLAS.  DAY.


In the window, CECILIA and ROBBIE are locked in a tender
embrace.

Below in the street, BRIONY turns away and sets off into the
distance.


INT.  UNDERGROUND TRAIN.

BRIONY sits on a busy train staring straight ahead, trying to
take in all that's happened, all she's learnt. Trying not to
cry. The lights flicker on and off, taking us finally to black.

OVER THIS, the tired VOICE of OLDER BRIONY.

>                    OLDER BRIONY (V.O.)
>          I'm sorry, could we stop for a minute?


INT.  TV CONTROL ROOM.  DAY.    1999.

Seen on dozens of monitors, BRIONY TALLIS, 76 now, has
interrupted an interview she's giving for television. Leaning
forward, she unhooks her radio mike.

>                    INTERVIEWER
>          Of course. Is anything wrong?

>                    OLDER BRIONY
>          I just need a couple of minutes to
>          myself.

The VIDEOTAPE rewinds and we're back to earlier in the
interview.

                    INTERVIEWER
          Your new novel, your twenty-first, is
          called <u>Atonement</u>; it's a period piece
          set before and during the Second World
          War...

He breaks off, concerned, as OLDER BRIONY buries her face in her
hands.

                    INTERVIEWER
          Briony?


INT.  BATHROOM.  DAY.

Alone, OLDER BRIONY grimaces at her over-made-up face in the
mirror, pours three aspirin into her hand and washes them down.
Then she lowers her head and closes her eyes.


INT.  TV STUDIO.  DAY.

The interview has resumed.

                    INTERVIEWER
          I'd like to talk now about your new
          novel, <u>Atonement</u>, which is coming out
          in a few days to coincide with your
          birthday.  It's your twenty-first
          novel...

<u>CLOSE on BRIONY, her face against black:</u> where we will remain
for the rest of her interview.

                    OLDER BRIONY
          It's my last novel.

                    INTERVIEWER
          Oh, really? You mean you're retiring?

OLDER BRIONY contemplates him calmly for a moment.

                    OLDER BRIONY
          No, dying.

Before the INTERVIEWER is quite able to reassemble his thoughts,
she resumes:

                    OLDER BRIONY
          My doctor tells me I have something
          called vascular dementia; which is
          essentially a continuous series of
                    (MORE)

                    OLDER BRIONY  (cont'd)
tiny strokes. Your brain gradually
closes down. You lose words, you lose
your memory: which, for a writer, is
pretty much the point. That's why I
could finally write this book; and
why, of course, it's my last novel.
Strangely enough, it would be just as
accurate to call it my first novel. I
wrote several drafts as far back as my
time at St. Thomas's Hospital during
the war. I just couldn't ever find the
way to do it.

                    INTERVIEWER
Because the novel is autobiographical,
is that right?

                    OLDER BRIONY
Yes, entirely. I haven't changed any
names, including my own.

                    INTERVIEWER
And was that the problem?

                    OLDER BRIONY
No. I had for a very long time decided
to tell the absolute truth. And I
think...

She hesitates.

                    OLDER BRIONY
You've read the book, you'll
understand why. I got first-hand
accounts of all the events I didn't
personally witness, conditions in
prison, the evacuation of Dunkirk,
everything. But the effect of all this
honesty was rather...pitiless, you
see. I couldn't any longer imagine
what purpose would be served by it.

                    INTERVIEWER
By what? By honesty?

                    OLDER BRIONY
Or reality. Because, in fact, I was
too much of a coward to go and see my
sister in June, 1940.

INT.  WATER TOWER AT ST THOMAS'S HOSPITAL.  NIGHT.  1940.

BRIONY sits at her typewriter.

                    OLDER BRIONY (V.O.)
          I never made that journey to Balham.
          So the scene in which I confess to
          them is invented, imagined.


INT. CECILIA'S FLAT IN BALHAM.  DAY.

ROBBIE's face; the empty bed.

                    OLDER BRIONY (V.O.)
          And, in fact, could never have
          happened...


INT.  CELLAR AT BRAY DUNES. DAWN.

CORPORAL NETTLE removes a piece of wood from the entrance to the
bombed out cellar. Light pours in.

                    OLDER BRIONY (V.O.)
          ...because Robbie Turner died of
          septicaemia at Bray Dunes on the first
          of June 1940, the last day of the
          evacuation...

ROBBIE lies dead amongst the rubble; beside him is the bundle of
letters and CECILIA's photograph. NETTLE picks up the letters.

                    NETTLE
          Cheerio, pal.

He covers ROBBIE's face and puts the letters in his pocket.


INT.  PLATFORM ON BALHAM TUBE STATION.  NIGHT.

A thick pipe, running above the platform, is dripping,
undramatic but regular.

                    OLDER BRIONY (V.O.)
          ... and I was never able to put things
          right with my sister Cecilia...

A WIDE SHOT shows the platform, dimly lit, crowded with sleeping
bodies, mostly women and children.

PAN OVER the bodies: one of them, CECILIA, as it turns out,
opens her eyes, quite calmly, at the SOUND of muffled explosions
from the first bombs falling on the street above. The lights
flicker and revive.

EXT. BALHAM TUBE STATION. NIGHT.

The illuminated sign above the station also <u>flickers</u> and goes
out. Out here the SOUND and flash of the bombs is far more
present.

> OLDER BRIONY (V.O.)
> ...because she was killed on the 15th
> of October, 1940...

INT.   BALHAM TUBE STATION.   NIGHT.

A vast wall of water cascades, in slow motion, down the deserted
escalators.

> OLDER BRIONY (V.O.)
> ...by the bomb that destroyed the gas
> and water mains above Balham tube
> station.

INT.   PLATFORM ON BALHAM TUBE STATION.   NIGHT.

CECILIA sits up as the lights flicker and, this time, go out.
The thunderous roar of the approaching waters.

INT.   UNDERWATER.

CECILIA's body, balletically graceful, hair fantailed out,
drifts through the tube tunnel towards a distant light.

INT. T.V. STUDIO.   DAY.   1999.

OLDER BRIONY looks intently at the CAMERA.

> OLDER BRIONY
> So my sister and Robbie never had the
> time together they both so longed for
> and deserved, which, ever since,
> I've...always felt I prevented. But
> what sense of hope or satisfaction
> could a reader derive from an ending
> like that? So, in the book, I wanted
> to give Robbie and Cecilia what they

(MORE)

                    OLDER BRIONY  (cont'd)
          lost out on in life. I'd like to think
          this wasn't weakness or evasion, but a
          final act of kindness.

She thinks for a moment.

                    OLDER BRIONY
          I gave them their happiness.


EXT. BEACH BELOW WHITE CLIFFS.  DAY.

ROBBIE and CECILIA crunch across the pebbles and splash
gleefully through the waves, below the towering white cliffs on
their way back to their white clapboard cottage.




                         THE END

**PRODUCTION NOTES**

## SYNOPSIS

The story of *Atonement* spans several decades. In 1935, 13-year-old fledgling writer Briony Tallis (Saoirse Ronan) and her family live a life of wealth and privilege in their enormous mansion. On the warmest day of the year, the country estate takes on an unsettling hothouse atmosphere, stoking Briony's vivid imagination. Robbie Turner (James McAvoy), the educated son of the family's housekeeper, carries a torch for Briony's headstrong older sister Cecilia (Keira Knightley). Cecilia, he hopes, has comparable feelings; all it will take is one spark for this relationship to combust. When it does, Briony—who has a crush on Robbie—is compelled to interfere, going so far as accusing Robbie of a crime he did not commit. Cecilia and Robbie declare their love for each other, but he is arrested—and with Briony bearing false witness, the course of three lives is changed forever. Briony continues to seek forgiveness for her childhood misdeed. Through a terrible and courageous act of imagination, she finds the path to her uncertain atonement, and to an understanding of the power of enduring love.

## ADAPTATION

Even before Joe Wright had begun shooting his feature directorial debut, 2005's *Pride & Prejudice*—which would ultimately earn him a BAFTA Award, among other honors—producer and Working Title Films co-chairman Tim Bevan realized, "We needed to plan on making this exceptional new director's *next* movie. So we started to look for material that we might work on with Joe after *Pride & Prejudice* was finished."

The new project would be another classic British romance from a great book; Ian McEwan's award-winning best-selling novel *Atonement* was already in development at Working Title with producer Robert Fox and director Richard Eyre. But, as Bevan reports, "Richard took on another movie and had a stage commitment as well. Very honorably, because he absolutely loves *Atonement*, he said that if we could find a director that we all agree we want to work with, then he would hand over the helm—and he did."

The director was intent on bringing *Atonement* from page to screen. He knew that realizing the narrative would be an exciting filmmaking challenge. He comments, "In making a book into a movie, the story reveals itself to you as you make it. You are questioning the structure, you are questioning points of view—and, for *Atonement*, we were questioning one single truth as opposed to multiple truths."

Academy Award–winning screenwriter Christopher Hampton had been adapting the novel. Wright explains, "When I was first sent the script, it had departed quite a lot from the novel. I thought the book was brilliant, and Christopher and I started again from scratch. The script was rewritten; we stuck to the book as faithfully as possible."

"That was the approach that worked best," confirms the screenwriter. "We returned to the structure of the book. The novel grows in power as the story progresses, and Joe and I wanted to stay true to that."

"It was quite a fluid collaboration," assesses Wright. "By the end, I felt I knew the book and knew the script totally, and understood every moment—or at least tried to. Then, I learned more and more about the material during shooting.

"A book is symbols and words on the pages; it happens in your head. As on *Pride & Prejudice*, I sought to make a film adaptation of the book that happened in my head as I read it."

Paul Webster had already rejoined Working Title co-chairs Bevan and Eric Fellner as producer on *Atonement*, following their producing *Pride & Prejudice* together. Webster says, "I thought the book was Ian's best, and most cinematic, work. Once our imaginative director started collaborating with Christopher, the script became richer and more complex. Joe brought a vast visual imagination to the film, and Christopher wrote a beautiful script—without what he calls the 'convenient crutch' of a voiceover.

"The themes *Atonement* addresses are so powerful and common to us all: emerging sexuality, intertwining fates, and that sense of 'if only I'd have done this instead of that, my life would have been entirely different.'"

Bevan recalls discussing the difficulties of bringing *Atonement* to the screen. He notes, "The film was going to have to be all about the detail, about the times and about precision. It was going to need three different actresses to play the same role, and would use the device of multiple perspectives of the same event. It was going to be a very complicated piece."

McEwan, who has witnessed his works being adapted for the screen on previous occasions, also knew the task would not be simple with *Atonement*. As he says, "It's a kind of demolition job. You've got to boil down 130,000 words to a screenplay containing 20,000 words. In this particular case there are greater difficulties for the screenwriter because this is a very interior novel. It lives inside the consciousness of several characters. I think Christopher Hampton has steered a wise and clever course through the book."

Hampton offers, "The best and most atmospheric of novelists are often the hardest to adapt. Yet, the adaptations that I've done that have given me the most satisfaction are from works—like *Les Liaisons Dangereuses*—that are masterpieces. I think *Atonement* is one of the best novels of the last twenty years, so to preserve its qualities was a great responsibility."

Michiko Kakutani wrote in *The New York Times* [on June 1, 2007] that, in *Atonement*, the author "beautifully [explores] the precariousness of daily life and the difficulty of achieving—and holding onto—ordinary happiness."

Wright muses, "*Atonement*, though set in the past, has contemporary relevance; it is about everyday experiences, relationships, emotions, choices, and decisions. As on *Pride & Prejudice*, I sought to interpret a period story in such a way that the modern-day audience is able to see beyond the time and setting of a story—and into the story itself.

"What I have learned from directing period pieces is that they free your imagination. If you utilize the specifics of a period very precisely in tandem with emotional truths, it all becomes relevant to a modern audience. In terms of the themes that *Atonement* deals with, it taught me a lot."

Hampton adds, "The more accurate you are with presenting a period, the more striking the modern aspects of the story become. Audiences watching

*Atonement* will see a completely different world than the one they know—and people in it relating to each other in wholly recognizable ways."

Bevan concludes, "There is a fascinating emotional journey at the heart of *Atonement*. We all have to live through the circumstances of what we do at any point in our life, and this story is a very acute rendition of that."

By the spring of 2006, the screenplay adaptation was at the 25,000 words it needed to be for a viable movie to be made.


## CASTING

As on *Pride & Prejudice*, Joe Wright made sure to cast actors who were of ages comparable to the characters they would be playing in *Atonement*. As before, he and the producers were set on Keira Knightley as their leading lady.

Wright clarifies, "I felt that Keira, who is such an intuitive actress, was ready to play Cecilia because the truth is that the part is a character role rather than that of the pretty leading lady. It's a very complex role; Cecilia is not a particularly likable person to start with, but she is redeemed by her love of Robbie and by his of her."

Knightley says, "I had a great experience on *Pride & Prejudice*; Joe is a sensational director. He makes sure that every actor sees the story from their character's point of view. After reading Christopher Hampton's beautiful script, I knew I wanted to play Cecilia."

Paul Webster notes, "The strong working relationship that Joe and Keira developed over the course of filming *Pride & Prejudice* meant they had a mutual understanding and respect that would enable them to effectively approach Cecilia together.

Wright enthuses, "Keira was not afraid of playing Cecilia as cold and difficult, and awkward in her own skin. She was brave in taking this role, since many actors are terrified of being disliked as the characters they play on-screen. The resulting performance is, I believe, her boldest and strongest to date."

For Knightley, there was considerable appeal in playing a character so different than any she has played in her career thus far. She explains, "The reason I liked this character is because she is a *woman*, of the kind Bette Davis might have played. She knows who she is, yet she doesn't know which direction to go in, so she's quite conflicted. She doesn't realize that actually she fancies Robbie; she's grown up with him, and at first won't admit that there's anything between them beyond a kind of brother-and-sister relationship. But, there is, and when we meet them they're on the brink."

The male lead role of Robbie Turner, the son of the Tallis family housekeeper with a Cambridge education courtesy of the Tallis family, called for an actor who, notes Wright, "had the acting ability to take the audience with him on his personal and physical journey."

McAvoy saw the story as "epic, romantic, and really about what it is to be a human being. It affected—and still affects—me hugely, and I hope it will do the same to audiences. *Atonement* also explores the truth of how we are at our best when we are being attacked, and Robbie Turner is forced to fight on two fronts."

Wright adds, "I'd first seen James in a play about seven years ago, and I could tell how good he was. I'd offered him parts twice before, and this third time was the charm. James has working-class roots, and that was very important; Robbie's story is that of a working-class boy whose life is often at the mercy of the snobbery of an upper-class family. James also has a deep soul, and isn't afraid to show it. The character is described by Ian McEwan as having 'eyes of optimism,' and James has those. When he smiles, you smile; when he cries, you cry."

McEwan adds, "Later in the story, it is written that 'there is a stamp of experience in the corners of his eyes.' Through James' performance, you feel the pathos."

Even so, as McAvoy notes, "Joe would tell me, 'Don't beg them to cry,' meaning, the audience. Robbie was one of the most difficult characters I've ever played, because he's very straight-ahead. In the 1935 scenes, the family doesn't see him as one of them, yet he doesn't have a chip on his shoulder. Joe was very keen not to be manipulative with the audience, so he emphasized underplaying. So, later in the story, when Robbie explodes, you really feel it.

"As a director, Joe knows how to choreograph his scenes, understands the story he's telling, respects his crew, and loves actors; he made me a better actor on *Atonement*."

Knightley reveals, "Joe would direct us to deliver our lines swiftly; he wanted the dialogue scenes to play as they did in classic British movies. He likened it to rain pattering down, or bullets firing. Doing that informed our performances and showed us who our characters were; it was exciting to play, because that particular style of speaking is now lost. It's like doing an accent, yet it made everything easier."

Wright clarifies, "The actors in 1930s and 1940s movies had a naturalism to their performances. I wanted to recapture that with this cast; I showed them *Rebecca*, *Brief Encounter*—which James and Keira particularly adore—and *In Which We Serve*, to name a few."

McAvoy laughs, "Keira just *flew* with that style of acting. For the rest of us, it took a little bit longer!

"Joe's basic instructions to me were very simple: 'Stop acting and stop trying. Less is more.' He taught me to do away with acting that you *think* you need to do."

McEwan says, "Keira and James are superb together. I particularly liked the scene in the library. This is a wonderful release of tension for Cecilia—a brittle upper-class young woman, divorced from her own feelings. In the library, she confronts them in a flood of strong emotion and erotic charge."

Bevan adds, "James is poised to become a movie star; he gives a fantastic performance in *Atonement*."

Casting not one but three Briony Tallises was a challenge the filmmakers happily met, albeit not in order of their on-screen appearances. While Academy Award winner Vanessa Redgrave was everyone's ideal to play the older Briony, and committed to the role after one meeting with Wright, the younger incarnations proved tougher to cast.

After many auditions and much searching for an actress to play Briony at age 13, casting director Jina Jay (who also cast *Pride & Prejudice*) came across Saoirse (pronounced "sear-sha") Ronan. The Irish actress, at the time 12 years old, has, according to Wright, "a keen sensibility which belies her years, making her perfect for the role of the young writer."

The young actress saw her character as "a girl with a very creative imagination; she can go off by herself and write stories and plays. She makes herself believe things, and after a while, she decides to go with her imagination and to believe herself instead of anyone else.

"I felt so lucky to have gotten this fantastic part. Working with Joe—who explains everything so well and so clearly—and everyone was just really special. Hopefully I'll be like Keira when I'm her age, making intelligent choices as an actress."

On the set, Wright only grew more and more impressed with Ronan. He says, "So much rests on her shoulders in that first section. Without a brilliant Briony at age thirteen, we would have been in trouble...A lot of actors draw on their own emotional experience; in a way they substitute their characters' emotion for their own emotion, and vice versa, and there's no right or wrong way of doing that.

"But Saoirse doesn't. She purely *imagined* what it would be like to be Briony Tallis, who is nothing like her. Saoirse has such empathy that she can feel and express the emotions of another human being. That's an incredible talent to have; every day she would surprise me, and fill all of us with awe."

McEwan marvels, "What a remarkable young actress Saoirse is. She gives us thought processes right on-screen, even before she speaks, and conveys so much with her eyes."

Speaking of which, adds Wright, "I consciously chose three actresses with strong eyes; Briony is the eyes of the film, which is conveyed when each of the three Brionys looks straight at the camera lens."

Hampton remarks, "With these three actresses, there is no doubt that you are seeing Briony Tallis throughout the course of her life. The hospital sequences are particular favorites of mine; Romola Garai has a quality of gravity that enhances the second section of the film."

Garai, who plays Briony at age 18, was the last of this trio to be cast. Accordingly, she was obliged to adapt her performance's physicality to fit into the Briony appearance that had already been decided upon for Ronan and Redgrave. Garai rose to the challenge, spending time with Ronan and watching footage of her to approximate the way the younger actress moved. All three actresses worked with a voice coach to keep the character's timbre in a similar range throughout the story.

Having read the book prior, Garai saw Briony as "an amazing character, and so precisely created. I usually play more outgoing characters, but after what happens in the first part of the story, Briony has become highly insular and not able to express herself.

"Joe does not have that problem; he's so honest with actors in his directions. Since I have to follow Saoirse's performance in the story, it was good to have someone who sees all for Briony and knows the character best; he was able to say, 'This is what she's thinking' or 'This is how she feels right now.'

With such a clear vision of what he wants the film to be, his was a working style that I really responded to."

Tim Bevan observes, "Romola is one of a very exciting group of new-generation British actors right now. Joe has four of them in *Atonement:* James, Keira, Romola, and Benedict Cumberbatch."

Cumberbatch is reunited with McAvoy after previously starring together in *Starter for Ten*; he was cast in *Atonement* as Paul Marshall, the chocolate company heir whose stay with the Tallises proves eventful in the first portion of the film.

In addition to Knightley, Wright was able to reconvene two more *Pride & Prejudice* actors: Brenda Blethyn and Peter Wight signed on for small but pivotal roles.

"They've cast *Atonement* superbly, and the precision of the performances shows how good a director Joe is," sums up McEwan.

## PREPARATION AND PRODUCTION

Even as *Pride & Prejudice* was still playing around the world, Joe Wright and the trio of producers were asking members of the team to ready for the new movie together. Executive producers Debra Hayward and Liza Chasin, and co-producer Jane Frazer, would again be on board.

More valued key collaborators encored: production designer Sarah Greenwood, costume designer Jacqueline Durran, composer Dario Marianelli—all of whom had earned Academy Award nominations for their work on *Pride & Prejudice*—and editor Paul Tothill. Cinematographer Seamus McGarvey and hair and make-up designer Ivana Primorac, who had themselves worked together on *The Hours*, newly rounded out Wright's team.

Greenwood affirms, "Joe likes to run a film like a repertory company, using the same team. It's a very creative way of working, and you can hit the ground running because there's a shorthand."

Paul Webster adds, "There's also a trust and a strength that are gained from a director having a team back together. The ideas and information flow."

Wright meticulously prepared for production, actively engaging with every department early on to communicate his vision, in order that the "book that happened in his head" could be dramatized on-screen and that once filming began, everyone was on the same page of that book.

"He's the most prepared director I've ever worked with," states Webster. "Once he has the film in his head, he designs it shot by shot and scene by scene with the cinematographer. He plots out every location. Then, he shares all this information with *everyone*, which is—in my experience—unique for a director.

"Before shooting begins, we are given a plan of the film, with everything down on paper: shot diagrams, storyboards, pictures. On those occasions when it changes during production, everyone gets the updates. What's especially exciting is that the camera becomes the writer."

"Joe has a strong vision," offers Durran. "He will be quite specific about the look he wants, but he will also be open to your suggestions."

The director conducted a three-week rehearsal period with the cast, ensuring that by the time the cameras rolled all the actors were comfortable with their characters and the environment(s) they inhabited. This afforded several members of the cast the chance to confer with fellow actors who were in different periods of the story.

Vanessa Redgrave says, "Saoirse Ronan and Romola Garai and I did some improvisations on body language, among other things, for Briony. Joe—who is brilliant with actors—was able to pick and choose what he wanted focused on during the filming."

Wright adds, "We had meals together and talked to each other so that everyone would be able to express their emotions, including when we began filming. This way, there was no tension blocking communication."

James McAvoy reveals, "We also learned dances like the foxtrot. Now, there's not much dancing in the film, but spending an hour every day for three weeks doing this made the cast bond."

Research was actively encouraged; Keira Knightley's extensive reading about WWII in the U.K. so fascinated her that she continued exploring those years even after production had wrapped. Actors met with real-life WWII nurses and war veterans, including soldiers who had been at the Battle of Dunkirk.

The three parts of the film were envisioned with very different identities and looks which Wright wanted to subtly convey to the audience through the camera work and different color palettes. This necessitated complete correlation between the director and his heads of departments—McGarvey, Greenwood, Durran, and Primorac in particular. Wright would communicate what he needed and wanted to the department heads, and the departments in turn would unify and enhance each other's work with a shared sensibility that would translate effectively on the set and to the final film.

The department heads worked with a historian and then went on to research and prepare for each part/period; they looked at paintings, photographs, and films, and searched archives for inspiration to fit the story. This was especially important with regard to the WWII era being re-created.

Given the director's preference for location shooting, Greenwood joined location manager Adam Richards (also encoring from *Pride & Prejudice*) in spending months scouring the U.K. for locales that could stand in for the French countryside and the French port of Dunkirk.

Webster notes, "The luxury and beauty of 1935 is fully conveyed; so, too, is war and loss during 1939 and 1940."

Primorac crafted hair and make-up that would subtly convey each period as well as how the characters' circumstances and experiences are affecting them through the years. She notes, "The 1935 segment at the Tallis house has a stylized 1930s look, one heightened to a level that the British aristocracy would not have practiced at that time; we have made their world more glamorous than it even was. There's something of a dreamlike quality, as in Briony's memories of happier times.

"In the second segment's London scenes, the hair and make-up reflect the harsh realities of WWII."

Marianelli was not on the set like the other department heads, yet in a way he was; Wright's preparation had extended to having the composer prepare a scene-setting score for the first day of shooting. The music, shared with the cast and crew, helped to set the tone for the shoot as a whole; other scenes were also shot to pieces of the score that the composer had readied.

Filming of the film's three sections was done almost entirely in sequence. The first part of *Atonement* is set on the hottest day of 1935, at the Tallis family home in Surrey, where the heat seems to affect the behavior of the individuals staying at or visiting the house.

Keira Knightley says, "As the day progresses, you sense unease in the air. In the heat, everything is languid. The people at the house are speaking very fast, yet they can't quite *move* the way they want to."

Wright notes, "The story reveals itself in layers in this section, and it was a wonderful journey for all of us while we were shooting this portion."

Set decorator Katie Spencer, who had been Academy Award–nominated in tandem with Greenwood for *Pride & Prejudice*, rejoined her in searching for the house that would best embody the one described in McEwan's book. The duo visited the archives of the U.K. magazine *Country Life* in the hope that they would come across properties which could be used to film the interior and/or the exterior scenes at the Tallis home on the fateful day and night. Stokesay Court, in Shropshire, had been featured in the magazine and was deemed perfect for both interiors and exteriors.

The script was modified to take into account the realities of the location once it had been set—"a fantastic way of working," enthuses Greenwood. Then, it took seven weeks of preparation to ready Stokesay for five weeks of filming. For the crucial sequence in which Cecilia and Robbie orbit each other as well as a fountain in the garden, Greenwood's team built a fountain over and around the existing Stokesay pond. This afforded a protective measure for the intact original structure, as well as creating a setting that even more strongly complements the actors' performances.

Knightley muses, "Stokesay was such a gift because it is a private home, so it was all ours; on *Pride & Prejudice*, we had beautiful locations where we would be doing intimate scenes while tour groups were there taking pictures...

"Joe brought us in a day ahead of the shoot, so we could spend time in our bedrooms and walk around the grounds. To be able to do all the interiors there as well was extraordinary."

McAvoy concurs, noting, "We stayed there for the whole shoot. There wasn't a couple of minutes' drive to the set each morning; it was a couple of minutes' walk. Joe knew we would get a sense of ownership, in addition to a sense of space and place. I think that familiarity comes across on-screen."

Greenwood adds, "We shot at Stokesay during the summer. It was very lush there, and luckily they'd had a lot of rain so there was a very verdant quality to the grounds. Even luckier, it really *was* very hot during shooting!"

Webster notes, "Sarah and Katie really got into the detail of the story, and paid special attention to what was going on in design in the 1930s. In the first part, everything is ripe to the point of corruption, and they have used the patterns of chintz—which are quite popular today as well. The wallpapers and fabrics and Jacqueline's costumes were all crucial to getting across this very dense and rich pattern-upon-pattern ideal."

Greenwood reveals, "The main difference between Jacqueline's costumes and the patterns that my department was using is that her colors are more vibrant than ours; ours were held back, so you have a separation that gives that much greater a contrast between what you see in Surrey and what you see subsequently in London and Dunkirk. The environments are at opposite extremes, so there has to be a juxtaposition of imagery."

McGarvey worked closely with Wright on how the different parts of the film would look. The director says, "Seamus and I used the camera not only to capture the story visually but also as a storytelling device in itself, through the movement and techniques applied."

"At the start of the film, there is dynamism with the camera," notes McGarvey. "There's a rhythm; Briony is restless and full of creative energy, so it's as if she is pulling the camera all over the house and the grounds. Joe didn't want to luxuriate in the period too much; certainly, everything is beautiful, but all the departments also concentrated on making everything look and feel vital to the story.

"The lustrous quality of the 1935 scenes was achieved by using particular filters—and older Christian Dior stockings!—over the lens, which created a beautiful glow. There's a lot of blue in the first part. When things take a darker turn in the first portion, we continue to use the filters, but that sweetness becomes more saccharine. There is a darkness that keeps surfacing, and which is progressed and built upon in the other parts of *Atonement*."

Durran adds, "Joe and I talked about how that summer day is the last perfect moment, before the fall—in both senses of that word.

"With Cecilia in the first part, the idea was that everything she wear be light and transparent, almost like a butterfly. For the backless evening dress, Joe wanted something that would flow because Keira would have to run in it. So we created a fuller skirt and narrower hips, and we picked this specific shade of green. Keira was involved in the process, so it really was a collaboration."

Knightley enthuses, "Jacqueline and her team made such beautiful clothes for me to wear as Cecilia in the 1935 scenes. They did an absolutely incredible job!"

Primorac says, "Keira has less vanity than anyone I've ever met. When we were working guidelines out for Cecilia in 1935—how stiff the waves in her hair would be, for example—Keira was ready for whatever was right for our story.

"When the war starts, we had to convey how Cecilia doesn't have as many resources; she still does her hair, though not as often. The temptation was to go outright from glamorous in the first section to dowdy in the second section. But that's not Cecilia; she would still put on lipstick if she could get one, or had one left over."

In the three parts, three different actresses progressively incarnate Briony Tallis. But a distinct look for the character, and the actresses, had to be maintained through hair and make-up as well as costuming.

Durran elaborates, "This meant keeping the color palate similar; so, because we start off in the first part with Saoirse in blue and off-white, we carry that on to the pale blue-and-white of Romola's nurse's uniform. These colors remain consistent for when you see Vanessa in the third part, wearing a dress that has elements of the dress that Saoirse wears in the first part.

"What I aim for, most of all, is that the costumes contribute to the actors' performances and add something for them and Joe to work with." Primorac and her department paid special attention to everything to the three Brionys. She notes, "We tried to make the lips into similar shapes, and matched their eyelashes and cheekbones. Giving them the same texture of hair tells you, 'This is Briony.' I think we succeeded because of the skill of these actresses, with Saoirse setting the tone.

"The London section was quite complicated because of Briony's working in the hospital, and the wounds that she tends to. But Joe's process is so detailed, and he has researched everything himself, so we knew what was called for."

Also for the second part, McGarvey and Wright adapted the camera technique to convey the change from the rich hues of the Tallis house to grittier wartime London and France. The cinematographer says, "The Dunkirk sequences are more symmetrical; with the homefront in London—

and the war hitting home—we adopt a more handheld and jagged approach to the cinematography. That applied to the light as well, which becomes harder and more brittle and abrupt; there's more contrast in the visuals."

Only eight U.K. military ambulances from WWII remain, and *Atonement* made use of them all. Uniforms from WWII were also used, but Durran had to have the majority made, given how many extras would be in the scenes. She notes, "We sourced original webbing, original helmets, and original hobnail boots, among other elements."

All of the nurses' uniforms had to be created, again with originals as reference points. Durran clarifies, "With the blue-and-white stripes, we did effect a change from the original lilac-and-white; we also modified what is worn in one scene, for dramatic purposes. All else, we got as right as we could, down to the Nightingale badges being reproduced for those qualifying nurses; you see Cecilia still wearing one, but by that point in the story she has moved on to another hospital."

When WWII sends Robbie and his British Expeditionary Force (BEF) unit through France, the full scale—human and spatial—of the army's retreat from and at Dunkirk is captured in a single shot worked out by Wright and McGarvey with steadicam operator Peter Robertson.

Wright says, "The sequence was originally scripted as a montage. But that would have required thirty to forty set-ups in a single day, with consistent light. So we went a different route."

McGarvey adds, "We wanted something that would evolve within the scene itself, and was appropriate for the context. The conventional way to shoot what Robbie is seeing would be to go for a wide shot with a longer lens. With this shot, you are with Robbie, so you share his point of view and also see his face, his reaction to it all."

The sequence was filmed on location at the seaside town of Redcar, with its existing beach and Corus Steelworks industrial landscape; 1,000 locals were employed to portray wounded or dying U.K. soldiers stranded on the beach at Dunkirk while awaiting safe passage home in 1940.

Greenwood notes, "Joe wanted the scale to be fully conveyed. To me, this shot says everything about Dunkirk—and about Robbie's journey."

Ian McEwan reveals, "My father was in or attached to the British army for fifty years. He was on the beach at Dunkirk, severely wounded and then evacuated. When he talked about it, you could see the darkness of the memory, yet also the sense that it was when he felt most fully alive."

McAvoy reflects, "We talked to one veteran who couldn't tell us a lot. He said, 'When you're doing it, boys, just think about how bad it really was.' It was hard for him to even say that to us."

All departments worked together to marshal for the sequence—among many other elements—a bandstand, French and British army weapons both vintage and re-created, a working ferris wheel, bombed-out buildings, a huge beached Thames barge, a choir in performance, and show horses.

In the five-and-one-half minute uninterrupted shot, the camera follows James McAvoy, Daniel Mays, and Nonso Anozie—as Robbie and the two other surviving British soldiers from his decimated unit—as they tenaciously search for any quieter space to try to decompress in.

Webster says, "James' powers of concentration and transformation impressed me all through the shoot. When it came time to shoot this sequence, he was moving through it all and reacting—which, in a way, is the hardest kind of acting. Robbie witnesses a lot, and James conveys his inner state brilliantly."

Tim Bevan comments, "In all of our movies, we've only ever done one sequence even close to this; this is epic, and spectacular—but the spectacle is there to emphasize the very emotional feeling of the sequence, of how it was for these young men nearly seventy years ago.

"The shot is also an example of the magic of cinema when you have something epic like this, you catch it on film, and then it's gone—in terms of the set and the moment. Then it lives forever in the movie."

McGarvey elaborates, "It was what filmmaking is all about—collaboration. Bear in mind that in addition to the 1,000 extras, there were 300 crew members at work—all without a weak link in the people chain."

Wright remembers, "It was very, very exciting and I loved doing it. We spent all day rehearsing it, from 6 a.m. to 6:30 p.m. The next day, we did one more rehearsal and then shot three takes. It became like a piece of theater. The light was amazing; I had faith that it would be. We were all so engaged and involved; everybody realized what we were trying to achieve."

Throughout post-production as well, departments worked in harmony, with special regard to the sound and editing processes. From the enhanced sound effect of rushing water when Cecilia emerges from the Tallis estate's fountain to the clipped upper-class accents of the Tallis family to the inter-weaving of the sound of typewriter keys into Dario Marianelli's score, every detail was worked out and unified.

Wright notes, "Our editor Paul Tothill is a master of sound, and we built up the sound as we edited. We wanted to make the picture and the sound-track into an integrated, cohesive whole. Dario would give us so much to work with."

For scoring, Marianelli reconvened key *Pride & Prejudice* collaborators, including—to perform the score he composed—the English Chamber Orchestra.

"*Atonement* is a cinematic symphony," assesses Redgrave. "In cinema terms, it's a real *film*—and a heartrending one."

Christopher Hampton says, "Joe has a strong grasp of what's doable in the editing room with Paul. The finished film moves like an express train."

Wright says, "The nine-month post-production process was delicate; we had to be sensitive to what the material was telling us. All the way through, our producers made me more confident on *Atonement* than even on *Pride & Prejudice*."

Bevan comments, "Joe is still hungry; he's always the one to leap from the front, be up earlier and work later, and always striving for a greater quality."

Paul Webster adds, "He's a great romantic who communicates philo-sophical themes and ideas in cinematic form so that they are comprehensible to the filmgoer. Like all good artists, he explores stories that reflect himself and his view of the world."

Wright concludes, "I'm honored to have had the chance to make this film, and to have worked with the people I did on it.

"*Atonement* is so close to me that I cannot look at it objectively; but, other people's work, I can look at objectively—and I am incredibly proud of what our cast and crew achieved."

## THE LOCATIONS

As with *Pride & Prejudice*, *Atonement* was made by the filmmaking team on locations all over Britain. Some of the specific shooting sites were:

## Stokesay Court, Shropshire

Stokesay Court is a Victorian house (built in 1889) which forms part of the privately owned Stokesay estate in the county of Shropshire. All the exteriors and interiors of the Tallis home and the Turner cottage were filmed at Stokesay.

## London

London locations included Whitehall and Bethnal Green Town Hall. The latter was used for the scene where Cecilia and Robbie are reunited in 1939 at a tea house.

The underground Balham station scene set in 1940 was filmed at the closed tube (a.k.a. subway) station Aldwych.

A street in the Streatham neighborhood was dressed for the scene set in Balham when Briony, at age 18, is looking for where Cecilia is living.

The St. Thomas's hospital ward interior and corridors were built as a studio set at Shepperton Studios. However, the hospital's storeroom, day room, and nurses' dormitory scenes were filmed at Park Place, Henley Upon Thames; the exterior of the hospital was actually University College.

The wedding scene was filmed at St. John's Church, Smith Square.

The third portion of *Atonement* was filmed at the BBC Studios in Wood Lane.

## Dunkirk and the French Countryside

The scenes with Robbie and his fellow soldiers making their way through the French countryside en route to Dunkirk were filmed in Coates and Gedney Drove End, in Lincolnshire; in Walpole St. Andrew and Denver, in Norfolk; and in March and Pymore, in Cambridgeshire.

The poppy field scene was shot in Cheltenham, Gloucestershire.

The light industrial quarter scenes were filmed at the Grimsby fish docks; the heavy industrial quarter, as well as the marshland, scenes were filmed at Corus Steelworks, in Redcar. The latter's beach was the site of the Dunkirk beach sequence, and also stood in for the Bray dunes.

The French cinema at Dunkirk that Robbie drifts through was in fact Redcar's venerable Regent Cinema, which is located on the pier at the beach.

# CAST AND CREW CREDITS

FOCUS FEATURES presents
In association with STUDIOCANAL and RELATIVITY MEDIA
A WORKING TITLE Production

# ATONEMENT

JAMES McAVOY   KEIRA KNIGHTLEY   ROMOLA GARAI   SAOIRSE RONAN  and VANESSA REDGRAVE
BRENDA BLETHYN  JUNO TEMPLE  BENEDICT CUMBERBATCH  PATRICK KENNEDY
HARRIET WALTER  PETER WIGHT  DANIEL MAYS  NONSO ANOZIE
GINA McKEE  JÉRÉMIE RÉNIER  MICHELLE DUNCAN

| | | |
|---|---|---|
| Directed by<br>JOE WRIGHT | Executive Producers<br>DEBRA HAYWARD<br>LIZA CHASIN | Costume Designer<br>JACQUELINE DURRAN |
| Produced by<br>TIM BEVAN<br>ERIC FELLNER<br>PAUL WEBSTER | Co-Producer<br>JANE FRAZER | Hair & Make-Up Designer<br>IVANA PRIMORAC |
| Screenplay by<br>CHRISTOPHER HAMPTON | Director of Photography<br>SEAMUS McGARVEY BSC | Music by<br>DARIO MARIANELLI |
| Based on the novel by<br>IAN McEWAN | Production Designer<br>SARAH GREENWOOD | Music Supervisor<br>NICK ANGEL |
| Executive Producers<br>RICHARD EYRE<br>ROBERT FOX<br>IAN McEWAN | Film Editor<br>PAUL TOTHILL A.C.E | Casting by<br>JINA JAY |

## CAST

(In order of appearance)

Briony Tallis, aged 13 . SAOIRSE RONAN
Singing Housemaid . . AILIDH MACKAY
Grace Turner . . . . BRENDA BLETHYN
Betty . . . . . . . . . . . JULIA WEST
Robbie Turner . . . . . JAMES McAVOY
Emily Tallis . . . . . HARRIET WALTER
Cecilia Tallis . . . KEIRA KNIGHTLEY
Lola Quincey . . . . . . JUNO TEMPLE
Pierrot Quincey . . FELIX VON SIMSON
Jackson Quincey
. . . . . . . . CHARLIE VON SIMSON
Danny Hardman . . . . . ALFIE ALLEN
Leon Tallis . . . . . PATRICK KENNEDY
Paul Marshall
. . . . . . BENEDICT CUMBERBATCH
Police Inspector . . . . . PETER WIGHT
Police Constable . . . LEANDER DEENY
Police Sergeant
. . . . . . PETER McNEIL O'CONNOR
Tommy Nettle . . . . . . DANIEL MAYS
Frank Mace . . . . . NONSO ANOZIE
Frenchmen . . . MICHEL VUILLERMOZ
LIONEL ABELANSKI
Naval Officer . . . . . TOBIAS MENZIES

Crying Soldier . . . . . PAUL STOCKER
Solitary Sunbather . . . . ALEX NOODLE
Beach Soldiers . . ROGER EVANS, BRONSON
WEBB, IAN BONAR, OLIVER GILBERT
Soldiers in Bray Bar . . . JAMIE BEAMISH,
JOHNNY HARRIS, NICK BAGNALL,
BILLY SEYMOUR, NEIL MASKELL
Soldier with Ukelele . . . PAUL HARPER
Sister Drummond . . . . . . GINA McKEE
Probationary Nurses . . CHARLIE BANKS,
MADELEINE CROWE, SCARLETT
DALTON, OLIVIA GRANT, KATY
LAWRENCE, JADE MOULLA,
GEORGIA OAKLEY, ALICE ORR-
EWING, CATHERINE PHILPS, BRYONY
REISS, SARAH SHAUL, ANNA
SINGLETON, EMILY THOMSON
Fiona Maguire . . MICHELLE DUNCAN
Briony, 18 . . . . . . . ROMOLA GARAI
Hospital Admin Assistant . . KELLY SCOTT
Soldier at Hospital Entrance
. . . . . . . . . . . MARK HOLGATE
Registrar . . . . . . . . RYAN KIGGELL
Staff Nurse . . . . . . VIVIENNE GIBBS
Second Soldier at Hospital Entrance
. . . . . . . . . . MATTHEW FOREST

Injured Sergeant . . . RICHARD STACEY
Soldier Who Looks Like Robbie. . JAY QUINN
Luc Cornet . . . . . . JÉRÉMIE RÉNIER
Vicar . . . . . . JOHN NORMINGTON
Pierrot, 14 . . . . . JACK HARCOURT
Jackson, 14 . . . . . BEN HARCOURT
Mother of Evacuees . TILLY VOSBURGH
Evacuee Children . . . ANGEL WITNEY,
        BONNIE WITNEY, BEN WEBB
Mrs Jarvis . . . WENDY NOTTINGHAM
Older Briony . . . VANESSA REDGRAVE
Interviewer . . ANTHONY MINGHELLA

### CREW

Production Manager . . SIMON FRASER
First Assistant Director
. . . . . . . . . . . JOSH ROBERTSON
'A' Camera/Steadicam Operator
. . . . . . . . . PETER ROBERTSON
Second Unit Director. . THOMAS NAPPER
Production Sound Mixer
. . . . . . . . . DANNY HAMBROOK
Production Accountant
. . . . . . . . . . . BETTY WILLIAMS
Location Manager . . ADAM RICHARDS
Script Supervisor . . . . . . . SUE HILLS
Supervising Art Director . . . IAN BAILIE
Set Decorator . . . . . KATIE SPENCER
Post Production Supervisor
. . . . . . . . . DEBORAH HARDING
Re-Recording Mixer . . PAUL HAMBLIN
Supervising Sound Editor
. . . . . . . . CATHERINE HODGSON
Post Production Accountant
. . . . . . . . . . . . TARN HARPER

### FOR WORKING TITLE
Chief Operating Officer
. . . . . . . . . ANGELA MORRISON
Executive in Charge of Production
. . . . . . . . . . MICHELLE WRIGHT
Production Executive
. . . . . . . SARAH-JANE ROBINSON
Head of Development
. . . . . . . . NATASCHA WHARTON
Head of Legal and Business Affairs
. . . . . . . . . . . SHEERAZ SHAH
Finance Director . . . . TIM EASTHILL
Development Executive
. . . . . . . . . . AMELIA GRANGER
Vice President of Legal and Business Affairs
. . . . . . . . . GRÁINNE McKENNA
Legal and Business Affairs Executive
. . . . . . . . . LUCY WAINWRIGHT

Executive Co-ordinator . . . ANN LYNCH
Legal and Business Affairs Manager
. . . . . . CHRISTINA ANGELOUDES
Assistant Production Co-ordinator
. . . . . . . . . . . JESSICA FORTE
Assistant to Tim Bevan
. . . . . . . . . . CHLOÉ DORIGAN
Assistant to Eric Fellner . . . ALIZA JAMES
Music Co-ordinator . . VICKI WILLIAMS
### PRODUCTION SERVICES
### BY SCION FILMS
Production Co-ordinator
. . . . SAMANTHA KNOX-JOHNSTON
Assistant Production Co-ordinator
. . . . . . . . . . . . . JO WALLETT
Second Assistant Director
. . . . . . . . . . . WILLIAM DODDS
Crowd Second Assistant Directors
. . . . . . . . . . CANDY MARLOWE
        NICK SHUTTLEWORTH
Third Assistant Director. . TOM BREWSTER
Assistant to Joe Wright. . ANNA EDWARDS
Assistant to Paul Webster and Jane Frazer
. . . . . . . . . . . . JESSICA COLE
Post Production Assistant to Paul Webster
. . . . . . . . . . . . . JO DAVIES
Production Secretary . . SARAH LINDFIELD
Production Runner . . . . SARAH PAYNE
Asset Manager . . . . . JULIE STREETER
Floor Runners . . JAE-SUNG OH, CARLY
        LEWISOHN, SARAH HOOD
Crowd Runners . . JO BRADMAN, SAM
                ROOK
Child Casting Director . . DIXIE CHASSAY
Casting Assistant . . . . ROBIN HUDSON
First Assistant 'A' Camera
. . . . . . . . CARLOS DE CARVALHO
Second Assistant 'A' Camera
. . . . . . . . . . . JENNIE PADDON
Grip 'A' Camera . . GARY HUTCHINGS
First Assistant 'B' Camera
. . . . . . . . . . . RAWDON HAYNE
Second Assistant 'B' Camera
. . . . . . . . . . . . IAIN MACKAY
Grip 'B' Camera . . . . . DEAN MORRIS
FT2 Trainee . . . . . . CHRIS McALEESE
Video Assist Operator . . NICK KENEALY
Apprentice Grip . . . . SIMON THORPE
Sound Maintenance
. . . . . . . . . ADAM LASCHINGER
Cable Man . . . . . . CHRIS ATKINSON
Unit Manager . . . . . ERICA BENSLY
Assistant Location Manager
. . . . . . . . . HARRIET SUTCLIFFE

Assistant Location Manager — Redcar
. . . . . . . . . . . . . MALLY CHUNG
Location Assistants . . JUSTIN GREGORY,
RORY SHAW, SARAH SHEPHERD,
TOM MAGNUS
Assistant Accountants. . DEBORAH LEAKEY,
CRISTIANO D'URSO, DIARMUID
COGHLAN, DEBBIE MOSELEY,
DAVID WILCOCK
First Assistant Editor
. . . . . . . . BRIDGETTE WILLIAMS
Location and Post Assistant Editor
. . . . . . . . . . . GABRIELLE SMITH
Second Assistant Editor
. . . . . . . . . . MATT STREATFIELD
Supervising Dialogue Editor
. . . . . . . . . . . . BECKI PONTING
Dialogue Editor . . . ANDRE SCHMIDT
Foley Recordist/Mixer
. . . . ALEXANDROS SIDIROPOULOS
Foley Editor . . . . . VIRGINIA THORN
Costume Supervisor . . DAVID CROSSMAN
Assistant Costume Designer
. . . . . . . . . . . ANDREA CRIPPS
Wardrobe Supervisor
. . . . . . . . . CHARLOTTE FINLAY
Wardrobe Master . . . . ANDREW HUNT
Wardrobe Mistress . . AMANDA TREWIN
Costume Makers . . . . JENNY ALFORD
JO VAN SCHUPPEN
Costume Breakdown . . EMMA WALKER
Key Costume Assistant
. . . . . . . . . . ANDREW FLETCHER
Fabric Buyer. . RACHELE VERRECCHIA
Wardrobe Assistants. . . BARTHOLOMEW
CARISS, DAVE CROUCHER, CARIN
HOFF, ADAM ROACH, ESTHER ST
JOHN GRAY, HOLLY WADDINGTON
Make-Up and Hair Artists. . . . . NORMA
WEBB, DEBORAH JARVIS, ANDREA
FINCH, LISA PICKERING,
ANDY SESTON
Make-Up Trainee . . . MELANIE DAVEY
Art Directors . . . . . NIALL MORONEY
NICK GOTTSCHALK
Standby Art Director. . NETTY CHAPMAN
Assistant Art Directors. . LOTTA WOLGERS
EMMA VANE
Assistant Art Director – Graphics
. . . . . . . . . GEORGINA MILLETT
Draftspersons . . SARAH STUART, TOM
WHITEHEAD, PETER NEWTON
DORME, TIM BROWNING
Junior Draftsperson. . OLIVER GOODIER

Art Department Co-ordinator
. . . . . . . . . . MICHELLE BARBER
Art Department Assistant . . LUKE EDWARDS
Art Department Runner. . POPPY LEATHER
Art Department Trainee . . . IZZI DUNHILL
Drapes . . . . . . . . . . . COLIN FOX
Drapes Assistant . . . LAURENT FERRIE
Prop Maker . . . . . ROWAN HARRIS
Action Vehicle Co-ordinator
. . . . . . . . . . . STEVE LAMONBY
Production Buyer. . . . ALISON HARVEY
Assistant Set Decorator . . SOPHIE TYLER
Assistant Production Buyer. . ALISON CARDY
Prop Buyer Runner
. . . . . . . . ELLY MARIE MEYRICK
Home Economist . . . KATHARINE TIDY
Property Master . . . DENNIS WISEMAN
Dressing Propmen . . MARK BILLINGHAM,
KENNY BURNETT, THEO HUTCH-
CRAFT, GARY MARTIN, ADRIAN
PLATT, LEE WISEMAN
Property Storeman . . . PAUL EMERSON
Standby Propmen . . . . . . ALEX KING,
ROB MacPHERSON, JOSH BARRAUD
Standby Greensman . . . . . JOSHUA LEE
Standby Painter . . SIMON HUTCHINGS
Standby Carpenter . . . . PETE LENNOX
Standby Stagehand . . . . . NIGEL ROSS
Standby Rigger . . . TERRY RICHARDS
Construction Managers . . . . . STUART
WATSON, ROB BROWN
HOD Carpenter . . . . TONY HOSKINS
Supervising Carpenter . . RUSS SARGENT
Carpenters . . . . . . . IAN BEE, DEREK
BELLCHAMBERS, CHRIS BROUGH,
DAVID CHETTLEBOROUGH, ANDY
GOOD, BARNABY INMAN, NICK
LLOYD, GRAHAM MITCHELL,
DOMINIC PIKE, LUKE SARGENT,
LEIGH THURBON, ALEX WELLS,
DAVID WELLS, JOHN WHITBY,
CHRISTOPHER WHITE, LES WYLIE
HOD Painter . . . . . DAVID T HAYNES
Supervising Painter . . . . . GLYN EVANS
Chargehand Painter . . . . . PAUL BALE
Painters. . . . . JIM FENNESSY, DAVID G
HAYNES, GARY GLEESON, ANTHONY
GODDARD, LEE GODDARD, JOHN
MALHAM, STEPHEN MARQUISS,
STEVE SIBLEY
HOD Scenic Painter . . JAMES GEMMILL
Scenic Painter . . . . . RUSSELL OXLEY
Signwriter . . . . . . TONY STATHAM
HOD Stagehand . . . . EDDIE O'NEILL

Supervising Stagehand . . . GARY EVANS
Stagehand . . . . . . NEIL ROBERTSON
Chargehand Plasterer . . MARK BEWLEY
Plasterers . . . ADRIAN AITKEN, KEITH
CHARLES, WILLIAM CLARKE,
STEVEN PONTING, PAUL TRIPP
HOD Sculptor . . . . . STEVE HUNTER
Sculptors . . . MARK BARNETT, DAVID
HERBERT, AMELIA ROWCROFT,
MARK STOWE
Gaffer . . . . . . . . . . PERRY EVANS
Rigging Gaffer/Best Boy . . . OSSA MILLS
Chargehand Electrician
. . . . . . . . . . RICKY PATTENDEN
Electricians . . . . REG BODDY, MARK
CLARK, MARK 'ROCKY' EVANS,
DAVID SINFIELD, JAMES SMART
Generator Operator . . . ALAN GROSCH
HOD Rigger . . . . . . . ROY ELSTON
Rigger . . . . . . KENNY RICHARDS
HOD Electrical Rigger . . PAUL HARFORD
Electrical Rigger . . . . RICHARD LAW
ROBERT 'NOBBY' CLARKE
Special Effects Supervisor . . MARK HOLT
Senior Special Effects Technicians . . JAMES
DAVIS, HUGH GOODBODY, RUSSELL
PRITCHETT
Special Effects Technicians . . . . MARTIN
GEESON, PETER KERSEY, NICK
KOOL, NEIL PETERS, MATT RYAN,
JOHN SAVAGE, MIKE TILLEY, JAMIE
WEGUELIN, TREVOR WILLIAMS
Trainee Special Effects Technician
. . . . . . . . . . . . . . . BEN COLES
Stunt Co-ordinator . . . . LEE SHEWARD
Stunt Performers RICHARD BRADSHAW,
ROB COOPER, GEORGE COTTLE,
JAMIE EDGELL, NEIL FINNIGHAN,
BRADLEY FARMER, DAVE FISHER,
GARY HOPTROUGH, PAUL HOWELL,
ROB HUNT, ROB INCH, TIDD JAMES,
MORGAN JOHNSON, DEREK LEA,
JULIAN LIGHTWING, GUY LIST, TONY
LUCKEN, MARK MOTTRAM,
BELINDA McGINLEY, SEON ROGERS,
MATT STIRLING
Miniature Effects . . . THE MODEL UNIT
Model Unit Supervisor . . MIKE TUCKER
Model Unit Director of Photography
. . . . . . . . . . . . . PETER TYLER
Model Unit Gaffer . . . ALAN GRAHAM
Model Makers . . . . . ALAN BRANNAN,
NICK KOOL, NICK SAINTON-CLARK,
SCOTT WAYLAND

Runner . . . . . . . . KELLY DUGGAN
Prosthetics and Body Effects
. . . . . . . . . . ANIMATED EXTRAS
Prosthetic Supervisor . . PAULINE FOWLER
HOD Sculptor . . . . COLIN JACKMAN
Prosthetic Make-Up Artist
. . . . . . . . . . . MATHEW SMITH
Prosthetics and Silicones . . DANIEL MEAKER
Prosthetics and Finishing . . CON McCLOSKY
Prosthetic Painting and Finishing
. . . . . . . . . . . . TRACY O'BRIAN
HOD Mouldmaker . . . NIGEL HEIRONS
Mouldmaker . . . . . DARRYL BROOKE
Underwater Photography
. . . . . . . . . MIKE VALENTINE BSC
Underwater Co-ordinator
. . . . . . . FRANCOISE VALENTINE
First Assistant . . . . . DEAN MORRISH
Second Assistant . . . . . . JAMES LEWIS
Underwater Gaffer . . MARK CAMPANY
Marine Co-ordinator . . . . . IAN CREED
Dive Supervisor . . . . LANCE PALMER
Marine Supervisor . . . . . IAN NICHOLS
Safety Divers . . . CLINT BAILEY, MARK
DYER, PHIL ANDERSON-HANNEY,
SIMON MURRAY
Unit Publicist . . . . RACHEL KENNEDY
Stills Photographer . . . . . ALEX BAILEY
EPK . . . . . . . . . SPECIAL TREATS
Dialogue Coach . . . . . . NEIL SWAIN
Choreographer . . . . . . . JANE GIBSON
Tutor . . . . . CHRISTOPHER PRING
French Tutor . . . . . . YVES BALLARD
Harmonica Tutor . . . DAVID MUNDAY
Chaperones . . . . . . . BELYNDA DAY
MONICA RONAN
Stand-Ins . . . . . JAMES PAYTON, AMY
IRVINE, REBECCA SURTEES, ELLEN
ORCHARD, FRED WINDSOR-CLIVE,
BEATRICE BRENNAN, JASON DEVIL
Historical Advisor . . JULIET GARDINER
Medical Advisors . . . . . . . JON SIONS
LUCY PLEASENCE
Military Advisor . . . . . ANDY LINDLEY
Health and Safety . . MEDIA SAFETY LTD
Unit Nurse . . . . . . SAM GOLDSMITH
ENIGMA NURSING AND CARE
Caterers . . . . . . . . . . REEL MEALS
MEGAN MORRISON
Transport Captain . . . GERRY GORE
Driver to Joe Wright . . COLIN SIMMONS
Driver to Paul Webster . . ERIC FRANCKS
Driver/Security to Keira Knightley
. . . . . . . . . . . MARCUS WARD

Unit Drivers . . . . . . . JOHN BURDEN,
GEORGE CACCAVALE, JOHN DAWSON,
EDDIE KAY, EDDIE McLAUGHLIN,
SHAHIN MOATAZED' KEYVANY, MARK
RICHARDS, BIROL SAHIN
Minibus Drivers . . . CHRIS HAMMON,
JOHN KEMP, GAVIN MULLINS
Standby Construction Driver
. . . . . . . . . . . . . TONY POWER
Camera Car Driver . . . . . ALAN JONES
Prop Truck Driver . . . . BRIAN HEATH
EDDIE RODMELL
Grip Truck Driver. . MARK HATCHWELL
Wardrobe Truck Driver
. . . . . . . . . COLIN BRESSINGTON
Make-Up Truck . . . . . . . PAUL JONES
Artist Trailers . . . . . . . DAVE JONES
Vehicle Construction . . . . REG CAPSON,
STUART HARRINGTON, DENNIS
PAPALEO, RONNIE PAPALEO, HANK
SCHUMACHER, PETER TOMBS, COLIN
WATERWORTH, GEORGE WILLIAMS
SECOND UNIT
Second Assistant Directors. . . . STEWART
HAMILTON, MICHAEL STEVENSON
Camera Operator . . . . . SIMON BAKER
First Assistant Camera
. . . . . . . HAMISH DOYNE-DITMAS
Second Assistant Camera . . . SALLY LOW
Grips . . . . STUART GODFREY, DAVID
MAUND, ANDY HOPKINS
Crane Operator . . . . . PAUL LEGALL
Camera Revolution . . . . JOE BUXTON
DIGITAL VISUAL EFFECTS
BY DOUBLE NEGATIVE
Visual Effects Supervisor . . JOHN MOFFATT
CG Supervisor . . . . . . RYAN COOK
Lead Compositor . . . ADRIAN BANTON
Executive Producer . . . . . ALEX HOPE

Producers . . . . . . . STUART McARA
KRISTOPHER WRIGHT
3D Artists . . . . . . . . PAUL DUCKER
JULIAN FODDY

Compositors . . . MICHAEL BELL, PAUL
NORRIS, GRUFF OWEN,
FLORIAN SCHROEDER
Matte Painting . . . . . GUREL MEHMET
Rotoscope Artists . . . . . BIMLA CHALL,
MATTHEW JACQUES, JOHN
MOFFETT, AMI PATEL
Match Move Artist . . ALLISON FARMER
Editorial . . . . . . . SARAH BARKER

Studio . . . . . . . . PETER HANSON

DIGITAL INTERMEDIATE BY
DELUXE DIGITAL ENTERTAINMENT
Digital Colourist . . . . . . ADAM INGLIS
Digital Intermediate Producer
. . . . . . . . MARCUS ALEXANDER
Digital Intermediate Editor
. . . . . . . . . . . . JOSH SUTCLIFFE
Digital Colour Assist . . . ANDREW LIM
Scanning . . . . . . . . . . BOB ROACH
Record . . . . . . . . . PAUL DOOGAN
Title Design by . . TOM HINGSTON STUDIO
Titles Produced by . . . . . GLASSWORKS
Sound Re-Recorded at
. . . . . . . BOOM SOUND STUDIOS
Re-Recording Mixer . . MARTIN JENSEN
ADR Recordist . . . . . STEVE HAYNES,
LIPSYNC POST
Foley Recordist . . . . . ALISTAIR RENN
Foley Artists . . . . . . PETER BURGIS
ANDI DERRICK
ADR Voice Casting
. . . . . . . . LOUIS ELMAN AMPS MPSE
ABIGAIL BARBIER
Insurance . . . AON/ALBERT G RUBEN
Product Placement and Clearances
. . . . . . . . . . . BELLWOOD MEDIA
Legal Research . . . MARSHALL/PLUMB
RESEARCH ASSOCIATES, INC.
Post Production Script Services
. . . . . . . . . . . . . MASTERWORDS
Camera, Lenses and Grip Equipment
. . . . . . . . . . . . . . PANAVISION
Lighting Equipment . . . LEE LIGHTING
Color by . . . . . . . . . . . . DELUXE
Laboratory Contact . . . CLIVE NOAKES
Telecine . . . . . . ARION FACILITIES
Arion Colourist . . . . . RAY CACKET
Negative Cutting . . . JASON WHEELER
FILM SERVICES
Dolby Sound Consultant. . CHRIS STURMER
Film Stock . . . . . . . . . . KODAK
Video Playback Equipment . . . SL VIDEO
Walkie Talkies . . . . . . . . WAVEVEND
Stills Processing . . . . . . LOFTY'S LAB
Armoury . . . . . . . . . . . . BAPTY
Location Security . . CONE ALONE LTD
Aerial Platforms . . UNIVERSAL AERIAL
PLATFORMS
Editing Equipment . . . . . . . OCULUS
Equipment And Facility Transport
. . . . LOCATION FACILITIES & LAYS
INTERNATIONAL

Horse Supplier . . . . . . DEBBIE KAYE
Horsemaster . . . . . . . . TONY SMART
Animals . . ALMOST HUMAN ANIMALS
Camera Action Vehicles . BICKERS ACTION
Fairground Props . . . . ALFIE GREGORY
ENTERTAINMENT
Boats . . . . . . . . HERITAGE MARINE
Costume Suppliers . . . HERO COLLECT-
ION, KRZYSZTOF KLOSKOWSKI,
COSPROP, ANGELS
Wigs by . . . . . . . OWEN KING & CO
Greens . . . . . . . . . FILMSCAPES LTD
Rehearsal Space . . . . . SANDS FILMS

PIANO PERFORMED BY
JEAN-YVES THIBAUDET

Executive in Charge of Music for Universal
Pictures . . . . . KATHY NELSON
Music Orchestrated by . . . DARIO MARI-
ANELLI AND BENJAMIN WALLFISCH
Conducted by . . BENJAMIN WALLFISCH
Cello Soloist . . . . . CAROLINE DALE
Music Performed by . . . . THE ENGLISH
CHAMBER ORCHESTRA
Harmonica Soloist . . BRENDAN POWER
Score Co-ordinated by
. . . . . . . . . . MAGGIE RODFORD
Music Recorded and Mixed at . . . . . AIR
LYNDHURST STUDIOS, LONDON
Music Recorded and Mixed by
. . . . . . . . . . . . NICK WOLLAGE
Assistant Engineers . . CHRIS BARRATT
OLGA FITZROY
SAM JONES
Music Editor . . . . . JAMES BELLAMY
Programmer . . . . . . . JODY JENKINS
Music Copyist . . . . . TONY STANTON
Piano Technician . . . MICHAEL LEWIS
Music Consultants . . . KIRSTEN AND
CHARLES LANE ON BEHALF OF
RIGHT MUSIC LIMITED
JEAN-YVES THIBAUDET APPEARS
COURTESY OF DECCA MUSIC GROUP

"O SOAVE FANCIULLA, O DOLCE VISO"
FROM "LA BOHÈME"
(GIUSEPPE GIACOSA, LUIGI ILLICA,
GIACOMO PUCCINI)
PERFORMED BY JUSSI BJÖRLING,
VICTORIA DE LOS ANGELES
AND THE RCA VICTOR ORCHESTRA
CONDUCTED BY SIR THOMAS BEECHAM
COURTESY OF EMI RECORDS LTD

"DEAR LORD AND FATHER OF
MANKIND"
(CHARLES PARRY, JOHN WHITTIER)
PERFORMED BY BEDE COLLEGE CHOIR
COURTESY OF UNIVERSAL STUDIOS

"(THERE'LL BE BLUEBIRDS OVER)
THE WHITE CLIFFS OF DOVER"
(NAT BURTON, WALTER KENT)
PERFORMED BY THE DUNKIRK
SOLDIERS
COURTESY OF UNIVERSAL STUDIOS

"KEEP THE HOME FIRES BURNING"
(LENA FORD, IVOR NOVELLO)
PERFORMED BY THE DUNKIRK
SOLDIERS
COURTESY OF UNIVERSAL STUDIOS

"BLESS 'EM ALL"
(JIMMY HUGHES, FRANK LAKE)
PERFORMED BY PAUL HARPER
AND THE DUNKIRK SOLDIERS
COURTESY OF UNIVERSAL STUDIOS

"HOT THROB"
(BASTIAAN MARIS)
PERFORMED ON THE LHPO BY
BASTIAAN MARIS
COURTESY OF UNIVERSAL STUDIOS

"MISS YOU"
(CHARLES TOBIAS, HARRY TOBIAS,
HENRY TOBIAS)
PERFORMED BY FLANAGAN AND ALLEN
COURTESY OF THE DECCA MUSIC
GROUP
UNDER LICENSE FROM UNIVERSAL
MUSIC OPERATIONS LTD

"CLAIR DE LUNE"
(CLAUDE DEBUSSY)
PERFORMED BY GORDON THOMPSON
COURTESY OF SANCTUARY RECORDS
GROUP LTD

SOUNDTRACK ALBUM AVAILABLE FROM
UNIVERSAL MUSIC CLASSICS AND JAZZ

THE RED CROSS EMBLEM IS A
PROTECTIVE SYMBOL USED DURING
ARMED CONFLICTS
AND ITS USE IS RESTRICTED BY LAW.

THE PRODUCERS WISH TO THANK THE
UNITED KINGDOM MINISTRY OF
DEFENCE AND THE BRITISH RED CROSS
SOCIETY
FOR AUTHORISATION TO USE THE RED
CROSS EMBLEM IN THIS FILM.

CLIP FROM "LE QUAI DES BRUMES"
©1938 STUDIOCANAL IMAGES
A FILM BY MARCEL CARNÉ
SCENARIO AND DIALOGUE BY JACQUES
PRÉVERT
BASED ON THE NOVEL BY PIERRE MAC
ORLAN
MUSIC BY MAURICE JAUBERT
FEATURING JEAN GABIN, MICHÈLE
MORGAN, PIERRE BRASSEUR
COURTESY OF STUDIOCANAL IMAGE

ARCHIVE FOOTAGE COURTESY OF ITN
SOURCE/BRITISH PATHE AND
GAUMONT

"BROWN TUBE SHELTER" BY HENRY
MOORE HAS BEEN FILMED
WITH PERMISSION OF THE HENRY
MOORE FOUNDATION.

HIS MASTER'S VOICE® AND DOG AND
GRAMAPHONE LOGO® ARE REGIS-
TERED TRADEMARKS
OF THE HMV GROUP PLC THROUGH
HMV (IP) LIMITED AND REPRODUCED
HERE BY THE
KIND AUTHORISATION OF THE HMV
GROUP PLC.

GRAY'S ANATOMY 24/E ©1943 ELSEVIER
LTD, USED WITH THE PERMISSION OF
ELSEVIER.

WITH THANKS TO
ROSAMUND PIKE, LYNDIE WRIGHT,
SARAH WRIGHT, KATHY BURKE,
DOMINIC DROMGOOLE,
SUSA GELPKE AND ALL AT PATERNO E
CORZANO, PHOEBE AND STELLA
McGARVEY

CHANEL JOAILLERIE

ASSOCIATED BRITISH PORTS,
GRIMSBY
THE BRITISH COUNCIL

COLEFAX & FOWLER
CORUS STEEL WORKS, REDCAR
CUMBRIA CRYSTAL
ENVIRONMENT AGENCY
KATE FORMAN DESIGNS
VÈRONIQUE HASSID
STEPHEN JONES MILLINERY
LONDON UNDERGROUND LTD
CAROLINE MAGNUS
NEIL MOCKLER
REDCAR & CLEVELAND BOROUGH
COUNCIL
THE RESIDENTS AND BUSINESSES OF
REDCAR
ROYAL CONSUMER INFORMATION
PRODUCTS, INC. AND VINCE
PORTELLI
ROYAL COPENHAGEN
R.S.P.B – OUSE AND NENE WASHES
ST JOHN'S SMITH SQUARE
DAVID SALMON FURNITURE
TURNELL & GIGON DESIGNS LTD
WESTMINSTER CITY COUNCIL, SPE-
CIAL EVENTS OFFICE
WILLIAM YEOWARD CRYSTAL

FILMED ON LOCATION AT STOKESAY
COURT, SHROPSHIRE AND IN LON-
DON, REDCAR, LINCOLNSHIRE AND
SHEPPERTON STUDIOS, ENGLAND.

THE CHARACTERS AND INCIDENTS
PORTRAYED AND THE NAMES
HEREIN ARE FICTITIOUS,
AND ANY SIMILARITY TO THE
NAME, CHARACTER OR HISTORY OF
ANY ACTUAL PERSONS
LIVING OR DEAD IS ENTIRELY CO-
INCIDENTAL AND UNINTENTIONAL.

THIS MOTION PICTURE IS PRO-
TECTED UNDER THE LAWS OF THE
UNITED STATES AND OTHER
COUNTRIES AND ITS UNAUTHO-
RISED DUPLICATION, DISTRIBUTION
OR EXHIBITION MAY
RESULT IN CIVIL LIABILITY AND
CRIMINAL PROSECUTION.

©2007 UNIVERSAL STUDIOS. ALL
RIGHTS RESERVED.

# BIOS

### CHRISTOPHER HAMPTON (Screenplay)

Christopher Hampton won the Academy Award® for Best Adapted Screenplay for *Dangerous Liaisons,* which he adapted from his own stage play (itself an adaptation of Choderlos de Laclos' novel *Les Liaisons Dangereuses*). The film version was directed by Stephen Frears and starring Glenn Close, John Malkovich, Michelle Pfeiffer, and Uma Thurman. The film also brought Mr. Hampton BAFTA, London Film Critics Circle, and Writers Guild of America Awards. Born in the Azores, he lived in Aden, Egypt, and Zanzibar as a child. As a teenager, he went to New College, Oxford, to study German and French, and graduated with a First Class Honours Degree.

While at Oxford, Mr. Hampton became involved in theater, and became the youngest writer ever to have a play staged in the West End. His early playwriting credits include *Total Eclipse, The Philanthropist, Savages,* and *Treats,* all staged at the Royal Court Theatre; and translations of such classics as *Uncle Vanya, Hedda Gabler, A Doll's House, Tales from the Vienna Woods, Three Sisters,* and *The Seagull.*

In addition to *Dangerous Liaisons* with the Royal Shakespeare Company, his subsequent theater work includes the stage adaptation of *Sunset Boulevard* for Andrew Lloyd Webber, which brought Mr. Hampton Tony Awards for both Book and Lyrics; *Tales from Hollywood*; an adaptation of *Tartuffe,* also for the Royal Shakespeare Company; and *The Talking Cure,* for the National Theatre. Mr. Hampton's translation of Yasmina Reza's *Art* won Olivier and Tony Awards, and ran for 2,500 performances in the West End.

His teleplays include *The History Man,* adapted from Malcolm Bradbury's novel and directed by Robert Knights; *Tartuffe,* directed by Bill Alexander; the BAFTA Award–winning *Hotel du Lac,* adapted from Anita Brookner's novel and directed by Giles Foster; the miniseries *The Ginger Tree,* adapted from Oswald Wynd's novel; and *Tales from Hollywood,* directed by Howard Davies.

Mr. Hampton's screenwriting credits include *A Doll's House,* adapted from Henrik Ibsen's play and directed by Patrick Garland; *The Good Father,* adapted from Peter Prince's novel and directed by Mike Newell; Agnieszka Holland's *Total Eclipse*; and, with Robert Schenkkan, *The Quiet American,* based on the Graham Greene novel and directed by Phillip Noyce.

He has directed and adapted three films to date. These are *Carrington*, based on Michael Holroyd's book, for which Mr. Hampton was awarded Special Jury Prize at the 1995 Cannes International Film Festival, where the film's star Jonathan Pryce was also chosen Best Actor; *The Secret Agent*, based on the Joseph Conrad novel and starring Bob Hoskins and Patricia Arquette; and *Imagining Argentina*, based on Lawrence Thornton's novel and starring Antonio Banderas and Emma Thompson.

Christopher Hampton was made an Officier de l'Ordre des Arts et des Lettres by the French government, and is a CBE (Commander of the Order of the British Empire).

### IAN McEWAN (Novel; Executive Producer)

Ian McEwan studied at the University of Sussex, where he received a B.A. degree in English Literature. While completing his M.A. degree in English Literature at the University of East Anglia, he took a creative writing course taught by the novelists Malcolm Bradbury and Angus Wilson.

Mr. McEwan's books have earned him worldwide critical acclaim. He has won the Somerset Maugham Award for his first collection of short stories, *First Love, Last Rites*; the Whitbread Novel Award and Prix Fémina étranger, for *The Child in Time*; and Germany's Shakespeare Prize. He has been short-listed for the Booker Prize for Fiction three times, winning the award for *Amsterdam*. Most recently, he won the James Tait Black Memorial Prize for his novel *Saturday*, and the Commonwealth Award for Literature. His latest published work is the novel *On Chesil Beach*.

His novel *Atonement* was published in 2002 and received the WH Smith Literary Award, National Book Critics Circle Fiction Award, the *Los Angeles Times* Prize for Fiction, and the Santiago Prize for the European Novel.

In addition to *Atonement*, other works by Mr. McEwan have been made into feature films. Among these have been *The Comfort of Strangers,* adapted by Harold Pinter and directed by Paul Schrader; *The Cement Garden,* adapted and directed by Andrew Birkin; *The Innocent,* adapted by the author and directed by John Schlesinger; the short story "First Love, Last Rites," adapted by Jesse Peretz and David Ryan and directed by Mr. Peretz; and *Enduring Love,* adapted by Joe Penhall and directed by Roger Michell.

In 1999, Mr. McEwan was named a CBE (Commander of the Order of the British Empire).